BOOKS BY SUZA KATES

The Savannah Coven Series
Whisper of a Witch
Conviction of a Witch
Binding of a Witch
Haunting of a Witch
Possession of a Witch
Deception of a Witch
Suffering of a Witch
Boys' Night Out (E-novella)
Vengeance of a Witch
Sacrifice of a Witch

The She Series
She Who is Hidden

Single Titles
Hallowed Eve
The Penance Stone

Coming Late 2014
Watchtower Maidens Series
Call to the East

SACRIFICE OF A WITCH

THE SAVANNAH COVEN SERIES

SUZA KATES

ICASM PRESS

SAVANNAH

This book is a work of fiction. The characters, names,
events and places are fictitious and products of the author's
imagination or are used fictitiously. Any similarities to actual
persons, living or dead, places or events is entirely coincidental.

Published by Icasm Publishing LLC
5710 Ogeechee Rd. Suite 200 #278, Savannah, GA 31405
www.icasmpress.com

Library of Congress Cataloging-in-Publication Data

Kates, Suza
Sacrifice of a Witch / Suza Kates
      p. cm.

ISBN-13: 978-0-9912002-1-4 (paperback)
ISBN-13: 978-0-9912002-2-1 (ebook)

I. Title

Printed and bound in the United States of America
10 9 8 7 6 5 4 3 2 1

Acknowledgements

Over the course of this series, several different people have contributed, whether with cover art, editing, or technical support. The books simply wouldn't exist, or wouldn't be in very good form, without the help of others.

I'd like to thank Sharyn Cerniglia for her undying patience with my unique "rhythm" and the sunny personality that accompanies her editing skills. It's rare to meet a person who is always so effortlessly happy, and I feel blessed to have you in my life!

Mandi Cranson also offered her wonderful editing advice, and along with that, she provided me a place to vent, to laugh, and to receive some much-needed counseling on the bad days. I am ever so grateful there is someone who talks as fast as I do and is also able to think straight at two in the morning. Thank you so much for your support and encouragement, and I owe you big after this one!

Donna Wood is always so easy to work with, and I appreciate her willingness to be flexible with her time. As the final pass-through, I know it can get tricky waiting for those last chapters, but you always hang in there, and I am grateful!

Finally, I have to thank my husband, David. Actually, there aren't enough words to tell him how appreciative I am. The last year would have tested the patience of a saint, and I am so glad to have had such a caring man by my side through all the ups and downs. I never even had to ask. He just knew when to make a run for Raisinets. So thank you, thank you, and I promise to manage my time better from here on out!

To Antoine and Jason,
saviors of lost little puppies

Special Thanks

I want to say a heartfelt thank you to all of the readers who have supported The Savannah Coven Series. From the beginning with "Whisper of a Witch," the shortest of the novels and one of my earliest books, you saw something in this coven of eclectic witches that kept you coming back for each of their stories.

I couldn't have done this without all of you, and I will forever be grateful for the last four years. I'm sure I'll look back at this time fondly as "the coven years," and I hope you've enjoyed this series, these women, as much as I have.

Thank you all and blessed be! --Suza

Anna St. Germaine
Hair: Long, straight, sable brown
Eyes: Sapphire blue
Color: Sapphire blue
Cat: "Ivy" gray female with lime green eyes

Anna sees visions of past, present, and future. She is the coven's head witch and is a descendant of the three women who originally banished the demon Bastraal three centuries ago. Her ancestral home is on an island off the coast of Savannah, Georgia and now serves as coven central.

Claudia Grant
Hair: Straight, long, flaming red
Eyes: River green
Color: Coral
Cat: "Rowan Von Ashbi" coloring of an American Wirehair with yellow eyes

Claudia is a history professor who only needs to touch an object to sense its past and previous surroundings.

Hayden Wells
Hair: Brownish red "caramel"
Eyes: Golden brown
Color: Pale pink
Cat: "Daisy" black tortoiseshell with yellow eyes

Hayden is a medium from San Francisco who sees and talks to spirits/ghosts.

Kylie Worthington
Hair: Long, wavy golden-blonde
Eyes: Hazel
Color: Yellow
Cat: Sassafras "Sassy" also a long-haired blonde but with bright yellow eyes

Kylie is a college student who's "on a break" to do her part for the coven and is able to control electricity in any form.

Lucia Ruiz
Hair: Long, wavy deep brown
Eyes: Brown
Color: Red
Cat: "Iris" black Persian with blue eyes

Lucia was born to privileged wealth in Spain and has the ability to find anything that is lost. She is an adventurer, world-traveler, and renowned relic-hunter.

Paige Reilley
Hair: Shoulder-length, white-blonde with ragged bangs
Eyes: Turquoise blue
Color: Turquoise
Cat: Tiger Lily "Tiger" brown and gray with white chest and belly, bright green eyes

Recently discharged from the military, Paige is a soldier in every way with the added abilities of super-strength and speed.

Shauni Miller

Hair: Long, straight, black
Eyes: Emerald green
Color: Green
Cat: "Cuileann" black short-hair with green eyes

Shauni is a nature-loving biologist from Colorado and communicates with animals telepathically.

Viv Sakurai

Hair: Shoulder-length, black, angled bangs
Eyes: Gray
Color: Purple
Cat: Kikoku "Kiko" orange tabby with yellow-green eyes and a grumpy disposition.

Relocated from Chicago, Viv is a physicist searching for an explanation for her own special power of telekinesis.

Willyn Brousseau

Hair: Wavy, shoulder-length, light blonde
Eyes: Pale blue
Color: White/cream
Cat: "Snowball" pure white with golden eyes

Willyn is a nurse, a mother, and a Christian. Raised in Alabama, she uses her healing powers to help those in need. She came to Savannah with an additional package, her young son, Tadd.

THE GUYS

Dr. Michael Black   *Whisper of a Witch*

This tall handsome veterinarian fell in love with Shauni in the first book of the series. He has dark blonde hair and gray eyes and is able to read a person's aura. He's a pretty calm guy until someone messes with his witch.

Dare Forster   *Conviction of a Witch*

Dark and handsome with deep blue eyes, this male witch came to the coven's island with his own plan. He wanted to partner with one of the women, but he never expected to fall in love. Especially with a gentle, Christian soul like Willyn. Now married, the two have made a family with Willyn's small son, Tadd.

Nick Reagan   *Binding of a Witch*

The coven likes to hang out in their favorite pub, and the owner of the bar always liked looking at Viv. His eyes are the color of the whiskey he sells, and his past is one of struggle. One night Nick finally got the nerve to approach the Asian beauty, but he got a lot more than he bargained for. The demon Bastraal had been destroyed once before, and his remains had been buried. Beneath Nick's very own pub.

Trevor Roch　　　　　*Haunting of a Witch*

One of Savannah's finest, this homicide detective clashes hard with the coven's ghost whisperer, convinced she's a con artist. Hayden has no choice but to work with the annoying man and find a serial killer who's working with the Amara. Staying true to form and following the coven's pattern, the two fall for each other. Against their better judgment.

Ethan Drake　　　　　*Possession of a Witch*

This demon hunter is well-acquainted with evil and has been chasing his own monster since childhood. When he offers to help the coven with their demon infestation, he has no idea he's about to be taken on the adventure of a lifetime. Lucia Ruiz is hard to resist, and is the one woman who might be able to save him.

Cole Lonergan　　　　　*Deception of a Witch*

As Trevor's police partner, Cole has been introduced to the coven and all of their secrets. While he admires the women and considers them all good friends, he never expects to feel anything more. But Claudia Grant is a long-legged-wicked-smart witch, and much like his favorite candies, Cole finds himself wanting to take a bite.

Quinn St. Germaine   *Suffering of a Witch*

Quinn is the younger brother of the coven's head witch, Anna. With sable hair and cobalt eyes, he is the masculine and handsome version of the siblings. His knowledge runs to occult history and magickal languages. He assists the coven in all things, and though he has his eye on a particular witch, he does his best to deny it.

Chris Decker   *Vengeance of a Witch*

An Army Ranger recently discharged, Chris was first introduced to the coven and their demon issues during a bachelor party gone wrong in the e-novella "Boys' Night out." Blonde-haired and blue-eyed, he's pretty laid back and easy going. Which is a good thing, since he's blessed with super-strength and speed, and has fallen in love with a rather temperamental witch.

1

Remember...be careful. Don't touch him.

Anna St. Germaine gave herself the silent reminder as she ascended the steps to the second level of a three-story townhome in the historic district of Savannah. The address was across from the stately and historic Monterey Square, a coveted downtown location. Early twentieth-century architecture enshrouded by monstrous oaks heavy with Spanish moss created a private enclave for residents and a picturesque scene that caused locals and visitors alike to slow down for a better look

Taking a moment to let her hair blow away from her cheeks as the October breeze eased past, Anna listened to the same wind ruffling the ivy that covered the brick building. After her repose and a moment to steel her nerves, she climbed the steps, trailing her hand along the black iron railing and marveling over the leaves still clinging to the townhome in their thick, vibrant green.

Many states would be deep into the rich reds, umbers, and golds of fall by now, but here in her Low Country hometown, the trees still preened, the air still warmed at midday, and autumn arrived at a drunken crawl.

She wouldn't mind slowing her approach as well, but the conversation ahead of her could no longer be delayed. Due to his hectic work schedule, it had been a week since she'd last met with the lawyer, whose large iron door knocker she now lifted to sharply rap twice. But given his unique circumstances, she couldn't afford to lose any more time to procrastination.

Born a witch with power to protect herself and prophecy to guide her, Anna had come across very few things in life that made her nervous, but the man who awaited her now affected her in peculiar ways. Ian Keller, with his arrogant demeanor and shrewd, appraising eyes could cast one look her way, and her heart would kick into a gallop.

It was the rare person who could raise her hackles as quickly and thoroughly as he did, but his bristly attitude wasn't the only reason for apprehension.

Don't touch.

The last time—and only time—her skin had brushed against Ian's, a powerful and painful vision had burst into her mind. Anna had been clairvoyant her entire life, but never before had her ability felt more like a sinister intruder than familiar friend. Never had an image scratched and clawed at the inside of her skull.

Not the way that vision had, the one caused—albeit indirectly—by the man she was about to see again.

She drew a deep breath, listening for footsteps to herald his approach. No sound carried from inside the grand home, but she spied movement through the oval glass of the door. Channeling composure, she conjured a warm smile of greeting.

The door opened to reveal a Saturday-casual version of the man she'd met on two previous occasions. Absent were the expensive suits and buffed-to-a-shine shoes, replaced by dark blue jeans and a pale blue button-up with sleeves rolled to the elbows.

She'd never seen him dressed down before, and her eyes were drawn to the tan arms sprinkled with golden hair. Odd, he didn't strike her as the outdoorsy type. Though now that she thought about it, he'd always had a healthy glow to his skin.

Maybe she hadn't noticed because of the hard time she'd had prying her attention from those piercing eyes of his, so deep, beautiful, and somehow knowing.

And so similar to those of another she knew. A woman, a witch, who was as cruel as they came. Ronja had been around a long, long time, and the depths of Ian's relation to her had recently come into question. The inherent risk of the connection between them—the modern man and ancient seiðr—was exactly why Anna needed to speak with him today.

"Hello," she said with a smile.

He gave her a slight nod in return and stepped aside to wave her in, the grace of his movement in stark contrast to the reserve etched into his stone-blue eyes, a blending of sky and granite that hadn't softened one bit.

Anna composed herself, called forth the charm bred into her Southern bones, and reminded herself why she was here. Why she had to be here, whether her host welcomed her or not.

His clothing might have changed, but the cool aloofness she'd come to expect was stolidly in place. She wondered if the two of them had somehow lost the headway they'd made during their last discussion. Gone was the man who'd called her for help, and in his place stood the rigid lawyer who'd once thrown her out of his office.

She'd dressed up a bit for today's meeting, eschewing her usual jeans for a black pencil skirt and crisp white blouse. The psychological undertones of dressing for confidence hadn't escaped her when she'd chosen the outfit, but faced once again with the standoffish version of Ian, she was thankful the high heels she wore brought her almost to his eye level.

Unfortunately, even at five seven and with a little help from her Louboutins, she still couldn't match his height. Built like the Nordic ancestors he likely hailed from, Ian was at least six-feet and then some. And with that icy glower of his...*Oh, yes. I can just picture him wielding an axe. One named Bloodseeker or Bonecrusher, no doubt.*

His indifference was nothing new, but she felt a quick drop in her stomach—like falling during a dream—when she realized today wouldn't go as smoothly as she'd imagined. So she hiked up her black leather tote on her shoulder and walked in the direction indicated by his extended hand.

She found satisfaction in the click of her heels across his tile floor. The man might be a snob, but Anna was a St. Germaine. Her ancestors had not only helped found the city of Savannah, but a certain trio of witches had also saved it from being decimated by a power-hungry demon.

She straightened her shoulders and walked with grace. *So give it your best, Mr. Keller.* She could blueblood it up with the best of them.

Pausing near the doorway of an open-layout living area, she perused the room and surmised he'd removed a wall at some point. The spacious room merged cleanly with the kitchen, sandstone tiles running throughout.

The timeless stone added to an overall style best described as old world modern. Here in his home, the staid counselor revealed more of himself, with both contemporary and classic art adorning the walls. Deep but vibrant hues of what appeared to be an Afremov original gave Anna additional insight into Ian's tastes, and she had to admit to a degree of surprise.

Carefully placed items like the Tiffany lamp and bronze sculpture of two hounds at alert spoke more of family heirlooms and stood out among the clean, stately lines. But at least they provided a touch of charm and personality for a stalwart man who could stand to have his edges softened.

The warmth of his home was encouraging, unlike the severe absence of character she'd seen in his office the day they'd first come face to face, when she'd tried to convince him to stop the real estate transaction that would grant Ronja ownership of a rural piece of land. The magical spread of property had a long history, and dark, deep wells of power, ready to be channeled by an evil practitioner.

Ready to be unleashed on an innocent world.

"Would you like some coffee or tea?" Ian led her to a sitting area near a window where bright sunlight filtered in through outdoor foliage.

"No, thank you." Anna could feel, and see, his stiffness, and her own posture grew straighter in reflection. So she forced herself to relax, unsettled by the influence he had on her.

"Let me at least take your bag. It looks heavy." He reached for the strap, his hand coming too close to her bare elbow for comfort, and the imperative of avoiding his touch leapt to the forefront.

Anna jerked away, moving quickly aside.

Ian froze in response, his hard expression conveying both insult and confusion. Carefully, he retracted his hand, and though he didn't ask for an explanation, he certainly didn't ask for her bag again either. Instead he inclined his head, inviting her to sit.

Moving to two of the three plush chairs surrounding a large arched window, Anna cast her gaze outside to a row of crepe myrtles that filtered the sun to create a shaded pattern on a curving stone path. She found herself longing to escape this uncomfortable moment and see where the path led. Likely to a large courtyard made private and romantic by high walls all around, a feature often found in the historic homes in the city.

After the tense and awkward greeting between Ian and her, she could use a few minutes among the plants and green life, a chance to step out of her shoes and press her soles to the inviting grass of which she'd caught a glimpse. *Earthing*, it was called, and she needed the centering, healing energy more than ever.

But her only real option was to deal with the man waiting in strained silence. "I have so much to explain to you," she started, still gazing at the peaceful scene instead of Ian's distant stare. "But I'll start with why I just reacted the way I did."

"There's no need—"

"There is." She settled her gaze on his. "We should get it all out in the open. All of it." Holding up her hand, she rubbed the center of her palm with the opposite thumb. "You already know I have powers. I showed you a small example when we first met, but I never gave you the full story behind my relationship with Ronja. And there's quite a lot to tell."

"About that." Ian shifted in his chair. "I've been considering everything since I last saw you." His smile was starched, forced. "I may have made a mistake by contacting you at all."

His posture was so rigid Anna marveled his spine didn't snap. You could take the man out of the courtroom... "I assure you, you did the right thing. Please," she said when he looked as if he would speak again. "It's important you have all the facts." She drew her brows together. "You would demand no less for any case you represented, right?"

With a superior nod, he seemed to relent slightly. "Go ahead." But the heavy sigh told her just how disagreeable he found the conversation. Or was it her he objected to? After all, she'd gotten the impression he didn't like her much, but particularly when she spoke of magic and evil, two things he seemed to pretend were non-existent.

Regardless of his persistent disregard for the truth, she barreled on. Protecting people was part of her duty, even when the protectee decided to resist. "The confrontation between Ronja and my family goes back decades, centuries. I've known since I was a child that I would play a role in fulfilling my family's..." she faltered, "duty."

She sensed that "prophecy" was too strong of a word. He'd clearly retreated since she'd last seen him and was again choosing not to recognize his new reality. But she could only do so much juggling with the semantics. Everything she had to say dealt with the supernatural, and nothing, she suspected, was going to be well-received.

"I'm a witch, it's true, but what you don't know is that I'm part of a coven. There are nine of us, and frankly, we are all that stands between Ronja and the hellish world she intends to create."

"Sounds a bit dramatic." Ian clearly found her admission entertaining, and his patronizing tone rankled. In fact, it created a tingle in Anna's hand, but she curled her fingers and kept the magic at bay.

Don't want to spook the civilian. Not when she needed the obstinate man to listen.

She crossed her legs and continued. "Each of the women in my coven has a particular gift, an ability, in addition to our shared magic." She glanced at his hand resting on the chair arm. "Mine is clairvoyance, and the last time I touched you, I had a rather visceral reaction."

"As in..." His ice melted a fraction as he considered her statement. "You saw something? Is that why you leapt up to run out of the restaurant?"

She didn't care for the summation but answered, "Yes. I saw an attack planned for that very day. Ronja and her followers intended to kill people at a funeral gathering, possibly even kidnap others to force them to be hosts."

"Hosts?" He tapped a finger to the brocade fabric, a quizzical crease in his forehead. "Hosts for what?"

Here we go. "People have gone missing in this city, and we know for certain they are often used as vessels, or bodies, to put it bluntly, for a certain class of demons."

"Demons?" Finally, his thick ice broke. Ian moved to the edge of his seat. "Are you trying to tell me—" He stopped speaking suddenly, eyes clouding over. "Wait. You mentioned a funeral?"

Then he stood and exited the room, leaving Anna to wonder if he'd decided he needed a drink. Or if she were about to be thrown out again.

After mere seconds, heavy footsteps preceded his re-entry.

He was holding out a newspaper and came to stand next to her chair. He held the paper out in front of her, his nearness allowing her a whiff of crisp, clean cologne.

With just a touch of warm male musk.

Anna lost herself for a moment but quickly refocused when he shook the paper in front of her face. "Is this what you're talking about?"

She merely glanced at the article he was pointing out, because she didn't have to read the headlines to know the story. Not when she'd been one of the main characters and easily recognized the picture taken at Laurel Grove Cemetery.

"You're telling me these reports are real?"

Anna nodded. If she'd expected him to relax when confronted with evidence of her claims, she'd made a serious misjudgment. His brow furrowed, his eyes darkened. "Impossible."

A light laugh full of frustration escaped as she looked up at the irate man standing over her with accusation in his eyes. "How much proof do you need? How many individual accounts of strange incidents will it take for you to delay your verdict and pay attention to what's right in front of you?" She drove home her point with a chilly tone. "Particularly the proof you've seen in your own mind?"

He opened his mouth but didn't reply, only shook his head.

She tapped the paper, causing the thin material to cave inward. "People are now witnessing paranormal events, because the prophecy is culminating, coming to an end. Ronja no longer cares who gets hurt or finds out about our existence."

"Prophecy? And demons? All here in Savannah?" Ian scoffed and folded the newspaper with an angry crunch. "I don't know how you expect me to respond to what you're saying. I can't place any real faith in visions or prophecies. Or in people who claim to be witches."

Anna felt as if she'd been sucked through a wormhole, back in time to the very first encounter she'd had with him. He had been all cynicism and demeaning attitude. An aggressive non-believer.

As he was being now. But at least she hadn't been booted from the premises. Yet.

"How can you say that when you were the one who called me about having visions yourself? You told me you believed the things you were seeing were memories of a past life and that Ronja was previously your sister."

"Well, I was wrong, and the episodes have stopped. I haven't experienced any strange dreams or other occurrences since before we met for lunch. And to be honest, you came here today for nothing. I'm sorry, I should have handled this over the phone."

Anna gripped her bag. "Actually, we couldn't have. I came prepared to safeguard your home, and you." She opened the leather flap and began to rummage. "I have what I need to place wards here, and I took the liberty of creating a protection pouch for you to carry. There's some rue and bay laurel, along with an obsidian stone to ground you to the earth. This will help with—"

Ian took a step backward, waving his hand at her and frowning. "No. I don't think so. I don't want any of that in my house. A little bag of stones and herbs is not the answer to my problems." He sighed and rubbed his jaw. "I really think it's time for you to go."

The edges of panic began to encroach on Anna. This was going all wrong. Why was he resisting? "But you can't face this alone."

"I don't intend to. I've made an appointment with a specialist, and I'm sure he'll be able to help me."

"A specialist? Who?" Anna was unaware of any other witch or practitioner he might call, particularly one close enough to provide the defenses he needed. That he needed *immediately*. "No one is better prepared to protect you than I am. And I'm here now, so let me do what I'm best at."

"There's our problem. I don't need protection. I'll be seeing a neurologist. Whatever has been going on in my head must be an organic issue. I need a doctor, Anna." His smile was patronizing. "Not a witch doctor."

"What you're saying makes no sense. You had your own misgivings about Ronja and came to me with suspicions about her and her acquaintances. You were upset the last time I saw you and fully believed in the danger she poses. What's changed? How can you explain it all away and think a physician is the answer?"

"Simple. I likely already had some sort of medical issue, and then you came to my office with wild stories about Ronja and her plans for evil deeds. My symptoms kicked in, and voila—instant paranoia, which then affected my dreams and caused..." he waved a hand as if searching for the right term, "visual disturbances."

Unbelievable. Anna stood to meet him and could almost feel the sparks flying from her eyes. "Let me get this straight. You'd rather believe you're sick, that there's something wrong with *you*, than accept the possibility of supernatural beings?"

He shoved his hands into his pockets and leaned toward her. "Would I rather have a brain tumor than lose my identity to some past life as the brother of a witch?" He turned up one side of his mouth in derision. "Absolutely."

So now we get to the truth. He was afraid, and with good reason. Anna should remember that not everyone had been trained and groomed since birth to deal with dark forces and the imminent dominion of a demon master.

She needed to give him some room, to not push him when he was clearly growing upset. So, drawing a cleansing breath, she eased down a few notches and spoke with concern. "Ian, I truly can't imagine how difficult this all must be for you."

She sucked in the smallest bit of air when he edged closer,

focused on her like a laser. Using the lapse in their discussion, Anna studied his clean-shaven face with its aristocratic angles and firm lips, the burnished hair in its neat, legal-eagle style.

Then he took her by surprise and smiled. *Really smiled*, causing a dimple to form in his right cheek. For a flash of time, he looked like a carefree man, the sexy been-sailing-all-day kind of ruggedness that affected any woman. Even a duty-driven witch.

Anna felt his smile in the pit of her belly and wondered if she should start worrying.

"I appreciate your concern," he said, drawing her back to the topic at hand. "I do, but honestly...which seems more plausible? Witches and magic? Or a more common and well-established physical illness? Everything I've seen or experienced, it can all be explained."

"Ian," she licked her lips as worry sprouted its first branches, "listen to me—"

"No." His eyes—the color, the coolness, so like Ronja's—flicked over her face in scrutiny. "I just can't."

She slowly rotated her head in denial. "What you can't do is shut me out. You're in danger."

"From Ronja? Even if that were true, I haven't heard a word out of her. She's not interested in me."

"That's where you're wrong. I know her, and she's just biding her time. Plotting, scheming." Anna knew she had to make him understand, even if it meant playing on the anxiety he was trying so hard to keep hidden. "But as you know, Ronja doesn't work alone."

Anna fixed him with a stare. She held him in place. "You have to let me help you, Ian, because as corrupt and bloodthirsty as Ronja is, she's not the worst thing you have to fear."

~

Ian knew he should make her leave. He didn't want to hear any more. Yet something in her warning touched on his deepest dread. The memory of a cold wind blew through him as he recalled the night in his bedroom, when he'd woken from a dream of Ronja.

And had almost been killed by an invisible force.

No. The feeling of wind was all in my head. I'm sick. I must be sick. Because what he'd told Anna was the truth. A tumor or mental illness could be handled; either could be treated. But what the hell was he supposed to do about unseen assailants wrapping frozen tentacles around his body and squeezing, *choking*, until the brink of death?

He'd much rather deal with medicine and the known ailments of the world. His world, Ian Keller, in the here and fucking now. What she was suggesting was inconceivable.

Still, he heard himself ask, "What could be worse than a witch plotting the demise of innocents?" He hated the scorn in his voice but couldn't seem to help it. Anna got to him, she drew him, and he still wasn't sure why or if his interest in her was wise. Or healthy.

Was that why he'd let her come all the way to the mainland and away from her island home? Just so he could see her again before telling her what he'd decided well in advance? Had he thought her presence would change his mind again?

Or had he simply wanted to see her? If he was so sure monsters only lived under the beds of children, then why had he asked her to elaborate? According to Anna, Ronja was treacherous and powerful, so as he'd asked, what could be worse?

Apparently, she was going to tell him. Her pink lips parted as she spoke. "Ronja has walked the earth for centuries, but not because of her own abilities. She's in collusion with a much stronger being."

Anna drew herself up, cleared her throat, and said, "His

name is Bastraal. He's a demon but of a different sort. He's been around longer than humans have known the heat of fire, and he's very, very strong."

Ian rubbed his forehead, the center of which felt knotted by a headache. "Demons again." He attempted to sound sarcastic, but a truth was in his soul, whether he wanted to admit it or not. Had this been the beast with which he'd come into contact?

But why would it attack and terrorize him only to disappear, leaving him essentially unharmed? The late-night assault had served only to frighten and confuse Ian, but why would a creature as mighty as the one she was describing even bother?

He was exhausted by all of this and actually yearned for a nice, boring dispute over construction zones. "I don't know what you want me to say."

"That you'll listen to me. We're running out of time, Ian, and I'm sorry to frighten you, but I can't afford to mince words. Lives are being lost." She moved closer to him and started to reach out before stopping herself. Instead she wrung her hands in front of her stomach.

She really was afraid to touch him.

He didn't understand why the notion irritated him, but the emotion showed itself unkindly. "If you're as good as you claim to be, shouldn't you be doing something to save those people?"

She stiffened, and he instantly regretted being cruel. He didn't trust her, but so far she'd done him no harm.

"Even with our power, we can't see everything or be everywhere." She looked down as true remorse passed over her refined features. Then she raised brilliant blue eyes to his. "We can't save everyone."

"Then why are you wasting time arguing with me?"

"Because you're important. You're at the center of it all. If you are Ronja's brother re-incarnated, she's going to want your allegiance. I know you're a man who believes in justice." Now she held out her hand again, fingers shaking.

Ian waited—the air held captive in his lungs, his heart pounding—as she reached out to touch him. He was partly curious to see her reaction, but he was equally interested in his own.

Anna pressed her fingers to his bare forearm, a feathered graze. But a jolt of something Ian didn't recognize ran through him. Not electricity, and not the familiar zing of physical attraction, but some sort of energy flowed into him, one that carried a warmth he'd never felt before.

His guest didn't seem to be affected the same way he was, as she only sighed and let a small smile flit over her mouth.

Ian swallowed his desire to press more of his skin to hers, to explore the fascinating current calling to a part of him he'd never known existed. Tilting his head, he steadied his voice and fought not to reveal his strange reaction. "No ill effects I take it?"

He wanted to experience the rush again, yet at the same time he needed to remove himself from her proximity. Her skin was far too hot, and the light caress far too pleasurable.

Anna took care of it for him, finally retracting her hand. "No. And I'm relieved. I don't want to be in constant fear of you." She eased closer to him. "And I don't want you to be afraid either."

His tone was low, raspy. "Yet you bring me stories of demons and tell me I'm in danger?"

"If you'll trust me, I can keep you safe." Her eyes were the truest blue as she pleaded with them.

"How can you make such an assurance? You just told me that people are dying." Knowing he was being harsh, he intentionally hardened his tone and crossed his arms. "If you have information about people being harmed, you should take it to the authorities."

"I should—" Her face flickered with confusion. "Why do I feel like I'm suddenly on the stand?"

"Ms. St. Germaine—"

"Now I'm Ms. St. Germaine again?" She rubbed her fingers together as if finally feeling a trace of what Ian had, but the tension around her eyes told him she was more concerned with his swift change in demeanor. "Distancing yourself from me won't solve your problem, Ian."

"I think you're the one with the real problem. I don't know what to make of your claims about magic and monsters, but I am an officer of the court. I have a duty to report any information about persons being harmed or any crimes that may be underway."

She held out her hands. "What is wrong with you? I came here to help."

"Or to misdirect?" He forced his mouth into a grim line. "No. I'm sorry, but I have no reason to take you at your word." He turned away from her. "What I do have is a responsibility to uphold the law, so if you won't notify the police, then I will. In fact, a detective has questioned me regarding Don Jacobson's murder. I have no choice but to inform him of your involvement."

He glanced back to see her lift her head regally, and admiration surged. She wasn't daunted by him at all. In fact, her expression conveyed pure annoyance with an undertone of insult.

"You're going to call the police and report me?"

"Yes. I've been dealing with a homicide detective since Jacobson's death, and I'm sure he'll be interested in anything you can tell him. By your own admission, you have specifics about the cemetery attack, as well as the strange deaths that have been occurring in this city."

When Ian fully faced Anna again, he was surprised to see a look on her face he couldn't decipher. With cobalt eyes glinting, she peered coolly at him, a queen to a bothersome peasant.

"Detective Lonergan," Ian told her firmly, still hoping to get a flicker of concern, to resume the upper hand.

"You're going to turn me in to Detective Lonergan?" Slowly

Anna began making her way across the room, clearly taking her leave of him. "Detective *Cole* Lonergan?" With heels clicking, she laughed softly and turned her back on him.

But before she rounded the corner, she tossed a final remark over her shoulder. "Call him, counselor. Be my guest."

2

Ian parked his silver Audi sedan on Perry Lane, since the only available parking spots this time of day were on side streets. He entered a gate to the back section of one of the city's main tourist spots, the sprawling and mysterious Colonial Park Cemetery.

Meandering the curving walks of tabby cement, he itched to remove his jacket as the sun blazed down on his shoulders. Today was the first of October, yet the burning orb in the sky was determined to keep her claim on the Southern city and all its inhabitants.

He passed smaller trees and shrubs as he moved, many of which were as heavy with moss as the sturdy oaks standing fifty feet in the air. Headstones were affixed to the perimeter wall of brick, placed there many years before, after the Northern Army had ransacked the burial grounds. The soldiers had broken and destroyed many of the markers, leaving them scattered across the grass so that no one could tell where they belonged.

Tourists loved the story, but Ian had heard it countless times. The history of Savannah was part of his makeup, another reason he took pride in his job. Why he wanted to protect the people and landmarks from any future destroyers.

Even if monsters and magicians were to be counted among them.

No, I can't comprehend that. The truth was, he didn't want to. So he'd followed his conscience and everything inside of himself that was determined to cling to normalcy. To the laws and regulations of a *human* world, even with all its imperfections.

Exiting a black gate onto Oglethorpe Avenue, Ian followed the sidewalk past the tall wall to the next building over, also constructed of brick. The Barracks were the downtown police headquarters, where he was expected by Detective Lonergan and his partner.

The police should be in charge of investigations into Anna, Ronja, Don Jacobson's murder, and any of the other crimes which had occurred in Savannah. They were the legal enforcers, and Ian would gladly let them take over.

He wanted nothing more to do with Anna St. Germaine, woman or witch, whatever the case.

Yet as he walked, doubt tried to wiggle its way in as his mind strayed again and again to Anna's tales of underworld dwellers come to take over the world. He just couldn't wrap his brain around the idea. None of what she'd told him was logical, and he still had no solid reason to trust her.

He only second-guessed his decision to come to the cops because of how he might sound to them. Surely like a madman, so he'd make sure they understood he was only relaying someone else's stories.

Ian would do his part to defend his hometown and hopefully help stop the strange murders, maybe even the kidnappings, if what he knew could steer the police in the right direction. Many people had heard about the abnormal corpses being left around the city and were anxious, unsettled.

A string of deaths like these just didn't occur, not in Savannah's normal, day-to-day society. Add the rise in missing persons cases, and the slow-moving city had been thrust into a state of semi-panic.

Ian didn't want to believe Anna could be involved, but she knew something. He'd cross-examined too many accomplished liars and professional bullies to allow himself to be coerced by one lone female.

Even if she did have mesmerizing eyes, long sable hair, and a regal air about her that drove him to distraction.

He shook himself, unsettled by the gut-deep attraction that pounded into him every time he pictured her. She was either unstable, highly eccentric, or she was a witch. And none of those were an option for Ian.

Then again, who was he to judge? He'd seen and felt some seriously unreal things in the past few weeks. The difference, though, was that he had the good sense to consult a physician.

Whether or not he'd imagined the horrible event in his home, he simply couldn't stand a repeat of his experience with the freezing cold entity that had entered the privacy of his bedroom and had almost smothered him to death. He couldn't go through such a vivid and realistic delusion again.

Because that's all it had been. There was simply no other rational explanation.

Finally reaching the Barracks, Ian walked in and was grateful for the cool embrace of air-conditioning. He tried to comfort himself with his plan of attack. Cops today, neurologist tomorrow. Then he wouldn't have to deal with any of this insanity again.

He'd kill the damned lunacy with law and logic.

Having had the occasional client who'd gotten into trouble when the court system hadn't worked quickly enough to suit, Ian knew his way around the station. In no time the elevator had whisked him to the appropriate floor where he stepped out and made eye contact with the receptionist known for her high heels and flamboyant dress code.

Just as she smiled and started to speak, a man's voice called out, stopping her with her pink-painted mouth open in an O-shape. "Mr. Keller." Detective Lonergan was striding across the room and motioning for Ian to accompany him. "If you'll come this way."

A taller and broader man stood from behind a desk that butted up to the front of Lonergan's. Both work areas were set against the windows for a view of Oglethorpe and the huge trees that lined the median between busy lanes of traffic. This would be the partner, but Ian didn't know his name.

He stopped to extend his hand. "Ian Keller."

The man nodded. "I've heard of you, Mr. Keller. My name's Trevor Roch." They shook, and the giant blonde indicated they should follow Detective Lonergan to the back. Eventually, they came upon a private room.

The door *snicked* softly as Detective Roch closed it, and despite the long meeting table and cool air, the space felt crowded. None of them were small men.

"You said you have information about the alleged events occurring at Laurel Grove Cemetery." Lonergan held out a hand for Ian to sit, and then he pulled out a chair for himself. "And that you believe it all might be connected to Mr. Jacobson's murder."

"That's correct." Ian met Lonergan's open and encouraging eyes, much preferable to the hard stare that had settled over his partner's features. "In fact, a woman told me specifically that she knows what happened at the cemetery. Her name is Anna St. Germaine. You should question her."

"Uh..." Now the bigger cop let his hard demeanor crumble and leaned over to place his palms on the table. "Anna St. Germaine? She told you what, exactly?"

Ian's throat seemed to swell. He wished he didn't have to repeat what she'd said, so he fell into lawyer mode. Clearly and concisely, that was the way to proceed. He was simply imparting pertinent information gained by legal and non-privileged means. "She claims to be part of a coven of witches and professes to have had a vision of the attack on the funeral."

Still he coughed, trying not to choke on the next part. "She said the attackers were demons. I know how ridiculous that sounds, but I believe she is somehow involved."

He waited while the two homicide detectives stared, eyes fixed on him with what may have been surprise or disbelief on their faces. He couldn't quite tell. "It sounds crazy," he added in the hopes of getting them talking, "but there *was* an occurrence at the cemetery. I'm only passing along the information I assumed you would want."

"Why," Lonergan began, "do you think she told you this?"

"What do you mean?"

The cops shared a glance, and Ian got the creeping sense they already knew about Anna and the incident at the graveyard.

The other one, Roch, glared at Ian with what amounted to sky-blue drill bits. "Where were you when you had this discussion?"

Bristling in response to the change in the man's tone, Ian leaned back in his chair. "I don't see how that's relevant."

"It's relevant," Lonergan said, and he too now tensed, taking on an adversarial posture.

Ian shook his head but answered the odd question. "She came to my home to discuss another issue."

"What issue?" Roch demanded.

Why the aggression? Ian felt his own muscles grow rigid and decided he was done with the interrogation. He'd come to offer information that may or may not be related to a crime, and now the detectives were grilling him over where he'd met the woman?

He cocked a brow, a move anyone who'd faced him in the courtroom would know well. The look was a warning that he was done playing nice. "That's not your concern and is immaterial to either the events at the cemetery or Don Jacobson's murder case."

"Why do you think she has anything to do with the murder investigation?" Roch asked, still eyeballing Ian.

Ian clamped his mouth shut. What could he say? Any

relation between Anna and Ronja and the suspicion that Ronja had something to do with Jacobson's death were all in Ian's mind. Weren't they?

Anna had admitted to having a lifelong animosity for the other woman, but that wouldn't be proof enough. The detectives already knew Ian had hired Jacobson to investigate Ronja, but would they doubt him if he told them he'd also had the P.I. look into Anna? The same woman on whom he was now casting suspicion?

He pulled at his shirt collar, feeling like he had to get his stories straight. He hadn't done anything wrong but was having trouble keeping reality separated from Anna's claims and his own imaginings.

"Look, that's all I know. If you want answers, you should call her." Ian made a move for the door. "She definitely knows more than I do."

"She told you some pretty unbelievable things, didn't she?" Lonergan delivered the question calmly, his even tone stopping Ian cold. Still facing the door, he paused to listen when the detective added, "She came to help you with a problem you've been having that's as crazy-sounding as demons. Isn't that right?"

How the hell could they know that? Ian turned around slowly, unwilling to betray the slightest response and hoping his face didn't give away his shock. "I'm telling you, the reason she came to my house has nothing to do with what happened at the cemetery or to Jacobson."

"Oh, but it does." Lonergan scrutinized Ian before heaving a sigh and raking a hand through his dark hair.

A knock sounded on the conference room door, prompting Roch to reach in front of Ian to open it. Then the towering man stepped out into the hallway and closed the door behind him, leaving Ian and Lonergan to stare at each other in silence.

After a moment, Roch returned and addressed his partner.

"We've got another one. Time to cut this short."

Ian was more than ready to take the reprieve before the detectives could dig any deeper. He'd been foolish to come here and talk of ghouls and magic, a subject he didn't want bandied about within his professional circles.

Then again, if his colleagues knew he'd been hallucinating and had gone so far as to seek out a brain specialist, that could kill his reputation just as quickly. *Damn it. I need to get out of here.*

"Wait," Lonergan said when Ian edged through the door. "I think you need to come with us."

"Where?" On the heels of the query, Ian swiped a hand through the air. "Never mind. I don't want to go anywhere with you. I'm sorry I troubled you."

Detective Roch didn't seem pleased by his partner's suggestion, but he only thinned his lips and said, "There's been a murder."

Ian exhaled quickly. "Why would I need to go to a crime scene? I have no business there."

"You should see what we've been dealing with," Lonergan said. "Trust me on this. It's in your best interest to accompany us."

"Is that some kind of threat?"

"No." Lonergan grabbed two bottles of water from a side table and offered one to Ian. "It's a favor."

~

The four-story building of dark gray was beautified by windows of mint-green glass, lawns manicured to perfection, and an art-nouveau patio out front with stone squares for seating. As Ian followed the detectives down the walkway, he admired the sleek, contemporary style and the way it was balanced by soothing tones.

The cops had brought him to a dormitory, part of the local art college known as SCAD, Savannah College of Art and Design. Since the two men worked homicide cases, Ian couldn't imagine why they felt he should tag along.

Their demeanor was solemn, the car ride quiet, both causing a cool tide of angst to roll through him, despite the day's persistent heat. Their behavior made him even more uneasy, yet his instinct told him to follow along.

He still couldn't decide if he should be relieved or troubled by the fact that Lonergan and Roch were already aware of what Anna professed was happening in the city. But instead of going into further detail about that, they'd asked him to come to the dorm.

And no matter how he felt about them or the witch they seemed to be familiar with, Ian's curiosity was even stronger than his dread. No, curiosity was too benign of a word. Something inside Ian was pushing him to find out more, to see whatever they'd brought him here to see.

He often relied on hunches when dealing with clients and adversaries, and right now, one was telling him to trust Lonergan and Roch. To follow them into whatever grisly scene they might be taking him.

He still didn't accept what Anna claimed. He couldn't find it in himself to believe in monsters and magic, but these cops were acting strangely. And above all, Ian needed answers.

He would take any explanation other than the notion that witches and demons actually existed. If he let himself accept that reality, then he would have to admit that something had come after him in his own home. And that idea was preposterous.

It was terrifying.

The glass doors opened to a cacophony of voices subdued but still noisy due to sheer number. Thirty or so students were cordoned off together in a lounge, the room's bright circus colors in stark contrast to the horror-filled faces of the young group.

The cold tide within Ian grew rougher, crashing into him relentlessly and threatening to take him under. He didn't have to be a cop to sense the morbid mood permeating the place, or to hear the soft crying and whispers, to see the wide eyes and stricken expressions.

Something terrible had happened here.

"Wait," Roch said before he and his partner moved to speak with officers already on-scene.

Two cops, a stout male with dark skin and a petite female with a blonde braid hanging between her shoulder blades, were standing guard at the bottom of the stairs. The man spoke briefly with Roch and Lonergan before the female waved Ian forward.

He didn't know what they'd said to explain his presence, and he didn't care to ask. He was simply moving, like a man set on auto-pilot.

When they reached the second floor they found the level of activity there was busier but quieter. The people milling in the corridor wore jackets or uniforms designating them as crime scene technicians, their swarm of activity centered outside of a dorm room.

The two detectives led him to a spot where he had a clear line of sight into the room. Two people were kneeling on the floor, discussing and gesturing to a mound covered by a white plastic sheet.

"Stay here," Lonergan told Ian, "and try not to draw attention to yourself."

No problem there. Ian's senses were heightened yet wary as he waited for any clue, any visual sign or overheard explanation to tell him what was going on. Clearly there'd been a death, but he still had no idea why he'd been brought here.

He stared into the room, watching intently as the two people stood to greet the detectives. Then they retreated to a corner to speak with Lonergan, leaving Roch standing beside the sheet. There appeared to be an irregularly shaped lump beneath the fabric.

Ian didn't have to be told what lay under the crisp, clean material, but he steeled himself when Roch knelt down. He held his breath when the detective turned his head to pointedly meet Ian's gaze.

And he clenched his fists when the cop flipped back the sheet.

Internally Ian recoiled, but physically he held his ground and forced his eyes to stay on the body. Or was it a body at all? He stared at the brown form—unnaturally twisted—trying to make sense of what he was seeing. What must have been flesh was now shrunken in on a skeletal form, bent and misshapen in an agonizing version of the fetal position.

As he studied the figure, he realized why the image wasn't computing. The body looked mummified, with skin so dry and cracked it looked like it had been resting in a sarcophagus for hundreds of years. But the clothing hanging limply on the corpse was new and undamaged.

Ian's mind rebelled. He could make no sense of what Detective Roch was showing him.

Then the strange outing made sense. This was why they'd brought him here, to shove even more incredible evidence in his face.

Why was everyone so determined to make Ian believe that something supernatural was happening in Savannah? Why did they all feel so strongly about his need to know?

Here were two cops, two men sworn to protect and serve, and they were showing Ian things he shouldn't see, and sure as hell didn't want to accept. They were determined to make him believe. Just as Anna was. And Ronja.

Yet Ian had kept convincing himself it was all untrue. He'd continued to deny.

Shaking his head, he took a tentative step backward and

hit the wall. He turned, intent on going back downstairs, but he came upon an older man with a balding pate speaking to another officer.

And what he said made Ian stop short. "Can you believe it?" The man shook his shiny head. "Another one."

The second officer's face was ashen. "What the hell is going on in this city?"

Ian had heard enough, and there was no way to convince himself he was imagining any of this. Reality was coming at him from all sides, breaking through the wall of denial he'd carefully constructed over the last few days. The hard shell he'd built to protect his sanity.

No. I don't want this. Keeping his pace in check, he moved to the stairwell and made his way down and then out through the front doors. He only made it as far as the cement seating area when Roch caught up to him with Lonergan close behind. "Wait," the big cop called from a few feet behind. "Ian."

The use of his name with such familiarity, and such understanding, from the more rigid of the two detectives finally made him slow and turn around. "Why did you bring me here? Are you trying to intimidate me?"

"No, we're trying to bring you around." Lonergan had been jogging to catch up and came to a stop with a heaving breath. "What if we'd told you why we wanted you to come here? What we wanted you to see?"

Ian let his gaze wander past them, back to the mint-colored windows that had seemed so nice before. Now they only held dark secrets, the pretty exterior of a safe world now shattered.

"I wouldn't have come," he said. Then he firmed his jaw and shifted his stare back to the detectives. "Fine then. Let's just say it's all true. I still don't want any part of it."

"That may not be an option." Roch shook his head. "If you really are connected to Ronja, if you were once her brother, you aren't simply a part of it." He frowned. "You're the damned linchpin."

They know everything. But Ian couldn't muster any more shock or indignation. He was simply worn down. "Why are you both involved? Why do you care?"

They glanced at each other before Lonergan said, "That's a long story. Suffice it to say, we both became involved with a couple of witches."

Ian laughed, but the sound was brittle. "I don't suppose they're part of Anna's coven?"

"We *are* on your side, Ian." Roch lifted a hand to shield the sun that suddenly popped from behind a passing mass of clouds. "All of us, but especially Anna. We had the luxury of being eased into all of this, but you..."

"You don't have time," Lonergan finished.

The same sentiment Ian had heard from Anna earlier today. He blew out a breath. "Well, I'm going to take some time. I can't tell if I'm the one losing it, or if it's the rest of the world that's gone mad. Either way, I don't know what's real anymore."

Shrugging, he took a step backward. "But I'm going to figure out what to do next. And I'll do it on my own."

"Don't take too long," Roch said. "Ronja already approached you once and brought you into her fold to be her lawyer."

"I've already severed that relationship."

"You need to stop thinking that Ronja or any of her kind play by the rules of human society."

Ian hardened at the reminder. "Isn't Anna one of her kind?"

"No way in hell." Now the big blonde cop's glower was back, and Ian could tell he was treading on sensitive ground. So he shouldn't insult the witches. Got it.

"You may not be safe," Lonergan told him.

Ian would have replied, but a young girl rushed up to them then, her eyes wide and anxious. "You're the two detectives?"

Lonergan nodded. "Yes we are, but any statement you want to make can be given to—"

"I tried, but they won't listen. Please." She clutched Lonergan's arm. "Jaime isn't irresponsible or some kind of a flake. Her purse and cell are still in her room. So's her boyfriend's phone."

Ian had a feeling this young woman's alarm wasn't just over the body found upstairs in the dorm, and apparently the cops agreed. "Ma'am," Lonergan said, "what are you talking about?"

"They're missing. Jaime and Rod were in her room last night, but now they're both gone," she sobbed. "They're just...gone."

3

In all of her previous visits to the pit, Ronja had been struck by the scent of recently-excavated soil in the subterranean room. Now as she edged through the jagged, broken cement wall leading from dungeon to earth, she was struck by the overwhelming stench of blood, infection, and copious human waste.

All of this came from the man strapped—and chained for good measure—to the stone altar at the bottom of the steps. The pit was in the center of the room, a space dug even deeper into the ground. The man's revolting condition was to be expected after enduring seven days of the most inhumane torture imaginable.

Yet Tyr, Ronja's lover, had suffered willingly. For her, for himself, for them all. The Amara.

His torture had been part of a ritual known as the Jin Deva, a ceremony rarely performed, because the subject usually didn't survive. But Tyr was strong, even without his normal intake of Ronja's immortal blood to give him longevity.

Ignoring the foul smell, Ronja moved closer and let her thoughts follow that path. Blood, the stuff of life, present at birth and often at death. And human blood had been the only sustenance Tyr had been allowed this past week. If people only knew the power they carried around in their veins—such potency, even if not blessed by a demon, as hers had been.

She took another step closer, her pale, bare foot scraping across the dirt. Tyr's eyes shot open, and she was pleased to see that his sclera and irises were consumed by black. The cold, obsidian orbs were evidence of his new state. His possession.

Even she didn't know how many demented souls now resided within Tyr's body. The ritual served a particular purpose: to invite demons and other malicious entities into his physical being, and therefore, into this realm. And though the beasts all lived within him, they did not possess and control Tyr.

He controlled them, along with all of their glorious and brutal power.

His upper lip curled in a snarl as Ronja eased closer. Something rolled beneath the flesh on his face, moving from his jaw, up over his cheek, and across his forehead before disappearing beneath soot-black hair. The normal shine was gone from his long locks, replaced by untold sticky substances that matted and knotted the strands.

But his time was done, and soon he would be cleansed, rehydrated, and fed whatever his heart desired. He would recover and reclaim his own natural stamina.

Then he would be set loose.

Before she could employ her new weapon, Ronja had to help bring Tyr out of his enraged trance. The feral and ravenous man she saw before her had been created by immense pain and the fever running rampant through his abused body.

Of course, the vile monsters now thriving inside of him were partly responsible. Each of the creatures wanted nothing more than to wreak its revenge on the society that had banished it to the netherworld. To Hell and all its darkness.

The underlands must surely be terrible. What fun could be had there, without humans to torment, brutalize, and…eat?

But Ronja would never be subjected to Hell. She and her master had much better plans.

"Tyr." She spoke calmly, concentrating on her lover's intensely furious eyes. The inky marbles were locked on her with such hate and craving she knew Tyr was not in control at the moment.

"Tyr," she said with more force. "Take command of your body and mind. You've done well, and now you will be set free. Rewarded." She risked another step toward the altar.

"Ronja," a tall, lean woman warned under her breath from the far side of the pit. Carson was her new second-in-command female, and she was concerned. Rightly so.

But Ronja did not fear the man writhing beneath his newly acquired cloak of evil. He worshipped her. He loved her.

"I want to set you free, my beautiful warrior, but first, you must come to me. Take control, Tyr."

Uncertainty creased his filthy forehead. And he closed his eyes.

"That's it, my darling. Come back to me. Own yourself and train your new servants to subside when you demand."

Tyr's bronze chest rose and fell in one long motion, the fierce musculature still amazing despite the muck covering his skin.

"That's it," she whispered, desiring her partner more than ever before. His ability to survive and become the Daevo was an aphrodisiac like no other. She wasn't sure she could wait until he was clean before letting him ravish her with his new viciousness.

Pus rolled from an open wound on his thigh, and she promptly changed her mind. No. She could definitely wait.

This time when his eyes opened, they were still a bottomless black, but a calm had entered his visage. More than that... recognition. "Ronja." His voice was a bare croak.

"Water," Ronja snapped, holding a hand out for Ross, the Amara's shifter, to hand her a cold bottle he held at the ready.

Knowing no fear, she went to Tyr's side and tipped the bottle to his lips, letting the cool liquid pour into his mouth and over his ravaged flesh. "Drink, my love. You have done well."

After he'd downed the drink, Ronja motioned to Ross and Carson. "Take off the restraints."

Ross showed all of the horror on his face that Ronja did not. "Shouldn't we wait a little longer to make sure—"

"Now." Her voice was steel and brooked no objections.

With a swallow so great it was audible to all, the shifter inched nearer the altar and began to untie the leather cuffs on Tyr's left hand. Carson moved in on the right, and then she retrieved a key from around her neck, inserting it in the lock that held the chains together.

Once Tyr was freed, both Ross and Carson moved far from the abused and starved man—the wretched creature who'd been tortured so terribly and driven to the very edges of death and madness.

With a grimace, Tyr rolled to his side and lowered one leg to the dirt floor. Ronja reached out to help him, but he lifted a hand to stop her.

Lust roared inside of her, and she smiled. Her Tyr, so proud, even now.

Once he was standing, Ronja eyed his tall, sinuous form with unabashed sexuality. She ran the back of her knuckles over the one clean spot she could find on his face.

And the entire room filled with a cold, overpowering presence. Their master had arrived, the demon Bastraal. His voiced echoed in the dark chamber. "Then it is done."

Bastraal's voice?

Ronja turned to the point from which the sound originated. "You can speak? But...I heard you, and not only in my mind."

"I heard him too." Carson had her arms at her sides, but tension racked her muscles as she stood in a combative stance. She was unnerved by the voice.

As was Ronja.

"My time draws near," Bastraal said, his raspy words blasting inside the underground chamber like explosions in a night sky. "Only during this moon can I become more and take true shape."

Ronja was both excited and disconcerted. For a millennium the demon had existed almost entirely in her mind, other than his brief entry into a mortal body centuries before. But recently, he'd found a way for his essence to cross over to this realm again, and it had been especially sweet that his summoning had come from one of the coven witches whom the Amara had deceived into helping them.

It had been too long since Bastraal had possessed a true sound. And a visible body, one that could be truly discovered by her seeking hands. Ronja licked her lips. *Oh, the possibilities.*

"What will you become?" she asked, only to have what felt like a hand grip her upper arm and begin tugging toward the steps, and away from Tyr. This sensation was new as well. Before, he'd only ever touched her with what seemed to be tentacles, and...*other* appendages.

"Let them tend to the warrior. You and I must confer," Bastraal said, his invisible fingers tightening around her.

She looked down at her arm. Was that a pale luminescence? "I see you," she whispered.

A riotous thrill ran from her stomach to her heart and made the organ pound. All was coming to fruition. *At last!* A thousand years gone by, and she was so near to achieving victory over the coven. Soon she would be able to look into Bastraal's eyes again, and with him truly by her side, they would reign over everything and everyone in this weak, pitiful world.

And Vanir would one day come to appreciate his position. Her brother, her second self, would return to her forever.

Finding him again—alive!—during the time of prophecy was no coincidence. They were meant to be reunited, and Bastraal had promised he would make it happen. He would make sure she knew her twin again.

She shivered and ran her fingers over those of her demon master and lover. "Now that Tyr has completed the Jin Deva, we can send him to the coven. He can destroy those witches and—"

"No." Bastraal tightened his grip on her, bringing a sting of crushing pain. He continued to steer her up the steps and through the hole in the wall that led to the dungeon, her own modern-day torture chamber, where three humans were currently chained.

They had provided blood for Tyr the past week, and now they were either rubbish to be disposed of or potential shells for other types of demons to reside within. Even with Tyr's transformation into the Daevo, Bastraal would demand his army of beasts.

And Ronja would supply.

But she did not understand his desire to wait one minute longer before ending Anna St. Germaine and her despicable coven. "Why not strike when they least expect it? We can lure Anna to town again, but this time our intent would be her death."

"Do you question me?"

Hearing him speak with such a thick, deep presence was not only satisfying but on another level…disturbing. Especially when he put such force into his words. She would swear his voice actually touched her, that the bass-like timbre vibrated into her chest.

"Never, Master." She bowed her head, while internally, she quivered.

At last, he released his crushing hold. "A thousand years we've waited, planned. I do not intend to rush now, not when I am just coming into my full power. We will wait." He stroked her shoulder, and then the wet texture of a tongue ran up her arm. A kiss to soothe the bruise he'd surely caused?

"Wait until I give the order."

"But what of my brother? What if he has more contact with the coven?" Ronja was distraught by his edict. "He could be swayed by their charms, or even their magic. They could turn him against me."

"No more!" His reprimand lashed out at her.

She cringed and expected a blow from his cold, cruel power. She knew better than to question him, but her brother meant so much. Vanir was the one thing for which Ronja would defy even the mighty Bastraal. She would have her sibling beside her again.

As if reading her mind, the demon's touch gentled, becoming placating and soft. He caressed the side of her neck, and Ronja shivered violently. Would he truly be kind now, or was his sweet stroke only a ruse?

"Do as I say, Ronja." Though treating her like porcelain, his tone was still thick with menace. "We will have more than enough time to coerce your precious brother." She felt his freezing breath near her face, on her cheek. "But first I must find a suitable vessel."

4

Anna gave a final stroke on the canvas with ivory oil paint and stood back to check her work. The magnolia was pictured up close and in full bloom, so vivid she could almost smell the airy perfume that personified spring in the South.

Setting aside the brush, she crossed her arms over her stomach and studied her creation. Painting soothed her, always had, and after her visit with Ian this morning, she'd come home in dire need of an outlet for her frustration.

She couldn't put her finger on what bothered her most. Was it his obvious abhorrence of anything supernatural? Or the very real possibility that he was her sworn enemy's brother reincarnate?

Perhaps it was both of these, combined with the fact that he'd come into her life just as her trial was due to arrive. Fate was a tricky, enigmatic force—as her sisters could attest—and Anna knew better than to accept anything at face value.

Whatever the man's role was to be, she had no choice but to offer her guidance. He was clearly unaccustomed to the mystical world in which Anna glided so effortlessly. He was a stranger to magic; in fact, he seemed to despise the very notion of its existence.

But he'd better get used to it. Because a coven of witches were all that stood between him and the truly dark magic that threatened them all.

Putting a finger to the royal blue stone in the center of her pendant, Anna reflected on all of the possibilities now facing her, some good, some...unpredictable. And for a psychic, not knowing could be the worst.

There'd been no clear sign that her challenge had begun, but she was the last of The Nine. She still had a trial ahead of her, and a man was most assuredly in her future. Each of the other witches had been united with her perfect match, though not all had accepted the pairing willingly. Not at first.

So Anna would reserve judgment or concern until she was certain her time had arrived, and she would welcome whatever man the prophecy had chosen for her. Her life, her essence, centered on magic, so it was easy for her to put complete faith in the powers that were.

She would never question her obligations.

With a glance out one of the rear windows that overlooked the sprawling gardens and stone patio, she noted the fading of day's final light. Everyone living here at her family estate would be in dinner-mode soon, so she made quick work of cleaning her brushes and oils and left her blooming magnolia to dry.

Rubbing a rose-scented lotion into her hands so she wouldn't stink of mineral spirits, Anna exited her chamber but paused before closing the door. Her cat, Ivy, had been reclining on the floor in a spot of afternoon sun while her mistress painted, but with the warm light gone, the sleek gray feline opted to leave as well.

The two females made their nimble way down the three stories of the large mansion bequeathed to her and Quinn upon their parents' deaths. She thought often of her mother and father, both skilled in magic to some degree, and both taken by that very power.

Over the years, the memories of the explosion—that horrible day—had lost some of their bitter sting. The happier images of her mother and father came with softer edges, and more often than not, brought tender emotion instead of pain.

But now that her challenge was drawing near, the pressure of fulfilling the prophecy sharpened all those memories. The depth of her loss threw everything into stark, clear reality.

She had to ensure the prophecy was fulfilled in the coven's favor. Her duty was to see Ronja and Bastraal defeated. Forever.

Yes, Anna stood to defend the lives of innocents.

But she also refused to let her parents' deaths, their sacrifice, be in vain.

For her it was simple. Faith in the prophecy equaled faith in her parents, as well as the gift of magic they had passed on to her and her brother. So she intended to honor it all by being victorious. No matter what.

Plastering on a mask of serenity for the sake of her friends, Anna entered the grand hall and looked about. The witches and their men had two favorite hangouts in the mansion—yet the first, the grand hall, was completely empty.

Willyn and Kylie weren't kicking back on the favored green velvet couch while watching one of their romances on the large flat screen on the wall. Neither Viv the physicist nor Claudia the historian were curled up in the elegant chairs reading a magazine. And Shauni wasn't romping about with Skid, the rescue-puppy who'd finally grown into his gigantic feet.

Anna hugged herself as a wind of things to come blew through her. The room felt positively barren and, not for the first time, she wondered how her life would be after things returned to normal. How would she pass the hours once the witches all moved out? When she had no more looming war for which to prepare?

There would be no more feminine squabbles or peals of laughter. No more sparring or weapons practice in the ballroom, and her dining room would once again be filled with tables and chairs instead of a chemistry-slash-spell-working lab.

She was both excited to complete her life's mission and saddened that her friends would be leaving. But the time for those sentiments hadn't arrived, not quite yet.

The kind of clamor that could only be created by a multitude of voices was coming from meeting place number two, the kitchen. By the goddess, they sounded like a horde.

So no, Anna thought, smiling to herself, she wouldn't have to worry about loneliness any time soon.

Veering toward the loud racket, she entered to find an almost full house, or kitchen as it were. The gathering was replete with the rest of her coven, multiple cats, most of the men who'd joined the group over time, and the ever-present kitchen fixture, Mrs. Attinger.

Amongst the chaos, Paige was seated at the center island with her boyfriend, Chris. The ex-Ranger was the most recent male addition to the clan, since Paige had just completed her challenge. As befitted the coven's warrior, her victory had come only after she'd taken the life of the woman who'd killed her mother and Chris's parents many years ago.

The required task was somewhat gruesome and unlike any of the previous challenges, but Scarlett, the woman Paige had beheaded, had been not only a murderess but also one of the Amara. After drinking Ronja's blood for decades to extend her life, Scarlett had delivered pain and atrocity upon innocents for far too many years.

So none under the St. Germaine roof would mourn her passing.

Anna eased over to the new couple, their blonde heads close together as they pored over a piece of paper. Avoiding the hot ovens and the women crowded around them, she took a seat on the black wrought-iron stool next to Paige. "What are you two so interested in?"

Paige lifted her head to reveal a dazzling smile and enthusiasm in her Caribbean-blue eyes. "My genius partner and I are coming up with a business plan." Paige clapped her hands together once and held her breath. Then, "We're going to open a nursery."

The center of her chest—where melancholy had threatened to grow—softened when she heard the news, as well as the hope, in her friend's voice. As a plant-lover herself, Anna had shared that passion with the coven's soldier and had always suspected Paige's tender touch proved there was more to the woman than her strength and fighting skills.

With her chest still warm with affection, she one-arm hugged Paige, holding her just a second longer than normal. "I can't think of a more perfect idea."

"That's not the best part, though," Paige said, reaching out to take Anna's hand, a rare display of emotion for the fiercest of the witches. "We're going to stay in Savannah. You know how I love the long summers."

Instead of words, Anna squealed and wrapped her arms around her friend, her sister in magic. As far as she was concerned, she wished all of her friends would stay close, along with Shauni and Viv, who'd both fallen for local men with businesses that grounded them in Savannah.

Hayden and Claudia were also a lock, at least for a while. They dated Trevor and Cole respectively, and the Chatham Metro Police would likely hang on to the detectives as long as possible.

Thinking of them, Anna slid her gaze to the two women now standing together, peering inside the top oven and presumably discussing whatever was cooking. Anna sniffed and detected a hint of herbed salmon, probably Hayden's choice. The ghost-whisperer was also a health advocate and urged them all to eat fish at least twice a week.

Laughter brought Anna around to see Willyn and Dare at the table at the far end of the kitchen, sharing something funny with Lucia and Ethan, as well as Quinn and Kylie. Anna couldn't guess what Willyn and her husband had planned for the post-prophecy years, but there was no doubt that Lucia and Kylie would be gone.

Lucia was a Spanish version of the popular tomb-raiding character in games and movies. Her new-found love, Ethan, was a well-traveled demonologist, so the two would surely return to globe-trotting soon enough.

And Kylie, the vivacious coed who'd fallen for Anna's little brother...well, she would follow Quinn anywhere. And after a lifetime of holding off his own dreams to help Anna prepare for the prophecy, Quinn was eager to see the world himself.

Anna wished them all well-being and happiness, even if their absence broke her heart on a daily basis. She'd always known she'd be one of The Nine, witches who would guard against encroaching evil and willingly give their very lives if required. All of that she'd been ready for, had trained for.

But she'd never thought of anything other than her duty. She'd never expected the coven to become her family.

"I'm telling you, it's done." Hayden grabbed a pot holder from the granite counter and opened the oven to retrieve two large cooking sheets of fluffy pink salmon.

"If you say so," Claudia said with her lips twisted up.

Sometimes, Anna thought with a smile, families tended to argue. Especially strong-willed sisters.

Falling into routine, Willyn and Dare came over to pass out plates while Kylie filled glasses with ice. The group that had once been a clash of various habits and personalities now functioned like well-oiled clockwork. Lucia and Ethan filled bowls with salad, and Mrs. Attinger took her mixture of diced yellow squash and zucchini off of the stovetop. Once situated around the crescent shape of the granite island, the group— more crowded than ever before—fell into banter and dug into the meal.

But it wasn't long before curiosity got the better of Kylie.

"How did your morning meeting go?" With long golden curls pulled back in a band, the youngest witch tilted her head in question. "When you came home, you flew straight up to your room."

Anna nodded, still chewing on a bite of her lettuce wedge with blue-cheese dressing. Then she replied, "I just needed some time alone, to decompress."

"So it went that well?" Paige the pragmatist asked.

"Just about." Anna reached for her tea before continuing. "Even though Ian contacted me for help, it seems he's talked himself into mental illness instead."

Viv set down her glass with a *thunk*. "Excuse me?"

Flicking her eyes to the Asian witch, Anna shot her a quick grin and clarified, "Let's just say he'd rather have neurological issues than face the truth."

Paige held up a hand. "So what happened?"

"Did he let you ward his house, at least?" Quinn was leaning forward on his elbows, his salmon forgotten.

Anna stopped eating and held her fork aloft. "Considering his last words were about reporting me to the police," she pointed the utensil at her brother, "that would be a no."

Claudia swallowed loudly and held up a finger. "And he wasted no time. He went straight to the Barracks to tell them all about Anna and how she might know something about the crimes recently committed in the city."

"What?" Viv gaped.

With a chuckle, Hayden glanced aside to Claudia then back to Viv. "No worries. The cops he called were Trevor and Cole. They...had a talk with him. Even took him to a crime scene." A shadow fell over the ghost-whisperer's golden eyes. "There was another murder reported."

Again Hayden and Claudia looked at each other before Claudia said, "And another kidnapping. We didn't see the need to tell any of you before now."

"Damn it." Paige thumped the granite with her fist, still quick to display her temper despite her new, calmer disposition. "It's time for this to end." She turned to Anna. "Any sign yet?"

"No." Anna knew what she was referring to, but so far, she'd had no blazing light, tingle in her veins, or any other signal to announce the beginning of her trial. Each witch's challenge had been preceded by some undeniable phenomenon, and she expected no less.

"Maybe you won't get one," Willyn suggested. "For the rest of us, we needed to know it was our turn, but since you're the last..."

"No heralding the great arrival," Kylie finished for her.

"That's a possibility." Anna stabbed a piece of fish. "Every time has been slightly different."

"And your trial definitely has the potential to be the most different of all," Quinn said.

Several confused stares jumped around the island until he added, "Come on, we're all thinking the same thing. Ian as part of Anna's trial. Ronja's brother. I mean, seriously, how bizarre would that be?"

"About as strange as a witch who talks telepathically to animals," Shauni said with a wink for Anna to show her support.

"Or," Dare put in with a hike of one dark brow, "as likely as a Christian witch and a pagan witch getting together." He shoulder-bumped his wife, and Willyn touched his arm in response.

Sparing a slight smile, Anna mimicked her brother and propped her elbows on the table. "The irony is he might have once been brother to a seiðr, may even have been a Nordic witch himself with his own power. But now he's suspicious and judgmental of anything to do with the supernatural. That is, when he's not trying to convince himself it isn't real."

"That's part of why Cole and Trevor took him to the crime

scene and," Claudia scrunched up her nose, "showed him the body. They were trying to get through to him and make him see that it's abhorrently real, and that we—meaning you, Anna—are actually the good guys."

"I'm all for helping him out if he truly is innocent." Paige, ever the realist, leaned against the back of her barstool. "But what if he's just another trick? Like the way Bastraal and Ronja manipulated Claudia's trial?"

"Thanks for the reminder." Claudia flipped a long lock of bright red hair over her shoulder.

"I've considered that," Anna said. "And we have to trust that whatever's meant to be will be." She gave a pointed look to Claudia. "Just like your trial, which went exactly how it was supposed to."

"I know." Claudia puckered her lips and hacked through her lettuce wedge with her fork.

"Or Ian could be the other thing." Kylie wiggled her brows. "He could be the one meant for you."

"I'm honestly not sure what's worse," Quinn said grudgingly, then lifted his hands when Anna made a scoffing noise. "What? I'm not crazy about being related to Ronja, even in the most distant, reincarnated kind of way."

Anna hadn't thought of it like that, and now that Quinn had drawn such clean, straight lines, she couldn't deny the potential relations. Her unease ratcheted up a notch. Or several.

"Why don't you just take a look?" Viv asked. "I know your visions can't be commanded or controlled, but you might as well try."

"I guess I could." Anna stared at her plate, realizing she'd barely touched her food while most of the others were almost finished eating.

"And we'll be there with you." Paige reached over and patted Anna's hand, while Shauni touched her shoulder from the opposite side.

Maybe it was the physical connection with her sisters, or—as Anna was fond of saying—because everything comes in its due time. Whatever the reason, timing, or trigger, a clear and vibrant picture flashed inside Anna's mind.

And she had her irrefutable sign. She sat up straight and whispered, "Oh."

Claudia's hand grasped her wrist now. "Are you okay?"

The images Anna had seen were fading now, but they'd left an indelible impression, one her psyche wouldn't and couldn't forget. "Well, I guess that answers that."

"What did you see?" Shauni asked. "Another attack? Ronja?"

"Ian?" Kylie chimed in.

"Not a person," Anna said, "but two items we're very familiar with." She drew a deep and somehow satisfying breath. "It's official. The ninth and final trial has begun."

She cast a look to Willyn and then to Lucia before allowing her gaze to encompass the entire group. "I need to get the book." She lifted her chin as determination flooded her body. "And the blade."

5

Still stunned by the day's events and his conversation with the detectives—who'd asked that he call them Cole and Trevor—Ian stood that evening with keys in hand to open the front door of his townhome. He'd gone to the office for a few hours in an attempt to distract himself but had done more staring into space than actual trial preparation.

Having opted for a quick bite at his favorite sandwich shop, he had no need to cook and didn't know what he would do to while away the hours. He was in no mood to watch TV or read a book, and he clearly wasn't in the right frame of mind to do any work.

Finding things to occupy his mind had never been a problem before, but tonight he just felt jacked up, like his skin was buzzing and his mind couldn't stay still. Images and worries jumped from picture to picture like a reel in his head, but one that had been spliced from different films.

A cool wind passed over him, and with it came a prickle at the back of his neck. No longer assured of a safe and secure world, he turned to peruse the square across the street.

Nothing seemed out of the ordinary as far as he could tell. A couple sat close to each other on one of the benches, their proximity and delicate movements telling him they were enjoying the romance of a pleasant autumn night beneath the majesty of ancient live oaks. The huge trees still held many of their summer leaves, and the lights of the square shone upward on thick foliage, creating a dramatic canopy.

Satisfied he was only feeling paranoid due to his discovery—his forced recognition that another realm had merged with the one he knew and trusted—he unlocked the door and stepped inside to a dark and quiet entryway.

He was still struggling with what to make of Trevor and Cole and what they intended to do to stop all the unruliness invading his city. His very life.

And there he went again, Ian chided himself, placing the responsibility at the feet of lawmen, when they'd both insisted that Anna was the one Ian should turn to. Anna, the witch. A practitioner of dark arts.

Though according to the two men, she was anything but wicked.

They'd seemed sincere, with a true concern for the murders that kept occurring, as well as the citizens who'd gone missing. Including, apparently, the young coed's roommate from the dorm.

Ian locked the door behind him, pausing as he wondered. Which was the greater likelihood, that two of Savannah's finest were in on a plan to destroy the city and kill its people? Or that they'd sided with a coven of witches to help stop that very thing?

Ian unloaded his pockets and tried to think of any other topic than a supernatural war. His brain was overloaded by all he'd learned, and he was in desperate need of one night, one single night of peace, without the threat of mystical anarchy weighing him down.

Setting his cell phone and wallet on a side table, he thought again of Anna. Trevor and Cole had dragged a promise from him that he would call her again. But he'd offered the assurance only because he'd wanted to get away from it all. From the crime scene, the cops, and the vile depictions of life to come if the coven couldn't find a way to stop the Amara.

The Amara, what a name. It meant "deathless" in ancient Sanskrit, according to Cole. The group served Ronja, who in turn bowed down to a demon. Bastraal.

Ian still couldn't shake the chills he'd felt since learning that name. A sense of familiarity stole over him whenever he thought of it. *Bastraal.* He'd never heard of the demon before, but somehow, he had a feeling he'd run into him. In person and in his bedroom.

You have no proof of that. His logical side took over in what surely was a measure of self-preservation, but Ian was fine with that. He'd had enough irrational and fantastic notions for one day and would gladly defer to sound judgment.

Which was why he couldn't contact Anna. Not tonight. He was still filled with distrust where she was concerned, no matter how sincere she might seem. Or how refined. Lovely and ...noble.

He shook himself and mentally stomped on the attraction he felt for her. The purely biological response was overshadowed by his first impression of her, an innate sense of suspicion that was still stuck in his subconscious.

On the first day they'd met, Anna's first go-to action had been to flash magic at Ian. And despite her claims of integrity and morality, he couldn't help comparing her actions with those of Ronja.

When that witch had gotten furious with Ian, when he hadn't immediately caved to her demands, Ronja's rage had blown through the room like a wind escaping the depths of Hell. She had also first approached him with smiles and sweet talk, but then she'd turned on him. She'd tried to intimidate him.

So how could he be sure Anna wouldn't do the same? He was back in the same predicament, not knowing whom he could truly trust. And now that his reality had been destroyed, replaced with an unknown and terrifying alternative, he needed someone with knowledge of that world.

Someone he could rely on.

A clank suddenly rang out deeper inside the townhome, wrenching Ian from his internal debate. The clink and hollow clatter sounded like a bottle landing on the floor to roll across the sandstone tiles. But no one else should be here now. Surely not his parents, because all of the lights were still off.

And Ian didn't have a cat.

Instead of calling out like the reckless heroine of some suspense story, he slipped quietly out of his shoes and began to ease toward the first door on the left, creeping into his study. Across the Persian carpet he tread without making a sound, calmly and with presence of mind, because this wasn't the first time he'd been broken into.

The second drawer on one side of his desk contained a Ruger, and though he'd rather not use a gun, it was better than being on the receiving end. He slid the drawer open silently to retrieve the pistol, and thumbed off the safety with a soft *tick*.

Last time the burglar had run, and Ian had never had reason to shoot his weapon outside of the practice range. He had the prickling sensation of dread again and wondered if tonight might be different.

Just as he began to move into the adjoining living room and come around the rear of the house, then through to the back entry of the kitchen, he remembered his cell phone still lying on the foyer table where he'd left it. His first instinct had been protection, but he scolded himself for overlooking the second imperative.

Calling for help in case there was more than one intruder. Maybe he was that foolish heroine after all.

As soon as he exited into the hallway again, a strange smell hit him and made him cover his nose in response. Rot. Something like death, but with an overlay of loamy earth.

He imagined a zombie having risen from its own decomposing grave. That's what it smelled like. Any time before, he would have laughed at himself for even thinking such wild things, but after what he'd learned today…hell, who knew?

He still needed that phone, so he moved toward the table, trying desperately to ignore the repulsive stench invading his nostrils and forcing its way down his throat.

The smell of decay was so awful he actually gagged. What was in his house?

Fuck the gun and the bravado. I'm out of here. He now had Cole and Trevor both on speed-dial and would call them from outside. No, from the park across the street. Because whatever was in here wasn't a simple home invader, not of the human variety—and while Ian might be proud, even stubborn, he wasn't an idiot.

And he didn't have a death wish.

He was reaching for the phone, skating past the table toward the door and his escape, when the first wave of cold swamped him. *No. No! Not again!* He tried to run, disregarding the phone or his lack of shoes. He just had to get out.

He knew that freezing sensation, and the last time he'd felt it, he'd almost died. Whatever the source of the chilling essence, it had come back for him. Maybe to finish the job.

He didn't plan to stay and find out, but as he ran, his right foot stepped into what felt like a snare. Freezing cold looped around his ankle to pull one leg and then the other out from under him. The icy presence had him in its grip and was pulling him back along the tile floor, down the corridor, and into the inky shadows at the rear of the house.

As he slid toward the darkness, his heart clutched in his chest. He had a split-second to wonder if his fine antiques and wainscoted walls would be lifeless and unsympathetic witnesses to his death.

The cold tendril continued its attack, snaking its way up around his calf to his knee, his thigh, and finally his hips like an out-of-control vine. As he was pulled to certain death, he had only one image flashing in his mind.

Anna of the pretty blue eyes.

He should have listened to her.

Now his lack of trust would mean his demise, and as the cold grew so intense that it became a burn, Ian sensed his end wouldn't come quickly. He screamed when arctic fire scorched his face.

So neither would his death be painless.

Still skimming over the tiles down the long, long central hallway, he grasped out blindly with his hands, trying to grab onto a doorjamb, a table leg, anything to slow his speeding skid toward the back door. He was moving so fast, he was afraid he'd burst right through the wooden panel and into the courtyard his mother had so lovingly designed, planted, and tended.

At least his collision with the door might end this awful agony. His skin was boiling, ripping from his face, yet beneath the ravaging of his flesh, he could still feel the cold. So cold.

He didn't ram into the back door as expected, but was caught in an invisible net-like structure that lifted him into the air and wrapped around him. He managed to open one eye and could make out a shimmering network of fibers, shining in the dark with a strange luminescence.

Whatever had him was surrounding him, wrapping him up. He was caught in a freezing spider web that damaged his skin wherever it touched.

Ian finally found his fury and would have cursed his attacker, but a strand fell across his lips, sinking in as if corrosive to the tender flesh. *My God. The pain!* It was everywhere, his face, his hand, his scalp, as the web cut through his clothing to rip into muscles and connective tissue.

The back of his neck suddenly tingled and burned worse than anywhere else on his body. He didn't just feel it; he *heard* the skin cells sizzle as they were blistered by the cold.

How much more could he take? His heart was beating so

hard and fast the throbs had bled into one unending beat.

Just when he began to feel unconsciousness closing in from all sides, the network of fibers released him. He dropped to the floor, landing hard on his back, but even in his injured state, he rolled to his knees and tried again to get up and run.

If he had a chance to get away, he would take it. His hands were numb, so damaged he couldn't even feel them anymore. His socked feet weren't in much better shape, but he would leave his destroyed flesh on the floor if he had to. As long as he got away. To safety.

As he made his way to his feet, the hallway lights flashed on, blinding him. He jerked a hand up to shield his eyes, and the brief action was enough to let him see the back of his hand, to see himself changing.

As he watched, his wounds began to heal.

Only able to move at a jog, he realized the burning was fading. The terrible cold was being pulled from his body, like poison being drawn by a poultice. But he was still caught up in the shock and fear, so he whipped around to face the back door.

Nothing was there. The hallway was empty. No more web, no glimmering strands to trap and sting.

Afraid to touch his face, Ian rushed to the console table in the corridor. He flipped on the small lamp there and studied himself in the oval mirror on the wall. He stared in disbelief.

Like his hand, his face had healed, leaving no blood, redness, scratches, or even any scarring. Whatever had happened had been temporary, just like last time.

But damn, he'd felt the burn, the awful sensation of his skin being flayed by threads of ice. And his clothing was still torn to tatters. *Proof.*

He put his hand to his nape, searching for further evidence of what had seemed to be the worst injury. For some reason, the back of his neck had felt especially cold, the damage deeper. But as far as he could tell with his head wrenched around, that area too was unblemished.

As he looked over at his destroyed clothing, felt his widened eyes and trembling mouth, Ian called himself a hundred times a fool. He had no choice but to keep that promise and finally, honestly, listen to Anna St. Germaine.

And he'd better do it fast.

While he was still alive.

6

In her ivory dressing gown, Ronja walked barefoot through high, uncut weeds, their sandpaper blades rough and hostile. Just as she preferred. The forest behind her home backed up to the marsh, and with the arrival of the tenth month, water levels had receded, allowing the smell of rotten aquatic life to permeate the air.

Pulling a deep draw in through her nose, she scented the aroma of the night. Death. Decay. Destruction. A pungent scent, and so, so sweet.

She pushed aside the sharp blades of two swamp palmettos and edged closer to the great fire that raged, snapping and crackling with a low roar as it fed on logs and tinder. The heat and the glow of six-foot flames caressed her skin, and the sounds—the lovely moans and growls of her brutish followers—were music to soothe her demented spirit.

Her eyes tracked the bright orange sparks as they lifted toward pine tree needles far above. She watched them still as they were lost to the midnight sky. Lifting her arms, she welcomed the dead of night, the witching hour, and the secrets they hid so well.

Long had bonfires burned during the month of Samhain, but especially on that most hallowed eve. Many believers, both good and evil, had thrown their end of summer crops into the flames, or perhaps the bones of animals. Offerings to the spirits, in trade for their protection.

A ghastly transaction and one Ronja approved of. Bone and fire. Bonfire.

So tonight's towering blaze honored those age-old traditions, though the gathering here needed no protection. If anything, they were the creatures of the night.

Those from whom others prayed to be protected.

The fire before her groaned and rumbled, its brightness a waving flag to announce the beginning of the final stage. The flames leapt and hissed as the Amara celebrated, as they prepared for battle. And the coals burned, hot and expectant, as eager for their sacrifice as Ronja was for victory.

She surveyed the various demon breeds that skulked all around, creeping in and out of the trees. *Here,* she counted hundreds of the mad, cruel monsters, *here, at last, is my army.*

And there, she thought as a thrill shot from groin to chest, was the fiercest of them all. From hooded eyes she saw Tyr step forward, into the amber light. Once a mere man, ever a warrior, and now…the unrestrained Daevo.

She'd always known Tyr was special, ever since she'd found him almost two centuries ago.

He'd been gifted with the sight and had a true fighter's heart, so she'd offered him the chance to live forever. With the first taste of her demon-blessed blood, the handsome Native American had accepted. He had greedily devoured.

And Ronja had given him a new name. Tyr. After one of the Old Norse deities, also known as the god of combat and heroic glory. In all the years she'd been with him, her brave lover had lived up to the title.

The fiends lurking in the forest this night were all so malicious, so sinister, that a layer of evil seemed to coat the environment, the air, the trees, and the pewter clouds roiling overhead. A film so vile, it added an ominous sheen.

Ronja reveled in the overpowering presence of evil. So intense, even moonlight dared not enter.

Across the clearing, on the far side of the fire, humans were being held inside bamboo cages. One of the demons bent its awful, round mouth toward a woman, making her scream and scramble away from the bars. The beasts were gruesome with their three sharp teeth, created to pierce flesh, and to extract life force. Those particular demons sucked life from their victims as easily as soda through a straw.

Ronja tilted her head, amused by her analogy and entertained by her pets' taunting of the captives. But she didn't worry overmuch—each of the beasts knew to restrain themselves, to follow Bastraal's one directive: leave the humans untouched and unharmed. For they would soon become soldiers, combatants for the Amara legion.

The Amara still had far more unbound demons than humans to place them in, but day by day, that disparity was diminishing. Even if their number didn't increase, the demons hunkering down by the fire or slithering through the forest were little more than dregs, grunt soldiers to pad the ranks.

They could be used to distract and kill the men who'd made themselves part of this war by joining with Anna's coven. And the witches themselves wouldn't be able to do a damn thing to save their lovers. Not when they had a greater force to face. Not when they—and especially Anna—were being decimated by the Amara's secret weapon.

A strong hand fell upon Ronja's lower back, and fingers trailed lazy circles. She shivered with delight as she lifted her face to Tyr. "The time draws closer," she whispered. "October has come, the final trial, Bastraal taking corporeal form." She rubbed a finger over his lower lip, "And you. My darling."

Tyr's eyes had once been deep brown, but since his transition to the Daevo, they'd remained a pure, depthless black. She slipped her finger into his mouth and let him suckle. The nature of his new existence was even more cruel, his depravity more extreme, and his...*appetites* more demanding. Ronja found she quite liked the changes.

Hardly able to wait to take him to bed again, she looked deeper into the forest. Perhaps a nighttime escapade in the woods? *Ah, yes.* With screams of terror and howls of demon enjoyment echoing across the autumn marsh.

"I've never made love to the sounds of murder before." She leaned into him, her other hand stroking his bronze chest while his mouth did wicked things to her finger. "Shall we try it tonight?"

He growled and turned her body toward him, dropping one hand to cup between her thighs. "Only if I get to do the killing." He forced the heel of his hand against her, grinding it in circles. Ronja dropped her head back to moan her pleasure.

She gasped as lust rose sharp and demanding. "Then you must deliver wounds that kill slowly." Her robe parted beneath his free hand as he bent to ravish her breasts. "Or you won't make it in time."

"To what?" he asked, lifting her quickly, wrapping her legs around his waist. "To fuck you as they fade away?" He took her mouth with his, in a kiss both brutal and unrepentant. Just like the man he had become.

"You're right." His feral grin lifted one side of his mouth. "We'll let Carson do the killing instead. She's much more talented than we ever gave her credit for. A worthy second to back you."

The reminder of Carson's new status crushed down on Ronja's passion. The Amazonian woman had only stepped into the role after a devastating loss. Scarlett's murder.

Memories of the red witch—her lover, her friend—bombarded her now, destroying the ardor she'd been enjoying. "Maybe later," she told Tyr, her voice turned petulant as she leaned away from his seeking mouth.

"Now," he insisted, baring fangs—another new development. He glared at her with such fury, she was taken aback. But only for a moment.

"Tyr, control yourself." This was the phrase she used whenever he was getting out of hand. She didn't know how many evil entities were inside of him—she wasn't even sure Tyr knew—but on occasion, the sheer number of degenerate souls began to seep through, their depravity overwhelming his. Which was quite a feat.

He dropped her unceremoniously to the ground, accepting her decree, but making sure she understood his frustration.

In a display of rage, he marched to the cage and ripped the door off, tossing the bamboo frame into the fire. Reaching inside, he pulled out a human, the same woman the leech had tormented before.

Backing from the cage, Tyr lifted her up and spun her around, her screams fading and growing with each rotation.

Then Tyr—No. The Daevo—stopped his game and dropped her into his thickly-muscled arms. Snarling, he bit into her neck and with his bite clamped like a vise, he began to shake her.

Ronja had the impression of a huge, vicious dog. One that chanced upon a cat in the bushes.

She heard the woman's neck snap, the pop ricocheting through the trees. Tyr screamed his triumph, his power to take and destroy at will, and lifted the dead body to toss it onto the bonfire.

The crowd of demons cheered.

And Ronja trembled with delight. *Now it truly is a fire of bones.*

But she shouldn't show approval of Tyr's disobedience, not in front of the dregs. Crossing her arms, she quirked one blonde brow when her lover turned a rebellious look her way. "Are you quite finished?" she asked blithely.

In answer, he licked the blood from around his mouth in one long, circular stroke of the tongue. Then he smiled at her. He roared his laughter.

Meanwhile, Carson and Ross were busy blocking the doorless cage as Jack used her super-speed and strength to round up the few humans who'd escaped. Ronja snapped her fingers at a nearby demon, one of the huge warrior caste. "Go get boards, something to help them make a door."

The beast disappeared into thin air, and Ronja contemplated the usefulness of always having the fiends on-hand. The value of their ability to transport between locations couldn't be overstated. And at the very least, they made exemplary servants.

With orders handed out and cattle being herded, she started toward Tyr but paused when the awareness came over her. Bastraal had decided to join the festivities.

Though his merciless chill still preceded an arrival, she no longer relied on temperature changes to detect his presence. She could see the outline of his monstrous form, the luminescence of his body more visible as it reflected the firelight. Bowing her head, she greeted her master. "Bastraal. I wondered at your absence."

His almost-transparent shape eased toward her, and from what she could tell, his head was well above hers. His form still didn't seem to be human, though he did have hands and arms, one of which reached out for her now.

Along with his arm, another long appendage curled around her waist. "Come with me." The fullness of his audible voice still stunned her.

"We were just about to begin. We have entertainment planned. More soldiers to create."

"I'll find my entertainment elsewhere." The demon pressed against her back, gently but insistently, letting Ronja know he desired her company.

Allowing one slow step, she bided her time, moving, but at a casual stroll. Bastraal had been secretive of late, vanishing for long periods of time, making no mention of where'd he'd been. And tonight, he'd gone away again.

"Tell me, what plans have you made for Anna and her witches?" She played the coy submissive well. "Is that what you were doing tonight? Off by yourself, plotting their demise?"

Perhaps he'd been to the stone yard, a collection of mystical rock formations. Far out in another forest on another piece of property now owned by Ronja.

Thanks to her previous lawyer. Thanks to Vanir.

She referred to her brother by his given name only, not this modern "Ian" to which he now answered. Bastraal had said nothing of how he would ensure Vanir's presence in her life, but he had promised she would be with her twin again.

"We are so close to our conquest, Ronja. Did you wait these last thousand years to only now become a nag?"

The insult was mild but well-placed. Ronja prided herself on her independence. She didn't need men. She ruled them.

Bastraal however... "I only want to know what you've decided. You've always told me what to do, kept me informed of your ideas, your schemes." Throwing his words back at him, she said, "These last thousand years, you've always turned to me."

She stopped and raised her stare up, up high, past massive shoulders to his semi-transparent face. "Do you reject me now? When we are indeed so close?"

"I am in this world now and becoming more corporeal every day, but this form will disappear when the veil between the worlds closes again. Finding my vessel is imperative. And, as I apparently must remind you, more important than your foolish brother."

He pushed her again, less sweetly this time. "And if I have need of your assistance, I will advise you of that fact."

Bastraal sounded like the aristocratic gentleman he'd taken possession of in the seventeen hundreds. He'd lived a pampered yet powerful life in the short time before he'd been discovered.

And then promptly banished by a trio of sisters. The original St. Germaine witches.

Ronja didn't appreciate his superior tone, but there was nothing she could do about his arrogance, or his evasiveness. Bastraal was the only creature in all the realms which could make her fear death, so once again, she would hold her tongue. She would question him no more.

Anger and violence would be her only answers if she continued. This she knew from painful experience. Added to that, his temper was high, more so than usual, and he wasn't dragging her away for mere conversation.

Tyr wasn't the only male in her life who'd changed, who'd become more aggressive and craved sexual release more often. Bastraal was practically insatiable of late.

As if sensing her thoughts of him, Tyr barked her name from where he still stood by the bonfire. She sent him a slanted look, full of warning. Had he lost his mind? Did he not see who required her attention?

Again, he yelled her name.

And all of the howling, screaming demons fell silent.

Crossing the clearing, Tyr bared his teeth, his fangs. The powerful muscles seemed to writhe beneath his skin. Then lines of maroon began to crawl across his flesh, like exterior blood vessels formed by his fury.

Ronja inhaled sharply. The fool! He was calling up one of his entities, one of the monsters that shared his body.

But Bastraal saw Tyr's intent and shot a stream of frozen power toward him. The blast would have knocked any of the demons off balance, but Tyr simply bowed his back, giving the impression he'd absorbed the blow.

Bastraal's deep vibrato rang out. "Remember your place, Daevo."

Sending an appeal with her eyes, Ronja shook her head

slightly at Tyr. She mouthed the word "No."

Inhaling deep, rapid breaths, Tyr halted, gave a growl of resentment. But then he nodded his acquiescence before turning to march back to the fire.

Ronja could still see the bizarre red marks growing over his flesh. She doubted any of the humans would survive this night.

Tomorrow they would have to double the raiders sent into the city, but that was a small problem. She was just grateful Tyr could use the captives to divert his attention. Better he spent his anger in a way that wouldn't get him killed.

Amazed by her lover's disregard for his own well-being, she lowered her face to hide her reaction. Tyr had never confronted Bastraal before, and though he'd had a slight animosity toward Scarlett, his jealousy had never gone further than petty snipes and rivalry.

His aggression tonight had shocked her.

The demon hand on her waist tightened. Bastraal, it seemed, was equally possessive. Without further comment, the towering demon lord urged her onward with a small shove.

Yet as they glided through the high grass, back toward her plantation home, Ronja's mouth curled upward. One of the most powerful demons in existence and the rare yet mighty Daevo had almost come to confrontation...over her?

Perverted romance or not, Ronja's body was alight with sexual hunger, she could barely walk from the trembling need. Two such formidable beings fighting to win her love?

She glanced up at the quietly seething Bastraal and gladly welcomed the month of October.

For all of the surprises it would bring.

7

Anna stood on her balcony to watch as dawn shed its gleaming light over the ocean horizon. With the rest of the mansion still silent with sleep, she made her way down the outside stairs and around through the gardens. As she eased through the stone gate and across the grass, she slowed to a stroll and took a moment to remember.

Here, she paused, was where she and her sisters had first practiced magic, creating poppets to protect themselves against the late R.J., member of the Amara, and his cruel mind invasions. The women had all laughed and teased, and felt the rush of power. It had been a heady experience, even for a long-practiced witch such as Anna.

She continued on, noting the tree under which Hayden often tried to encourage them to do yoga. And on the edge of the forest, where they'd once set up hay bales as target practice. Viv had helped them hone their telekinesis skills, hurling wooden spheres, each of them finding new sources of strength.

How far they all had come, Anna mused, after embracing their destiny and overcoming uncertainty. She not only respected and loved the women of her coven, she admired them. They'd all jumped right in, despite never knowing or even suspecting their true fates and the important roles they would play.

Anna had been raised with prophecy, had years to prepare—magically, physically, and mentally. Her sisters had taken a great leap into danger, unsure of what would come or what they would be required to do.

Yet each of them had handled adversity, banding with the other women and battling through to success.

Yes, Anna consoled herself, no matter what happened from here forward, she felt sure her sisters had earned a restful place among the spirits, whenever that time should come.

She passed into the cooler, denser shade of the forest. Within the canopy of island vegetation, she passed another place which stirred memories. The cellar in the ground, where Willyn and Dare had searched for the book.

The sacred tome had been left behind by the original three St. Germaine witches, hidden so that only the modern coven could find it. The enchantment and information within those pages had been left for The Nine, Anna and her coven. Those who'd always been meant to battle Bastraal when he returned.

And prophesied as the only ones who had a chance of defeating the demon. The only power in the world that could banish and abolish him. Once and for all.

Now as her bare feet fell upon the ground, she let her energy feed the earth. And in return, she was fed. Magic could be found in every particle of soil, each leaf or insect, but the synergy of all those things was especially strong here, on her island.

This place with its wild forests and calming shores had been her inheritance, her fortress, and her blessing.

A black snake zigzagged across the path in front of her, but despite its arrow-shaped head, she feared no strike or even a hiss. She was a woman of the woods, a witch of the natural world, and while she did not possess Shauni's powers to communicate with animals, she sensed a communion of sorts. A mutual acknowledgement and respect.

Every hour of every day of her life had been building toward this special time, when she would take the final duty upon her shoulders, the most crucial task. And she was determined to do the one thing for which she'd been created.

The sun's warm light had traveled across the seas and found its way to the marsh waters. As she knelt in the grasses and inhaled the briny scent of stagnant pools, the brightness fell across her cheek.

A ray of that light beamed upon the deep green surface. And there a bubble popped, as if guiding her hand to its depths.

Wearing a sleeveless nightgown, Anna reached long, elegant fingers into the marshy water, her arm following until the olive-colored liquid covered her elbow. Her hand easily found the rope, for she had been the one to place it there. And with her grip tight, she pulled.

Water was one of the elements of magic, and salty inlets had been part of the island, part of her legacy, since the prophecy had been cast centuries before. The thick marsh had been the perfect place to hide the box and the treasure it held. Here where water and animals alike would guard the blade.

The dagger destined to end Bastraal.

She'd always known she would be the one called for the final battle, yet still her hand trembled as she untied the wet knot and wound the rope into a tight loop. Hefting the box in her other hand, she turned to face the woods.

Walking the path that would take her home, and back to her coven, she listened to the birdsong.

And readied herself for what was to come.

~

For once, all those living in the St. Germaine mansion chose to skip breakfast, opting instead for another source of nourishment. Magic. Every corner of the great home was quiet and the mood serious, while the witches dressed and readied themselves.

Today's circle might be the last they created during this time of prophecy. So apprehension and hope both contributed to the solemnity pervading every corner of the home.

The women would wear satin today, each in her signature color. Just as they had when they'd become a true coven and their amulets had been chosen.

Rather, Anna mused, when the enchanted necklaces had chosen them.

Her trial was the culmination of all the challenges, battles, and hard-won victories she and her sisters had seen. It was the end point of a life spent serving Fate, and the goal her parents had died trying to help her fulfill.

Even they had known Anna would be one of The Nine. Somehow, her family had always known.

So it was only right that the tap on her doorframe came from Quinn. His cobalt eyes, the same as hers, were steady with love and support.

Anna smiled at her brother. She could always count on Quinn.

"Ready?" he asked, the single word filled with so much.

Anna wondered if he was also recalling their first lessons in the craft, when he had been just a toddler, and Anna barely big enough to hold her first wand. Wands are associated with the element of fire, the element of power, and it wasn't long before she'd harnessed the flow. Magic had always come easily to her.

Her soul recognized the gift. Her heart remembered.

And the acceptance of her destiny had been ingrained in her, from the very first stories her mother had read at bedtime. Tales of three women, witches, who'd saved the very city Anna lived in. Savannah.

How exciting it had been for her then, imagining her ancestors banishing a demon! But her delight would turn to goose bumps when her mother came to the end, to the ominous prediction that the beast would one day return.

And that another St. Germaine witch would rise, to face the monster once again.

Anna tied the black robe and let it lay loosely on her shoulders. The front fell open to expose her royal blue dress underneath. The color of her eyes, her enchanted amulet, and—coincidence or no?—the coven's magic.

"After all these years." She turned with a mischievous smile meant to encourage her brother, to calm him as he calmed her. Because she knew he worried beneath that mask of bravery. She tossed the sides of her robe back with a flourish. "Surely, by now, I should be ready."

Catching on to her intent, Quinn laughed and fell into step with her as they made their way toward the wide mahogany stairs that would lead them down three stories to the main level. He too understood the importance of Anna's role. Ever the leader, never to falter. The other witches depended on her, just as she'd come to depend on them.

When they made it to the grand hall, the central enclave of the mansion, her sisters were all waiting for her. As Quinn made his way to Kylie, Anna felt a cord snap. As if she were truly handing him over to the young woman he'd fallen in love with.

Quinn had always stood by Anna, but now his place was with another. Anna's heart pinched but quickly released, flooding with warmth and love for Quinn and Kylie, as well as all the others.

Shauni and Michael were here, as were Willyn and Dare, and Viv and Nick. Even the detectives had traveled to the island, Trevor to be with Hayden, and Cole with Claudia.

Though the two men were tasked with solving the murders and stopping the disappearances in the city, they realized the importance of being with the coven.

Today the book, blade, and burial ground would be brought together in ceremony. And every open heart was welcomed on the island.

Every available source of coven energy—and the men were

now a part of that—would be present to support the witches as they cast their circle. Mr. and Mrs. Attinger were nearby, in the kitchen with Claire and Joe, who'd come from the mainland with Joseph and Sylvie.

There were no flowers out for Anna today, yet she understood that was Mrs. Attinger's way of showing her faith. Instead of blossoms, Anna had her family.

Lucia and Ethan stepped forward then, completing a semi-circle to stand beside Paige and Chris. As if on cue, the cats of the house all filed into the room, and if Anna hadn't already known what a portentous day this would be, the feline presence would have given it away.

Even the dog, Skid, was somber today as all of the animals sat near their humans. And all of them faced Anna, awaiting her smallest gesture, her simplest word.

Awaiting her command.

Anna's chest filled with golden heat, her heart burned with emotion, and she knew—she just *knew*—that with these amazing friends at her side, she could never fail. She would complete her challenge.

Sensing her rush of joy and confidence, Skid leapt to his hind feet and stood briefly to bark one sharp retort. Then he lowered to stand on all fours.

Anna inclined her head to the hound as he shook with excitement, his tail wagging forcefully and whapping against Shauni's thigh.

She knew her friends were on edge. How could they not be? After all the uncertainty, the riddles, and missions, everything rested on this last trial. They'd all been through so much and had come so far. Now it all fell to Anna.

For the first time ever, there would be no men in the great room. Anna couldn't say why she'd made this decree, but the others knew her instinct came from a greater place than her own wisdom. They would be nearby, their energy felt, but none besides the witches and their familiars would be exposed to whatever came from today's ritual.

So as she moved across the slate floor, the other witches left their men to follow. Only the cats accompanied the coven, for they had been called to defend the women. As surely as the women had been called to fight.

Anna tossed a look over her shoulder to Quinn and the other men. To the Attingers, Joe and Claire, and Joseph and Sylvie, who'd all come out of the kitchen. They would guard the gates while the coven was engaged in magic.

Feeling bolstered, Anna faced forward again. She glanced down to Ivy, the feline silent and serious as she strode forth. At the end of the corridor, Anna pressed her hand to the door, its ancient wood still intact.

She entered the great room to find that Quinn had done his usual duty and had set up the altar in the middle of the room, directly below the epicenter of the pentagram on the ceiling. The long wooden beams had been placed almost three centuries before, and the room had long been the heart of the island's power.

Anna flowed across the floor past the altar, where the sacred book stood on display. She made her way to the twelve o'clock position as the other women formed the circle, their bodies aligning outside the symbol of the sacred feminine, the star above them.

Pointing their hands to the floor, casting with flesh instead of athame, the women worked in unison. Visualizing a beam of light inside herself and then sending it out through her fingers, Anna—along with her sisters—first cast a circle for protection, then one for focus, and the third for power.

Once this was done, they called for a meeting of the human and the divine, a union as timeless as life itself. With the words spoken and the blessing requested, Anna lowered her hands and moved to the front of the white stone altar.

Before opening the book, she ran her fingers over the deep blue leather, taking just a moment to appreciate the fine copper embossment, imprinted in a language even she didn't understand.

But the book had helped Viv and then Lucia during their trials, as Anna expected it now would do for her.

Guided by knowledge from a source she couldn't name, she reached beneath the folds of her robe to an inner pocket. She withdrew the blade and held it aloft, balancing its weight across her open palms.

A line of light ran down the silver edge and lit upon the gleaming onyx stone set within the hilt. Reverently, she set the dagger on the altar in front of the book, then reached back into her robe to retrieve a tiny sack.

Inside the small burlap pouch was all that remained of the enchanted soil from Bastraal's previous grave, the one in which the original St. Germaine witches had put his remains years ago.

Pausing, Anna glanced around the room to her sisters, gaining strength from their confident expressions. They believed in her. And she had faith in magic, not only her own, but the source, a well of energy that was generations-old.

Though clairvoyant, she had no idea what to expect. But with this small amount of dirt, she would at last be bringing the three sacred items together. Her veins trilled as her very blood sang, the flutter of her heart providing the rhythm.

Only The Nine could defeat Bastraal, and they needed these three objects to do so.

Anna drew a deep breath, unashamed to feel her fingers shake, her throat catch. She lifted the bag and untied its string, ready to bring the three together at last.

The book. The blade. And the burial ground.

Anna poured out the mixture of soil and ash. She and her coven watched, entranced, as the glittering particles drifted slowly downward, carried not by gravity, but by magic alone. Finally the particles settled atop the closed cover of the book's blue leather, and the dagger's sharp silver edge.

For a moment, a thousand tiny bells rang through the air of the great room.

Then a blast of power erupted from the altar, shoving Anna backward two steps. A light came from above as winds with no origin rushed over them all. Anna looked above to find the pentacle glowing from within.

And as the gale picked up in strength to become a screaming tempest, she nailed her gaze to the quaking altar.

Just as the book flew open.

8

Light was a physical presence as it rushed through every cell of Anna's body. She felt warmth. She smelled sea salt and sage. And for the briefest of moment, she felt afraid.

But soon a sense of familiarity joined the powerful surge, filling her soul, calling to her spirit. This was a magic she knew well. The trilling sensation was born of her ancestors, the modern coven's predecessors.

She should never fear this source of power but cherish the solidarity with her elders. The St. Germaine sisters had been the first and had gone on to create a powerful lineage. One that ran down through Anna's maternal grandparents to be inherited by her mother. And embraced by her father.

Those who'd come before Anna had carved the path and kept the way well lit for others to follow. Retelling stories, teaching spells, and instilling courage. Her personal strength and code of honor had been handed down through the generations. Now both would be called upon as she faced her future.

Not just the future, but her present. Anna opened her arms and embraced the light. Her destiny, the prophecy, had come full circle.

The flood of light filling her veins was as much a part of her as the women forming the protective barrier around the room. Like the witches of the coven, power was her friend, her support system, and many times in her solitary life, this gift—magic—had been her sole companion. The love of her life.

As illumination whistled through her, she let the pulsing surge fill her with joy. At last she would serve as she'd been called to do so long ago. And, she thought with a glimmer of a smile, doing so would be a privilege.

Confidence rose up in Anna, pride in her family, her friends, and her role in this battle of light versus darkness. She had been chosen to defend the innocent, to stand against evil when none other could.

She would not fail. Could not. So much depended on her actions and her choices. Time and family had prepared her for this, her trial, and she would do whatever had to be done.

Paper rustled, pulling her gaze to the open book. Even with the bright glow of the pentacle overhead, a white-hot inscription was forming on the pages, a blazing light to outshine everything else in the room.

The mystical artifact was revealing itself to her, providing information that would guide her in the right direction. It had done the same for Viv and Lucia during their challenges; only then, the writing had been an electric blue.

Stepping closer to the altar, she surveyed the text. Reading swiftly, she discovered a mixture of eighteenth-century English and Latin. She wasn't as proficient as her brother when it came to the second language, so she passed her finger over each line, stopping occasionally to work out a word's meaning.

With the touch of her hand, the mystical storm within the chamber began to calm. No longer did the air move as if born of fury, and the pentacle above dimmed to a soft glow.

Certain her sisters would want to know what she was seeing, Anna paraphrased the essentials of the script, explaining as she went. "The text tells of a great battle, one that will decide the future of our world." This she and the coven already knew.

Her friends had each engaged in various confrontations and tasks, magical, mental, and physical. And they all knew Anna would be the one to end the demon, as well as the only one who could go head-to-head against Ronja, a witch who'd had a thousand years to hone her skills.

She began with the next paragraph. "Thirty-one days…" Trailing off, she studied the odd syntax, deciding how to best interpret what came next. "One sanctified month. This month I have to assume, since October has thirty-one days, and because my trial has begun. This month will constitute the final days of the prophecy."

She perused the next passage. "Um…create change. No, wait. That's not right." She bit her bottom lip, stare fixed on the section she was struggling with. "*Tribuo*."

The light still emanated from above, but the book's pages were no longer magically writing themselves, and the winds had died down completely. Anna turned to her sisters. "I think I'm going to need Quinn's help after all. Unless any of you are fluent in Latin?"

Claudia stepped forward, her loose hair a flaming river over the black robe. "*Tribuo*? No. I can't be sure about that one."

"I'll get Quinn," Kylie offered. "One language specialist coming up." The youngest witch hurried out of the great room, but her golden-haired cat, Sassy, merely watched from her place on the floor. Then she lifted a dainty paw to lick.

Kylie returned less than a minute later with Quinn, but the other men remained elsewhere.

Anna's brother crossed to the altar and studied the passage she indicated. He was much faster with his translation. "*Tribuo*. To grant, or granted. And *formo*." He sighed, a frown pulling at his mouth. "Your enemy will be granted body." He looked to Anna. "The only one of your enemies who is in need of a body is Bastraal."

Viv spoke up. "We already know he intends to take over a man's body."

"No." Quinn glanced to her then back at Anna. "That's not what this refers to. The word here, *animus*. That can mean vivacity or will. The way it's written means your enemy will be granted a body for his will, given a form to carry out his intentions. I think they mean Bastraal himself will become wholly physical."

Quinn studied the text again, crossed his arms, and stepped back. "At least for one night."

Anna slid her eyes to the page again. *Thirty-one days.* "All Hallow's Eve. Bastraal will take form on the night when our world is most closely linked to the spirit world, to the realms we can not see or sense any other day of the year."

Paige chimed in then. "So what we've got is the final battle occurring on Halloween, and Bastraal will have an actual demon body to fight us with."

"Sounds like," Shauni agreed as her black cat, Cuileann, sat by her feet staring at Anna and Quinn with piercing green eyes. The felines all seemed fully aware of the grave topic under discussion. Their knowing eyes held steady as they looked to Anna and Quinn. Tails barely twitched. Pointed ears stood at attention.

They were on full alert, as they always were when Bastraal was mentioned.

Thus far, they'd been the only creatures able to detect Bastraal, even see him when no one else could. The felines and Skid, Shauni's dog, had warned the witches to the demon's presence when he'd burst into their dimension and directly into the coven mansion.

It had taken several of the witches firing into Bastraal at once to force him out of their home, and that's when he'd been no more than an invisible presence. They'd felt his cruel, cold touch, but he'd still been without an actual form.

Anna was both revolted by the idea of seeing what Bastraal looked like and encouraged by the fact she would have a clear target. Positive and negative. Yin and yang.

Magic was all about balance.

"Is that all it says?" Willyn asked, kneeling now to pet Snowball. Even the gentle white cat was agitated.

"Not quite." Anna continued her perusal of the ancient vellum pages. There had been only a few paragraphs written, but everything she needed to know was there. "*Sepulcra* and *lapideus*." She glanced aside to her brother. "Graves made of stone?"

"Essentially," Quinn confirmed. "We all know the place it means."

He slanted a look to Kylie. The two of them had discovered the ominous house in the forest, as well as a towering rock formation. Inside an oval-shaped barrier of thick shrubbery, they'd come upon the stone yard, boulders and rocks of various forms with one great misshapen plate of black in the center.

Ronja had fought to acquire the property—by using Ian— and the coven had suspected the gloomy place in the forest would play a role in the prophecy. With a halting smile for the woman he loved, Quinn turned from Kylie and gave his attention to the book again.

This time as he read, his face fell into hard lines.

"What, Quinn?" Anna read over the last paragraph, the one detailing how Bastraal must be destroyed. The demon couldn't simply be banished this time, but abolished forever, not only in this world but in all worlds.

Ending the beast was Anna's ultimate task, the one thing she must do to complete her trial.

So she read the words as Quinn had done. Then she checked them again, allowing their meaning to fully register.

A place inside her chest congealed, even as the throb growing there became painfully strong. Her heart thundered its denial of what the book was instructing her to do, and she closed her eyes, wishing she could go back, even a few seconds before.

She didn't want this knowledge.

Before she could explain to the others, Viv began pacing and tapping a finger to her chin. The scientist of the group was working those brilliant wheels in her head. "We shouldn't see this as a bad thing. Bastraal taking form could be good."

"Why is that?" Lucia asked, lines of tension around her brown, Spanish eyes.

Anna stayed silent as they spoke, still trying to find her balance. Trying to understand how Fate could be so punishing. So vindictive in its demand for equality. For give and take.

"Think about it," Viv continued. "If Anna's going to be able to use the dagger on him, then he has to be corporeal, at least physical enough for her to drive the blade into."

Hayden snapped her fingers, joining in. "That's how you'll be able to kill Bastraal," she said to Anna with a light in her eyes. "If he becomes real by Halloween night, you can see him, hurt him."

Paige pointed at Hayden as if backing the theory she and Viv had formulated. "And then Anna can shove the dagger straight into his chest. Because we all know the bastard doesn't have a heart."

"You're right." Anna heard the defeat in her own voice. She felt the tremble and knew it was impending grief. "He doesn't have a heart."

"I wasn't being literal." Paige angled her head, but when she caught Anna's gaze with her own, she stilled. Her smile fell away. "What's wrong?"

Anna shook her head. "You are exactly right. He doesn't have a body, a soul, compassion." She pressed a fist to her belly, where horror churned with cruel blades of inevitability. "And he doesn't have a heart. That's why I have to wait until he's taken possession of whatever man he chooses."

"What? Why?" Hayden moved closer, with Claudia and Kylie flanking her. The other women drew near as well, giving their immediate support, their comfort. They tightened the circle, falling into a protective formation.

But even they couldn't save her now.

"The final sentences tell me how to defeat Bastraal for good, but to do so…" She stopped, swallowed against the angst and terror. Then she whispered, "*Vasa…interficio.*"

Claudia gasped and Quinn clenched his fists.

"Quinn." Anna cast pleading eyes to her brother, hoping against hope. "Please, tell me I'm wrong."

He shook his head, the shadow of heartbreak in his eyes. "No. I'm sorry, Anna. However you translate *interficio*, it means make something cross over to the underworld." He squared his shoulders, doing his best to stand firm. For her. "Or to kill. And *vasa* means—"

"Vessel," Anna whispered. The stone floor seemed to plummet from beneath her, and darkness crowded in from all sides. "That's it then. To kill Bastraal, I must wait until he inhabits a living, breathing body. One with a true, beating heart."

Anna's eyes burned, her throat closed. But this was what she'd been trained for, the moment she'd awaited her entire life. And she knew better than anyone, that there was no avoiding Fate's decree.

Her one duty in life was to protect the world from Bastraal. At all cost.

So with the weight of ten hells on her shoulders, she placed her palm on the open book. "There is no choice. To end the demon…" she inhaled shakily, "I have to murder an innocent man."

9

Anna sat in the library, where she'd been since the ceremony. Finally the book, the blade, and the burial ground had all come together, but the results were not what she'd expected. And despite her loyalty to her family and belief in Fate, she was here searching, hoping for another answer. Praying that either she or magic had made a mistake.

Surely she'd been wrong. Her challenge couldn't possibly include the murder of another human being, one who'd done no wrong to her or anyone else. Something had to have been lost in the translation.

She'd read everything she could that might possibly give her an alternate meaning of the book's instructions. The others were here too, all of the witches and their men, the many hands making quicker work. The library was huge, with shelves rising to the high ceiling, and Anna had fewer than thirty days to figure a way out of the mess that was her long-awaited trial.

Her friends tried to appear optimistic, hiding their solemn expressions and worried eyes. Even Quinn—whom Anna could tell felt the search was in vain—was there with her, scouring the oldest materials, searching for anything that referred to destroying a demon's chosen vessel.

But so far, every mention had supported what they already knew, what they feared. The only way to rid the world of a creature like Bastraal for good, was to kill him in his most vulnerable state. On Halloween. As soon as he was inside his brand new host.

The transition required energy, so while Bastraal was taking over the poor man's life—whomever he chose—Anna would have a slim opportunity to destroy the beast within.

Ethan and Lucia had focused on tales from Peru, the country where they'd found and recovered the dagger. But from what they could tell, the demon destroyed there centuries ago had also infected a human being first. There seemed no other way.

To die by flesh, the demons had to first possess flesh.

Sunset was growing near, and the day had taken its toll. Rubbing her tired eyes, Anna looked outside, losing herself in the view from the long bank of French-paned windows. The countdown to Halloween was on, and day-by-day, the sun would lose its mastery of the sky.

She shuddered to imagine the darkness closing in. She dreaded the passage of time.

Sickness was a sly invader within her stomach, her heart. She would be forced to perform an execution—because that's exactly what it was—and that went against everything she stood for and fought for.

But the prophecy had made its request, made its condition known to the St. Germaine witch responsible for seeing it done. One horrible act of cruelty to serve the greater good. Take one life or endanger thousands more. Either way, she was doomed.

With one hand on her stomach and the other around her amulet, Anna was still trying to overcome nausea when the doorbell chimed. The harmonious bells echoing throughout the mansion were too cheery, too hopeful, for the gloomy afternoon.

She glanced at the clock atop an antique trestle table and wondered who would be visiting this late in the day. Her second question to herself was why she hadn't seen them coming.

Closing the book, she stood and stretched, disgruntled by the fact her gift, the clairvoyance she would likely need to complete her challenge, had chosen this time, of all times, to go on the fritz. She'd never been able to dictate her gift or call it up with a wave of her hand, but in the last few days, her sight had become exceptionally unpredictable.

Ambling down the corridor, hoping someone else would beat her to the door, she continued to clasp her necklace between two fingers. Halfway there, an image popped into her mind, as if someone had decided to plug the movie projector back in.

She knew who was waiting on the other side of the doors, and frankly, after the damning revelation she'd had, she was in no mood for this particular visitor.

Ian the judgmental, come to judge the wicked witch.

She paused, hand reaching for the door. Because it seemed she would now become exactly that. A murderess.

She shook off the anxiety and focused on the here and now. She would still help those she could, including Ian. Though the scales would never be balanced for her again. Not after October thirty-first.

But he needs me. I can't forget that. Can't shirk my obligations. Even those that would leave blood on her hands.

With her head weighted by the troubling thoughts, she sighed deeply and opened the door. Late-day rays of sun lingered stubbornly and further burnished Ian's golden hair. His stone-blue eyes were still hard and sharp, if a bit bloodshot, and his clothing was slightly rumpled, with what seemed to be more than the average end-of-day wear and tear.

Again, his shirtsleeves were rolled to his elbows, tempting Anna into a quick glance. She admired the corded muscles of his forearms, the strong, capable hands that could heft a weapon as easily as they shuffled papers.

She cringed inwardly, telling herself she had to stop picturing him as an Ian-Vanir hybrid. That line of thinking wouldn't help either one of them.

Yet as he stood there, tall and broad-shouldered yet lean through the hips and waist, she couldn't help feeling a bit awed by his formidable presence. His stance told her he hadn't exactly come in peace.

Or rather, he wasn't *at* peace.

She noticed the tiredness around his eyes, the strain. "You look like you've had a rough day." She bit her lip wondering where her manners had fled. He hadn't even had a chance to insult her yet.

Ian scanned from her bare feet and poppy-red toenails all the way up to meet her gaze again. With a frown, he barked, "We need to talk."

And the concern she'd almost been feeling was effectively squelched. He'd managed rudeness in under three-point-five seconds. A new record.

"Then by all means. Come in." Attempting to be the ever-gracious host, Anna allowed a soft smile to play over her lips as she gestured for him to enter. "Would you care for a drink?" His strong, straight nose and carved cheekbones were flushed, whether from heat or anger, she couldn't say.

"Yes, thank you." Silent for the longest stretch she'd heard from him yet, Ian walked with her to the grand hall. Finally, he said, "Do have any scotch?"

Without his usual stiff but appropriate manners, he moved past her to drop into the upholstered captain's chair, one of Viv's favorite reading spots. As Anna made her way to the liquor cabinet across the room, she glanced back to see him lower his head to his hands.

This was a man who never had a hair out of place, no wrinkles in his clothing. His office and home were both immaculately modern, and he gave the word "propriety" a whole new meaning. But today he appeared almost disheveled, absent the staunch reserve he usually wore like a cloak.

What had happened to him that he would let down his defenses? That he would reveal an all-too-human side, and to her of all people?

Anna set aside her own issues and dredged up sympathy for Ian. He'd come all the way out here, and all she'd done was bristle at his surly tone and make snide remarks. She normally had much greater patience, but this man stirred her in ways that were completely foreign, unsettling.

Physical attraction, indecision, and fear all melded together in one heavy weight in her gut. And if she were being honest with herself, Ian wasn't the only one with suspicions. The only one with trust issues.

What if he turned out to be Ronja's brother? What if he remembered fully and became Vanir? Was that why he was part of the final trial? What was she supposed to do? Help him, maybe even come to care for him?

Or would she end up fighting him? The loyal Viking brother standing by Ronja's side.

The image shook her, and she considered a brandy for herself. But she needed a clear head, as much as was possible now, with guilt already crowding out every other emotion or thought.

To save, she would have to kill. There was no logic or magic in the world that would save her now.

With Ian's drink in hand, she rounded the front of the chair to stand before him. He looked perfectly miserable, dejected and run down. And if this was some charade to get close to her, Anna thought, to infiltrate the coven's inner sanctum? Then she'd happily eat a pile of toadstools.

As sympathy bloomed, she handed him the scotch. "Do you take it on the rocks? I didn't think to ask."

"Perfect," he said, taking the tumbler and downing the drink.

She stepped away and waited, observing as he sat back and rolled the glass of ice between his palms. His mind was a million miles away, it seemed, but eventually, after minutes passed, he shot those eyes her way. "I went to the cops about what you told me."

Anna hiked one brow. "Yes. I know."

His attention remained fixed on her, his gaze open and direct. "Of course you do. But then, you know far too much for one person."

That was truer now than ever before. But she smiled softly, revealing nothing of her tainted musings. "It's been my life's blessing and curse. Another?" She held out her hand for the glass.

In answer, he set it on the table beside his chair. "I've had reason to reconsider my options."

Except he really didn't have any alternatives. He was in danger from the Amara, and the coven was all that stood in front of him. He needed to accept their help, and Anna believed he was coming to that awareness slowly. Methodically. Which suited him.

Standing by, she used silence to encourage him to continue.

Ian stood, ran a hand through his hair. "Since you have the police department in your pocket—"

"No." Anna stopped him there, as she didn't care for the implication. "That sounds as if I've used money to sway or influence the authorities, but only two detectives know the truth of what's happening in this city, and only because they were drawn into it."

"Drawn how?"

"By Fate, or destiny, if you will. Cole and Trevor are part of the prophecy now and are attached in more ways than one." Placing her hands on her hips, she tossed back his righteous stare. "And they are both good men. Without question."

His eyes homed in on her, narrowed, and then he nodded. "I agree. And, to be honest, I had that opinion supported today by more than one other person."

Anna felt her mouth flatten defensively. "You checked up on them?"

"Of course I did." Holding out a palm, Ian again let his

expression settle into lines of annoyance. "I don't know why you expect me to simply fall under your spell and accept everything you say without question." Then he gave a sardonic grin. "No pun intended."

She didn't respond.

"Look, I know people are dying and even more may be in danger, but I just can't see my way through the fog of all this. And I don't understand my involvement. It's crazy to even consider being related to an immortal witch. One who expects me to re-enact a previous life."

He shook his head insistently. "I just don't want to think about what it all means. If I accept it as reality, if I believe the visions I had are real…"

"Then you have to accept that they're flashbacks from a past life," Anna said softly.

"Yes." He reached for the tumbler again but only ice was left inside to clink against his teeth. "Damn it all!"

She saw his fingers clench on the glass and expected him to heave it against the stone wall. But he only returned it to the table and began to pace. He spoke without looking at her. "I believe in the law, in justice, and a system that serves everyone equally. There is no room in my life for something as ludicrous and unpredictable as magic."

He spun on her now. "I may be a blood-sucking lawyer in your eyes, but I did nothing to cause any of this. Regardless of what you think, I actually help people."

Anna remained calm. "So do I."

Blowing out a breath, Ian let his shoulders sag and rubbed two fingers over his forehead. "I believe you."

She could tell what the three simple words cost him. He was admitting that his life was changing, and by coming to her, he was saying he didn't know how to deal with it. Not by himself.

"Ian," she said softly, starting toward him, but he lifted his head and stopped her with an expression she couldn't name.

He strode several steps away before turning back to her, his shiny shoes pivoting cleanly on the old slate floor.

He shoved his hands into the pockets of his expensive black pants. "I haven't been completely honest with you."

Bumps raced over Anna's skin. "You haven't?"

"No. I told you about the visions, but that's not all I've experienced."

She wanted to appear serene, but her witch's instinct was clawing its way to the forefront. "I'm listening."

"Last night when I returned home..." He lifted his hands, stared at them, rotating palms to backs to palms again as if inspecting them. Then he dropped his arms to his sides. "Something was in my house."

The ice in his glass shifted, the only sound between them. "And I think it wanted to kill me."

~

Anna's eyes widened almost imperceptibly, but Ian saw. He'd been focused on her, watching, amazed by the blue of her irises. Like cobalt glass—rare, soothing, and so beautiful he couldn't tear his own gaze away.

She rushed to him in three quick steps. "Were you hurt? What happened?" Then her concern faded into irritation. "And more importantly, why didn't you call me?"

"I was hurt, yes, but I healed. The attack was different from last time, but—"

"Last time? You've been attacked before?"

He flinched. "Yes, a while ago. It's what prompted me to reach out to you, to meet for lunch." He had the good sense to try and look shame-faced, but that didn't cool her ire. It didn't come close. If anything, the lady of the manor was working herself up into what his mother would call a *tizzy*.

"Do you mean to tell me," Anna paused to lift a hand, her

fingers splayed, "that you were attacked by some sort of entity and didn't think it important enough to mention? Not only that," she said, raising a stern finger when he opened his mouth, "but you were attacked *again* last night, in your own home, yet you still waited the whole night and an entire work day before contacting me?"

"I had to make a court appearance." He crossed his arms, wondering how he'd become the defendant. He hadn't asked for any of this. "I have people who rely on me. My work is important."

"I'm sure it is, but I'm also fairly certain you'll do a better job representing your clients if you're still around to do it." She threw out a hand. "I could have at least cast a spell to give you a small measure of protection. Why didn't you listen to me? For the sake of the goddess, Ian!"

When her voice echoed up to the walkways a level above, Anna lifted her gaze and frowned. Checking to see if anyone was witnessing her display of temper?

Whatever the reason, she closed her eyes briefly and then pressed her hands together prayer-style. She lowered her voice. "Now do you understand what you're up against?" She tapped her chest and gestured to the interior of her home. "What we are *all* up against?"

"Yes, dammit! More than you know." And why did that statement ring so true with him? Why did he have this innate resistance against the entire idea of magic?

He'd been motivated to tell her about the visions, but not the assault. Why did the images, the memories of another life, scare him more than the vicious attacks?

Maybe because his skin had mended, because he'd lived through both experiences, no matter how terrible. But if he truly had been this other person, this Vanir, what if the visions came back, or even escalated? What if they overtook him?

Ian pulled at his shirt, trying to straighten some of the

wrinkles. When that didn't work, he rubbed his jaw and was dismayed to feel stubble. He was already losing too much control.

"I don't know why I didn't tell you. It felt like I would be giving away too much information, handing over everything and letting you take over my life, when I already have plenty of others who are trying to do the same thing. First Ronja manipulated me into helping her, then I kept seeing myself in another's body." Ian had never rambled like this, further evidence of his mental state. "Only to have you follow up by telling me the world and life as we know it may soon be obliterated."

He laughed and held out his hands. "That a demon wants to take over the world."

"Tell me about the attacks," Anna said, expression stern.

Ian knew when to dodge and evade a line of query. And now was not that time. "They were different, yet similar. The first time I was being strangled, smothered by a force I couldn't see." He put a hand to his throat. "But I could feel it, so cold."

Anna stiffened visibly.

"What does that mean to you?" Ian asked.

She only shook her head. "Later. Tell me about the other. What happened last night?"

"The cold came back again, a temperature, a sensation that was so much more than the one word can accurately convey. *Cold* just doesn't do it justice. But this time, I saw something—glimmering strands, like threads, frozen and solid enough to cut into flesh. A sharp, icy spider web. That's about the best I can do to describe it."

He stepped backward until he felt the edge of the chair against his legs. Then he sat. "It all happened so fast, and I just panicked, scrambled to try to get away." His heart banged, paused, banged, a shutter slamming in a storm. "If it hadn't released me, I would have died."

Anna waited, listening, her soft eyes on his face. "I'm sorry," Ian said. "And, yes, I should have listened to you."

"I'm the one who owes an apology. I should have handled this more delicately."

Ian found the statement ludicrous yet amusing and laughed. "I'm being smothered and inflicted with cuts and burns by an invisible monster, and you're worried about being delicate?"

She smiled back at him, and for the first time, the very first time, they shared a genuine moment. He saw past the barrier of magic, the shield she tended to hold in front of herself, whether or not she realized.

He looked to the woman and considered her, the people she surrounded herself with, the family she'd come from. Could he not find a modicum of trust when they had much in common, and she'd only ever offered him help?

And now, he knew he needed it.

With hidden truth no longer weighing him down, Ian relaxed enough to ask for another scotch. When Anna nodded, smiled, and took the tumbler from the table, he used the opportunity to have a good look at the surroundings.

The stone floor had been laid long ago, and his eye for antiques—forced upon him by his mother—assessed the gleaming mahogany wainscoting and stairwell to determine they too had been in existence for decades, maybe even centuries. Maintained by caring hands? Or by magic?

The large painting on the wall intrigued him, as he could tell by its distance from the wall that it was on tracks. An expensive and authentic work of art covering a flat-screen TV? He listened as Anna walked across the floor, returning to him with his scotch.

How could this all feel so...normal?

A woman chose that moment to breeze in, causing Ian and Anna to look in her direction. She had silver hair in a short, efficient style, and her eyes were just as lively as her step. "Oh, hello." She beamed at Ian, then slowly angled her head to his hostess. "Anna, who's your friend?"

"This is Ian Keller." Anna handed him his drink again, just as he rose to meet the new arrival.

"Wonderful." She apparently knew who he was, though he couldn't say the same.

The silver-haired woman stopped in front of Ian. "You can call me Mrs. Attinger. They all do, and I rather like it." She winked. "Sounds more authoritative, and lord knows I need as much of that as I can get around here."

"If you had any more authority," Anna said, "we could all sit back and let you take on the monsters."

Ian started at the comment. How easily they bantered about such dire topics.

The woman, Mrs. Attinger, pursed her lips and waved a hand. "Oh, now." Then to Ian, "You'll stay for dinner." Not quite a question, not quite a command, but somewhere in between.

"Thank you, but I'm afraid I—"

"Young man," Mrs. Attinger tucked her chin, "do I strike you as the kind of person you can outmaneuver?"

Ian was quite familiar with the classic Southern woman's set-down of an impertinent youth. No judge's reprimand could ever come close. "Um...no, Ma'am."

"Good. Now, for the record, and since you're spending time with my Anna, I manage to keep nine witches, nine cats, eight men, and a spirited dog in line, so even a man who argues for a living won't be able to talk his way around me."

Straightening up, and feeling a sudden affability for the iron-fisted Mrs. Attinger, Ian bowed slightly. "Then I defer to your judgment."

She practically cooed. "Oh, I like the sound of that."

Anna rolled her eyes.

"I saw that," the older woman said.

"Of course you did. I'm the psychic, but," Anna laughed,

"*you* see everything."

With a wink and pointed finger, Mrs. Attinger continued on her way, leaving the two of them alone once again.

With the mood lightened, he hated to bring up the previous discussion. Anna had more to tell him, that was clear, but he decided the details could at least wait until he'd finished his second drink. Perhaps even until he finished dining with the witches.

Witches. Could this week be any stranger? Tossing back the liquor and enjoying the burn, he let the much-needed warmth sink in.

10

Ronja was still abed late in the afternoon after her previous night with Bastraal. The demon had not been gentle after all, and even she, an immortal seiðr, needed rest to regain her energy.

Shoving the thick bedcovers down, she glided the flat of her palm over the silk sheets, a deep, dark purple that perfectly matched the marks Bastraal had left all over her body. All because she had displeased her master, doubted him, and such a sin was never overlooked.

Across the room, candles burned on the fireplace mantle, as well as on her vanity. In the oval dressing mirror, she saw that her face was far paler than the porcelain tone she usually wore, that she much preferred. Now she appeared sickly. Weak.

She was about to summon someone, tell them to prepare a meal, when a tap sounded lightly on her boudoir door. The meekness of the knock made her suspect Beth, the newest member of the Amara, and the lowliest. The little mare knew her rank despite her abilities.

With her influence over nighttime wanderings, Beth could wreak devastation on an unsuspecting person's dreams. Scarlett had been working with the younger girl, teaching her to actually cast people into a deep sleep, thereby putting them at her mercy.

Ronja stilled as she recalled the horrible truth. *Scarlett.* Her dear would work no more magic.

Irritated by the grief now infusing her, she snapped, "Who is it?" When the timid knock came a second time. Then she was surprised to see Tyr enter. He had never been terribly genteel, even before the Jin Deva ritual, but surely not after.

Yet he glided inside and quietly closed the door. "Are you all right?" he asked.

Now Ronja could see his shaking hands, his barely suppressed anger and concern. He'd been more than jealous last night when the demon had hauled her away. He'd been worried.

"Yes. I'm fine." She held out a hand, and he was instantly at her side, sitting on the edge of the mattress.

"I've let you sleep as long as I dare."

She was immediately alert. "What's happened?"

"Now that I've regained my strength and cooled my wrath," he put his palm to the center of her chest, over her cold heart, "I was able to calm down enough to see something."

Tyr was not only a fierce warrior and deliciously handsome man, he was also a seer. He had visions, a useful talent when Ronja desired information she couldn't gain through magic. Another reason she'd chosen him as a life mate.

"Vanir, he has gone to the witch."

"What?" Ronja sat up fully. "Anna?"

"Yes. He went to the island, only an hour past."

"You should have woken me immediately!"

"You needed rest." His face hardened. "After last night. Besides, the demon bastard was still here then. He might have overheard us."

Mulling over his concern, Ronja assessed the risk of going against Bastraal's orders to leave Anna alone until he could deal with her directly. The demon's pride had festered for too long, and now his desire for vengeance on the St. Germaine descendant could cost her her brother, and she couldn't allow that.

She would rather face Bastraal's fury and deal with the punishment—which would be horrific, no doubt—than lose Vanir to that bitch's charms. "There is no time to waste. We have to remove Anna from the equation before she does irreparable damage."

"What do you intend?" Tyr assisted her when she slipped out of bed to stand.

Ronja narrowed her eyes at him. "To kill her. Just as we have planned all along." She felt her priorities shift as swiftly and violently as a mudslide. Her sole purpose had always been to fulfill Bastraal's every wish, but since she'd seen Vanir, miraculously alive again, getting him back had become her primary objective.

"Do you feel this is wise?" Tyr asked, dark eyes filled with concern beneath a furrowed brow. "Bastraal—"

"He is wrong on this matter." Once the words were said, Ronja and Tyr both waited, eyes darting about as if lightning might strike. Or to see if Bastraal had somehow heard. His strike would be far worse.

What they were planning was conspiracy at best—treason if the demon took her betrayal to heart. But what good was living forever if those long years were polluted by grief?

No. Vanir meant more to her.

"Tyr." She took both of his hands in hers. "Do this for me." She drew a halting breath. "I beg of you."

"Sssh." He put a finger to her lips. "Never beg. The act is beneath you."

"But I am desperate." And she was.

He cupped her cheek and pressed his lips to her forehead. The Dacvo was one of the most fearsome creatures ever to exist, yet he yielded tender kisses to her, and only to her. The love she felt for her warrior swelled so quickly she was afraid her chest would burst.

"Sit here," he instructed, pointing to her bed. "Do not move from the center."

Doing as he commanded, Ronja scooted to the middle of the plum-colored sheets and tucked her knees up against her chest.

"Don't be afraid," Tyr said. "I will maintain control."

Ronja understood then what he meant to do. Whatever his plan, it involved releasing one of his stored-up beasts.

"There is a creature, an *infidus*. An untruth. The entity is a creator of false truths. Its will to deceive is so strong, whomever he casts his magic upon will believe that whatever they see, whatever they are *shown*, is real."

"What are you going to do?"

"If we are to destroy Anna, one of the strongest witches we've ever encountered..." At her frown, Tyr inclined his head and continued in a chastising tone. "You are too smart to deny the strength of your adversary. Doing so will only make you vulnerable."

Biting the inside of her cheek, Ronja bobbed her head. "You're right. I shouldn't underestimate her." She glanced around, still nervous, afraid Bastraal might show up at any moment.

Then she and Tyr would both be punished severely.

"If we are to have an opening for attack," he went on, "we must first get her off of the island. The land there, even the waters surrounding it, are too protected. We will never be able to enter."

"We need a reason for her to come to town."

"Precisely. Which is why I will allow the infidus to escape, briefly, just long enough to do my bidding."

"You will have it create a false truth?"

"Yes."

Ronja sat up on her knees, growing excited. "Anna will see it in a vision. She'll think it's real."

"And because she is who she is, she will come straight to Savannah. Her trial has begun, and she won't be able to stay away. Then we will have the advantage. She won't realize what's truly happening until it's too late."

"You're brilliant!" Ronja let her head fall back as she cackled. "How better to trick a psychic than with a vision that lies?"

"Now." The smile that had graced Tyr's handsome mouth fell away. "Do as I said and don't move. Stay. In. That. Bed." He cocked his head. "Trust me?"

"Yes, Tyr." And the depth of her faith in him warmed her all over. Tyr had always been loyal, and he'd always loved her.

When he held both of his arms out to the side, an intense buzzing sound vibrated from within his body. His black eyes were closed, but his mouth fell open as a churning, roiling mist began to seep out from inside.

The vapor was the color of rust with small moving parts, like millions of ants all swirling in a tornado. Ronja had seen countless terrible deeds—she herself had performed a hundred times more—but what she witnessed now, coming from Tyr's mouth, was deeply disturbing.

A long, keening moan accompanied the raging brown formation.

Yes, she would do as she'd promised. She wouldn't budge from the bed.

~

Okay, so he didn't think he'd been poisoned. Or bespelled.

In fact, Ian thought as he handed his dirty dishes to the young woman named Kylie, the women of Anna's coven—he still stumbled over that word—had all been gracious, charming, and understanding.

And none of them had held it against him that he'd turned Anna in to the police.

Well, except for the blonde ex-soldier, Paige, who'd tapped her nails on the granite counter when the story had been recounted. They'd all eaten at either the side table in the kitchen or crowded around a huge granite island in the shape of a crescent moon. He felt the shape was befitting of an ancient stone mansion inhabited by a witch.

His head swirled at the oddity of it all. Anna and her friends had explained about the trials, the three St. Germaine sisters from three centuries before, and the legacy they had left behind. A mission for the current Savannah Coven, a duty only The Nine could fulfill.

Very little about Anna, her home, or her acquaintances fell under his accepted definition of ordinary. Even the nine cats running about seemed to be eerily cognizant.

They were all lined up in the huge main room of the mansion when Ian and Anna exited the kitchen. Shauni was handing out treats in regimented manner and reportedly—as the current feline behavior supported—was able to communicate with animals.

One by one the cats took their snacks and scurried off in different directions. Finally, the lone dog was given a chewy bone, and he also departed for a large cushion on the floor in one corner. A single cat with short gray hair and lime green eyes stayed behind.

She—and Ian felt sure it was a female—studied him intensely. She was still continuing her perusal when Anna touched his arm. He actually jumped, so drawn into the staring contest he hadn't realized she'd come close.

"That's my Ivy." Anna said. "The plant symbolizes constancy, and Druids often used it in their rites and rituals." She smiled at the cat, who instead of offering Ian a friendly greeting, lifted her tail and sauntered away.

"Hmmm." Anna frowned. "That's not like her."

"Guess she doesn't take to strangers."

"No. That's not it. We've had a houseful of people for months, all of them strangers at some point." Anna slanted her eyes at Ian. "She must sense your dislike of me. That you still don't trust me or anyone else here. Cats can be very sensitive that way."

Though a lawyer, Ian didn't confabulate as a rule. So he wasn't going to lie now. "I wouldn't say I don't *like* you. But the trust...well, lets just take things one cautious step at a time."

"I thought we had been. The first time I came to you, tried to tell you the truth, that was this past summer. Almost three months, and in that time you've seen for yourself what Ronja can do."

Ian bristled at the reminder. He'd been taken in by the woman, fooled by her polish and apparent wealth, which was why he was still taking careful inventory of the witch beside him. "Her guilt doesn't automatically equate to your innocence."

"Right you are." Her pink lips curved daintily, and he had to force himself to look elsewhere. Anna's smile, her eyes, her voice, they were all so calming, each like a soft touch on his senses.

And then there was her sweetly floral scent. Thinking of it prompted him to inhale, to see for himself if it was as enchanting as he remembered. And yes, it was, like roses after the rain.

Dammit. Why couldn't she have smelled like rancid stew from a cauldron, maybe some eye of newt? Those stereotypical items seemed more apropos for a woman who so proudly claimed the title of witch.

He wondered if she actually had a cauldron. "Do you really cast spells on people?"

She tilted her head, a bemused response to his question. "I generally cast spells *for* people." She leaned in to whisper. "Unless they're very, very bad."

When she laughed, Ian couldn't help laughing with her. Just another part of her character that was infectious. "You're making fun of me."

"Yes." She lifted a shoulder. "But you keep making it so

easy."

Their light-hearted repartee didn't last long.

"Anna." Hayden, with the golden eyes and ginger-hued hair, hurried in but stopped when she looked at Ian. "Trevor just called."

Ian listened to her melodic voice, studied her sweet face. He was still trying to understand the pairing of this gentle woman—who talked to ghosts, of course—with the tall, brawny man who was as rigid as a rock. Just like his last name suggested.

"I hate to be the bearer of bad news, but two more men have been reported missing." Hayden glanced over her shoulder toward the kitchen.

"What else?" Anna asked, as if she too had picked up on her friend's additional concern.

"They were both Rangers."

"Oh, no. I assume Chris knows them."

Ian had met Chris tonight as well, and that man was the perfect match for tough-as-nails Paige. He had once been in the Ranger Regiment, and Ian felt a swift punch of sorrow to hear that two of his colleagues, two men who'd served their country so valiantly, had been taken by a different kind of enemy force altogether.

Anna continued to surprise him. Friends with cops, with soldiers...the coven's list of allies was forcing Ian to reassess his doubts. Military and law enforcement personnel he was familiar with, he respected. So if they supported Anna enough to fight alongside her...then who was Ian to second-guess them?

"Yes. They're friends of his," Hayden said. "He called them by their first names, Antoine and Jason. I can't stand to see him so upset. He thinks they were targeted because of him, and he's ready to storm Ronja's plantation to get them back."

"But he won't do that, will he?" Ian asked.

"No. He's just upset, and understandably so." Anna went to

the comfortable-looking green couch but didn't sit. She paused before walking around to stand behind it, resting her hands on the back. "It's not his fault. I hope he knows that."

Ian saw her fingers grip the velvet of the sofa. "Poor Chris. During the trials," her stare was centered on the wall behind Ian, "we've all had to deal with guilt at one time or another, whether deserved or not. Remorse can be an insidious weapon. A slow death."

Hearing the change in her tenor, the sadness, Ian watched Anna as she worried the edge of the green fabric with her fingers. Did she have something to feel guilty about?

Still holding on to the back of the couch, her eyes still fixed on a spot beyond him, Anna's face suddenly relaxed, but not in the way a person did when they felt relief. More like when they'd been give a huge dose of morphine.

"Cut." Anna uttered the word as she stared into space.

"What did you say?" Ian asked, just as Hayden hurried to her friend's side.

"She's seeing something," Hayden spoke quietly, holding herself still, not touching Anna or the couch, but standing nearby, just in case.

"Cut. Smoke. Victory."

Looking more closely, he could see Anna's pupils were huge, dilated as they had been that day at lunch. He held his breath, trying to not make any noise.

"Cut. Smoke. Victory." She released air through her lips, the breath wheezing out slowly, rattling as if it might be her last.

And Ian was suddenly afraid. For her. "Anna?" He moved in quickly, worried she might be in pain again, like she'd been when she'd touched him and triggered her clairvoyance. "Anna, can you hear me?"

"Wait," Hayden started, but just as she held out a halting hand, Anna began to blink. Her shoulders slumped.

"Victory," she said, rubbing her temples with two fingertips on each side. "Victory Drive." Like a bird who'd detected the noise of an approaching predator, Anna looked up sharply. "We have to go there. Now."

"Victory Drive?" Ian went to her and, motivated by feelings he didn't recognize, he grabbed her hand. She was cool to the touch. "Anna, that spans most of downtown. Can you be more specific?" And since when did he believe, unfailingly, in her gift to see what others could not?

Perhaps when he'd finally let himself see what all the others here in her home had. That witch or not, Anna St. Germaine was a good person who put the needs of others before her own. Why else would she have kept pursuing Ian, even after he'd cut her down time and again?

She helped people, she'd told him, echoing his own sentiment. And he was sure that's what she was trying to do now.

He rubbed her fingers, sharing his warmth. "Where on Victory, Anna?"

"I'm trying." She clenched her eyes tightly. "Cut. Smoke. I saw those words too, but I don't know what they mean. I'm just sure wherever we have to go is on Victory Drive." She angled toward him, her features grim. "Three men will be there, young men."

Casting a quick glance at their joined hands, Anna tightened her fingers on Ian's for a heartbeat before turning to Hayden. "I need Claudia."

Whether they'd heard this last statement or had picked up on the ensuing trouble through some witchy talent Ian didn't know about, several of the women came out of the kitchen, including the red-haired history teacher Anna was referring to.

"Claudia," Anna said, her brisk manner of speech urgent and demanding. "You said that Bastraal had deep brown eyes when you saw him in the past."

"Yes."

The past? Ian felt his chest constrict. What the hell were

they talking about?

"And they had flames in them?" Anna persisted.

"Yes. Yes. But why?" The tall woman wore tight black pants and a black, sleeveless shirt that showcased her flaming hair color. "Tell me," she said, putting a hand on Anna's shoulder.

"I'll tell you on the way. We have to get downtown, now. I don't have a time frame, but more men are going to be taken tonight."

With only that for explanation, Anna's friends fell into what Ian would describe as a well-practiced fire drill. No one exchanged directions or commands, simply spreading out to disappear and then return with weapons. Meanwhile, Mrs. Attinger went to a long antique table and dialed a rotary phone.

Anna whirled on him then. "You're staying here."

Ian expelled a gust of irritation. "Out of the question."

"You'll be—"

"Safer. I'm sure you're right, but that doesn't matter." Standing with legs apart, Ian fixed her with a willful stare. "Up until now, you've all done your damnedest to convince me your world is real and that I should accept it. You did everything you could to force me into it. Now that I'm listening, now that something's happening, you want to hold me back?"

"You aren't prepared for this. I haven't even had a chance to tell you—"

"I'm going with you," he said, his tone cutting straight through any argument she might make.

With an exasperated huff, she threw up her hands. "Fine. We don't have time for this." She looked to Claudia again when the woman returned with a belt on her hip and two long knives attached. "Have you called Cole yet?"

"Just about to."

"Good, they can meet us. And tell him the kidnappings aren't just about building a demon army anymore. I know why the Amara took that young man from the dorm, and the Rangers. I can't believe I didn't make the connection before."

Hayden was back as well, and she put a hand to her throat. "Bastraal. You asked about his eyes."

Anna nodded solemnly. "At the end of my vision, I saw one of the three men, but he was lying on the ground, on a huge black rock."

"The stone yard," Hayden uttered in a voice half reverent, half revolted.

"He looked dead." Anna's mouth trembled as she glanced to Paige and each of the other witches who'd filed back into the room. They were all loaded up with weapons of various sorts.

"But then he opened his eyes," she continued, "and they were so dark, empty. Other than the flames."

"What does that tell you?" Ian asked. He was no longer following the discussion but could see her discovery held great significance. That whatever Anna had seen had impacted her, hard, almost stealing her breath and her composure.

She avoided meeting his eyes, still speaking only to her coven. Ian could see her jaw clench from where he stood. "The most recent victims are all young, healthy, attractive men." She latched onto the necklace hanging from her neck, gripping it like a lifeline. "Bastraal is collecting his candidates."

11

"There!" Anna tapped at the side window of the SUV. Her brother, Quinn, was driving and slammed on the brakes to veer into a parking lot behind the building she'd indicated.

The concrete lot they rolled over was cracked and filled with weed invaders, and broken windows added to the rundown look of the place. Ian knew the warehouse was abandoned and had been for some years. "I know this building, had a client ask about this address once, but it never came on the market."

He said aside to Anna. "I'm sorry, but I would have never guessed by your description."

"No, of course you wouldn't. Even I don't understand my visions half the time." She slid him a glance. "At least, not at first."

The car skidded to a halt and everyone jumped out. The two other cars copied form, just as Quinn made a quick call to Trevor, letting him and Cole know where they were.

Ian kept quiet as a quick decision was made to spread out in groups. The building was large and sprawling with two wings jutting off from the main section, basically a giant T. Ian fell in behind Anna, Paige, Chris, Quinn, and the caramel-haired woman who'd earlier introduced herself as Hayden. In a group, they headed around front, to the main entrance facing Victory Drive.

Ian had become comfortable with quite a bit in the last twenty-four hours, more willing to believe there was more in the universe than what was controlled or understood by mankind. But he was still stunned when he read the faded white lettering on the bricks.

Even in the low light of night, he could see the remnants of advertisements from long ago. The word "cut" was barely legible on the upper left corner with "smoke" still clear in the middle of the wall. He was indeed now standing on Victory Drive, and Anna's declaration of "Cut. Smoke. Victory," was, he had to admit, dead accurate.

"That way is chained tight," Chris reported after dashing up the front steps to test the double doors. "No way anyone got in through here."

"Let's keep moving then." Paige scanned the windows on the front side, but like the doors, they all appeared to be sealed. "We'll eventually meet up with the others. One of the groups is bound to find the point of entry."

"What would those kids be doing here, anyway?" Ian walked side by side with Anna now.

"Now that I think about it, I saw a camera around one of the men's neck. Maybe they work for the city, or a developer? Art students?" She rubbed her hand against the side of her thigh in an agitated, nervous gesture. "I don't know."

"What did you mean before when you mentioned candidates?"

She paused, her mouth open slightly. She snapped it shut before speaking calmly. "I have more to explain to you, but we should save it for later."

Hurrying off, she jogged to catch up with Paige and Chris. Ian let her go, because as she'd said, they would discuss it later. He intended to make sure of it.

Traversing the long side of the structure and around the wing, they found only a few broken windows, and even those had wire mesh across the frames. Chris gestured to them. "No one got in through here either."

Still moving, they made it to the rear where the overgrown

lawn terminated at an alley. A few lights glowed from houses across the way, and other than two men sitting in chairs and smoking—Ian could see the vibrant burn of orange in the dark when they puffed—the narrow street was empty. Ominously so.

"Wait here for the others?" Paige asked.

Anna nodded, but then her body jolted, as did Ian's, when a thunderous noise reverberated through the neighborhood. Far away, on Victory, cars began to honk and brakes squealed.

"That was an explosion." Chris shared a knowing glance with Paige before they both lifted their gazes skyward.

Ian did the same. He could barely make out the deep gray smoke in the night until it rose high enough to contrast with clouds backlit by the bright moon.

"They're here," Anna said. "They want to draw us away." She looked to Chris. "Go to the others. Send half of the group to check it out. The rest will stay at this location."

Ian blinked, and Chris was gone. "Did he just— Where did—"

"He's like me," Paige said, giving Ian a whole new insight into what Anna had meant before when she'd described Paige as lightning-fast.

Before he could comment further, Paige asked Anna, "You think it's a trick?"

"Yes. Just like during your trial." She shifted her face to Ian. "The Amara's done similar things before, causing a commotion to pull us in different directions to divide us."

A ball of tension began to turn in Ian's gut. "But you're still sending half the group to check?"

"We're seventeen strong," Paige said with a grin. Then she surprised him by punching him in the arm. "Well, eighteen now."

He rubbed his shoulder as she moved away and wondered if she truly knew her own strength.

In response to the boom and shudder of the explosion, a few

people had come out of the homes on the other side of the alley. The two smoking men walked across the street and into the parking lot of the abandoned building, heading to investigate.

Shortly afterward, those who would be staying behind arrived. Chris returned along with Lucia and her boyfriend, Ethan.

It was then Ian noticed a window with the mesh pulled hallway off. He pointed. "I think I found the way in."

"Then let's go." Hayden jerked her head toward the opening. "There's no sign of the Amara, so let's see if we can avoid a fight. Just this once. Besides," her mouth turned down, "we'll get plenty of that on Halloween."

Apparently in agreement, Anna was the first to move. Ian wanted to ask Hayden what she'd meant about Halloween, but she too had already started walking. Lucia and Ethan followed and then Paige, with Chris hanging back with Ian.

While the others worked on removing the rest of the mesh from the window, Ian turned to Chris. The Ranger was staring down the shadowed alley, eyes narrowed, body tense and still.

"Something's not right." He swung a soldier's experienced eyes back to Ian. "I can't pinpoint it. The air is…"

"Static," Ian said. Because now he felt it too.

Hayden gasped suddenly and stumbled backward. "What are you doing?" she cried. She was standing with her hands on her hips, looking at the window where the others had just climbed inside.

"Who is she talking to?" Chris asked before shaking his head. "Oh, I forgot."

Hayden was a medium. Ian hadn't understood her exclamation at first either, had thought she was talking to Paige. But he felt a little better knowing he wasn't the only one still acclimating to this world of witches.

"Why not?" Hayden asked into thin air, talking to the ghost no one else could see or hear.

She took a step, listening intently to whatever the spirit was saying. Then with a leap forward, she yelled for her friends. "Lucia! Paige! Wait!"

As the last to crawl through the window, Paige whirled to look back outside. "What?"

Hayden went to the opening but stopped short. "It's a trap!"

Paige didn't argue but turned to speak to the others already in the building. Ian saw the soldier shrug and speak again before turning back to reach for the windowsill. Her fingers seemed to bump against thin air, crumpling from the impact.

She glared at the open space and tried again. The same result. Finally she pressed the flats of her palms against what should have been nothing but air.

Anna joined her at the opening, testing the area herself. After a quick survey of the edges, she looked out to Hayden. "It's been warded. Strong magic too. Ronja's work."

"Shit." Paige thumped her fist on the invisible barrier. Again.

"You can't break it, not that way." Anna looked up and around, searching. "And I don't have what I need to undo this."

Ian and Chris rushed to the window, but Paige held up both hands in a halting gesture. "Don't! Stay out."

Chris nodded, but he didn't look happy about being apart from her. "Try to find another window or door that you can break out."

She gave a sharp nod, tossed her choppy blonde bangs out of her eyes, and dashed away.

"This isn't good." Hayden had her hands in fists, looking up and down the back street.

Ian moved and studied the brick exterior. He didn't see anything, no markings or symbols like he would expect from a hex. Maybe Ronja was so good she didn't need such rudimentary tools like runes or...

Ian froze as a tingle raced over his scalp. How the hell would he know anything about runes or their uses?

He met Anna's serene gaze through the hole, but she only nodded. "We'll figure something out. Don't worry."

Ian cleared his throat, trying to push aside his own concerns. First, they had to get the others out of the building. Then he'd figure out where he'd learned about runes. Probably just a magazine article or a documentary on television. The History Channel, most likely.

Anna spoke to Hayden but angled her head gently in Ian's direction. "You should get him away from here."

His self-concern fled. "Forget it." He advanced on the window but stayed far enough away for safety. It wouldn't help Anna or the others for him to get trapped as well. "Instead of worrying about me being out here, focus on getting yourself out of *there*."

Dismissing Anna's surprised expression, he turned to Hayden. "Why would Ronja want them trapped here, with no one else inside?"

"I have no idea." Hayden was also looking more closely at the window.

Ian looked around, but he didn't know why. It wasn't like he was going to see the ghost. "Can your friend tell you anything else?"

"No. He's already gone." Hayden stood back from the wall and sighed. "Message delivered. I just didn't get it in time."

Inside the building, Paige reappeared beside Anna. "Every opening has been warded. I can peel away the boards and wire mesh, but I can't get a single finger outside."

Ian and Hayden shared a glance while Chris eased away from them, toward the back street. Paige's attention went with her boyfriend. Anna's followed.

Ian turned as well, apprehension crawling over his skin like tiny spikes, each one a stab of chilling instinct.

Wind rushed down the alley, sending leaves dancing across the pavement. A green glass bottle rolled until it came to a stop with a *clink* against the curb.

Silence was heavy on Ian's shoulders as he and the others watched. They waited.

The few back porch or streetlights in the alley all began to flicker. On and off in a mad dance of light versus dark. Finally, they were all snuffed out. Leaving only one lamp shining where the alley intersected with a cross street.

Two hulking oak trees stood as sentries, their leaf-ridden branches framing the scene. In the middle of the road, Ian saw the black silhouette of a man. He didn't have any special powers of foresight, but neither did he have to be told.

This was what they'd been waiting for.

Keeping his eyes locked on the man, Ian lowered his voice. "Chris."

"I see him." The Ranger's body became one lean line of taut muscle.

The wind lifted the figure's long, unbound hair, and Ian locked onto a memory. The man's wide-legged stance was also familiar. "I've seen him before. At Ronja's."

"His name is Tyr," Hayden said, her voice a whisper threaded with fear. The wind picked up, and she made a sound of distress. Then her words rippled through Ian like cold, noxious fluid.

"He's...*different*," she said. "Can you smell that?"

Ian drew a breath through his nose, and he did smell it. The strong scent of scorched matter, like a variety of materials— rubber, wood, meat—had all burnt to cinders to disperse on the night wind.

A sound that was part scream, part groan rolled toward them. The force of the wail was so intense that Ian swore and covered his ears. Sound waves assaulted him, thumped physically against his torso. The baneful wail came from Tyr, yet...it did not. The man began to laugh, but the scream continued, increasing in force and growing louder.

Two separate beings seemed to be making the sounds, yet both emanated from the one body.

Tyr raised his hands to the sky, and a white wisp flew from his torso. The ghostly form literally flashed into being as if expelled from the man's chest.

"Shit." Chris stared at Tyr but angled his head slightly, speaking to Anna, Paige, and the others within the building. "He's become the Daevo."

Another scream scraped over Ian's eardrums but he stood unmoving.

He didn't know what or who this Daevo was, but something inside him held him in place. He would stand between this unnatural creature and its victims. He had been gifted not only for his sake but also for others.

Ian shook his head and blinked. Had those been his own thoughts? They didn't make any sense.

Before he could waste any more time on his own mental confusion, two more screams filtered through the night. But these were human. Two teenage girls were standing in the shadows of a great oak tree. Ian hadn't seen them before. Had they come from one of the nearby homes to check out the explosion?

They alternated between screams, cries, and whimpers, but the noise they made drew the notice of the creature that had flown from inside Tyr. The whisper-thin apparition stilled, flapping in the breeze as it floated.

Then the thing shifted, drifting straight for the girls.

Ian didn't think. He didn't seek counsel from the others. He simply bolted toward the two teens who stood immobile and terrified. One girl had the other's arm in a death grip, and both were screaming over and over again, the tempo increasing as the beast—demon?—closed in on them.

Ian heard Hayden cry out after him, and then felt a heavy wind brush past him. Still sprinting, he glanced to see a blur and realized he hadn't felt the wind at all. Just the backdraft caused by Chris as he raced towards Tyr.

With a wave of his hand, the black-haired man toppled the Ranger and sent him skidding across the pavement. The strong, powerful ex-soldier slammed into a parked car, his body out of control as it rolled up onto the hood.

Limb by limb, he was splayed over the hood, an unseen force holding him down like an insect pinned to a specimen board.

Paige yelled Chris's name and started battering the invisible wall that still prevented her and the others from leaving the abandoned warehouse.

Thinking only of the two scared girls, Ian threw himself in front of them and turned to face the pale streak that was homing in. The mist-like entity slowed its approach and lingered above Ian. He stared up at what amounted to little more than the wispy vapors of a cloud.

Yet he could feel the evil intent rolling off the creature.

The mass began to undulate, shifting into something more. Was that a head forming? Were those arms spreading wide?

The girls must have seen what he did. Their breaths rasped in and out, screams pitching higher. "What is it? What is it?" The one with her hands clamped onto her friend decided to grab onto Ian's waist instead.

A strange sensation rose up in him now. His entire body began to tingle. He spread his legs and lifted his hand to the creature as if he could summon forth a weapon against the beast. Part of Ian was baffled by his own behavior. But the other half, the one that was intensifying, roared to life and demanded he act.

That he defend.

Tyr's voice sounded abruptly, harsh words that sounded like a command. As Ian stood in a battle-stance with one arm raised, the apparition halted its forward motion, and then slowly retracted itself.

The white mass floated backward and returned to Tyr as if being reeled in. Then it hovered behind the man, like a dog come to heel.

"Go inside," Ian said to the girls. "Get back to your house." He whirled on them and gave the one still holding him a little push. "Now. Hurry!"

The two finally broke free from their daze of fright and ran between the two closest houses to disappear.

"This is your doing." The deep voice was directly behind Ian now, but with caution in mind, he eased around to face its owner. Tyr now stood less than a foot from him, but Ian hadn't heard his approach. Not a sound.

Ian faced him down, the two both close in height. "What do you want?"

"Remember what happens here tonight." Tyr spread his mouth into a malicious grin. "It's because of you."

"No." Ian reached for Tyr's arm when he started to walk away, but his hand missed by inches when the other man jumped to the side. He'd progressed several yards in one motion, as if the distance hadn't been there at all. The move wasn't the same streaking speed as Chris but more of an instantaneous leap from one location to another.

Ian stared after Tyr as he leapt forward again, moving down the street toward the vacant building.

Metal groaned beneath Chris's weight as the force holding him down diminished, and he was able to slide off the car's hood to his feet. "What did he say? Why didn't he attack you?"

"I don't know." Ian started after Tyr, picking up his pace when Hayden ran forward to position herself between Tyr and his apparent destination—the window where Paige, Anna, Lucia, and Ethan were trapped.

He and Chris were sprinting, but even the Ranger couldn't reach Hayden before she lifted both hands to send a flood of blue light toward Tyr.

Tyr only waved his hand again and redirected Hayden's magic toward the ground. Then he moved to her with a jump through space and lifted her by the waist. He threw her backward through the window, where Paige caught her and dragged her inside.

But not necessarily to safety.

"They can't get out," Ian said to Chris. "They can't get out!"

Chris went for Tyr again, but another flick of the bastard's wrist sent Chris to the ground. The Ranger swore under his breath, finally comprehending what Ian had already pieced together. He made it to his feet and yelled, "Paige, run!"

Ronja had laid the wards, imprisoning anyone who entered the building.

Ian saw Anna's eyes widen. Saw her wave a hand to urge the others back before she vanished into the depths of the building after them.

Tyr was closing in, moving straight to the open window.

Ian ran, but neither he nor Chris would catch the beast that had once been a man. Tyr made it to the opening. He disappeared.

Ian understood Ronja's plan now. The danger didn't come from being imprisoned inside the abandoned warehouse.

But from being trapped inside with the Daevo.

12

Anna sprinted through the dusty building at a breakneck pace, arms out in front of her as she barreled into pitch black. When Lucia stumbled up ahead, Anna regained her senses and threw a stream of power into one of the exterior rooms as she passed. They might not be able to get out of the doors or windows, but she could at least destroy some of the covers and let a little light in.

She was still reeling from what she'd witnessed. Tyr tossing Hayden aside like a doll, coven magic—no effect. And while Anna and the witches normally stood and fought, she knew, as her friends knew, that they were running for their lives.

The beings inside of Tyr came with a host of abilities, all of them available to the man who now housed them inside his body. He'd become the Daevo, an inhumanely tortured soul gifted with fierce powers. And he'd been set free on the population.

Tyr was clearly the one who'd undergone transformation once before, turning into the monster when Chris and Paige had been young. Then as the Daevo, he'd helped Scarlett scour the earth for children with special strength and speed, searching for the one predicted to one day grow up and put an end to the red witch.

And Paige had done exactly that, killing Scarlett and passing her individual test. But now all of the witches would have to face the Daevo. The impending final battle between the coven and the Amara was drawing near, and Tyr had revived his inner monsters.

The strength he'd just displayed shook Anna to the core. Her palms were clammy, and her heart tumbled within her chest.

"We can't touch him," Lucia said, echoing Anna's distressing thoughts.

Paige was up ahead in the lead, blowing out the occasional window as Anna had, letting in dim illumination from street lamps outside. She skidded to her right when she came upon a metal door, a symbol above indicating a stairwell. Ethan and Lucia pushed through behind the soldier, then Hayden and Anna, just as a furious bellow roared down the corridor behind them.

Anna stalled, chanced a look down the empty hallway. She met the solid black orbs that were Tyr's eyes. He glowered at her. He grinned. And Anna knew.

He's come for me.

She slid through the doorjamb but not before a ghostly shape speared through the air from behind Tyr. The thing was gunning for her and moving fast. She launched herself through the door and turned to slam it shut behind her.

With her hand still on the handle, she channeled fire into the lock. Mastery of the elements had come to her as a child, and fire had always been the most natural, the most familiar. Many witches understood that magical abilities weren't actually learned, so much as they were remembered.

The fires she created were often bold, dancing fiercely due to the emotions she summoned forth. Be it rage, defensiveness, or vengeance which formed the flames, they were always full and glowing, as comforting as a candle in the lonely night.

But the heat she generated now was sharp and thin, filled with sparks. Evidence of her overwhelming fear. No matter its appearance, the magic coursing from her still did the job, smelting latch, bolt, and strike into one solid slab of metal.

She doubted the quick fix would hold for long, particularly against the brute force pursuing her and her friends. Speeding up the stairs she rounded the landing just as loud thumps hammered on the other side of the door. Either Tyr or his strange beast was pounding to enter.

When she reached the top, the door slammed open and against the wall below. "They're too fast!" she yelled to the others before spinning to face whichever threat came at her first. Her hands glowed blue, and a split second later the white entity dove at her face.

Calling forth the magic created by the coven's union, she flooded her assailant with crystalline light of bright azure. As the mist-like creature drew back and began to shudder and shake, she added an extra thrust that was all her own, shoving it back down the stairs where it crashed into the cement wall.

Whatever the fiend was—demon or malevolent spirit—it was no match for the coven's unique power. The transparency of its form sizzled and then evaporated into a thousand sparks, like tiny, glowing sapphires.

No ash erupted, so not a demon. But she'd puzzle over that later.

Tyr was still coming.

"Move it!" Paige shouted, grabbing Anna's arm and yanking her into the upper hall. Wild panic was in the warrior's eyes, for she too understood the danger Tyr posed. "We still can't get out, Anna. And we can't avoid him for long."

You mean I can't. Nor could Hayden, Lucia, or Ethan. And though Paige might be able to stay out of Tyr's reach, she'd never allow her friends to fall to him. She'd die trying to save them all.

"At least he doesn't seem to be in a hurry," Hayden pointed out, looking back to the door as if expecting him to burst through at any second.

"That's because he knows we're trapped." Paige heaved a

breath. "It's just a matter of time."

"We'll think of something, but you're right. We need to keep moving." Contradicting herself, Anna skidded to a stop to stare at two sets of windows. She caught a shimmer, an outline of markings. So Ronja had left her mark after all. "Wait."

"We can't, Anna." Ethan was of the same mind as Paige. "Come on!"

Anna nodded and started to move again, but as they ran she told Paige, "The wards are around each door or window."

"We already know that."

"But listen. They don't go from one opening to the next. The spaces in between aren't protected. If we can find a regular wall..." Anna trailed off, growing more winded every minute.

Paige caught on, and then she grinned. "Brick, cement." She puffed out a short laugh. "Who needs a regular wall?"

From up ahead, Hayden yelled back to them, "How can Tyr be immune to our magic? How are we supposed to fight him?"

"We aren't," Anna squeezed out, trying to reserve her stores of oxygen. "Not tonight."

By the time they reached the opposite end of the building, Anna was beginning to feel a persistent stitch in her side. Fatigue was wearing on all of them except Paige, and they sounded like a herd of wildebeest as they tramped down the cement stairs.

At the bottom, Paige ducked into the next room, searching for any possible exit. Anna tried blasting out one of the warded windows again but with no luck.

"We don't have a choice," Paige said, "and the walls are all brick on the outside, no matter where we are. But I can handle it. I just need some space. The more distance between Tyr and me, the more time I have to work."

They ran back out into the corridor just as the floor seemed to shift, rocking beneath Anna to throw her off balance. With her forward momentum still going, she careened out of control and fell, landing hard on her hip.

Ignoring the stab of pain, she swiftly rolled and stood again. Brushing aside hair that had come loose, she lifted her gaze.

And saw Tyr standing at the end of the hall.

His eyes were void of life, but a wicked smile stretched across his face. He raised his foot, stomped on the floor. The torn linoleum, flooring, and support structures below all shimmied. Anna threw out her hands, afraid the entire hall would drop from underneath her.

Tyr's chest was bare, so she saw when he tensed his muscles, saw him prepare to leap forward. He would be on her in a flash. And then she'd be dead.

Anna couldn't believe this was it. All her years of training, her ancient forms of power, and here on a dirty worn-out floor, she would meet her death. As well as her greatest failure, and a catastrophic end to the prophecy.

Tyr shot forward several feet, but purposely fell short, laughing sadistically when Anna flinched. He was teasing her, playing with his prey. He tensed again, and Anna tried to turn and run, but strong arms locked around her and picked her up.

Before she knew what was happening, the dingy walls around her began to blur as she suddenly flew away from Tyr. She was being carried—no, she was being rocketed—down the corridor.

In the center of the long stretch, Paige stopped and set Anna back on her feet. "Okay. Here's the plan."

"I'm listening." Winded and dazed by the abrupt speed and subsisting terror still numbing her mind, Anna threw a glance back at Tyr. He was strolling toward them, unconcerned. Paige had been right. He was simply waiting for them to tire out.

And at this pace, that wouldn't take much longer.

"Let's go!" Hayden cried when she and the others caught back up with Anna and Paige. It was becoming clear to everyone that Tyr was only interested in Anna. She was the witch at trial, and the one destined to destroy Bastraal for good.

Her death would ensure the Amara's victory and guarantee their world domination.

Anna ran side by side with Paige, while Ethan, Lucia, and Hayden brought up the rear. No one took time to slow down or even look over their shoulders. Dust kicked up with their steps, various debris rolled over the floor, and glass crunched under their feet.

"You said something about a plan?" Ethan asked.

"I want all of you to keep running. Stay together." Paige wasn't even winded. Super strength and speed were her norm. "When we get to the other end of the building, I want you guys to go back up the same stairs we used the first time. Retrace the path we just took. Make the entire circuit one more time."

"What about you?"

"I'm going back. Toward Tyr."

"That's crazy!" Hayden rasped out, holding her side.

"Don't worry." Paige gave a sardonic smile but came to a skidding halt when they reached the stairs. He's fast." Now that smile turned vicious. "But he's not *that* fast."

She started backing up. "Listen. When you come back downstairs again, take the turn in the middle of the building and head to the front."

Anna nodded. "Got it. Down the base of the T."

Paige's features were set with determination. "By the time you get there, I'll be sure we have our own damn door. One with no wards around it."

Paige all but flew down the hallway, straight toward the hulking Daevo who was slowly yet purposefully tracking them. Then Anna heard the soldier say, "Hey, asshole," before slipping past a surprised Tyr. He swiped an arm at her as she passed.

But missed by a mile.

He seemed to consider going after Paige, leaning in her

direction with fury contorting his features. But he apparently remembered his real objective and refocused his hateful stare on Anna.

"No more talking," Ethan said. Then he pushed Lucia and Hayden, one hand on each of their backs. "Go! Go!" He paused and grabbed Anna's arm, swinging her ahead of himself.

There was no time to argue or protest. Witch or human, no one knew how to defend against the Daevo, and all were in a perilous position. Up the stairs they ran again, each of them panting by this point. Bursting from the door at the top of the stairwell, they sprinted down the hall.

Anna and Ethan were still in the rear when they heard a rush of wind behind them, right on their heels. Then another gust blew right by.

But the force they'd felt hadn't been a simple rush of air. Tyr now stood in front of Anna and Ethan, placing himself between them and the others.

Anna stopped so fast she went up on her toes. Ethan did the same.

Her mind spun frantically as she tried to think of a way out for her and her friends. "Keep going!" she called to Lucia and Hayden. She lifted her hands, and when they only stared back at her, she shouted with more emphasis, "Trust me. Please go!"

The two witches didn't budge, with Lucia sending an anxious look to her boyfriend. But Hayden finally relented and started tugging Lucia with her. "They'll be okay."

Tyr paid the fleeing women no mind, his attention all for Anna. His intended goal. His target.

"I see you've sunk to a new low, Tyr. That your nasty friends give you additional powers." Anna pulled magic from her deepest wells. She let her fear and rage swell, combining into one great surge.

"But I wonder," she taunted him, "can you walk through walls?" Using the strength of her emotions, she let it all burst free and directed it to the ceiling over their heads. She wasn't the strongest telekinetic of the group, but fear for her life and those of her friends gave her gift an extra push.

She pulled down a portion of the ceiling and the roof, letting a huge sheet of plaster and an avalanche of wooden framing and bricks rain down between her and the Daevo.

Wasting no time, she and Ethan flew into reverse, dashing back down the stairs. They both jumped the final steps, stumbling out of the door to run as fast as they could back down the corridor.

Hayden and Lucia were barreling in from the other direction, the four of them now racing toward each other and the turn that would take them to Paige. And hopefully, a way out.

Anna could feel both panic and fear increasing as imaginary fingers reached for her flying hair to yank her back. Her legs were numb and weakening from exhaustion. Still she ran, dragging much-needed air into her lungs with deep, gasping breaths.

She and Ethan rounded the corner right after Lucia and Hayden. Then they gave it all they had, a final push for freedom, and for safety.

Paige was standing at a wall near the termination of the corridor, punching out bricks one by one. Both of her hands were bloodied and dirty, but the hole she'd created wasn't large enough for them to get through yet.

"Almost there," Paige said, but the tension in her voice betrayed her concern. Even if the women could slide through, no way was the opening going to be wide enough for Ethan. Not soon enough.

Tyr roared from the depths of the building, furious now and no longer enjoying his game.

"Paige!" All of a sudden, Chris was looking in from the outside. Viv stood beside him. "You're bleeding." He eyed his girlfriend's damaged fists. "Let me take over."

"No." Viv put her hand on his shoulder. "Let me." Pulling him back several feet, she turned to shout, "Everybody get back!"

The Asian witch took a few more steps away from the outside wall and turned to face Paige and the others still trapped inside. Anna knew what was coming. "Step back," she warned.

They didn't dare go far, since Tyr was closing in from the other direction.

"Anna!" Her name was a curse from the monster's mouth. A promise of death.

Viv had her hands up, directed at the wall. The bricks around the opening began to shake, slightly at first, and then with enough force to create a thundering, scraping noise. All over the wall, the blocks began to shift and crush against each other.

Those at the edge of the hole began shooting outward and away as Viv used her gift to move the very wall itself. At first a few bricks at a time. Then many all at once.

From Anna's perspective, the wall simply caved outward. In a stream of reddish-brown, the bricks disappeared, veering to both sides where Viv finally let them fall into the overgrown grass.

Chris reached inside and hauled Paige out, despite her gasp of protest. Then he was there to help Anna—since the others had shoved her to the front. Tyr was advancing, and now they heard his quick, pounding steps.

He was running.

"Out, out!" Ethan helped Lucia and Hayden with Chris waiting on the other side. Then at last, the demonologist practically threw himself out. Chris grabbed his arms and dragged him the rest of the way out.

Once the group was clear, Viv went back to work.

Performing her previous feat in reverse, she curled her fingers, her delicate face twisted with rage, and lifted all of the bricks again. But this time, she wasn't careful or precise. With a forward thrust of both hands, she sent every piece of the wall blasting inward, straight through the hole. Then the individual chunks turned into well-placed missiles.

Tyr roared again, and Anna caught glimpses of him ducking the projectiles. Then he caught two in his hands and crumpled them into brick dust.

Viv responded with a yell of her own. And for good measure, she crushed the sidewalls and the roof, crumpling the end of the building as easily as a tin can.

Most of the others had returned from the explosion, and when Viv lowered her arms, they all crowded around her.

Quinn gestured to the squashed section. "Can he get through that, you think?"

Anna was shaking worse than ever, her system overloaded by adrenaline and the aftereffects of good old-fashioned panic. "I don't know." She shook her head and took her brother's hand. "And I don't want to find out."

~

The mood was still grim when the cars rolled into the driveway of the mainland estate. The yellow house was alight with warm, glowing lamps, inside and out, but Ian wasn't comforted by the inviting welcome.

The vote to leave downtown had been unanimous, with the only reservation being Tyr's presence in the city. After agreeing he'd come for Anna, and only Anna, they decided that he'd leave the city in peace and return promptly to Ronja.

To report his failure.

"I don't see how we're supposed to combat Ronja, Bastraal, and now that *thing*." Claudia slammed the door of the SUV, but her irritation was understood—and seconded—by all.

"I hate to say it, and it doesn't seem fair," Quinn stood in the lamplight of an exterior bulb, "but Ronja and Bastraal have had almost three centuries to figure out a way to tip the balance in their favor."

"Then they certainly spent their time well," Hayden said, her observation thick with sarcasm. "I might as well have been a child throwing crayons at him for all the good my magic did."

Like the rest of them, Ian had cycled through varying degrees of anxiety, defeat, and disbelief. As the reality of what he'd witnessed—no, that he'd *experienced*—saturated his once logic-driven mind, irritation slowly gurgled to the top.

Anna must have noticed his restlessness, his hands clamped together behind his back. "Are you all right?" she asked, placing a lingering touch on his elbow.

"Yes. I'm fine." His reply was clipped, and he immediately heard the sound of avoidance in his voice. Apparently, so did she.

She barely turned her head, continued to scrutinize him. "You didn't have a vision, did you?"

"No. No episodes." *Just thoughts and intentions that weren't mine, or at least, not completely mine.*

The alien words that had formed inside of him had unnerved him, but still, wasn't the occasional stray thought better than losing himself to another's point of view? He'd still been himself, just with a few new ideas flitting through his head.

He might convince himself, if only the internal surround sound hadn't been in another's foreign and halting accent. The way a Swede or Dane might sound when speaking English.

A revelation struck home, and he found himself whipping his hands to the front, clenching his knuckles, short nails biting into his own palms. Perhaps tonight's incident was actually worse than the visions he'd had before. In those, he'd gone to Vanir's world, transferred into the dead man's once-living body.

But tonight, the opposite had occurred, and Ian was more than a bit unsettled to realize Vanir had encroached on his world for a change. Had entered *his* body.

When Anna withdrew her hand but persisted in her perusal of his face, his eyes, searching for a telltale sign, he gave her what he hoped was a reassuring smile.

Then he looked past Anna and caught Quinn eyeballing him.

Averting his gaze, Ian shifted back to the friendlier St. Germaine sibling and said to Anna, "Just a lot to take in. That's all."

She nodded. "I understand. And you can take it all in and process it, like I know you will, from a guest bedroom out on the island."

The offer surprised him, but he'd already been thinking how nice it would be to get back home, gather his thoughts, and make peace with all he'd become acquainted with.

"No." Ian said, his tone thick with resistance. "But I'll take one of those protective..." He bounced his palm up and down, searching for the word. "One of those pouch-things you mentioned with the herbs. I'll keep it with me, and tomorrow you can come over and ward my house like we talked about.'"

"Ian." Anna put her stern face on.

But he wasn't done with his rebuttal. "My coming to stay with you is not a good idea."

"It's more than an idea. It's a necessity." A hand on her hip, she pressed on. "You saw what Tyr's become, what he's capable of doing."

He kept shaking his head, and where he would have grown more insistent, more demanding in an attempt to argue his position, Anna simply moderated her tone. And something in her mild manner told him just how serious she was. "Warding your home is no longer enough."

"I understand your concern, but Tyr passed me by tonight. He's not interested. Came right up to my face, as close as you are to me now. But he didn't touch me."

Quinn had gradually drawn closer and had his arms crossed. "Yeah, why is that? He hardly gave you a second glance."

Ian paused to study the younger man, the planes of his face hard with suspicion. Protective brother or not, a punch to the face would have been less insulting.

Ian finally let his frustration boil over. "It appears to me that you all need to make up your minds. What's it going to be?"

He looked to Anna. "Do you want to help me?" And over to Quinn. "Or do you think I'm the enemy?"

"He didn't mean—" Anna began.

"I don't appreciate your line of questioning," Ian told Quinn, ignoring Anna's attempt to mediate. "Do you honestly believe I'm secretly in league with the Amara?"

"No," from Anna. "He doesn't. We don't."

Quinn shook his head. "No."

"Everyone just got caught off-guard." Anna reached back and pulled her long hair from the band that held it back.

Headache? Ian thought. After tonight, it wouldn't be surprising.

She rubbed her temple. "This is the final trial and everything is at stake. Added to that," she swallowed and took a breath, "the obstacles being thrown in front of us this time seem insurmountable."

Ian again got the feeling there was more to her statement than its literal meaning. She'd said she still had things to tell him, and he was ready for her to come clean. Soon. Maybe then her words, her actions—hell, the woman in general—would be less of a mystery.

"Ian, listen to me." Anna cleared her throat. "The next time you encounter Tyr, he might not give you a pass. Ronja's allegiance is weak, so I doubt she'll tolerate your dismissal of her for very long. And when she does turn on you, she'll send Hell's fury in search of you."

Ian exhaled and frowned. "It couldn't be any worse than the Daevo."

She lowered her voice. "I'm *talking* about the Daevo. Look," she added quickly, "surely you have others you work with who can represent your firm in court. The bulk of it is research and trial preparation, right?"

"No. No. That won't work, and even if it could, I told you. I can't just stop my business mid-stream. I refuse to give my life over to this mystical war." He couldn't say he had nothing to do with the events. Not anymore, because he no longer believed that.

"It will only be a month," she urged.

"You said that already, but how can you be sure? What happens on Halloween?"

Her eyes darted away but returned to meet his. "There will be a confrontation, the final battle. It's set for the last night of the month." She spread her hands, imploring him to listen. "After that, you'll be free to return to your home. No more worries over Ronja or Bastraal."

"If you win, you mean." He moved in closer, spoke with an intense whisper. "But what if you don't?"

Anna's solemn eyes locked with his. "Then it won't matter where you go."

13

The following day, Anna led Ian into her sitting room. She'd missed him when she'd gone down for breakfast and had been informed by Mrs. Attinger that he'd risen early, gone for a jog on the beach, and had returned to his bedroom, not to be seen since.

Anna had given him his solitude, sure he was still picking apart all the occurrences of the last few weeks and trying to restore them to some semblance of order. The lawyer in him needed logic, it seemed, rationale to make sense of things. Yet the man he was had a black and white sense of justice, a straight and strict outlook on what was right or wrong.

Anna, on the other hand, felt most things came in a rainbow of possibilities and degrees of good or bad. So now she hoped to merge their views, and hopefully settle on some common ground.

So after hunting him down in his room, Anna now led him into her quarters. Just past the threshold, he paused to take in her personal space.

Penetrating eyes roved over the fawn-colored walls and dark wood trim, her family heirlooms, as well as her own modern additions. Was he searching for hints to her personality, her lifestyle? Trying to discern any secret motives?

Looking for her cauldron?

"You paint?" he asked with a nod at her work in progress.

The magnolia had gone untouched since...she stopped to

consider. Since the day Ian had come into her life for the third time, and at a most crucial juncture. "Yes. Painting is a release for me. An escape."

She needed the mental vacation her art provided now more than ever but couldn't settle herself long enough to work. Not now, when so much hung in the balance and her mind rolled in circles of confusion.

"You're good," he stated matter-of-factly, the absence of false flattery making his appraisal all the more valuable.

"Thank you." Anna gestured to the peacock-blue sofa near a bank of windows. She hoped a clear view of the gardens might encourage him to relax. To open up. "I thought we could talk in private." She offered a smile along with a cup of tea from a pre-set tray. "I'm sure what you're experiencing is hard enough without the constant audience my friends create."

Ian took the beverage and picked up a wedge of lime to squeeze into the steaming brown brew. "As it happens, I'm used to an audience. The difference is your friends aren't sure whether they want to applaud or throw things at me."

Anna added cream and sugar to her own tea and sipped to warm her throat. "Well, since you brought it up, let me apologize for what my brother suggested last night. We're all in a state of heightened awareness now, a little more sensitive to changes, more alert for signs of danger."

"And your brother thinks I'm dangerous?" The question was delivered without a change in demeanor or flinch in facial expression. The deceptive calm of an accomplished litigator.

"He's...being vigilant. We all are. And to be blunt, your past association with Ronja added to the fact you likely have a deeper connection with her, well..." Anna blew on the steam still rising, then returned his direct stare. "Can you blame him for being cautious?"

"No, actually. I understand him completely. It's you I'm having trouble with. If you believe there's good reason to fear me, then why did you insist I come here?" Now he cocked one brow. "Keeping your enemies close, Ms. St. Germaine?"

With a shake of her head and a long, weary sigh, Anna set her cup on the walnut coffee table. "I can always tell when you've got your back up." Her hands crossed primly in her lap. "Because you stop calling me by my name."

"Got my back up?" Ian laughed, and his smile burst out like sunshine after the rain. Along with that perilously charming dimple. "You wrap things up in such pretty little bows, don't you? I might turn into a man that lived a thousand years ago, and *died* a thousand years ago. And then what? Attack you and your family while you sleep? Start channeling my Viking heritage?"

Anna sat silently as he got it all off his chest.

"Rape and pillage. No wait, those were pirates." Now he put down his cup as well and shifted on the couch, moved closer until their knees grazed. "Tell me right now, no more playing Ms. Polite Hostess. *Anna.*" He said her name with emphasis. "Do you believe I'm going to become Vanir and try to do you harm?"

She opened her mouth—paused—and then gushed out a breath. "I don't know." Another lie or evasion would just be too poisonous on her tongue. To her mind, she was already deceiving him, and subversive behavior didn't sit well with her.

There were still important details she had to tell him, but she couldn't yet bring herself to reveal her dirtiest secret, the truth of what her trial really entailed. Her integrity was being diluted gradually, like a daily drop of blood into a cold, black lake.

By the time she reached the end of the month, all that she represented, all she valued, would be gone, leaving only what the gods had dealt her. Emptiness.

She already despised herself for the murder she was bound to commit, and for some inexplicable reason, she couldn't bear to have Ian's hate as well.

He stared at her for several seconds before inclining his head and relaxing, his broad shoulders rolling free of tension. "I appreciate your honesty."

Anna's own muscles released as well, though she wasn't sure if her dread of Halloween night had caused her discomfort, or if it had been the sudden shock of awareness when his body had come into contact with hers.

Just a simple brush of legs, really, but between that and the dimple, the sun streaming in to highlight the masculine ridges of his face, and the rich sound of his voice when he grew edgy, Anna had become far too aware of Ian.

Not as the man who needed her help, the standoffish and sniping lawyer, or even as Ronja's potentially reborn brother.

But as an attractive and virile man who, frankly, she had begun to admire.

He hadn't run from Tyr last night, one of the deadliest and most evil forces in existence. Nor had he complained about having to take a leave of absence from his law office for the remainder of the month.

Yes, he'd argued at first, but once he'd been convinced, his decision was immutable. No grumbles or objections. Ian had made an agreement, and he would stand by it. He took his word and his honor seriously.

"So now I'd like you to be honest about something else," he said, jarring her from her daze. "I need to ask what you plan to do about the missing people. I know the police are searching, but given your talents..."

"Yes." Anna answered, feeling a blush rise to her cheeks. Did he think her so cold-hearted? Would she forever be the evil witch in his mind?

Then she turned her thoughts to the final battle. If he ever found out about the man she was doomed to kill, he would think far, far worse of her.

Her attraction to Ian was normal. He was a handsome, accomplished man.

And it wasn't strange for her to fear for his safety. She lived every day with apprehension, with worry for the innocents she had pledged to defend.

No, what had Anna feeling nervous and had sweat forming between her fingers was her need to have Ian's approval. As it turned out, she cared what he thought of her. Ronja's stuck-up counselor with the dust-free world.

And as high school as it sounded, especially now when destiny was at hand, she really, truly wanted him to *like* her.

Each of the coven challenges had had its own twist, turn, or I-didn't-see-that-coming, but aside from Kylie's return from death—actual death—Anna felt she had a lock on first prize for most heartless hand of Fate *ever*.

Emotion was suddenly overflowing. Guilt and dread she might be able to handle, around her friends, when she was with her family. Because they understood.

But here was one person who'd always made her feel judged, and it was no coincidence he'd come into her life during her trial. Right when she was supposed to fall in love.

She already knew Fate was a bitch, but to throw more acid on a raw burn? It was beyond sadistic to send her a man who didn't trust witches, who thought them evil.

And then force her to turn to the dark.

With the sting of rejection climbing her throat, she coughed to push it away. "I do look for them, Ian. Every morning and every night, as well as at noon, when the sun is at its apex. Pure light is guidance, and I use everything at my disposal."

Feeling the need for a break, and for some distance, she rose and went to the antique desk where she kept the bulk of her supplies. She trailed a loving finger over the ancient carvings before removing the slip of fabric that covered her gazing ball.

She stared for a moment at the sea-blue reflection of herself.

She damned the woman who stared back.

Lifting the orb, she breathed in and pivoted to show the shiny ball to Ian. "Reflective surfaces are wonderful for meditation or psychic visualization. You can use water, a mirror," she tossed her head, "the hood of a car after it's rained. The most important thing is to be open-minded."

Gently, she replaced the ball on its stand and picked up one of her sets of Tarot cards. "These have been used for centuries, and are often more revealing of the answers you already know, those hidden in your subconscious. The representations, the fool or death, empress or moon, they aren't always to be taken literally."

She set the deck down, too soundly. "They're perfectly harmless, but often misunderstood."

Anna heard the stridency in her voice, felt the vicious curl of resentment in her stomach, but despite her normally calm deportment, she couldn't seem to find her way back.

After picking the cards up again and returning them to their proper place, she opened a cubby to retrieve a candle from her stash. "A dancing flame? Perfect for letting your mind fly to other places. And notice the color? Black. Dark as space, as an abyss, as a crow, or a devil's den."

"Anna…" Ian tried to interrupt.

But she kept rolling. "But black is used to *banish* negativity, not always to invite it in. The color also helps induce a meditative state, and I've used this as well," she hoisted the candle, "to search for those innocent people."

Ian stood and took a few wary steps toward her. "I don't understand. Why are you showing me all this?"

"Because this is who I am. I'm a witch. I practice, I *live by* magic, and if you're ever going to be able to trust me, you have to accept that. With no reservations."

"Well, you don't ask much," he said, running a hand through his flaxen hair. "But let's be fair here. Have I asked you to accept me completely? No. I haven't. Because I understand what's happening to me and who's causing it, so I wouldn't put you in that position. I wouldn't ask you to lie to me by saying you had no concerns."

Anna lowered the candle to her side. She was at a loss for words.

He just kept surprising her, and now here, in the face of her temper, he had gained another level of respect. Though she might not always like what Ian had to say, she could count on him to shoot straight. And to always play fair.

There was an extra sting in that knowledge, because for the first time in her life, Anna couldn't say the same of herself. Not only was she hiding the truth about the final battle, the sacrifice, but she was also holding back her own suspicion.

Quinn's observation the night before had stuck with her, had needled her mind even in sleep. Tyr had passed Ian by, because Ronja wouldn't have wanted her brother hurt. And Anna couldn't help wondering if the sibling loyalty went both ways.

Would Vanir's love for his sister be strong enough to surface? To overcome even Ian's staunch morality?

The unfairness of the situation didn't elude her. How could she ask Ian to believe in her, when she was now having her own doubts?

"I didn't mean to imply that you didn't care about them," Ian said softly. "The missing people."

Anna's residual upset faded, leaving her only tired...and scared. "I know." She set the candle back down. "It's just so frustrating. We know exactly who's taken these people and for what purpose, but their location is blocked, from my sight especially."

Clasping her hands together, she tried to lighten the grim atmosphere they'd created. "I've apparently got some unresolved issues when it comes to you and your views on the supernatural world."

Ian dazzled her with *the smile*. "No. Ya' think?"

In spite of herself, the situation, and her gruesome destiny, Anna laughed. She trudged back to the sofa and sat. Ian did as well. She found her tea slightly cooler but still needed to soothe her throat. Along with her raw nerves.

"What are they being taken for?" Ian asked, and when she made a sound of query, he clarified, "The missing people. You said you knew why they were being taken."

Anna took a huge gulp. And prepared to evade the whole truth once again. "They can be used as hosts for demons."

"Ah...that's right. I remember you mentioning it that day at my townhome. I honestly didn't believe you then." His gaze wandered out the window. "I was in denial. *Hard* denial, just like you'd said."

Still staring out, he asked, "Is that what you meant by candidates? For demon possession?"

Technically... "Yes." If she told Ian about Bastraal's need for a human body, it would naturally lead to a discussion of how she planned to defeat him. She held her breath, but the answer seemed to satisfy.

Eventually he turned his eyes—still stone-blue but softer at the edges—to her. "Will they die?"

"We do everything possible to prevent that. Even if we come up against them during a fight, we have ways to expel a demon from its host. Once the person is free, we can kill the demon."

Anna licked her lips, wishing to all the stars that she could do the same for whomever Bastraal decided to inhabit.

"What about the town? More and more people are paying attention, especially after the bombing last night." Ian was full of questions, but Anna wasn't surprised that he'd thought it all through, dissected every problem. And she couldn't blame him for worrying.

"Two months ago," he said, "the first thought in everyone's

minds would have been terrorism. Now it's of monsters being spotted lurking in town squares, or people moving at lightning fast speeds on a bridge to save jumpers." He captured her with a look. "And yes, I heard about that one too."

"My family kept this secret well, and my coven, too. Up until recently." Anna put her arm on the back of the sofa, curled her legs up under her. She was oddly comfortable with him now, after her outburst.

Because he hadn't fired back at her. He hadn't run.

He was still here.

"But eight of my sisters have now triumphed, and no matter how foreboding the situation seems to be, I have to maintain faith that I will also overcome. I have to believe that no matter how wrong things seem," *no matter how cruel*, "it's all happening because it's supposed to."

"Everything is meant to be?"

She couldn't tell if he was mocking her or not.

"Magic and the prophecy have guided me my entire life, Ian." She rubbed her amulet, closed her eyes briefly, and then met his. "I can't give up on them now."

"We...I mean *you*...should try to help the community understand." He leaned toward her. "People are scared."

"They should be. And actually, we decided to stop putting so much effort into hiding the truth. Lives are at risk, so the people of Savannah should be on guard. Now more than ever. We haven't overtly exposed our presence, but we've stopped trying to conceal it." She shrugged. "And truth be told, we can only track so many people down so Dare can alter their memories."

She'd managed to shock him, his eyes gone wide. "He can do that?"

"Mm-hm." She sipped again.

"Do you think he could take a whack at mine?"

Ian had tried to force humor into his voice, but the unease

beneath showed through. At least to Anna. And she didn't need a gazing ball to see how distraught he was.

Better to go ahead and get it done, address the rest of the problem head on.

"I guess that brings us around to why I asked you here." Anna leaned to the service tray atop the coffee table. "More tea?"

"No. Thanks."

"I'm having some." And once she'd poured another cup, doused it with sweet and creamy, she got to her feet.

With the tea in one hand, she extended the other to Ian. "Come with me to the bedroom."

14

Holding on to her long, ladylike fingers, Ian let Anna guide him into the adjoining room. He was surprised by how delicate her hand felt against his when she had always struck him as bold and assertive.

His next surprise came when he entered her bedroom. The grand centerpiece was a king size bed, topped by a gauzy canopy of deep blue above a rich brocade coverlet, white with azure stitching. The place where she slept was whimsical, inviting, and suitably magical.

Yet the wall of built-in bookshelves was sturdy and worldly. Contradictions, the room was full of them. Just like the woman who resided here.

"Wow," Ian finally managed. "Even with the library downstairs," he swept his hand to indicate the high shelves, "you have all of this?"

"Yes. My mother was a woman of magic with a fondness for books. My father was a man of books with a penchant for magic." The smile she gave him was hampered by sadness. "It's no wonder Quinn and I turned out the way we did."

Sensing a wound, a core event that had formed this witch he was now thrown together with, Ian pressed for more, but gently. "What happened?" His tone was soft. "To your parents."

Though she faced the back of the room, he saw her lips pinch together. "They died when we were younger." With this she glided away to the opposite wall.

And that, Ian could tell, was all that would be said on the matter.

Stopping beside a writing desk, Anna looked back and crooked a finger. Several books, most of which could likely be classified as relics, were spread out over the surface. He moved to her, stopping at what felt like an appropriate distance. But still he could smell the light floral scent he was starting to associate with the enigmatic Lady St. Germaine.

That's how he thought of her, regardless of her other unnatural talents. Her regal bearing and tranquil fortitude were reminiscent of royalty, traits possessed by those who had no choice but to balance leadership with compassion.

And after what he'd learned of her prophecy, her duty, and her role within the coven, he felt the comparison appropriate.

But as he leaned in, he found nothing unapproachable about her scent. The last time he'd noticed it, he would have sworn the teasing fragrance had been one of roses, but today, she reminded him of lilies.

Ian sniffed again, but subtly, so she wouldn't notice. Did he even know how lilies smelled? And if so, why did he not banquet his home with the flowers?

If he could be surrounded by something so sweet every day, a sensation so—

"You all right?" she asked.

Ian realized his eyelids were at half-mast, so he coughed and rubbed at the corner of one. Just a little dust, he pretended.

Or stardust, maybe?

Ignoring the fact he felt the room's colors were too vivid and the light too enchanting, he gestured to the books. "What are these?"

"These are my family's journals. They date back centuries, all the way to the original three."

He knew the story of the sisters and understood whom she meant. He nodded to show he was following.

"There are more than these, many more, but I only pulled some to show you. I don't expect you to read them. I only wanted to share some of my history with you. I know you still aren't completely comfortable with what I represent, but I hope you can at least feel safe here."

Ian locked eyes with her, held just there. "I'm beginning to."

Her hand fluttered to her amulet, a giveaway movement she did when she was nervous or he said something she didn't expect. After a quick grip on the necklace and its sapphire-hued center stone, she ran a reverent hand over the wrinkled leather of one of the books. "I don't invite just anyone to come here."

He said nothing but inclined his head, marveling that she trusted him. At least on some level. He could admit now, looking back, that he'd been hard on her. Prejudiced and assumptive.

Henceforth, he would behave in accordance with his mother's strict etiquette guidelines and would persevere to act the perfect houseguest.

Though he didn't recall a section in Emily Post titled "Deportment Amongst Covens."

He caught her studying him again, with that calm and steady focus he found unexpectedly sexy. Then she drew herself up and resumed the mantle of astute and experienced leader, preparing to share her wisdom.

He relaxed into a comfortable stance, ready to listen.

"You should know everything that I know when it comes to the Amara, and most of what I've learned over the years came from these books." She patted a cover, the leather colored like mustard. "What I didn't get from reading I received in oral storytelling or from my occasional vision."

She turned to him and leaned back against the edge of the desk. "I've garnered little pieces over the years, one nugget at a time. But I still don't know everything there is to know about Ronja. Or about Bastraal."

"Tell me more about the beginning," Ian said. "When Bastraal and Ronja first came to the area."

Anna's face flickered with indecision, and he wondered if she'd been about to say something else. But after a decisive nod, she answered him. "Bastraal succeeded in gaining a body once before, almost three hundred years ago. He had a short but gory run before the St. Germaine sisters banished him. By all accounts, Ronja didn't play a large role that time, but she was around. The three sisters wrote of her. They knew what she was and where she came from, but not much more."

Tilting his head in thought, Ian cast his eyes to the beige wall, the ornate tapestry hanging there. He was starting to grasp the significance of Anna's legacy. Sure, he'd heard her when she'd said things like "demon," "prophecy," and "world domination," but staring at the needlework that must have been more than a century old, he found a new appreciation for her responsibilities.

She was the end of the line. Her coven, Savannah, and even her long-gone ancestors were all depending on her. The weight of her obligation had to be severe, and add to that, she'd never actually had a choice in the matter.

Ian, on the other hand, had been lucky by comparison. He'd chosen to work with the law because he'd seen his father do so. He'd witnessed the long days and nights spent poring over research documents and volume after volume of legal precedents. He'd also seen the difference his father had made in people's lives.

So he'd wanted to do the same. Work wasn't as hard when you loved it, when you believed in it, and the worst thing Ian had ever faced was an ignorant judge with a heavy gavel.

He could hardly fathom how Anna carried her duty on such slender shoulders. The gravity of it all had kept her tied to this island, to Savannah, and in reality, to demon-crafted evil from which she could never escape.

Not until now, her trial.

So with this new perspective, Ian focused on his expert witness. "Do you think Ronja has been causing my visions?"

Her chest rose and fell with the depth of her breath. "I think your association with her may have triggered them, yes. And it's time we started calling them what they are. Memories."

The assertion shot straight to the deepest recess of Ian's psyche, jarring loose a terrible sense of acknowledgement. Half of him knew she was right, but the other half still insisted on putting forth an argument. "I've never had a memory I couldn't get out of."

When she raised her brows with meaning, he added, "I know I'm splitting hairs, but I'd be just as happy to continue calling them episodes."

"You can't beat Ronja if you don't face who she is to you. Which is why we should look further for answers."

Ian was still reeling, but what she said made sense. To make any progress, to preserve his own sanity, he had to consider the stark possibility. Then deal with it. "So you believe I am her brother."

Deliberately, Anna held his gaze. "I believe that you *were*. Once she found you again, she may have created a spell or performed a ritual to make you see the past. She *wants* you to remember."

"Because she wants me to be Vanir. Or she wants me to become Vanir." The notion of the dead man's thoughts penetrating time and death to invade Ian's mind was horrifying.

"But her magic can't touch you here," she reassured. "And I'm hopeful the visions will be gone forever. Just as soon as she is."

With a determined expression, Anna spoke quickly, getting in her next bit before he could veer to another question. "There's another reason I fought to convince you to come stay here. We have very strong protection on this island, spells that even Ronja can't break." Her pause was heavy, deafening. "Or any demon."

Ian's eyes became slits. "What are you getting at?"

"You described a terrible cold that accompanied both attacks."

He nodded as a fist of apprehension bunched in his stomach.

"The freezing temperature is a telltale sign. The creature that did those things to you...was Bastraal."

Ian stepped back reflexively. "The master demon? The one even Ronja fears?"

"Yes."

"But why would he do that if Ronja wants me unharmed?"

She released a breath and looked up as if the answer would be found floating in the air. She shrugged. "Beasts from the underworld don't function the same way we do. Their motivations are driven only by their desires, their cruelty, and their fury." She looked at Ian again. "Remember, Ronja answers to Bastraal, not the other way around."

"And Bastraal doesn't seem to want me in the picture. That's just perfect." Thumping his fist against his thigh, Ian edged around the bed and over to the windows. Here the view was still of the gardens.

But he could find no solace in the carefully-planned pathways and green-shrubbed borders. "I don't understand Amara politics at all. The immortal witch is determined I return to her side and play dutiful brother, while her demon master wants to drive me away."

He whirled around. "And last night, Tyr did the exact opposite." Still reeling, he raised his shoulders and then let them fall. "This doesn't add up. The Daevo won't raise a hand to me and neither will Ronja, yet Bastraal lashed my skin to pieces, tried to smother me."

"Bastraal can't enter here." With easy, casual steps, Anna made her way to him. "I will keep you safe until this is all over.

If you continue to allow me."

"I won't give my life to them, Anna. I won't." He'd heard her assurances but was struggling with the fact that even with the prophecy drawing nearer to completion, Ronja was still focused on Ian.

Correction. On Vanir.

"I am not this other person." His voice was calm, belying the fear still growing inside. "When I see these visions, they're like watching a movie that someone else is starring in. The guy may look like me, and I may sense his feelings, but that's all they are. *His* feelings. Not mine." He clenched a fist, pressed it to the glass. "Not mine."

Anna was beside him now, a hand on his arm. Her gentle touch soothed. "I may be able to discover more about Vanir and Ronja. That is, if you're willing."

Ian glanced down to the point of contact between them and grasped her meaning. "You'd do that willingly? What if the vision is painful for you?" Protectiveness surged, another surprise. "I don't want you hurt."

"I needed the last vision you gave me, and I needed it quickly. I credit the urgency of that situation for the headache it caused." Removing her hand, she dropped it to take his, then repeated the act with her other.

They were linked, forming a unit of two. Liquid warmth flowed from her, heady, almost intoxicating.

"If you'll let me look, I'll tell you what I can," she whispered. "If you'll trust me."

Ian hesitated, more concerned for her than himself. And when had that transference occurred?

"There's a chance nothing will happen." One side of her pretty mouth lifted. "We might just end up holding hands for a minute."

Then she sobered. "But you are connected to Ronja, so we might as well use that to whatever advantage we can."

Ian liked the sound of turning the witch's nasty tricks back around on her. He didn't like being used or manipulated, even by someone who purported to love him like a sister.

And he definitely didn't care to be a conduit for a man who'd already had his chance, who'd already had his life. "We won't know until we try, and considering what's at stake," he gently squeezed her fingers, "I think we should go for it."

"Okay then." She gave a slight nod, rolled her shoulders, and let her face relax. "And Ian," she said, "no matter what happens, I won't let go of you."

When she closed her eyes and inhaled slowly, he did the same. Though he didn't feel as calm as she seemed to be.

He'd never meditated before, had heard it took some practice. But he and Anna must have created a powerful psychic conduit, because at once he was overcome by the sensation of falling backward. His stomach dropped, so he clenched his eyes more tightly. Just when he should have hit the ground, he found himself floating instead.

In all of his previous visions, he'd been looking out through Vanir's eyes, but this time he was more of a spectator, a ghostly voyeur hovering above a room. It must have been an effect of linking with Anna, seeing for himself and being in control instead of at the vision's—no, the *memory's*—mercy.

Taking in the new surroundings, he had the impression of crudely built walls, a dirt floor, and dry heat permeating a shadowy chamber. When a woman screamed, he narrowed his eyes to see better, but the scene popped into clarity of its own volition.

Flames were leaping in the fireplace, their blaze providing warmth to the woman who lay upon a mess of blankets and straw. She was abundantly pregnant. And she was definitely in labor.

Time recognized no rules or limitations in this half-light state of being, and though Ian witnessed the events, they all seemed to flash by at great speed. Finally, after long, painful hours, a child was delivered. A boy.

A tall man with long blonde hair and braids on each side of his face stepped forward to accept the infant once it had been wrapped up in a coarse blanket and had its eyes wiped clean.

The man held his son—Ian knew they were father and child—in front of the fire. He laughed heartily as the child kicked and wailed. Glowing both with happiness and firelight, the man proclaimed the boy "Vanir."

Ian observed without great emotion, but a trickle of dread made its way in when another scream tore from the woman on the floor. Judging by her contorted grimace and raised upper body, she wasn't done yet.

The second baby entered this world much more easily, and more rapidly with her smaller female form. This time the woman collapsed into the supporting arms of other females and laughed the tired, joy-filled laughter of one who'd just become a mother.

The man had moved to kneel by her side and was whispering what appeared to be endearments. Then he took the girl child in his other arm, repeated the ritual by the fireplace, and boomed with equal pride, "Ronja!"

Ian had no time to be shocked by the revelation that Vanir had not only been Ronja's brother, but her twin, one of the most steadfast bonds found in human nature. He didn't have the opportunity to worry, because he was swept away to another time, another place.

Here he floated above a village. He watched as two young people, likely in their late teens and both impossibly attractive, circulated amongst the small community. The golden twins interacted with people, they counseled, and upon occasion, they offered help or healing.

They performed white magic.

Ian's mind knew this was Ronja and Vanir, but seeing the

witch as a kind, generous soul was now so foreign to him, he found himself trying to shake his head in rejection. But with no other option, he continued to watch. And he wondered.

How would this information help him? How would it help Anna, her coven? And did any of it affect the prophecy?

He wished he could communicate with Anna and ask her opinion. Vanir struck him as a good person, a responsible practitioner of magic. For that matter, so did Ronja. So what had happened to change everything?

Pain lashed at Ian, and he jerked in response. He was still sealed inside the alternate dimension, but the scenery was changing again. Suddenly there was a crowd gathered below him, but their dress, their language, both were out of place.

A long-buried instinct whispered low to Ian and he knew. *They do not belong here.*

The shouts and yells bursting from the invaders were in a foreign tongue, but their zealous rage transmitted loud and clear. In the center, several men were struggling to subdue a single male. They were punching him as they dragged him to a wooden pole.

It took all of them to restrain the man as they fought to tie him to the thick stake. One attacker's head popped backward when the captive landed a solid blow, and in that instant Ian caught sight of Vanir's bruised and bloody face, his crimson-soaked tunic with its blue-embroidered rune turned purple.

The trauma of this barbaric deed made his chest tighten as if a boulder had just landed on top of him. For whatever reason, he was beginning to feel his actual body again. He was returning to reality, to the island, and to Anna.

But what happened to Ronja?

And in swift answer, he was shown her fate.

The beautiful young woman, the sweet and kind healer to her people, lay broken and shattered on a damp cavern floor. Though she shivered from the cold, she made no attempt to cover her skin, exposed from where her clothes had been ripped.

From an assault? A desperate run through the forest?

Sprawled across the stone surface, she sobbed, moaned, and pleaded for salvation. For rescue from her awful pain.

A freezing wind slapped at Ian's back, so he turned his gaze to look out across the lands. A thunderhead was rolling in from the frigid blue ocean, an angry, seeking storm that was not of this world.

The bank of pitch-black clouds raced with preternatural speed, overtaking everything and engulfing Ian in its mad rush to consume. Throwing up his arms, he braced for the cold attack he'd learned to expect, but the pulsating storm caused no ill effects.

Its stench, however, was shocking. Rancid earth and decay of death.

The depth of the storm was endless. Soon it filled the cave, covered the sky and, it appeared to Ian, swallowed eternity.

In the center of the rolling gloom he could see only Ronja. The bleakness in her eyes stabbed him once, a needle-thin puncture of sympathy. If he could, he would stop what was about to happen.

Still lying helplessly on the ground, still cold and crying out her heartbreak, Ronja looked up and gave herself. Opening her arms, she embraced the darkness.

Ian sucked in a breath so hard and fast it scraped his lungs. He awoke, his gaze clashing with Anna's. "It was Bastraal." They were still holding hands, but even her warmth couldn't thaw the chill that had settled into his marrow. "He found her."

15

Paige tapped the screen to end her phone call just as Ian strolled out from behind a tall garden hedge. She was seated on a stone bench out of sight, so he hadn't seen her on approach and still hadn't noticed her.

Aside from that, he seemed lost in his own thoughts, even now with a deep crease on his forehead, the kind that came from serious introspection. These last few days since he'd come to the island, he was usually in his room, wandering outside, or quietly observing the other occupants of the house.

He'd seemed especially withdrawn since his experience with Anna. The coven leader had filled them all in on the visual experience she'd shared with Ian, as was the norm among the witches.

And with the climactic conclusion of the witches' trials on the horizon, this was certainly no time for secrets.

Wondering if this rule applied to Ian, Paige started to speak up, but he chose that moment to rock back on his heels and groan, rubbing his fingers on his forehead. Right where that line of tension had been.

Carrying around that much seriousness all the time, it was no wonder he had a thumper of a headache.

She'd been mildly irritated to have her private moment interrupted, but her own concerns vanished. The guy was clearly stressed out, and unbidden empathy suddenly sliced through her. It wasn't so long ago that she and Chris were going through the tortures of the damned.

Or the destined.

And it didn't take a math genius—or a psychic—to see that Ian's arrival coincided nicely with Anna's challenge. And Paige kind of liked the pairing. Even if he had brought some massive baggage with him.

Hmph. Paige shook her head. *And I thought I had it bad.*

Certain issues from her trial were still unresolved, but at least she'd found Chris, the only man who'd ever made her stone heart make any sort of movement resembling a *pitty-pat.* He loved her and all of her shortcomings and had also been instrumental in helping her heal some old, persistent wounds.

Her fingers tightened on the cell phone. Yes, she was on the mend, but her injury had been so severe, almost permanent, that she still suffered the occasional phantom pain. Like the past several minutes spent talking with... With *him.*

So yeah, she could put herself in Ian's buffed-to-a-shine shoes. She could dredge up a little compassion.

But what she couldn't do was sit here any longer and let him think he was alone. Breathing deeply, she asked, "Out for a fresh breath?"

Ian swung around, a flash of surprise passing over his features just before recognition settled in. He nodded in greeting, then looked over her head to do a quick scan of the gardens.

At last, he spoke. "Yeah. I just need to get out once in a while. It's only been a few days, but..." He shrugged a shoulder.

"I know." Paige leaned forward, elbows on knees. "Believe me, I know. I have excess energy to burn, and even in the Taj Mahal back there," she hooked her thumb toward the mansion, "I can still get stir crazy."

She tapped the phone on her leg as she searched for conversation starters, which wasn't exactly her forte. She stared down at the flagstone path. "Things around here have been even twitchier lately, and I find myself going for walks a lot more often."

Lifting her face to let the sun warm her cheeks, she sighed and said, "Truthfully, the waiting is killing me, especially now that we have an actual countdown."

"A what?" Ian seemed perplexed. Then he tilted his head back. "Oh, right. Halloween. The big battle."

When he added nothing more, Paige stole a peek at him. Didn't he know the rest? About the sacrifice Anna was being forced into?

And if not, Paige rubbed a knuckle beneath her chin, why hadn't Anna told him?

On second thought, she mused, this was the same man who'd run straight to the police only a few days ago. So Anna certainly wasn't in any hurry to spill her I'm-planning-to-dagger-a-guy beans.

So neither would Paige.

With the sun beating down and a light breeze floating through the greenery, the two were content to bask in the light as well as the silence. Until the cell phone started to feel like a hot oven brick in Paige's hand.

Without knowing why she spoke, or why the words that flew out were of such a personal nature, she inhaled sharply, held it, and expelled the breath in a rush. "That was my father."

Ian quirked a brow.

She held up the phone.

"Oh." Still, he remained mute. He didn't press.

"He and I are not on the best of terms. I mean, things are better now that we're talking, now that we *can* talk to each other. But that's another story, another challenge." She laughed at her own joke, so Ian lifted one side of his mouth in solidarity.

As if mirroring her own emotions, he also grew serious with her when she sensed melancholy taking over and frowned.

Maybe that was too strong a word, though. Regret was better, regret for the years and memories she'd never get back.

She didn't know why she all of a sudden felt the urge to share her problems with the one person on the island who was a virtual stranger. But then again, maybe that was exactly why. He was a lawyer, he knew how to listen, but best of all, he came with a completely unbiased opinion.

Ian didn't care enough about her to say nice things just for the hell of it or try to make her feel better. If ever there was a blunt and factual person, honest to the point of rudeness at times, it was the man standing here in the quiet garden.

Waiting patiently for her to continue or not, her choice.

"I didn't know him growing up," she said. "He couldn't have me near him, because he wanted me to stay hidden." Paige dashed her bangs from her eyes and twirled her finger in a circle on the back of the phone. "From the Amara, or as it turned out, from Scarlett."

Ian nodded, and Paige remembered he knew most of the story.

"He also ended up raising Chris instead of me."

"Chris, as in your boyfriend?"

"Yeah. Weird, right?" She stood, stretched. "But we're good, Chris and me. It's a long, sordid story, and I know my father stayed away from me for all the right reasons, but it's hard getting to know him. Now. As an adult."

"I bet." Ian kept his blue eyes on Paige.

She tried not to think of Ronja and how much he favored her. It seemed like a betrayal, even if Paige hardly knew him.

His next words caught her off-guard. "But I think you'll figure it out. You strike me as the forgiving sort, if given good reason."

At that, Paige guffawed. "You aren't very observant, are you?"

He stayed cool, barely moving a muscle when he said, "On

the contrary."

"Well, I don't know about that, but we'll see." Paige heaved a sigh, wondering what she could do to keep herself distracted for the next few hours. So she wouldn't hear the imaginary sound of *tick-tock tick-tock*.

"I appreciate the talk," she told him.

"Short and direct," he said. "My preference."

"Mine too." Hands on her hips, Paige felt herself slip across that line, moving from "stranger" side to "acquaintance." The guy was kind of growing on her. "You know," she offered, a drawl in her voice, "we are all here to help you."

"Why do you say that? I've made peace with our... arrangement."

"Have you?" She lowered her forehead. Grinned.

"Well, let's say I'm still adjusting to fire sprouting from fingertips and hearing only one side of a discussion being carried on with a cat." He laughed when Paige did. He scratched his cheek. "But I didn't know I was being so obvious."

"Yeah, well. You've heard of the proverbial stick up the—"

His hand spiked up to halt her. "I've heard."

"Well, no offense, man, but you've got a hundred-year oak up there." She cringed, picturing her own analogy. "Anyway, all I'm saying is that it's okay to relax."

"Relax?" he scoffed. "You were there the other night when that thing went after Anna and your friends, right? The Daevo? When he came over to me, I swear I thought those girls and I were dead."

Paige had heard the account from Hayden and Chris, about how Ian had run to shield the teenagers. Tight-ass or not, her respect for him had tripled after that. For a man who was supposedly freaked out by the supernatural, he'd dived right in, ready to fight. Ready to defend.

"Then he looks right at me, not half a foot from me," Ian continued, "and tells me that all of this was because of me."

"Because you're Ronja's—" She stopped herself, but knew that he knew what she was going to say.

"That's what I inferred." A kind of tired acceptance made that crease reappear on his forehead. "Protecting myself is one thing, but I don't want anyone else put in danger because of me and my," he grunted, "whatever it is."

After they each mulled in silence for a while, Ian stuck his hands in the pockets of his gray slacks. Paige pulled her mouth down. Didn't the man own a pair of jeans?

"What do you do about it?" he asked, breaking into the quiet again.

Paige cocked her head and wrinkled her brow in question.

"When you get stir crazy? What do you do?" He gestured. "Watch the gardens grow?"

"Not usually. My entertainment of choice is…" Paige paused as an idea began to creep around the edges of her very-bored brain. *Oh. Yeah.* "I'll tell you what, Ian."

He lifted one blonde brow in a way that made her think of a super-British-spy, all cool and aloof.

So she chuckled again, and man, she was actually feeling better. She pulled her head to the side, indicating he should follow. "Come with me and I'll show you.

~

Quinn hit the blue gym mat with a *whack!* Then with a groan, he rolled over and crawled up to his knees. Once he was standing on unsteady feet, he rubbed his stomach. "Tell me again why we spar with Paige. As much as it hurts my male pride to say so, it's not exactly a fair fight."

Paige stood with hands on her lean hips and a cocky grin on her face. "Because you'll be ready when a demon comes at you—the slower ones with a physical shape, or the ones that can flash through the air."

Ian was glad he'd managed to have clothes picked up and sent out to the island for his extended stay. The workout clothing had been especially handy, since his daily runs helped alleviate some of the built-up tension.

But as he glanced around at what used to be an elegant ballroom now turned gym, he had to agree with Paige. There was nothing like letting off steam with a good brawl. Wrestling, boxing, you name it.

His streamlined life with the law created little opportunity to let go, to lose control and show an opponent how he really felt about them. That's why he led an active life outside of his professional demands—SCUBA, running, martial arts.

There was more to him than legal analyses and wing tips. He just didn't feel the need to spout off about it.

So it was a furtive smile that crept to his lips when Paige asked, "Who's next?" Hiding his true response, he whipped out an I'm-not-sure-about-this expression and lifted a timid hand. "I guess I'll go."

"Good." She surveyed the group. "Let's put you with..." Her smile was as mischievous as the one he'd hidden. "How about Trevor?" The glint in her eye told him she wasn't one to go easy on fellow trainees and was throwing him in the deep end by pairing him with the towering cop.

But big often equaled slow. Just how Ian liked them.

Ian met Trevor in the middle of the mat, the other man giving a respectful bow with hands steepled together. Mimicking the act, Ian nodded to his sparring partner and fell into a relaxed stance.

The first punch came at him faster than he would have expected, but he managed to sidestep in the nick of time. The big guy wasn't as slow as he'd expected, and Ian was beginning to see the benefits of Paige's special sessions.

Still, this wasn't his first time in the ring. Or on the mat, as it were.

Again Trevor drove his right fist forward, a blow that was meant to put a man down. But even though he was tall and broad-shouldered himself, Ian was limber and knew how to become fluid.

Leaning his upper body to the side, he simultaneously brought up a swift knee kick to Trevor's gut. The grunt the detective expelled was deep and satisfying. At least to Ian.

Trevor whirled away and brought his hands up, still winded from the jab to his abdomen but ready for whatever Ian threw at him next.

These people were better trained than Ian had given them credit for. So he decided to get serious. Dancing around to Trevor's left, he faked a swing to get his attention and, as predicted, Trevor swung around to protect his face.

Ian then used the cop's momentum in his favor, sweeping a leg to take Trevor's out from under him. The bigger man went down hard. With a muttered, "Damn," he eased onto his back and blew out a long breath. Then he lifted a hand to Ian.

Paige gave a few claps of applause while the others who were there offered congratulations or—he wasn't shocked to hear—whispered to each other of their surprise. Ian reached down and hefted Trevor up, feeling more than a little proud that he'd given this group of warriors an unexpected show.

Across the training arena, a door opened, allowing a few late additions to enter. Still catching his breath, he watched as Kylie and Viv walked inside wearing exercise clothes. Ethan strolled in after them but held the door open for another person. Then Anna walked in.

And Ian felt like Trevor's right hook made contact with his chest.

She too was dressed for a workout, but the tight black pants and sleeveless sports tank showcased a sleekly muscled figure, tight in all the right places. And softly rounded where it counted most.

Afraid he was ogling like a horny teenager, Ian shifted his attention to Kylie and Viv and lifted a hand in greeting. But Anna and Ethan were trailing along after them, and he couldn't keep his eyes from straying back to the gorgeous coven leader.

And the only unattached female in the bunch. *Just thirty days without rain. A perfectly natural response.* He tried to convince himself it was the banishment from the mainland and his normal habits that suddenly made Anna so appealing.

Hell, he'd had stretches without female companionship before. It's not like he was desperate.

But seeing her made him feel distracted…in a desperate sort of way.

She noticed him staring and gave him a wide smile in return, her cobalt blue eyes…happy to see him? And Ian found he couldn't tear his own away.

That's when the room tilted and he somehow ended up on his ass. He was staring at the far away ceiling when Paige flashed to stand over him. "Lesson one. Never turn your back on a demon."

Ian frowned but accepted her offered hand. "I thought the match was over."

"You were still on the mat." She punched him in the arm. Why was she so fond of doing that to him? "Which brings us to lesson two," she said with a wink. "Don't expect a demon to fight fair."

"Duly noted." Smarting in his butt *and* his shoulder, Ian glanced aside to look for Anna, but she'd already moved a good distance away and was standing in front of what looked like a tic-tac-toe board with swinging panels. Symbols had been painted on each square.

He realized why when she, Willyn, and Lucia took turns sending fire, water, and what he assumed were gusts of air toward the board. They cheered each other when a hit was made. Which was every time they made an attempt.

"Good match." Trevor's voice rumbled beside him.

"Thanks. You too." Pivoting to look around at the other activity areas, Ian added, "I needed that win too." When Trevor only shook his head, Ian explained. "The girls are over there throwing fire and water from their hands. Paige just handed my ass to me." He rubbed his throat and met the cop's stare. "I swear my testicles are shrinking where I stand."

The roar of laughter his wry comment received caused Ian's mouth to quirk and jerk in return. Then he finally gave up the battle and let loose a grin.

"I know exactly what you mean," Trevor said. "And," he said in a lower tone, comrade to comrade, "I happen to know the cure as well." Swinging his arm out, he cocked his finger like a gun and pointed toward a far corner where several of the men were gathered.

Ian couldn't see through the line of male bodies to fully appreciate what was going on. But he would soon find out, since Trevor had already started off that way. And Ian followed, fully intent on re-sizing his manhood.

On the other side of the row of men that consisted of Quinn, Cole, Nick, and Chris, a long table was draped in brown fabric. Along the top, a variety of weapons were displayed, ranging from small but deadly black stars with wickedly sharp points, all the way up to hatchets and full-metal swords that looked as if they'd been designed for this particular sport. Throwing.

Michael was currently showing them all how to turn it into an art form. Settling in next to Trevor, Ian crossed his arms and watched, fascinated. The mild-spoken veterinarian was one mean mother if handed a knife. He hit the bull's-eye. Every. Single. Time.

"Yeah, yeah." Chris uttered, doing his part to fulfill the quota for the obligatory shit-talk they all expected. "Let's see you do that with a hatchet."

Cole leaned forward and spoke over the others to Chris. "No,

man. Don't." He smirked at Michael who was happily headed
for the hatchets. Then back to Chris. "Just don't."

Putting on an act of false disappointment, Michael lifted
his hands. "You're lucky there's a new guy who needs a turn,
Chris. So I won't have to make you eat your words."

At the mention of "a new guy," Ian perked right up. He'd
considered purchasing throwing knives before but hadn't
gotten around to it. "Yeah. Sure." He joined Michael beside the
table. "What do you suggest I start with?"

"A butter-knife," Trevor said, causing a round of male
chuckles.

Ian shook his head and sent the cop a grin that let him know
he was a real smartass. And that it was appreciated.

"Here you go." Michael held out a moderately sized dagger,
plain metal with no embellishment.

Ian accepted the weapon. And sizzling heat rushed up his
arm. For a moment, he was sure the blade was electrified, but
the current subsided before he actually dropped the dagger.

He was still gripping the hilt, his breathing still ragged. The
shock was fading, but his body was still reacting to the charge.
With his glower pinned to the weapon in his hand, Ian gritted
out, "What's in this thing?"

But a part of him knew. A part of him recognized.

"What?" Cole had come over and the others all circled around
too, probably concerned over Ian's reaction. He'd jolted and
jerked when the metal had first touched his palm. "Oh, you
mean the magic?"

Ian met Cole's light green eyes. His throat felt dry and tight
when he asked, "Magic?"

"Yeah." Cole nodded. "The coven magic. The women imbue
it into the weapons, so we can fend off demons. You know, we
can't just spit it out like they do." He took the dagger from Ian
and shrugged. "Must be some residual left in here."

"But why did you sense it?" Michael asked. The vet didn't

seem very friendly any more.

And Ian noticed the light-hearted banter had disappeared. Now the other guys were all quiet. Confused? Or concerned?

"I just got a shock. Too much static in my clothes or something." Ian told them, playing it off. Then he spoke to Trevor. "Maybe a delayed reaction to getting put down by Paige. She likes to hit, doesn't she?"

"You have no idea," Chris mumbled.

The guys all laughed. And just like that, all was right again in the man-world.

But Ian decided he'd take a break, leave the room under the guise of getting a drink. "Here." He handed the dagger back to Michael. "I'll pass for now."

The blonde vet's stare turned to slits. "You sure?"

"Yeah, yeah. But I want to learn. Just...later." Ian stepped back and turned away, raising a hand to the guys in departure. He definitely needed some alone time, because now he had two things to worry about.

One. Why had he picked up so easily and so *violently* on the magic in the dagger?

Heading for the door in a clipped pace, he resisted looking back again.

And two. Why had Michael looked at him that way?

16

After another few days had passed without issue, Anna found herself in the kitchen rummaging in the fridge for one of Hayden's special drinks. One of the fruity options that was supposed to boost a person's energy.

She wasn't exactly tired, she told herself, craning her neck to look over the orange juice. But the daily routines on the island had become too predictable, less enjoyable, and unbearably... well...routine.

Having spoken to the other witches, she knew she wasn't alone in her feelings. Kylie had only this morning described the slowly passing days as a dream-walk. Everything seemed foggy and thick, as if the hands of the clock were having to push their way through tar.

Anna agreed with the assessment, but added to that, she was also functioning through a constant cloud of dread. She'd had no other sign from the sacred book, and no new vision that might steer her—she prayed to the goddess—along another path.

As far as she knew, she was still compelled to do as the book had outlined. Stab Bastraal's chosen victim in the heart, therefore actually piercing an organ controlled by the demon.

Stab. Pierce. Puncture. Tear. She repeated the words in her head, envisioned various male faces staring up at her, pleading for mercy, but every image, every repetition was just as awful as the last.

Faced with the most wretched task of her life—the most horrific she could even imagine— she'd been trying a psychological method similar to what was known as trauma-focused cognitive-behavioral therapy. Since it was often used to treat PTSD, Chris was familiar with it and had been the one to suggest Anna try her own version.

Even he, the newest of the group, could see how affected she'd been to learn of her final role in the prophecy. He was offering what help he could.

The technique was used to help trauma victims deal with thoughts and feelings that reminded them of their tragedy. Only Anna was doing it in reverse, attempting to numb herself, to remove the emotions that naturally accompanied such a violent act.

As yet she could tell no difference, and part of her was glad of that, while the rest of her dreaded the eventual event. There was no preparation to be made, no trick or diversion to make things easier. How was one to accustom herself to the idea of committing murder?

The idea still nauseated her, and she'd broken down in tears no less than three times in the last couple of days. There was no escape and, despite her normally stoic attitude, she kept asking what she could have done wrong. What misdeed could she have possibly done to deserve such punishment?

When all her life she had faithfully and lovingly served magic.

So no, she wasn't tired, not in any physical way. But she was mentally and emotionally beat down. Honestly, how could she stand another twenty-three days of this anguish?

Her fingers tightened on the edge of the door. *Stop being self-centered. Think of the poor man who will give his life to save everyone else.* No, she corrected, the life she would *take* to accomplish that goal.

Swallowing down more tears, more of the bile that threatened continuously, she searched further for that drink. She had an irrational need for the healing properties it was supposed to contain, as if the ancient recipe could help her feel better. Make the dread go away.

Finally spying the label with the word "Kombucha," she grasped the bottle by its thick neck. And was disheartened to see the only flavor available to her was green. Fermented tea was hard enough to swallow when it was a cheery pink, let alone the color of chlorophyll.

She let the refrigerator door drift shut and was still trying to get the plastic off the lid when Ian's voice broke through the stillness of the midday kitchen. "I'm leaving," he announced.

He startled her and she almost dropped the precious bottle, the ambrosia of the gods that was sure to cure what ailed her. "What did you say to me?" she snapped, giving the plastic one hard twist before it finally gave way. She crumpled it in her fingers with a loud crackle.

Ian held up his hands and retreated a step, sensing her subsurface temper. "Sorry. Let me rephrase. I really need to get away from the island for a little while."

As her upset deflated, Anna eased to the trash can, disposed of the wrapper, and removed the lid. Leaning against the creamy-brown masonry of the pizza oven, she took a long drag of greenish tea with cultures of...something she'd probably rather not think about.

"Whoa," she said, rearing her head to read the label again. "This stuff is..."

"Awful?" he supplied. "Because it looks awful." He eased into the room and came to stand beside her.

"No. This is really, really good. The green stuff. How about that?" She offered the bottle. "Try it?"

His hand went back like a tortoise to its shell. "Not today, thanks."

But as she shrugged, sipped again with an "Hmmm," he

studied her, amused.

Cutting her eyes his way, she took another long slug. The smile that formed on his full lips took its sweet time, drawing out and up on one side before creeping over to the opposite cheek.

Anna paused. She watched his mouth, the chiseled jaw, until the other side curled, lifted...just a little more...and then—Bam! He hit her with the dimple.

Lowering the drink, she caught herself rubbing the exposed skin above her V-neck. He was too close, smelling of crisp, clean male. And on top of his alluring scent, his smile had struck a chord inside of her that thrummed pleasantly, vibrating all the way down to her toes.

Then she recalled his previous declaration. "I'm sorry. You want to leave? Where do you want to go?" He wasn't a prisoner, and she could only do so much to persuade him to stay, to do what was wise for his own protection. Still, the notion of his being off-island made her uneasy.

"What I'm really in the mood for is a dive." He looked at her expectantly, hopefully.

"As in scuba?" She blinked a couple of times, sure she'd misheard. "You've got a powerful demon who enjoys causing you pain and near-death experiences, yet being beneath sixty feet of water strikes you as a good idea?"

"I was thinking eighty. I know a place—"

She raised the bottle between them. "All I will say is this. If you really feel the need to risk your life that way," she shook her head, "then I won't try to stop you."

He had the gall to look offended. "You won't?"

A bare inch of green goodness remained in the bottle, so she tipped it back while she gathered her wits. But it didn't help. "Ian, you know good and well I can't let you do that. But you also know I won't force you to stay here." She turned and walked over to chunk the empty bottle in the recycling bin.

She spun back to him. "Which means I'll have to pull out my BCD and regulator and get dressed to—"

"Wait." His eyes lit up. "You dive?"

Thinning her lips, Anna asked, "Why is that shocking?"

"It's just... You're so..."

"Careful there."

Cocking his head and coming across as entirely too charming, he made the save with, "So dignified."

"Mm-hm." She wasn't buying it. But how was she supposed to stay frustrated with him? How could she be depressed when he was standing there grinning at her like that?

"So, no diving then. You're right about it being a bad idea." He clasped his hands together. "But I really need to get out on the water. You've got boats. How about a quick run?"

Moving closer, he let his charm turn syrupy, but in a manner designed to make Anna laugh. "I'll have the prettiest, most powerful witch in the South with me. What could go wrong?"

"Hmph," was her answer. "We've learned not to ask questions like that. They're almost always a jinx." But the knot in her stomach had relaxed at last, and she could practically feel the salty wind in her hair, smell the ocean, and see the deep blue. Boating was one of her favorite recreations.

A sensation of recklessness stole in to replace her usual caution, and before she could think twice—or think better—she matched Ian grin for grin. "What are we waiting for?"

~

Kicked back on the front of the boat's sun deck, Anna and Ian reclined with leisure, and she had to admit, this was the most free, happy, and relaxed she'd felt in days. Joe and Joseph had both opted to come along for the ride, and after skirting around the island to give Ian a tour they'd headed farther out to sea where they could anchor the liveaboard and absorb the serenity.

For hours they'd dealt with nothing more than the warm sun, the occasional squawking seagulls passing overhead, and the liberating scent of open water. Anna and Ian were both clad in shorts and T-shirts, comfortable in the fall weather despite a strong breeze blowing in from the east.

Since the boat was idle, Joe and Joseph had ducked into the kitchen to throw together sandwiches, chips, and drinks, the typical day-on-the-water fare. Head tilted back to soak up the descending sun—which was close to giving its final bow—Anna blinked her eyes when she heard Ian shift beside her.

He'd pulled up his legs to prop his crossed arms on his knees. Still staring out toward the horizon, he spoke in a deep, gentle timbre. "Thank you for today."

Stretching her arms above her head, she said, "I needed this, so no thanks are necessary."

"Deal. But only if you promise you'll dive with me sometime."

Her lips kicked up quickly. The man was nothing if not persistent. "Deal."

"So, how'd you get into it in the first place? I took my first lesson in college, and I'm not ashamed to say that it was to get closer to a girl."

Laughing low, Anna remained in her recumbent position. "How'd that work out for you?"

"Pretty well, actually. I threw back the girl. Kept the sport."

At ease, because Ian had put her at ease, she decided to answer his harmless question. "My parents both loved diving." No shadows were chasing her memories today. Just a sweet nostalgia of family daytrips spent swimming, laughing, and for her and Quinn, learning all about scuba.

He nodded, and she caught the mild tightening around his mouth and eyes. Worried he'd brought up a sore subject?

Anna sat up and touched his elbow. "It's fine. I was abrupt with you in my room the other day, but only because we were digging deep into the past, and I was still…"

"Unsure about me? How I'd react?"

She lolled her head side-to-side. "Something like that." Taking off her sunglasses, she shielded her face with her hand and turned to him.

He returned the courtesy by taking off his own and showing his eyes as well.

"I told you that my parents both knew magic. But what I didn't say, is that's also what killed them." She waited a heartbeat, heard the cry of a gull, and then added, "They were trying to meld magic with metal for the purpose of imbuing weapons, creating a sort of backup of power."

"Like the ones you have now." He nodded. "They did that?"

"They came up with the idea and laid the chemical foundation." She shrugged. "There was an explosion. A fire." She turned to the sea. "Quinn and I didn't work on the project until recently, during Lucia's trial. It was time then, and Ethan came along to provide a couple of missing pieces to the puzzle."

"Lucky he showed up," he said.

More than that, Anna thought, but she kept the truth about Ethan's arrival to herself. It was becoming clear her attraction to Ian wasn't a passing phase or harmless crush. But today she was finally at peace and was keeping her fears at bay. Or at least buried where they couldn't disturb her rare tranquility.

She wasn't ready to tell Ian everything about the trials, especially since he'd only just stopped throwing suspicious glances her way all the time. He'd finally accepted her gifts as normal. Okay, maybe not normal, but not quite as horrific as he'd first thought.

So it bothered her that more than one lie now stood between them. She hadn't told him about the requisite sacrifice slinking closer every day. And neither had she mentioned the very crucial role that romance played in every witch's challenge.

It was bad enough she suspected Ian was her intended

match. She could handle the extra strain.

But how would he react to the news? He barely tolerated the supernatural world to which he'd been introduced. She certainly didn't expect a joyful response to hearing he might be fated to love a witch.

With a sigh, she tried to relax again, letting the last of the warm rays cascade over her skin.

But Ian still wanted to talk. "After losing your parents that way," he angled his body toward her, "do you ever resent the prophecy? Do you blame the magic for causing their deaths?"

Her nails dug into the deck, but she maintained a mask of calm. "I've had my moments of anger, but in the end, magic and the energies that flow through it, through us all, demand balance. Every reward has its cost. I've made my peace, for the most part, but it helped when I learned to accept one fundamental truth."

"And that is?"

She swung her gaze back to him. "Even tragedy can bring about better days. As hard as it was for me to admit at one time, I know I'm better prepared for what lies ahead because of my loss. When my mother and father were killed, I threw all I had into the craft. I studied, practiced, and studied and practiced some more, determined to make sure they hadn't died in vain."

Comfortable with him on a level that shook her to her core, Anna turned her body in his direction, leaning in so their shoulders were almost touching. "What they gave to me, what they nurtured within me, is a gift. No life is without pain, and I would be selfish to deny my destiny and my ability to help others because of my grief."

His eyes, too full of insight, caressed her face. "And your parents wouldn't have wanted that."

She shook her head. "No."

"Anna. I hope I'm not out of line here." He waited until

she nodded, giving him the go ahead to say whatever he was thinking. "I didn't know your parents, but based on what I've seen, what I've been told by others," his gaze locked with hers, "I believe they would be very proud of you."

A place in her heart squeezed painfully, pinched a tiny bit more, and then released with a sigh. She rarely spoke of her parents or the accident that had taken them from her and the others who'd loved them. Now that she had shared her private pain with Ian, she was touched and a little unnerved by how clearly he could read her. How much he'd learned in the last week, and how quickly he took small parts and pieced them together.

No, he hadn't known her parents, yet he had touched upon Anna's one wish.

That she would make them proud.

This man had many layers, and just as he had judged her too quickly, she was coming to believe she had done the same.

Once she reined in her sentiment, she felt physical awareness starting a slow sizzle inside her. Then a flame leapt to life between them. Without words, they looked at each other, and in that one shared moment, Anna felt the shift.

Ian was thinking of her in a new way as well, seeing her as a woman instead of just...a witch. "Anna," he whispered, and that was all. His granite-sky eyes said much more.

A breath lodged in her throat, her skin ran with heated chills.

But a great flash of light drew her attention over Ian's shoulder and out to sea.

She cleared her throat, lifting a hand to point. "Storm's coming in." She used the distraction as an excuse to escape. Whatever had just happened between her and Ian was powerful, more consuming than any magic she'd ever wielded.

She got to her feet, just in time to feel the whip of wind lash through her hair. Gentle waves began rocking the vessel, enough to make her widen her stance to keep her footing. "I'd better let Joe and Joseph know. Looks like we're heading back in."

Ian was standing now. "I think they probably feel this." With a scowl he studied the growing clouds on the horizon. "Moving fast." He slid a worried look to Anna. "Too fast?"

"Something's not ri—" Her reply was lost when the boat lurched viciously, this time hard enough to thrust her against Ian.

His arms enfolded her. "Are you okay?"

"Yes. But we need to get the boat started." Still locked in his embrace, her hands on his firm chest, Anna gasped as another wave rolled in. But this time, it wasn't water that crashed but intuition. She was flooded with sensation, a sick, oily feeling of misery and hate wrapped up together.

The ocean had turned choppy with violent waves, and they now slammed the boat from every side. Not rogue waves. Because they were definitely being controlled.

The building tempest was no natural storm. Something was stretching inside Anna, being pulled, as the magic within her recognized its foe.

And then she felt the cold, so much cold, blowing in from the seas, hurtling across the water to buffet and toss the vessel. Bastraal had found them.

No, Anna thought with a strike of terror more jolting than any slash of lightning. He'd found *Ian*.

The engines roared to life, creating a mild rumble beneath her feet. Joe and Joseph were able-bodied seamen, familiar with the risks and rigors involved with any outing. And they'd felt the change in the sea, recognized the unnatural source, and were even now preparing to flee toward land.

I should never have risked Ian this way. The cold was closer now, licking its way over her flesh with tiny, sickening kisses of greeting. The demon had already sought to harm Ian, and now that she'd given him protection, he made an even more tempting target.

"We have to get below deck!" she shouted.

"It's him, isn't it?" Ian glanced around, then he spun, throwing his arms backward to enclose her, to shield her with his body.

Anna could see the bumps rise on his skin as the temperature dropped. The immediate skies were black as obsidian, blocking all light, turning their lovely day into treacherous night.

The seas bucked and thrashed, sending them both tumbling toward the handrail of the sun deck. She went to her knees, hands sprawled outward, as Ian slid closer to the edge, closer to the roiling deep.

Anna prayed to the goddess and all the gods that she hadn't made a mistake that would cost them all. She tried to scramble to Ian, to reach out to him. He'd gained his feet and was reaching back when an iridescent shape formed behind him.

"Ian!" She screamed a warning, but a mass of inch-thick cords wrapped around him, cocooning his body before Anna could draw breath, before she could move her legs, or even summon her magic.

And because she'd stalled, because she'd let horror override her years of training, Ian was seized by Bastraal. His eyes met hers an instant before he was jerked up into the air, then plunged down into the cold October sea.

He disappeared into what was now a death trap, below the turbulent waves, surrounded by freezing cold, and his arms locked against his body by that demon bastard.

"Anna!" Joseph was edging his way toward the front of the vessel, slow-moving due to the tumultuous rocking.

Her panicked eyes met his. "Tell Joe to wait!" Readying herself, she cast a final glance toward Joseph. Then she dove overboard, slicing straight into the churning ocean.

The cold almost knocked the breath from her lungs, but she

clamped her lips tight. There was no way in hell she would draw another breath until Ian was beside her to do the same. She wasn't leaving him down here alone.

Darkness saturated the water, surrounding her with Bastraal's malignant essence. But the demon's own form shimmered from within, allowing her to catch sight of the tentacles still coiled around Ian. And the beast's massive shape floating nearby.

Kicking her feet, she knifed toward Ian as he thrashed and struggled against the bindings. She allowed her anger and terror to rise as one as she sped toward them. She would need to harness every ounce of emotion if her magic were to stand a chance against Bastraal's.

This was not the setting in which the two were ordained to face each other. Fate had decreed she would meet him on the unholy ground of the stone yard. And for that reason, Anna knew she would survive this day.

But Bastraal would reap such pleasure if he could hurt her, wound her in other ways. And killing Ian would be right up his sadistic alley.

Bubbles abruptly burst from Ian's mouth, and he grimaced, threw his head back. Bastraal was squeezing the air from his body.

Not going to happen! Holding out her hands, Anna exploded her magic, shooting the blue stream toward Bastraal's immense shape. But the burst of power was strong, thrusting her into a backward flip through the water.

Mentally cursing herself for lack of control, she fought to gain her sense of direction. Ian was running out of time.

Finally she righted herself and started down again, only to see that Ian had been freed and was swimming his way up to meet her. She'd expected to see panic, terror, or a combination of both after what he'd just endured. But even from yards away she could practically feel his burn of fury.

And her heart kicked with pride.

Yes, he was an accomplished scuba diver, and yes, he was growing more accustomed to the presence of magic, both light and dark. But the resilience and willpower that had him barreling toward the surface—slowing to snag Anna's hand in the process—was an indication of the man himself.

He'd apparently had enough of being blind-sided by the demon. And now looked killing mad. He let her go, so they both could swim faster, and seconds later she broke the surface a split-second before him.

As one they dragged in the precious oxygen. Ian waved, and Anna glanced up to see Joseph on the rail with a lifesaver in his hand.

"Keep it!" Ian yelled. "We're coming up." The steely determination in his tone sent a shiver through Anna that settled in her chest. She'd been the one who'd come to rescue Ian, yet when they made it to the ladder, he pushed her ahead of himself, urging her to climb.

When she was halfway up, a monstrous light came from below, bright enough to reflect in Joseph's wide eyes. "Hurry!" He grabbed onto Anna's forearms and hoisted her up the final two rungs before leaning over to lock a hand on Ian's elbow.

But Ian's strong legs made easy work of the leap onboard.

Joseph rushed to the center of the vessel to shout to his father. "Go! Now!"

The engines that had been purring beneath now sputtered and died. Bastraal wasn't done toying with them yet and had affected the motor.

Anna cursed the beast and waited for him to reveal himself again.

Together she and Ian stood their ground, side by side, watching as an enormous ball of fire began a slow rise from the depths. Beside her, she heard Ian's sharp intake of breath. She glanced over to see his features gone slack, his pupils dilated as hers often did when she was seeing another place in her mind.

Still focused on the flames, Ian choked out, "Fire." But he didn't move, transfixed by the demon's show of strength.

Anna stood in front of him this time and threw up a wall of ice between the boat and Bastraal's inferno. The thick shield ran the length of the boat, fore to aft, high into the air, and down into the sea.

As the fire pounded on the other side of the ice, melting with each blow, Anna stood with fists at her sides. "I may give my life, Bastraal, but not theirs. You will not harm them!"

The boat heaved as the demon began to attack from underneath, still able to affect the vast ocean. Even a vessel as large as the liveaboard was but a speck on the endless seas.

"You will not harm him!" She lifted her palms to send another spray of ice and water toward his leaping flames as they started breaking through her barrier. "You will fail! Do you hear me? Just as your Daevo failed when you sent him to kill me before Samhain!" She showered her magic up and over her own wall. "You coward!"

At her words, a roar of rage shook the icy partition. Bastraal pounded his power against the wall until it cracked.

Anna readied another surge, but the demon's presence suddenly faded. Above, the leaden clouds dissipated. The churning seas calmed. And even more quickly than it had risen, the unnatural tempest died.

All at once, the boat was bobbing gently as the final remnants of the angry waves disappeared. The vessel and all her passengers were left to bask in the golden light of late afternoon.

Anna's pulse still beat rapidly in her throat, her chest. Her magic still burned, craving release.

But Bastraal was gone.

Ian came to her, put his hands on her shoulders as Joe throttled the boat and circled toward home. "What did you do?"

he asked, his hands now roaming up and down her arms as if he needed to make sure she was intact.

Anna felt the urge to do the same. Turning into his arms, she put a hand to his face, searched for any traces of pain. But found only stoicism. "I don't know what happened," she said, then she hugged him tightly, pressed her head to his shoulder.

She shivered now, because she could. "He just...left."

17

Ronja was alone in her parlor, enjoying the receding daylight. Every evening she grew more excited, standing at this very window to watch the dying of the light. Waiting for time to pass each night while darkness approached, slithering over the land.

For each day that was put to rest was one step closer to the Amara's victory. And, she mused, scraping a black fingernail over the window pane, once Bastraal was in control and the coven was no more, her master was sure to fulfill every promise he'd ever made to her.

Yes, she still had faith in the demon, even though his very nature was one of betrayal and deviance. She alone had served him for centuries, and she would therefore receive appropriate compensation for her loyalty.

But until that time, she would continue to work toward her ultimate goal. Tyr had failed to destroy Anna and sever the witch's burgeoning relationship with Vanir. Ronja sneered and mocked in a sing-song voice, "Oh, forgive me. I meant to say Ian."

But she wasn't beaten, wasn't devastated. She was ever-optimistic. Because when Bastraal ruled over the afterworld— of charred cities and blood-filled streets—her brother would eagerly return to her side. He would come to know her again, and love her, as a sister deserved.

Caught up in her dreams of conquest, she was stunned to feel the silk of her robe whirl around her legs as sudden turbulence rushed into the parlor. Such bracing, ripping winds shoved her from behind that she spun around and bared her claws, ready to defend against whatever force had infiltrated her sanctum. But at the last second, she sensed Bastraal and recognized his bizarre new form in the doorway.

Her mouth opened to question the furor of his arrival, but the demon sailed across the floor and grabbed her by the throat. With a roar he lifted her high, slamming her back against the navy-papered wall before thrusting her up toward the ten-foot ceiling.

He stopped just short of braining her with the plaster above her head, but she could feel his barely-restrained violence, the fury that quaked throughout his semi-visible shape. And she knew fear.

Ronja was immortal. To a point.

But that didn't mean she couldn't be killed by the right kind of magic.

The grip on her throat clamped down harder. "Why did you go against me?" Bastraal thundered. "Do you not value your life and all that I have pledged you?"

She flailed in the air, held in place only by the hand on her neck. Unable to speak, it was her mind that screamed in terror. He'd somehow discovered that she'd sent Tyr after Anna, that she'd gone against his directive. But how did he find out?

After days with no mention or eruption of anger from the demon, Ronja had believed the secret safe. Now that Bastraal was tethered to the physical world, he hadn't demonstrated quite the same degree of omniscience he'd once possessed. So she'd grown bold, arrogant.

But now he knew. She grappled at the fingers that choked her, nails clawing at his huge hand. The pitiful attempt only made him growl.

Then he abruptly released the hold on her ruined throat,

dropping Ronja to the floor in a pile of her own weak limbs and the silver satin of her robe. While she had the chance, she tried to rasp out her plea. "Please, Bastraal. I had to act. Vanir has gone to the island to be with those witches. They will sway him, turn him against me!"

"He is already against you, foolish woman!" The floor shuddered as he stalked across the room. Providing a much-needed distance, so he wouldn't be tempted to finish what he'd begun? So he wouldn't kill her then and there? "I told you the matter of your twin would have to wait."

He turned his head to the side to growl at her, "You must be patient, lest your actions ruin everything!"

"How?" Water rolled over Ronja's cheeks and, aghast, she wiped a finger slowly over her face. Tears? She was crying? How shameful and weak. How human!

As distraught as she was now, she couldn't gather the appropriate disgust for herself. She was too overwhelmed by grief, too consumed by the gaping hole the death of her brother had left behind.

She still mourned, after all these years.

"How can I be patient? I've waited so long for our success, and all along I mourned Vanir. Now that I've found him, why should I wait?" Finding a small, growing flame of resentment, she struggled to stand on aching legs. "Better yet, how can you ask me to?"

Instead of responding to her questions or commenting on her reprehensible tears, Bastraal gradually turned. And his eyes grew more visible. They lit from within, orange flames flickering inside a black abyss. "How did you know that?"

Caught off-guard, she stammered, "Know wh-what?"

"That Ian had gone to the witches?"

She squared her shoulders. "His name is Vanir."

"Answer me!" The explosion of sound pressed her to the wall, but Ronja kept her mouth firmly closed, as there was no reply that would satisfy his rage.

"Ah...of course," he ground out. "Your little whipping boy who can see things in his mind. Tyr." His tone changed then, growing lighter, placating, but the amiability was fake, the cheerfulness mocking. "Would you like to keep your pet, Ronja? Rather, would you prefer your Indian lover to keep his skin?"

In a rush of air, he was back, his hand again on her body, but now the curled fingers dug into the center of her gut. He held her aloft again, the hard ball of his hand ramming into her. "You would be wise to remember who will rule in the end. And I assure you, it won't be your Daevo. His power is a temporary thing, borrowed ability and strength."

Bastraal crowded her, pressing his glimmering body against hers and lowering his face, frigid breath against her cheek. Then he sunk his sharp teeth into her neck, ensuring she would never forget this lesson.

Rarely did Ronja show any sign of pain. Rarely did she scream.

But she did now.

The freezing burn hit her bloodstream and paralyzed her upper half. A disgraceful whimper squeaked from her open mouth.

Bastraal pulled his teeth from her flesh and rasped, "But my power." He shoved his mouth to her ear, so she could hear him licking her blood from his lips. "Mine is eternal."

He backed away, removing his overwhelming essence yet keeping her within his grasp. "Test me again, and you won't be the one I punish." He didn't drop her this time but flung her across the room to crash into a solid oak buffet. She struck her face on the corner of the sturdy wood, knocking silver candlesticks to the floor and crushing a fragile vase from the Yuan dynasty beneath her when at last she fell to the floor.

Lying amid the refuse of her fine things, Ronja put a hand to her throbbing cheek and came away with bloody fingers. She raised terrified eyes to Bastraal. To her *master*.

He stomped over to her, his words pulled tight and thin with rage. Spoken low with promise. "You have lost your way, Ronja." A tentacle crawled under her chin to hold her face. "Perhaps another would serve me better."

~

Quinn was coming out of the kitchen with a grilled sandwich of cheese, ham, and tomato on a plate when Anna and Ian entered the grand hall. Their clothing hung heavily with the appearance of wetness, and Anna's hair was bedraggled, a knotted mess.

"You decide to go swimming?" Kylie asked from where she sat on the green velvet couch waiting for Quinn.

Anna and Ian glanced at each other. "We shouldn't have gone out," Anna said. Then moving forward, heading to the stairs, she tossed aside, "We had a run-in with Bastraal."

"Whoa, whoa, *whoa*." Quinn set his plate on an end table and called after his sister. "That's it? That's all? You deliver important news in that clipped, clinical way and keep walking?"

At the base of the wide mahogany staircase, Anna pivoted, and he could see her irritation in that flat expression she wore whenever she was feeling emotional and wanted to hide the fact. He'd seen that face since they were kids, her impervious veneer, perfected soon after their parents' deaths.

And that's how he knew she was truly upset.

"I'm tired, Quinn." Anna released a pent-up breath. "And I would like a hot shower."

Michael and Shauni appeared then. They'd also been in the kitchen making a huge salad to share when Quinn had left them. Michael was in the lead, hands bunching and releasing as if he considered making fists. He took in Anna's disheveled attire, and then whipped his head to Ian.

Quinn was watching the interchange as Michael studied the newcomer to the island, and he clearly saw Michael's eyes narrow, his jaw tighten.

What is going on there? As if in answer, Michael shot his attention to Quinn and stared hard at him before furtively sliding his eyes to Shauni.

Quinn understood the surreptitious gesture. Michael had something to say. But he didn't want to say it in front of the entire crew.

Quinn's hackles stood straight as concern for his sister stole through him. So because he was worried—and because he didn't want her to realize it—he acted casual and went back to pick up his sandwich. "Fine. Whatever. You clearly survived and don't want to talk about it."

He shrugged nonchalantly, then sent her a fake look of despair. "But did the boat get damaged?"

"Nice, Quinn," Kylie said from behind him, clucking her tongue and shaking her head when he gave her a What-did-I-do? look.

But as Anna continued up to her chambers and Quinn settled in next to Kylie to watch a movie, he again studied Michael.

Who was watching Ian walk up the stairs after Anna.

~

The clock in the library struck twelve midnight as Quinn was closing the double doors firmly behind him. He and Ethan were the last two to arrive, and his friend, like all of the other men gathered there, appeared none too pleased.

"Okay, what's with all the cloak and dagger?" Dare asked. "Willyn is a light sleeper, and it took me three tries to slip out without waking her. Because if she had," he added, pointing at Quinn, "I wouldn't have lied to her."

"I'm sure whatever Quinn and Michael have to tell us all is

important." Cole yawned and sat on the side of a long study table. "At least it better be, because Trevor and I have to be back at the station early."

"Should never have left," Trevor groused. "Not with all the people still missing."

Cole dropped his gaze to the floor, dejected. "Captain made us leave," he explained. Then he lifted his eyes to Quinn. "He told us to get our asses home and get some *sleep*."

"It's important." Michael spoke for the first time, his sharp tone making everyone sit up straighter and listen a little harder. "I'll be quick, but you all need to hear it."

Choosing to stay standing where he was, guarding the doors, Quinn crossed his arms and waited for the vet to explain further.

"I should have said something the other day when we were in the training room." Michael dragged in a monster of a deep breath. "It's about Ian."

"I knew it." Quinn's terse statement came out through gritted teeth.

"What did you see, Michael?" Nick asked. Viv's boyfriend was quietly perceptive and had also grown tight with the veterinarian since the two men had been involved with the coven and the prophecy longer than anyone here.

Except for Quinn and Dare, who'd both been young male witches, attached by family or friendship to Anna, and both with a heavy load of Fate to bear. Which was now coming to fruition.

"When Ian touched the dagger, when he had that reaction?" Michael waited until all the men who'd been present nodded or spoke to affirm that they remembered. To the ones who weren't, he said, "Ian acted like he'd been shocked by something when he touched it. Claimed it was static."

Michael shook his head. "It was the magic he responded to, and I think I know why." He gestured to Chris, Dare, and finally

Quinn. "You three can pick up on the coven magic, right? Feel its hum or something?"

"Yeah," Chris said. He turned to Quinn, held out a hand. "But it's a little different for each of us."

"Uh-huh." Quinn was keeping quiet, letting Michael play it out slowly. Because in truth, he didn't like where the discussion was headed.

"Damn." Dare pressed his knuckles to the table where he leaned. He'd figured it out. "Because we all have magic."

Ethan took two strides toward Michael. "You're saying that's why Ian reacted to the dagger? He felt its magic because he *has* magic?" He grunted. "The guy hates all this supernatural stuff." Then he tilted his head. "At least he did. Before Anna."

Yeah, Quinn thought. He wasn't the only one who could tell that Anna was looking to Ian during this final trial.

And that Ian was looking right back.

"I know." Michael's features turned grim. "But Ian doesn't have magic."

Some of the men turned to each other. Voices began to rise in debate.

After slashing his hand through the air as he talked with Cole, Trevor pushed up from the chair where he'd been sitting and headed to Michael. "But you just said—"

"It's Vanir." Nick's quiet tone broke through the growing clamor. The pub owner raised whiskey-hued eyes to his friend. "Vanir's the one who has magic."

Michael patted the pocket on his shirt, looking for his perpetually-misplaced glasses. "That's what I think, anyway. That day, with the dagger, Ian didn't just react physically. I also saw him change."

Whatever hope Quinn had been holding out on collapsed. He'd wanted Michael to be wrong. Hell, he'd wanted his own suspicions to be wrong. But this proof was irrefutable. "You saw his aura change colors?"

"Yes. Not the normal colors that indicate mood and emotion, but a base tone." He circled his hand in the air as he searched for a way to explain. "Say one chair is red and one chair is blue. If you layered white on top of them..."

"They'd look different," Ethan said. "So you think Ian's core personality changed."

"That's sugar-coating it," Dare said roughly. "He fucking *became* Vanir for a minute. That's what Michael's saying."

"And I knew I had to tell you guys now, because I saw it again tonight, when Ian and Anna came back from the boat. But this time, it was different. It was all mixed up, like Vanir's base coat was mixing with Ian's."

"Well, they came into contact with Bastraal." Cole tried to interject a little devil's advocate. "Now he and Anna have both agreed to stay on the island until Halloween. Maybe the... *mixing* will pass."

"But it didn't pass when Ian walked inside this house." Quinn turned around, his fist raised and ready to punch the solid wooden doors. But he checked himself just in time.

Choosing to pace instead, he gestured wildly with his hands. "And Ian was on the island the first time Michael saw him change. So it wasn't caused by Bastraal or Ronja. They aren't getting past our protection spells to affect him."

He stopped and looked around the room to encompass all the men when he said, "The problem is *inside* Ian. Now he's here for good, and you all know we aren't going to change Anna's mind about protecting him."

"We don't know what will happen, Quinn." Cole moderated his tone, but the fear was there, underneath. "He might get control of it, or Anna will. Maybe it's part of her trial."

"Yeah, I hope so." Quinn swallowed down the rage. He wanted to curse Fate but knew he had to stay steady. He had to support Anna in whatever she chose to do. This was her trial, her turn. "But it's all just so damned unfair."

He moved to a chair, fell into it. "She already has to do the unthinkable. And if she really does end up killing a guy to save everyone and everything else, she will never be the same. Added to that, the man she's supposed to be able to rely on, the one who's supposed to help her find her way through her challenge..." Quinn spit out a disgusted breath. "He may end up being her enemy."

"So we keep an eye on him," Dare said. He looked to Michael. "And we'll need you around more."

"Already considered that. I've taken some time off. My partner will cover, and we've been thinking of adding another vet to the practice anyway."

"And if he does change?" Trevor was still scowling. All of them were. "What if he remembers so much he finally shifts and becomes Vanir? Completely? If Ian is gone, we don't know what will be left behind."

"Yes, we do." Quinn felt lifeless as he stared straight ahead, focused on nothing. "Anna told us about their shared vision."

He rose to stand once more. He looked to the other men, all gathered around and ready to do whatever had to be done to protect the final witch, the coven leader, and a woman they'd all come to love and respect.

"Vanir was a great magician and a battled-hardened warrior," Quinn said simply. "In short—no one you'd want to fuck with."

"And if he does change," Ethan added, "he'll be here. Dead center of his beloved sister's enemies."

"We can take him." Chris stood, letting his muscular arms hang slack by his side. The deceptive calm of another battle-hardened warrior. "Eight men, three of us with magic. But the real problem is going to come when we all haul off and kick his ass like we've been expecting him to change all along."

Cole groaned. "You mean the women."

"But should we tell them what we know?" Ethan asked. "You

recall how they were after we all kept Chris a secret."

"No. We don't tell them, especially not Anna." Quinn crossed his arms. "Not yet, and not unless we have to."

"So we watch," Dare said. "And we protect her at all costs."

Quinn nodded, even as his chest ached for his sister. "Even if we have to protect her from the man she's falling in love with."

18

In his temporary bedroom on the top floor of the mansion, Ian stood at the rosewood dresser and poured himself a scotch. He'd take it neat tonight, since he didn't want to go roaming around the sprawling house, potentially waking someone else. As little as he'd been out of his quarters in the last few days, he might easily be mistaken for a trespasser.

Kicking back the two fingers of liquor, he stared at the ivory-toned wall. Lately, a home invader is exactly what he felt like any time he ventured downstairs. The men of the island had taken to tossing him strange looks, and though they tried to go unnoticed, the numbers just weren't on their side.

One man giving him the evil eye, like Michael, he could brush off as no big deal. But all eight of them? One or two were always lapsing, sliding him suspicious glares and showing their true feelings.

So Ian was doing everyone a favor, himself included, by keeping busy upstairs and helping with what little office work he could from his laptop. Only once in a while did he feel crowded in the spacious bedroom, and during those times he'd come to be truly grateful for the balcony outside.

Pouring himself just one more for the night, Ian took his Glenfiddich 18 and decided to make use of the outdoor space. The nights had finally turned cooler, and from the stone terrace he had an expansive view of the island forest, then the vast Atlantic beyond.

The natural scenery was soothing to his fractured mind, and he made use of it quite often. Ever since the encounter with Bastraal. His thoughts wandered to that day again and again, and out of everything that had gone wrong, he was fixated on one particular moment.

The only thing he could think of was the huge, roaring ball of fire lifting from the ocean, and how he had gone numb. The sight of the licking flames had terrified him, rendering him almost speechless.

"Fire," was all he'd said, paralyzed by the blinding glow, the searing heat, the hungry hiss. The demon's display had been his only focus.

Because that was how they'd killed him.

Not *him* him, of course, but Vanir him.

Ian swirled the scotch, though there was no ice, and stared into the shadowy mix of pines and hardwoods. The clash of personalities still going on inside him was taking its toll.

As was the fact he had a demon for a stalker. So he tossed the whole glass back and relished the smooth, mossy hit.

Leaning against the ancient railing of stone, he sighed and let the briny wind caress his face, his bare arms and chest. At least one good thing had come from the attack and his third— count them, *third*—near-death experience.

And that was his new perspective of Anna.

When he'd gone under, she'd dove in right after. And when he'd been thrown into shock by the sight of fire, she was the one who'd stood in front of him. So when Ian accounted for the people he trusted with his life, Anna St. Germaine was now indelibly on that list.

Which meant something else had been happening over the last few days, now that his distrust was no longer a barrier. With his suspicions gone and doubt out of the way, he'd been able to honestly evaluate his feelings for her.

And admit that they were changing.

Somewhere along the way, she'd gone from potential nemesis, to cautious acquaintance, to now being the first person he went to with his problems. Whenever he had wandered the mansion or grounds, they'd always seemed to find each other.

During these times, she'd talked to him of her passion for gardening, painting, and the island she called home. Benign topics with no mention of witches or demons, as if she'd known he needed a break, a chance to get his head straight. And in turn he'd shared his fascination with the law, how he loved its intricacies and complexities, and breaking them down to make pieces useful to a client.

He'd learned all about Joe and Claire, their son Joseph, and the elusive Mr. Attinger. Anna had been orphaned young, and Ian was glad for the extended family that had stepped in when she and Quinn had needed them.

He replied with stories of his civil rights attorney father, and how the brusque, no-nonsense man had inspired his son. And was really a teddy bear underneath the bluster.

These were the kinds of things a man and woman shared when they were getting to know each other, whether as friends or as lovers. Yet each time he and Anna had pulled apart and gone back to their own little corners.

And each time, Ian had felt her absence more keenly.

Was he grateful for all she'd done for him? Did he see her as simply a friend? His saving grace?

Or was the loss of gravity he felt when he saw her an indication of something more?

His lids began to droop, blocking his view of the woods and their nighttime secrets. *And that's an indication it's time for bed.*

The scotch had gone from his glass and straight to his bloodstream. So he lumbered back inside, slipped off his pants, and climbed into bed. He left the balcony doors open wide, so he could sleep through the night with the pleasant breezes blowing in.

As he dropped his head against the dark blue pillowcase, he spared another minute to contemplate her, the woman—the witch—who was always in his thoughts. Then he stretched, relaxed, and settled into sleep almost immediately.

The instant he fell, he continued to drop. Much farther down, much farther back.

Suddenly he was on alert, blinking against the terribly bright light, sun reflecting on a monochromatic world. All white with a smattering of green and brown.

His eyes cleared when he felt her calling him. She was in trouble, scared, and she was hurt.

Ian trudged through the mid-winter snow, following only his internal compass, the intrinsic knowledge that told him he was going in the right direction. His sister's energy was a bold and panicked orange, the color of warning. The color of danger.

Ronja was his other half, and so her terror echoed within him.

Ian had a vague recollection of who he truly was and knew he had been hijacked once again. But Vanir's fear for his twin sister was primal, powerful, and Ian's rationality didn't stand a chance.

No, he wasn't Vanir, and he recognized the separation. But still he was overridden, compelled to follow the other man's instincts.

Allowing the strange, invisible connection to Ronja to lead him, he moved as if pulled by an unseen rope. Until he stumbled across tracks in the snow and trailed along after them instead. The small imprints had been made by his sister's feet and would surely take him to her.

His optimism rose. He could get there in time. Whatever force put her in peril, he would rescue her.

And then he saw two more sets of footprints intersect with hers, larger tracks, made by men. A mass of brown interrupted the pale landscape. Ronja's pack of medicinal ointments. She always carried the bag with her, but it had been tossed haphazardly in the snow.

Or dropped, Ian realized racked by chills that were internal. She'd lost her things when she'd had to run.

Now Ian was running as well, moving as quickly as he could through the thick layer of winter white. His breath was harsh in his own ears. His chest was tight though not from exertion. Dread was a vise on his torso, pressing him with unwanted images, choking him with the brutal truth of human nature.

His skin shot with a cold crawl of electricity when he heard his sister scream. Her absolute fear bounced through the majestic silver birch, up the jagged mountains, and onward to the cruel gray sky.

The next time she cried—half scream, half wail—Ian responded with a resounding roar.

He crested a hill, and she was there. The two men she'd encountered had caught her. They were upon her.

Pure, flowing rage covered his eyesight, but his hand knew where to go, and it gripped the sword, ripping it from its sheath. With the patterned-metal piece raised high, he yelled a cry that warned of bloodletting. And charged.

One man was holding Ronja's arms above her head while the other moved on top of her. It was clear what base and animalistic act was being done to his sister, so when the first man released her arms and stood, backing away with his own hands out in supplication, Vanir didn't pause. And Ian didn't flinch.

The sword slid home like a stick into a summer pond, so sharp the man's gut simply caved as the blade struck deep.

Seeing his companion cut down by the blow, the second man pushed up and tried to flee. But Vanir would not allow his escape. Throwing forth his other hand, he gave his second weapon free rein, using his magic in a way he'd never done before.

The power wrapped around the man's pumping legs and brought him down. The snow was wet, and the villain was panicking. He was still struggling for purchase when Vanir closed the distance. In three leaping strides he was standing over the man, and with one deft move he shoved the bloody blade into his quarry's back.

With the sword lodged between ribs, Vanir adjusted his angle, before giving another wrathful bellow and thrusting upward. To pierce the rapist's heart.

His magic returned to him, though now it felt tainted. Rarely had Vanir been undone by such ferocity, and his power, his gift, had been discolored by hate.

After several deep breaths of the frigid air, he quickly glanced over to find Ronja trying to hurriedly cover herself. To give her more time and privacy, he moved to a nearby shrub and used the prickly foliage to clean his blade.

At last he heard her say his name, softly but steadily. Though her shame leaked through.

He turned and went to her, with fury still pumping through his veins, still clouding his sight.

His sister's eyes were red from crying, her cheeks dirty from where she'd tried to wipe away the tears. "Let us go. I want to leave this place."

Vanir stepped forward. "I will carry you."

"No!" Her outburst surprised them both, so she offered a smile and gentled her tone. "I can walk." She looked aside to the first man he'd killed, and she whispered, "I want to walk."

At a loss for what to do now that the two attackers had been dealt with, he simply nodded. Until a blemish on the ground caught his eye. Unable to look away, he stilled, his only movement the pounding of his heart.

The red was so bright. The blood against the snow.

And he knew this stain was Ronja's innocence.

Grinding his hands into fisted balls, he tore his eyes away from the evidence of her pain, her humiliation, and glared at the two corpses. "I would kill them one hundred times, each more torturous than the last."

Avoiding her eyes, Vanir kept staring at the second crumpled form. He stiffened when he felt her hand slide into his. "Come, brother. We should return. There is no more to be done here."

Trying to dispel his own grief and anger, he let his sister guide him away. Side by side they walked in silence, as they had so often done. When they stopped to pick up her pack, she gripped his arm and whispered, "Don't tell."

"No," he said. And for this solemn promise, he finally looked into her eyes.

"It's all right, Vanir." She touched his cheek, her fingers like ice. "I'll be fine."

And back in the bedroom, Ian's eyes flew open. His heart galloped, just as it had for Vanir. *But she wasn't fine.* He gasped for air. *She was never the same again.*

A soft, rustling noise had him angling his head sharply to find the source. But it was only the lightweight curtains performing a slow ballet, with the island breeze for partner.

He'd left the doors open to the balcony. He remembered the night and where he was. So now he was back again. He was himself again.

But the residue of the terrible ordeal still coated him.

Sitting up, he rotated and dropped his feet to the hardwood floor. And waited for the punch of disgust to fade. Whatever he thought of the present-day Ronja, no woman deserved...

A harried knocking filled the bedroom just before Anna's concerned voice called, "Ian?"

"Yeah," he said, hoping to quell her obvious alarm. But he hadn't expected her to burst through the door.

"Oh, Ian. Are you..." She let the question die as her eyes raked over his partially-clad form.

Ian slept only in his briefs.

Unabashed, he stood to face her. "I'm okay." She'd been connected with him and had also seen the vision. Somehow, they were still linked.

Despite the awful vision, Ian felt a smile easing out. Because even in dreams, she worried about him.

When she eased farther inside, she stepped into the soft glow of the lamp he'd left burning. And once he got a better look at bed-tousled Anna, his tender feelings changed. They grew carnal.

She was barefoot, her toenails painted a light color he just knew exactly matched the shell pink nightgown she was wearing. The silky material hung to her ankles, but the thin straps up top revealed every luscious inch of elegant arms, shapely shoulders, and a neck he had to taste. Right then.

Ian closed in and saw her eyes flicker. Did she think he was still Vanir?

He stopped just short of touching her. "It's me, Anna. Only me."

She exhaled, and his eyes were drawn to the amulet hanging from her neck. That might be her talisman, her mark of magic, but it was the woman beneath that Ian wanted.

And he would make sure she knew it.

Without asking permission, he swept her into his arms, held her against his chest. With those big blue eyes locked on his face, she made a sweet, female sound. Then her arms stole up to encircle his shoulders, to cling for support.

Maybe he shouldn't have imagined kissing her, and perhaps this would add another layer of complication. But he caught a glimpse of the butterfly pulse in her neck, saw the royal blue of her eyes flare, the pupils widen.

And knew her response had nothing to do with a vision.

Lifting her up to her toes, he locked her in place with his arm around her waist, his hand buried in her long sable hair. As he lowered his mouth to hers, Ian caught the scent of lavender.

And truly understood what it was to be lost.

19

Flames of pleasure licked through Anna's body as Ian held her, as he kissed her like his sanity depended on it. She'd come to his room in a rush, anxious because of the dream, but he'd headed her off with one hot look.

She'd had only a moment to appreciate his tall, brawny form in nothing but black briefs before he'd crossed to her like a man on a mission and wrapped her up in steel-banded arms. Then his hungry mouth had seared away the last of her concerns, leaving nothing behind but an aching need.

Her blood raged, her skin tingled as his smooth flesh slid against the satin covering hers.

I want to paint him. The urge popped into her head as her hands roamed over hard curves and ridges, enjoying the musculature he normally kept hidden by loose athletic wear or starched business suits.

But now she'd had an eyeful. And the man was a masterpiece. There was no other word to adequately sum up his long, powerful legs, lean hips, and shoulders that flared wide with strength.

And that face. Sure, she'd seen his shapely mouth and compelling eyes many times before. But never with the scorching intensity he'd possessed as he arrowed straight for her.

Even now the imagery caused her fingers to curl as she gripped his back and wanted every single part of him...*closer*.

Good thing she was locked around those amazing shoulders, because his deep, delving kiss was making her weak. Lust came upon her quickly, and without mercy. All she could do was hang on and abandon herself to sensation.

She pressed her hips to his and was again surprised. Ian concealed *a lot* beneath his reserved and stalwart surface.

To Anna's mind, he was the perfect male specimen, and the passion in his kiss swept away every coherent thought. But she didn't fight, wanting nothing more than to forget the disturbing vision of Vanir's.

And to fill her head with Ian.

His hands were moving up the small of her back, as if sculpting her with the firm but gentle pressure. Up to her shoulders he trailed his fingers, then traced her neck with a delicate touch. He ended the kiss and pulled away, just before pressing his mouth to the hollow of her throat.

Right where caressing fingertips had been.

Anna let her head fall back. She moaned as he applied sweet yet insistent strokes to her skin. Her chest felt heavy, while a delicious yearning swirled farther down.

Dropping his hands, he rested them softly on the outer curves of her breasts. She gasped, the expectation exciting and torturous at the same time. Her nipples hardened in response, as desire stronger than she'd ever felt before swamped her.

But Ian paused, his eyes flickering to her face. He placed one last kiss on her mouth while skimming his palms back up to her shoulders and down her arms until both of her hands were captured in his.

Anna was intrigued to find him gazing at her with an expression more of affection than lust, as if he'd just remembered something. And whatever it was had altered his course. The dark sexuality was still in his stare but had been tempered by his sensible nature.

Normally she admired this particular trait of his, but at the moment, she silently cursed the interruption.

"I hate the reason," he started off, confusing her. Then he clarified, "But I'm glad you came to me."

Recalling the dream she'd had, the dream-*travel* she'd experienced with Ian, reality came crashing back in, sufficiently dousing the sinful fire inside of her. "I'm not crazy about the reason for my visit either." Did her voice sound husky?

Running a hand over her hair, she cleared her throat and straightened her shoulders. But it was difficult to feel imperious in a light pink nightie. "And even though I was caught off-guard, I can't find it in myself to complain about your style of welcome."

One side of his mouth curved upward as he tugged on her hands. "Let's go to the bed."

"Oh. Well now that we have our senses back, I'm not sure—"

"To sit down, Anna." His wicked grin said he was enjoying her sudden return of decorum. "I don't think either of us is going to be able to sleep right away, so we might as well go over what happened while the memory is fresh."

No. I definitely won't be sleeping after that kiss. But what she said was, "Right. That makes sense."

Spying the bottle of scotch on the dresser, she considered having herself a midnight-cap. But then she took another look at Ian—who hadn't yet bothered to get dressed—and decided she should keep her faculties intact.

She'd known from the first day she'd met him that he would be a point of contention in her life. He'd been legally involved with Ronja, and over time it had become clear he would be part of the prophecy.

But Anna had never expected him to play this role in her trial. She'd never known he would be her weakness.

They sat side by side on the edge of the mattress. Ian's feet were firmly on the floor, so when hers dangled just shy, she opted to tuck her legs lotus-style and face him instead.

He then hiked one leg up to angle casually toward her. Just two friends having a late-night chat.

If only that were all. Anna was torn between her desire for another kiss and her conscience that prodded her to do what was right, what was needed, in this moment. So she launched into a discussion of the terrible dream-vision-memory the two of them had just experienced.

"What were you doing before you fell asleep?" she asked in a steady I'm-not-looking-at-your-lips tone of voice. "What were you thinking about?"

"You," he said without a trace of embarrassment. "The day on the boat specifically, and how my opinion of you has changed." He cocked his head. "You may have noticed, but I like you more now."

Anna pursed her lips. "This is a serious matter, Ian." Though inside she did a happy-girl dance. "How much scotch have you had anyway?"

"Not that much. But you're right." With an attempt to smile that was more just a squint of his eyes, Ian lost his playful expression. "This is serious."

Anna detected the underlying discomfort he'd been hiding. The dream had disturbed him as much as it had her.

"I was thinking of you, Bastraal, and what happened on the boat. Truthfully, I have no idea why the dream took us to that particular moment in Vanir's life." Ian stared past her. "Unless I was meant to understand how they were both affected."

He swerved his gaze back to Anna. "That day left a mark on both of them, scarring them, but in different ways. Vanir was appalled by his actions. Not the use of his sword, but of his magic to do harm."

Anna nodded but kept quiet.

His expression darkened. "Ronja never trusted again after the attack. She no longer had faith in anyone besides her brother."

"How do you know all this? We only witnessed one day."

Ian shrugged but the movement was stiff, evidence of his unease. "How do I travel through time in my head? I can't explain it, but every time it happens, I glean more inherent knowledge of both Vanir and Ronja."

He rubbed the back of his neck. "And I'm beginning to feel sorry for them both."

Anna studied his troubled face as she wondered how to respond. She wasn't sure what bothered her more. Ian's new sympathy for the dark witch...

Or the fact she had some of her own. The scene had been brutal, sordid. Her gut had clenched as she'd shivered from instinctual horror, one with which every woman could identify.

And a small portion of her heart had softened toward Ronja.

No, she told herself. For the girl Ronja had been. A thousand years past was literally lifetimes ago, and no trace of that innocent young woman remained.

The compassionate white witch who'd once healed people now relished the idea of bathing in their blood.

"Part of me understands his actions." Ian shrugged, swallowing. "But the feel of the sword as it slid into that man's stomach. So...easily," he said, his words strained by agitation. "It shouldn't have been that easy."

Abruptly, his expression turned hostile. "Killing him, killing both of them, wasn't about punishment, but ending their existence. I don't believe in taking another's life, even if it seems justified."

His words were a dart to her center. She froze, trying to take full breaths, but she couldn't seem to move past the sudden blockage in her throat. She had been about to reach for his hand but couldn't do that now, too terrified he would hear the pounding in her chest or feel her erratic pulse as it thrust into overdrive.

Ian had voiced his belief, and there'd been no waiver of his convictions. With that one sentence, he'd given credence to her fear.

He would never condone the sacrifice set to take place on All Hallow's Eve. The one in which Anna had no choice but to execute. Even if he could be made to understand, he would always remember. He'd never forget that her hand had dealt the killing blow, that she'd willingly taken a life.

No matter the circumstances.

Too intent on their discussion of Vanir, he hadn't noticed her sudden stillness. "When I was inside Vanir, I supported his need to deliver punishment. Now that I'm back and myself again, I hate what happened."

With a shaky laugh, he rubbed his neck again, then the base of his skull. "I just don't know where my head's at anymore."

"Yes, you do," she said sternly.

He gave a weary sigh. "Yeah, I do. But it's not the physical departures that shake me. The visits to other times and places aren't what terrify me most. It's the slow takeover, the sly replacement of my own will with his."

Now his hand dropped to the mattress as he formed a fist. "It's a damned sneak attack." A vein ticked in his temple. "And every time I gain a new memory from Vanir's life, it feels like I lose a piece of my own."

He sounded miserable, and that in turn made Anna furious. With Ronja, Vanir, and the fates that were allowing this to happen to a good man like Ian. He hadn't asked for this. He'd just had the misfortune of being born with Vanir's shape and form.

But she'd be damned if she'd let them win. "I can work with some spells," she said, finally taking his hand and forcing her pulse into a slower cadence. "Maybe I can repress Vanir. Keep him down."

"No." Ian frowned.

Anna let her mouth fall open, surprised by his prompt

rejection. "But you just said—"

"I know." He waved her argument aside. "But my instincts tell me I have to go through this. Vanir must have something to say, and everything I'm learning might end up being important.

"Besides," he continued, "aren't you the one who likes to say everything happens for a reason? If we try to divert what's meant to be, we may hurt our own cause in the process."

"*Our* cause?" she asked. "No, Ian. All you need to do is stay here and stay safe."

"But the images, the visions keep finding me, even on your island. So what does that mean?"

Anna couldn't see any way to avoid this particular answer, the same one she'd come to upon waking from the dream. "Neither Ronja nor Bastraal can penetrate our wards. Not here, especially inside the house."

Instead of gentling, she steeled her tone, because that's what he would want. What he would need. "These memories are coming from inside of you."

His features hardened. "Because I was once Vanir, and he's still here. He wants back out."

"This month is a very active time when it comes to spirituality. Planes of existence can intersect. Coincide." She edged closer to him. "Especially on Halloween. Especially with your—" She trailed off, hearing a hint of accusation in what she'd been about to say.

He waved his head in a tell-me gesture.

She pressed her lips together. "I was with you, shadowing you the whole time, and I could feel how upsetting it was for you. The rape. The deaths. You may be getting too close to Vanir."

She had a solid psychic bond to Ian, and he to Vanir, and therefore to Ronja. The intimacy was growing far too intense for Anna's peace of mind—too tight, and too crowded with intricate connections.

"But you did nothing to deserve this," she said earnestly. "So let me help you."

"You're right. I didn't." His jaw tensed. "But neither did you, any of you. Neither did the people out there." He thrust his chin to the window, and she knew he meant the mainland. "People who've died or been taken."

"And it's still going on," he said. "So while you and your coven are doing your part, I can at least do mine. I don't know why, but keeping Vanir down is the wrong answer."

Though his hand was warm on hers, Anna couldn't help but worry. What if Vanir ever gained control, if only for a while? As far as Anna and Ian could tell, Vanir had been a peaceful practitioner.

Right up until the moment someone had hurt Ronja.

And how, Anna asked herself as her fingers threaded with Ian's, how would she respond if the man she was falling for turned and raised his sword—or his magic—against her?

"I don't want to lose you to him," she heard herself murmur. "I know it's selfish, given everything else that's going on, but I—" She broke off when Ian put his hands on her sides, fingers splayed over her ribs in a dominant, possessive way that thrilled her despite everything.

"Not selfish." He assaulted her with a smile, killed her with the dimple. "I just hope you aren't speaking simply as the witch who has to defend the innocent."

He inched closer, his body heat rolling in waves across her skin. And all her attempts to keep judgment intact melted beneath his strong, capable hands.

"I hope," Ian said, leaning closer, eyes intent on hers, "you see me as something more."

"Ian," her voice was a bare whisper, "we should be cautious with this." She didn't have to say what *this* was. The force between them was palpable.

And judging by the way his eyes flicked to her mouth, he not only acknowledged it, but was about to reinforce their newly-acquired intimacy.

So she put her hand on his chest, his skin burning her like the Savannah sun. She struggled to maintain composure. "Once is enough for tonight. I think we've both had a bit of a shock."

"And you have to be in control of every facet, every single thing that might affect your challenge."

"Yes."

"You have a great battle looming on the horizon."

"Exactly." She was glad he understood.

"And I could lose myself at any time. Vanir could just take me over."

"What?" He'd abruptly switched lanes on her. "No. I won't let that happen."

"You're sharing both my visions and my dreams now, Anna. You know as well as I do—he's getting stronger."

"I told you, I might be able to help."

He shook his head. "That's not my point. You're the clairvoyant. You're the one who can see things. So tell me, are we both guaranteed a happy future? Will we both be around come November first?"

"I..." She envisioned what her state of mind would be after she'd murdered a man. "I can't make any promises."

"Then why shouldn't we be together now? I know we've had our differences, largely on my part, but we're both capable of change, of realigning our opinions. And it's clear we find each other attractive."

She hiked a brow. "Oh, really?"

So he slid a single finger up her side. And grinned wickedly when she sucked in a breath.

He closed the distance. "As I was saying."

"Yes. Yes." She brought up her other hand, trying to hold him off. Trying to think straight, because his kisses drugged her system. "We are attracted to each other. I'll allow that."

"But? I hear a but."

"But," she said, pushing her way from the bed to stand. "It's not the time to leap forward. We can't afford to become distracted. Emotions can be funny things, and right now, we're both overflowing with a lot of new feelings."

Knowing she was making an escape, Anna beelined for the door. And even as she fled, she was afraid yet hopeful he would chase her down.

When she flung open the heavy oak panel, a gray blur all but flew inside the room and up onto the bed where Ian still sat. He apparently wasn't coming after her, and she pretended she wasn't disappointed.

For now she'd simply deal with her cat, since Ivy was standing on Ian's lap and giving him a slanted stare.

Ian put up his hands. "I give up. I won't kiss her anymore, oh fanged guardian." Then he slid stormy blue eyes to Anna. "Not tonight, anyway."

Despite his teasing, she could see his shoulders were tight, and he was being very careful not to move. Then he glanced warily at the cat.

Anna laughed at the huge man sitting perfectly still and under Ivy's control. "I see. So you trust me at last, but you're afraid of my cat?"

Ian grimaced. "Look where she has her claws."

Shifting her gaze to his groin, Anna tsked and called her pet. Ivy only glared at Ian and growled.

Hurriedly now, Anna moved to the bed and scooped the feline into her arms. "Sorry. I don't know what's gotten into her."

But she trusted the animal's instinct implicitly, and her dislike of Ian filled Anna with a creeping dread.

Walking with her pet firmly ensconced, Anna stopped just outside the doorway. After all they'd shared, she didn't want to end on a bad note. "Good night, Ian."

Now that he was no longer being held prisoner, he stretched out and lay back on his pillows, arms behind his head. "Good night, Anna."

He was so enticing, with his blonde hair slightly mussed, a devil's grin on his face, and all tucked up in bed, ready for—

Stop that. Anna pushed the fantasy aside and gave him what she hoped was a chaste smile. She backed into the hall. "Sleep well."

"I will," he said in a voice like melted sugar. "But if I don't," he held her with a look, "I know you'll be there."

With a firm nod she closed the door soundly, and once certain Ivy couldn't get back inside his room, she set the suddenly rancorous cat on the floor. With a final spit toward the closed door, the feline sprinted down the corridor in the direction of Anna's chambers.

With a growing sense of trepidation, she followed slowly after her cat. And wondered what Ivy knew…that she didn't.

20

"No, no, no. Not that way." Claudia scurried from one side of the grand hall to the other, waving her hands at Kylie and Paige. Anna stopped with the box of orange string lights in her arms, pulling up short as her friend whizzed by.

Claudia was now pointing a French-manicured nail. "You should put the green pumpkin there, in front of the haunted house."

"Why?" Kylie argued. "The orange pumpkin is a little smaller, closer to scale."

"But the green matches the witch's striped stockings. Trust me." Claudia whipped her finger back and forth until Paige groaned and rolled her eyes.

Giving in to stronger forces—when it came to any sort of color coordination—the soldier removed the orange pumpkin from the table she and Kylie had been decorating and replaced it with the green. "There." Hands on her hips, she scowled at the flame-haired witch. "Happy?"

"Claudia, you are so right," Kylie agreed as both fashion mavens smiled and ignored the disgruntled Paige.

And this, Anna thought with a grin, was a familiar routine. Her friends, her sisters, squabbling over insignificant details and contrasting priorities. Where she used to cherish her solitude and quiet time, she now found the daily mansion chaos exhilarating.

Who would have ever thought she'd be sad to lose the sound

of raised and often bitchy voices? Not her, not once upon a time.

But now she'd come to adore the *clomp-clomp* of Kylie coming down the stairs for her morning aerobics, or Paige's noisy blender as she made her disgusting brown shakes. And how dull would breakfast be without Willyn and Hayden giggling in the corner or Claudia flipping through a magazine in search of the latest must-have apparel?

Or Skid, she laughed to herself, sliding across every smooth surface of the house? Shauni and Michael would be taking the dog with them. In fact, the only reason the newlyweds hadn't yet moved Shauni into his townhome was her need to stay with the coven.

Until the end, the completion of trials. Which was drawing ever closer.

Examining the pretty lights that would twinkle like orange stars, Anna sighed and chided herself for being sentimental. She couldn't believe she'd waited this long to decorate for Halloween. That she'd almost allowed outside forces to rob her and everyone else of one of their favorite times of the year.

The annual adornment with all things ghoulish and grim was a special festivity for her and her extended family. Every witch deserved his or her share of Halloween fun.

Yet here it was, the fifteenth of October, and she was only now pulling out the boxes. In deference to her needs, and considering the ordeal that was inevitably part of the current trial, Mrs. Attinger had held back and let Anna decide whether or not to celebrate the holiday.

While it had taken her far too long, Anna was glad she'd finally gotten the party under way. She cast a furtive glance to Ian as he helped Viv and Hayden hang a tapestry. She admired his strong arms as he easily hefted the huge swath of dense fabric.

Ian the honest, the stubborn, the brave. He was yet another thing she'd been denying herself. At least in the physical sense.

Of course they still spent time together each day, and she kept a cautious eye on him during his nighttime wanderings. But only his visitations with Vanir, eerie trips on which she always seemed to be invited.

Otherwise, it was as if she and Ian had an unspoken agreement. He sensed her unease with their attraction, their new closeness, and Anna couldn't bring herself to approach him in that way. She carefully avoided sending him the wrong signals.

Not that she didn't think about kissing him again, dream of being held again. Because she did. Quite often.

But she held herself in check, because it just wouldn't be fair to him. As the coven leader, she knew better than anyone that trying to dodge Fate was a fool's game. Each of the witches had been matched with a worthy mate during their challenges, and Anna couldn't deny the extreme attraction she harbored for Ian.

And, she believed, he felt the same way. Yet Ian was already dealing with so much. How could she add to his problems, his already out-of-control life, by telling him he had been picked for her? That he really had no say in the matter?

What would be her approach? *Don't struggle. It's easier if you don't fight, and destiny wins every time.* She crossed her arms and let annoyance rear its head. Real romantic, and just what a strong-willed man like Ian would want to hear.

Still watching him, her dour mood lightened a bit when she heard his laugh. Viv had "accidentally" dropped the tapestry over his head. But Ian simply held it up to her again, quirking his handsome mouth in a way that told the telekinetic witch he knew her game.

Anna sighed like a lovelorn teenager. He looked so tall and fierce, helping lift the colorful tapestry, one depicting fairies and other woodfolk dancing around a bright bonfire. The scene was one of merriment and celebration, but whether it was a harvest festival or dance of the dead, Anna had never been able to tell.

Her favorite part had always been the round yellow moon hovering over them all, acting as watchful guardian. Particularly on the night of Samhain, when the veil between worlds became so very thin.

There was another thing Anna had changed her mind about. She'd always thrilled at the idea of Halloween, with its crisp night air and huge glowing moon. Now the waxing cycle terrified her.

So did the idea of Ian being anywhere near Ronja when the auspicious night arrived, one reason she was determined he'd be here in her home when the final battle raged. The other was so he wouldn't witness her evil deed firsthand, a bloody act of butchery he'd probably never erase from memory.

And yes, she would be committing evil. That's how she saw it. The many, many lives she'd be saving might be a balm to her conscience, but even they couldn't take away the pain. Their survival couldn't bring her back. Not after she'd sacrificed her true self as surely as the blameless victim.

"Here. Let me get that." Dare was suddenly hoisting the box into his arms, relieving a startled Anna of its weight. "Trevor volunteered to help hang lights," he said loudly, drawing the detective's attention.

"I did?" Trevor looked up from where he was icing cupcakes. A treat for the workers, as Willyn had decreed, before she'd drafted the burly cop to not only ice, but also to apply the cute little bats and mummy faces she'd found. A task he'd studiously tried to avoid.

"Right," he said, leaping up in one move to drop an unfolded napkin from his lap. "I did volunteer. To do that." He pointed at Dare. "Lights. Outside. With the men."

"Oh, go on." Willyn faked a disapproving moue, then winked at Hayden as that one chuckled over her boyfriend's frantic flight.

Tadd was seated with his mother and looked up to Willyn with solemn eyes, sky blue, like hers. "I thought cupcakes *were* men's work."

"That's right, my darling." Willyn sent a withering stare to her husband when Dare started to speak up. "Girls *and* boys can both cook."

"Good." Tadd grabbed a tube of red icing and drizzled it all over the mummy face he'd just applied to his creation. "Because I love making cupcakes." Then he grabbed a tiny sword from the table and jabbed it through a bandaged eye. "Arghhhhhh!" he cried pirate-style, jumping up to take the treat to Dare for inspection.

Dare took one look at the mutilated mummy and patted his small stepson on the back. "That's my boy," he said with a wink for Willyn. His wife pouted, stuck out her tongue, and returned to spreading orange frosting.

"I'll help you," Shauni offered, plopping down cross-legged to take Tadd's place. She was soon joined by a large black shadow named Skid. Who promptly divested the women of another cupcake.

"Skid!" they cried in unison, before doubling over laughing as the dog gushed purple icing from the sides of his mouth.

"Ewwww!" Tadd cried. Then, "That's awesome. Give him a red one so it'll look like blood."

"That's exactly what we need." Quinn swooped in and picked Tadd up to toss him over his shoulder. "More blood. Blood and slippery entrails."

Tadd giggled, his words jarring as he bounced up and down. "Wh-what's en-en-entrails?"

"You know, the stuff that spills out in the movies." As soon as the words popped out, Quinn hunched his shoulders and sent Willyn a look to see if he'd overstepped. By her expression, he was teetering on the edge of too-much-for-a-six-year-old.

Anna's brother placed Tadd gently on the floor. The little boy plucked the sword from his cake and held it up. "You have one of these, right?"

Since Tadd had seen Dare practice with weapons, Quinn knew this was safe territory. "I do. I also have a great big *dagger*." The single word ricocheted off of every hard surface and bounced right back to Anna as everyone in the large room fell silent.

One by one, heads turned to her with expectant faces. All of them wondering how she would react.

Tadd didn't notice the adults had all stopped talking. "What's the difference between a knife and a dagger?"

Ian, however, was fully aware of the atmospheric shift. He too studied Anna curiously.

So she broke the heavy stupor and went over to kneel beside Tadd. "The two are very similar, and many people will say there's no real difference. But generally," she continued, "a dagger will be double-edged, used mainly," she took his little sword and poked the cupcake, "for stabbing."

She realized she'd gone too far in her attempt to redirect conversation to fun and frivolous topics when her stomach lurched. The slick slide of plastic toy into soft cake was far too close to what she imagined her real dagger would feel like.

As it pierced the human heart of the faceless body she always saw in her nightmares.

She stood quickly, rubbing her hands to release nervous energy. "An easy way to remember," she added hurriedly, trying not to bolt, "is you'll probably never end up peeling an apple with a dagger."

Tadd scrunched up his face. "Huh?"

"Um. Why don't we go have a demonstration in the kitchen?" Dare gave Anna a sympathetic glance and steered Tadd away. "Come on, Quinn. You started this."

"Wait." Willyn held up a finger. "What exactly are you two

going to teach him?"

"Trust me, sweetheart," Dare said lovingly. "The focus will be on food."

Lucia and Ethan had been in the storage room hauling out more boxes, and Anna was extremely grateful when they barreled in, laughing and talking. "What have you got?" she asked, then cringed at the overly-chipper ring of her voice.

Hoping the previously-festive mood would return, she did her best to focus on whatever was in the boxes. But when she looked down, all she could see was a blur of orange, black, and purple. She blinked several times before she heard Lucia calling her name. "Anna. Anna."

She looked up and was baffled by her friend's sorrowful expression. "Oh, sweetie." The Spanish witch set her load down and came to her. "What's the matter?"

The once cheer-filled room began to press in from every side like the shrinking traps in horror movies. She wiped at her cheek, and only then realized she was crying. "I don't know. I don't know. Everything, I guess."

Sniffing, Anna lowered her head. "I need to get away before anyone else sees."

Ethan moved to stand by her, the large box still in his arms effectively blocking her from view. "No one's looking," he said softly. "Why don't you head back down that way?" He lifted a shoulder to indicate the back corridor.

"Okay. I'm sorry." Anna started to take a step, but Lucia stopped her with a hand on her shoulder.

"After everything you've done for us, all the tantrums and tears you've helped us through, that we've all helped each other through, you should know better than to ever," she lifted Anna's chin with her finger, "*ever*, apologize to us."

Her friend's sweetness and understanding almost did her in, so she nodded quickly and murmured something that might have been "thanks" before hurrying toward the hall.

This particular passageway led to the tower, the place where her parents had been killed. But getting out of the grand hall before Ian saw her crying was paramount.

And the tower workroom no longer haunted her as it had before. During Lucia's trial, she and Quinn had cleaned the upper room, of soot, cobwebs, and bad memories. So it was to this re-claimed space, one of her parents' favorite hideaways, that Anna now ran in an attempt to salvage what was supposed to be a happy day.

Dammit! I don't want it all to be spoiled. Wasn't it bad enough that she'd been cast into the role of killer? That the man she was coming to care for might one day wake up and forget who she was? Who *he* was? That he might become another man entirely?

And one, she thought, falling against the old wooden door where the hallway ended, who might just decide he hated her simply because Ronja did.

So yes, the mighty and composed coven leader was having herself a good bawl. Wasn't she entitled to one now and then? For the sake of the goddess, she'd carried this weight since childhood, and now Fate had stacked on another hundred stones.

Overcome by the crying jag, she was satisfied to stop where she was and lean against the scarred yet durable door. Like many elements of the mansion, the wooden planks had been in place for decades, maybe even centuries. Since magic was one hell of a preservative.

So the wide door with its pointed top felt like an old friend of sorts. A good place to finish her pity party, a comforting spot to get it all out.

But the footsteps behind her put an end to her plans for privacy, and when she whipped around to Ian, there was no hiding her tear-stained face. "What are you doing here?" Her shame at being caught made her churlish.

When Ian only reached out and cleared a wet strand of hair from her cheek, she regretted lashing out. "I'm sorry. I didn't mean to snap."

"No problem." He eased closer. "I've been bitten by worse. You forget," he stroked her jaw, "I *am* a lawyer."

She could hardly believe it when she felt laughter bubble up. Only seconds before she'd been cursing her fate and bemoaning the unfairness of destiny. Yet now she stood in the shadows with the man who'd been sent to her by that same fickle force.

And all of the sadness, the very real dangers she faced, everything else seemed insignificant. If only Ian would smile at her.

He did. And she all but fell into his arms.

"Sshh," he soothed as she sobbed anew. He rubbed her back in small, reassuring circles.

As her crying subsided, she found that Ian was also comforting, a good place to lean, and like the old door, he'd also managed to become her friend. He was sturdy, and probably, she was coming to realize, just as dependable.

At last she was able to lift her head without new streams running down her cheeks. But she couldn't bear to imagine what she looked like. It seemed Ian was getting to see her in all her worst states. They'd already been through angry, defensive, haughty, and stubborn.

Now he was getting a dose of blubbering Anna. And still his eyes were adoring.

"Why did you come after me?" Her hands remained on his shoulders, his arms around her waist.

"Anna," he pressed a gentle kiss to her forehead, then to her lips. "Do you really need to ask?"

Pure white light seemed to come from within as she lifted her face for another, more meaningful kiss. No more running from what was meant to be.

And when she was in Ian's arms, there was no escaping the

fierce pull between them. She felt as if a long, meandering line of energy had always existed, but since they'd found each other it had shortened, tightened. It had become unbreakable.

A shrill beep intruded on the tender moment. The insistent sound came from Ian's hip, more specifically, his pocket. "That's...not my normal ringtone," he said, pulling out the smartphone. "And it's not a phone call but a face-to-face call."

He frowned, lifted his eyes to hers. "It's an unknown number."

Anna didn't want to keep him from anything that might be important. "Go ahead."

As she made sure her face was dry and her appearance as put-together as the dark and mirrorless corridor would allow, he swiped a finger across the screen.

As soon as he did, his eyes filled with shock, followed by rage. "Ronja," he said between clenched teeth.

Something akin to lightning stabbed at Anna's gut. She angled so she could also see the small screen.

"Ah, of course. And there's the St. Germaine whelp." Ronja's insult told Anna she'd become visible on the other end of the call.

"I'm hanging up now," Ian began, but Ronja's smug expression fell to one of despair.

"Wait. Please," she cried.

Anna widened her eyes. Had Ronja just said "please?"

"I just want to speak with you, Vanir. I need to see you."

Voice terse, Ian bit out, "That is not. My. Name."

"I'll call you whatever you like," the Nordic witch said docilely. Another uncommon occurrence, as Ronja was never compliant. "Anything. Just please come."

Ian scoffed, his derision clear. "And let you set your Daevo on Anna again? I don't think so."

"He isn't with me. I swear." Ronja curled her lip, proving her colors hadn't changed at all. "And you don't have to bring *her* with you."

Now Anna was the one to speak. "Think again, Ronja."

"Whatever you need to say to me, you can say right now." Ian was holding firm.

"No. I insist on seeing you in person. You can bring the witch with you if you want. I swear on our bond as siblings that I won't hurt her, and neither will any of my people." She narrowed her eyes. "But that promise is only good for today."

The witch knew just as Anna did that Halloween night would be no-holds-barred. A magical free-for-all.

"Sorry. No deal." Ian made as if to hang up, but his hand froze, suspended over the screen.

Ronja was holding her phone farther away, revealing more of the background scenery.

Anna could sense the change in Ian as he turned to stone beside her.

"I'm sorry to do this, Ian, but you leave me no choice." Ronja panned the camera around her location, revealing a stately home, a blend of beige and brown bricks with a sweeping staircase leading up to the front door. Then she zoomed in on the house number before filling the screen with her face again.

She didn't speak, only stared at Ian.

He stunned Anna by saying, "I'm on my way. But hear me, Ronja. If you hurt anyone, I swear my own oath. I will despise you. And you will *never* see me again."

"Then don't waste any time." With that, a red "Face-to-Face Ended" icon popped up. And the witch was gone.

Anna could see it was her turn to be supportive, because Ian's face was ashen. "What's going on? What can I do?" She hated the alarm so clearly etched into his visage, the panic in his eyes.

"I'm going. I have to."

"All right." She didn't argue. "Then I'm going with you."

Grabbing her hand, he held her close to his side as he all but ran down the hall and back toward the great room. "We have to hurry." His voice was harsh with fear. "She's outside my parents' house."

21

Ronja stood waiting on the sloping green lawn that led to the home of Ian's parents. Two women he didn't recognize were there as well, a tall blonde with muscular arms bared by a sleeveless shirt, and a small, more compact female with jet-black hair and matching leather jacket.

Anna strode beside him, filling in the blanks. "Carson and Jack. The small one is fast like Paige and Chris."

"The other?" he asked as they edged into the grass.

"Carson is stronger than the average person, but her real gift is her viciousness and complete lack of compassion."

Ian pictured his mother's delicate build, thought of his father's advanced age, and flexed his hands. "Good to know."

He'd asked the other men to stay at the island, as well as half of the coven. Though Anna had argued, he'd finally convinced her to bring only four other witches. He just had a feeling Ronja would react badly to a show of strength.

Today wasn't about fighting or one-upmanship. Today was about getting his parents free and clear. And then far away from Savannah until Halloween had passed.

Ian glanced over his shoulder to see Paige, Viv, Claudia, and Shauni spreading out behind him and Anna. Each of them wore intense expressions, because they too were uneasy with this arrangement.

None of them trusted Ronja, and neither did Ian. But he wouldn't risk his parents.

When he faced Ronja again, he noticed her eyes burned more brightly. They'd narrowed to slits, exposing the depth of her hatred. All of which was directed at Paige.

Ronja trembled from head to foot. "My promise for non-violence does not extend to *her*." She pointed at Paige, her hand quaking. "You murdered my Scarlett!"

A sound filled with both shock and disgust burst from the coven's warrior, but Ian turned to her and shook his head, silencing whatever comeback she'd been about to make.

Twisting her mouth into a tight ball, Paige nodded at him and kept quiet. Judging from her taught muscles, however, she'd like to give Ronja a lot more than a verbal response.

So Ian spoke to draw the Nordic witch's attention back to him. "I'm here, Ronja. Tell me what is so important that it couldn't wait until the thirty-first." The jerk of her head gave away her surprise. "So you know it all."

"I do." But Ian's reaction mirrored hers. He'd managed to surprise himself. Until this moment, he hadn't acknowledged his intentions, the driving urge to see his involvement with Anna, Vanir, and the witch standing before him all the way to its culmination.

He wanted to be there when light clashed with dark. He was intimately related to the struggle between Anna and Ronja, as well as the one between himself and Vanir. He couldn't say why, but a deeply-buried intuition was speaking through him.

And now the plan was set.

"Yes, I'll be there." He answered the question in Ronja's eyes. Then he tossed a glance aside to Anna. Based on her tightened jaw, she wasn't pleased by his announcement. Not in the least.

But that debate would have to wait until they were alone again. Safe again.

Right now the environment practically crackled with energy, with restrained fury. He was surrounded by supernatural females who all wanted to tear into each other.

To prove his point, Ronja shouted, "She has to go!" Anger was beginning to override her desire to speak with Ian.

And her temper was quick. Before he saw it coming, she angled her hand toward Paige and drove a line of magic straight toward her. The power headed for the ex-soldier was so intense Ian could actually see it buckling the air into waves as it moved.

But just as rapidly, Anna intervened. She blasted magic that acted as a reflector, bouncing Ronja's strike toward the ground. A patch of grass the size of a Mini-Cooper sizzled to black death.

Ian grunted. His mother wasn't going to be pleased.

Thinking of her, he shot a look toward the house where he saw both of his parents through the beveled glass of the front double doors. His mother's eyes were locked onto him, her mouth tight with worry. His father stood behind her, brow furrowed and jaw clenched.

But it was the third figure that filled Ian with fear. "Who's with my parents?" he demanded of Ronja, taking three steps in her direction. His slow movement belied his displeasure, the unease shooting speedily toward rage.

"Ross. He is only keeping them...out of danger."

"You mean he's keeping them in check," Ian said, his tone cool yet laced with steel.

Ronja must have sensed his fury, for she held out a hand in a placating gesture. "You don't want them running out here." Her reasonable tone was meant to convince him of her pure motives. "They might get hurt."

"And if they do, you will answer for it."

"I only swore I wouldn't hurt that bitch there!" She jerked her head to Anna. "You can't hold me—"

"Don't play word games with me, Ronja." Ian lowered his head, glared at her. "You're not good enough to beat me in that arena." He took two more steps as his blood burned, his muscles tightened. "You may not keep your word, but I do. So hear me now."

He stopped several feet away. "If you harm anyone here today, or if you *ever* hurt my parents, you will lose much more than your honor." He raised his head, standing to his full height to stare down on her with loathing. "What's left of it."

"How can you speak to me so?" Sorrow swept over her visage, changing her from dangerous witch to pitiful victim in an instant.

And Ian flashed back to the dream. He remembered the innocent girl on the cold, snowy ground, struggling beneath a beast of a man.

Shaking his head, he looked beyond her to the grand old oak where his childhood swing still hung, then to his parents, both confused and terrified. "No. No tricks, Ronja. Stay out of my head."

"I'm not doing anything." She held out her hands. "You know I'm not." Then she pointed wildly to Anna. "And *she* knows I'm not. If you don't believe me, ask her. Ask her!"

Overwhelmed by the images filling his mind, the conflicting storylines that fought to claim him, Ian shook his fist at her and shouted, "What do you want?"

Ronja made a mewling noise. "I want you to come with me, Vanir. That's all I ask. I will never harm you, and I'm sorry if I frightened you when you came to my home. I was upset when you denied me."

She eased closer to Ian, and he heard Anna move in response.

But Ronja gave no hint that she cared about Anna, Paige, or anyone else. Her focus was on Ian, eyes glistening with unspent emotion. "I love you more than anyone ever could. Please let me help you through this. Please," she whispered. "Brother."

"No. Your idea of love is warped." Despite his words, Ian's head was spinning, a merry-go-round of his memories combined with Vanir's. They whirled so quickly, all blurring together, making him dizzy. Sick.

Pressing the heels of his hands to his temples, Ian tried to dislodge the antagonistic images. They warred against each other, pushing and pulling.

He closed his eyes and thought of Anna. He pictured her diving after him into a dark abyss that could have taken them both down forever.

Her actions could have been motivated by duty alone, but the way she looked at him, the way she responded to his touch, his kiss, told him she was driven by more than her conscience.

"You don't know love," he heard himself say, and then he opened his eyes. The nauseating whirlwind disappeared, leaving so abruptly he would swear he heard a suction of air as it went.

Ronja curled her fingers, green-tipped nails befitting her rancid personality. "Do you have any idea how I suffered when I lost you? How I've mourned all these centuries? Let me tell you, if you did, you would never say that to me. Never!"

Lifting her hands to the sky, Ronja screamed and called forth a black bolt of lightning. She captured the stream of heat in her hands before shooting it back out in two different directions. One line of electricity struck the side of Joe's SUV parked on the street.

The other hit the old oak tree, frying the majestic limb that held Ian's swing.

She was losing control, and there were too many people nearby. Neither of the two women with Ronja spoke, only gaped at her sudden tantrum. They would be no help.

Neither Anna, nor the other witches, could do anything. If they acted, Ronja would lose it completely.

That left Ian. As hesitant as he was to reach out to Ronja, he was the only one who could calm this storm.

"Ronja, listen to me." He gentled his tone but remained firm. "I know you suffered during the lifetime we once shared. I know you were hurt, and I'm sorry for that."

The flashing light behind her eyes dimmed, so he continued. "If I could help you, I would." He put a hand to his chest. "But I am Ian Keller. Please understand. Your brother is gone."

A smile snaked across her lips. Her eyes danced with madness. "But he's not. He's rising again." She pointed a finger, twirled it in tiny circles. "I can see him in there."

Opening her mouth, she wheezed out a dry laugh. She stepped past Ian toward Anna, and Paige closed in at warp speed. Viv, Shauni, and Claudia were right behind her, closing ranks.

So, of course, Carson and Jack advanced as well. But instead of positioning themselves for a fight, they shared a glance before the tall blonde put her hands on Ronja's shoulders. "We should leave now."

Ian didn't understand, but the two seemed apprehensive, as if they actually wanted to avoid an altercation. Because they were outnumbered by coven witches? Or something else?

Ronja didn't try to pull free of Carson's grip, but she wasn't finished with Anna yet. "As for you, time is ticking away. You have less than a month to live."

Her features morphed from glee to animosity, as if she couldn't settle on one emotion. Finally, she said with force, "You will be dead. Dead! And then you can't stop it! Vanir will return. He will return to me!"

The one called Jack frowned and started assisting Carson, dragging their leader away. Carson lifted a hand to wave at the man inside with Ian's parents. Ross.

Ian released a painful breath of relief when the strapping man exited the house.

But he was equally upset to see his father storming out after. And then his mother.

Ronja and her entourage were now halfway across the yard, headed toward a black sedan. She was leaving without objection, but she whipped her head around when Ian's mother ran to him, calling, "Ian! Are you all right? Ian!"

Stopping in her tracks, Ronja stabbed her hands down by her sides, her neck straining as she yelled, "His name is Vanir!"

"This would be a good time to go inside." Anna walked to him, put a hand on his back.

But then his mother was there, pressing her hands to the sides of his face. "Who are these people, Ian? What's this all about?"

Paige had intercepted Ian's father and was likely urging him not to go for the shotgun he was mentioning between every other word, and all of them profanity. So Ian took the opportunity to say, "Mom, this is Anna. We need to talk, to explain."

"Yes, yes."

"You and Dad need to go away for a while, only a couple of weeks."

Releasing her hold on his face, his mother stepped back and studied Anna shrewdly. Biting her bottom lip, she scanned the other women who were still hovering.

Ian saw the precise moment she'd determined the women were to be considered friends. She nodded, her gaze lingering on Anna as she tried to work up a smile. "We can talk over coffee."

Then concern blanketed her face, and the smile she'd tried to build just wouldn't hold up. "But Ian," she cupped his face again, a mother needing to assure herself of her child's safety, "did I hear that woman correctly? She was screaming, but I would swear..."

Ian's eyes fixed on his mother's and held. He felt a cold surge of awareness, as if a part of him knew what she was going to say, but the rest of him still needed to hear it. "What, Mom? What is it?"

She dropped her hand to wring it with the other. "Did she

call you Vanir? Surely I heard wrong."

Anna spoke evenly but had a catch in her breath. "Do you know that name?"

"Yes. Oh, yes." Then his mother's features crumpled as dread completely took over. "Oh, Ian. Is it happening again?"

The question was a blow to his sternum. His mouth opened but no sound came out.

So it was Anna who answered, "I believe so." She gestured toward the house. "But maybe we should all sit down."

Ian barely noticed the trek inside, his mind scrambling for something solid to grasp on to. What did his mother mean? She'd heard the name Vanir? This had happened before?

Recognition stirred as Ian paused inside the living room. Then a distinct memory came to him. Here on this very carpet, he had opened a gift for Christmas. He remembered being disappointed by the magician's set, wondering why his parents didn't understand.

"Oh, my God." Though the words were but a croak, Anna heard. She stayed behind with him as the other women followed his parents to the kitchen. "I used to tell them I wanted to do magic. For a while, it was all I talked about."

Then the image was gone and he was standing there, stiff as the little black wand he'd stuffed back inside the unwanted box. "This is crazy. I remember my life, my childhood." His gaze leapt up to meet Anna's. "And Vanir was part of it."

"Let's hear what your mother has to tell us," she said, unwavering. "We will handle this. Together."

Ian's mother had always been most at home in the kitchen, so that's where they congregated. Renovated several years back, the room boasted ivory-hued cabinets, creamy marble countertops with dark swirls, and brushed-nickel fixtures.

He and the witches gathered at the center island. Though his brain buzzed with unanswered questions, he would wait until his mother was ready. Her hands were shaking as she prepared the coffee maker, but by the time she was filling their matching green mugs, she was steady.

Once the fresh Bundt cake was cut and served, her expression had grown serene, the competent mother-in-charge he was used to. "Yes, I know the name Vanir well. Very well." She picked up exactly where they'd left off in the yard.

Ian worked his jaw but kept his eyes on her.

"Ian, when you were four years old, you spent over six months telling your father and I, anyone who would listen, actually, that your name was really Vanir."

He set his cup down before he spilled hot coffee in his lap. "I what?"

"At first we thought it was normal, just part of a child's active imagination. Many children have imaginary friends, why not an alter ego?" His mother set aside her cake and laid her hands flat atop the marble. "It became an issue, however, when you started insisting we call you that in public, at church, everywhere we went. And if we refused, you would become… quite agitated."

"I don't remember, not clearly."

"You wouldn't, would you? Being so young." She turned to the refrigerator all of a sudden. "Oh, I forgot the flavored creamers." Then she returned with hazelnut and French vanilla before topping off her own drink with a little of both.

The discussion was making her nervous, old memories coming back, old concerns for her son she'd probably believed long forgotten and done with.

"It's all right, Mom." Ian gave her an encouraging smile. "It's better to talk about it, and I know it's unexpected, but I promise you, we will take care of this. Once and for all."

She gave him a baffled look, and then she shifted her attention to Anna. Her mother's antennae had picked up on the connection between the sable-haired beauty and her only son. "Yes," his mother finally said, and she gave Anna a small smile.

She cleared her throat. "What truly alarmed us was your use of words we didn't understand. They sounded like a foreign language and only popped out of your mouth when you were very upset, angry when we didn't call you by that other name."

"He spoke another language?" Anna asked.

"Oh, yes. He'd spit out strange sentences like a little Tommy gun. Scared your father and I to death." She shrugged daintily and pursed her lips. "But then one day it all stopped. You came over to me, so solemn for a little boy, and you told me that Vanir was gone. Just like that." She snapped her fingers.

Ian was perplexed, but this was important information. Maybe something he could use to exorcise Vanir again. He could stand another thirty years without the guy. "Did something special happen that day? Did we go somewhere?"

"No, nothing." Now his mother took a bite of her cake. "We were at home, a Saturday afternoon. I'm sorry, I never knew the reason." She reached across the countertop and patted his hand. "But I was grateful. I'd finally gotten my little boy back."

Releasing a sigh full of love and relief balled into one, she pulled away. "And I'll never forget that day. March fourteenth, nineteen-eighty-six."

Beside him, Anna gasped. She started coughing on the cake she'd apparently inhaled, then took a long drink of coffee to wash it down. Casting haunted eyes to his mother, she put a hand to her chest, her fingers on her amulet.

Then she slowly turned to Ian. "That's the day I was born."

~

Two hours later, his parents were packed up and headed for a cabin in the Rocky Mountains. While Ian was relieved to have them out of harm's way, he was still off-kilter, his head reeling from a whole new perspective of Vanir, Anna, and the explanation he now had for his deep-seated fear of the supernatural.

His distress over being invaded by forces he hadn't understood.

They were aboard the boat and bouncing across open water, heading back toward the island. He enjoyed the bracing winds, the fresh, salty smell of ocean.

But even though pieces were clicking into place, he was still stunned by his mother's story. And by the link he had with Anna, one they'd shared their entire lives. Neither of them aware.

So it was no wonder his mind was still stumbling along, trying to understand what it all meant. His hand glided over the seat of the boat in search of Anna's, found her warm skin, and grasped.

He'd been right to give her his faith. Because whether or not she'd realized it, she'd been helping him since the day she was born.

That didn't mean he wasn't unsettled by his history with Vanir. For Ian, it was like discovering he had a second shadow, a lurker that had followed him, watching, waiting for the right moment. And the unseen force had been with him for decades.

The motors slowed, prompting him to look up to where Joseph was positioned at the helm, surprisingly unfazed by his damaged SUV. He was throttling down to ease up beside the dock.

Being back on the island was a reassurance, so Ian released Anna's hand long enough to disembark. But as they walked across the beach and onward through the forest, he kept her close, within arm's reach. He needed her calming presence.

Today had been the first time he'd come into contact with Ronja since his hasty retreat from her plantation home. And while his head ached, churning with the new information, he couldn't seem to stop thinking of the Nordic witch and how she'd implored him to go with her.

"Brother," she'd called him, and with such heartfelt tenderness. Such love in her eyes, the exact color of his own.

So each time he thought of Ronja, he touched Anna or held her tighter. She was his anchor now, when his thoughts and emotions were so unpredictable, so turbulent.

Only a few minutes until the mansion was visible through the trees, and Ian was more than ready to get inside, go up to his room, and lie down on the bed. He wasn't in the mood to deal with the other men.

Yes, he understood their concern. He knew they worried about Vanir. It didn't take a genius to add up their suspicious glances and Ian's ever-increasing visions from a past life.

But the confrontation with Ronja, followed by his mother's revelation, had knocked Ian's world off its axis, and he wasn't feeling like himself.

He laughed internally at his own terrible pun. Welcome to a day in the life of Ian.

And his trusty sidekick, Vanir.

The grand hall was filled with the other residents, as if every one of them had decided to wait there, eager to hear about the meeting with Ronja. They were all concerned. They just wanted to help.

But even the vast space of the main room felt stuffy and overcrowded. Ian's head was already overflowing with noise, and he desired nothing but peace and quiet.

But the others weren't of the same mind.

"What happened?" Quinn asked, stepping in front of Anna. "What did she want?"

"To convince Ian to go with her." Paige's sarcasm was thick, her head shaking with irritation as she went to stand with Chris. "She actually pleaded with him. Called him *brother*."

Ian flinched to hear the word repeated. He didn't need a play-by-play just now, and frankly, he was sick of it all. Ronja.

Vanir. The impending battle that had Anna upset to the point of tears.

Why the hell should he have to answer to anyone? Why did Anna? Who'd decided they should fill these roles?

And what would happen if they just left? He and Anna could take his car and join his parents in the mountains. Just run away.

He stopped and drew a deep, cleansing breath. He was having crazy ideas. But probably as a result of the pain in his head. The throb was growing stronger, a giant's fist banging at his mental gate.

Putting a hand to his temple, he turned to Anna. "I'm going up. My head is splitting, and I need a break from all of this."

"Of course." She nodded, squeezed his arm with her free hand. "Do you want to be alone?"

"I—" Black circles bloomed in front of Ian's eyes, and the ache in his head became a jagged shard driving up from his spine to the base of his brain. Staggering, he reached out for the nearest stable item and stumbled a few steps until he hit the mantle of the fireplace.

He heard Anna call his name as if from the far end of a tunnel. But he couldn't find her. His vision was almost entirely gone. Sliding his hand around the edge of the mantle, he sought anything solid, something he could lean against.

Hands were on his shoulders now, but all he could see were inky Rorschach blotches erupting and fading over and over. Suddenly they disappeared, and he was staring at the stone wall, inches from his nose.

Then his legs gave way, his mind imploded, and he opened his eyes. He still saw stone.

But this one was flying toward his face.

He reacted and tried to move his head out of the way. But the dodge came too late. The rock caught him on the cheek and glanced painfully off the bone beneath. All around him people were gathered, shouting, their spittle flying, their fists thrusting into the air.

These weren't faces he knew. Anna and her friends were gone.

Then Ian realized that wasn't quite accurate. He was the one who'd left. *Again.*

He'd experienced pieces of this vision, this *memory*, once before, but never in such a visceral way. He smelled blood, sweat, and dirt. He felt the bruises he'd gained from brawling with the invaders, the more severe pain in his side from where a man had stabbed him with a blade.

The sky above was metal-gray and as cold as the eyes of the men standing nearby. The ones who'd brought him down and tied him to the pole.

He shook his head when blood ran into his eyes, but the motion made him dizzy, nauseated. The sensation of freezing cold crept up on him, and he realized his clothes were drenched. The moisture soaking him was thick and oily, rank with the odor of animal.

Fat. He'd been doused with melted fat. And then a rush of sound told him why. A man with a torch backed several feet away. And smiled at him.

His hands were tied behind him, around the hard wooden stake pressing into his spine. More ropes encircled his torso and arms, ensuring there would be no escape.

He was trussed up tight, immobile and vulnerable. So those who'd attacked his people, who'd conquered his lands, could feel safe as they threw stones and cursed him.

The man from the North.

The one with magic.

The words they flung at him were of an unknown language, but their twisted faces and aggressive behavior made it clear they were chanting for his blood, for his death.

And when the awful smell of smoke reached him, he knew

they would have it.

Flames began to lick at his toes, the terrible heat searing through the material covering his feet. Soon his soles began to burn, but the pain was lost among so many others as the flames danced higher, as his body was consumed.

Once the oil caught, his clothing blazed like the torch, and his hair, his skin, became a living shell of agony. He thrashed on the pole but didn't scream. Instead he was intent, eyes on the mob, searching, searching, but for what he didn't know.

He needed to see her, to make sure she was alive. But who? Perhaps his sanity was being destroyed along with his flesh.

Then someone was yelling at him, a voice so near his ear it drilled into his skull. "Ian! Ian! Wake up!"

He was burning, dying. Why were they doing this? Was there no one who would show mercy? No one who would put him out of his misery?

Finally, he could stand no more. The flames had engulfed him, and he heard the sizzle of his face. Why was he still alive? He was in agony! Torture!

Then someone was there, grabbing his arm and shaking him. Again they screamed, "Ian! Ian, wake up!"

With a roar borne of fury and pain, he opened his eyes and locked onto the gathered crowd. They'd come to steal his home, his family, and his very life.

But he'd been given another chance. And he would take it.

Rolling to his knees and then his feet, he saw the glint of steel on one marauder's hip. He snatched the knife and whirled to face his aggressors.

"Ian!" a woman cried, her hands held out in a plea.

But he had no sympathy for her anguish. He was free from the fire. He had a weapon in his hand. And as his chest filled with light, he knew.

He had his magic.

Staring down his adversaries, he brandished the blade. He

called forth his power and stood tall. "My name," he growled, "is Vanir."

22

Anna stood in shock and stared. One minute Ian had been on the slate floor thrashing and flailing, and the next he was on his feet grabbing the knife from Claudia's belt. Now he brandished the weapon back and forth, his countenance racked by pure hatred.

"Ian," she said, breaking free from her emotional lockdown, ignoring the words she thought she'd heard him say. Her tone was calm and kind, but he responded with a glare and a hostile lunge in her direction.

And Anna knew she'd heard correctly.

As one, the others moved closer, especially Quinn, who stepped in front of Anna. But Ian didn't make good on the threat. He retreated, careful to keep the wall at his back so no one could sneak up behind him.

Expression rigid and furious, he spat words at them, things Anna didn't understand. There was no doubt the man she knew was now ruled by another force. Another person had moved in and taken over, one who was ready to do violence, and was fueled by fear.

Not Ian, she thought with despair. They were now facing a ferocious warrior and talented practitioner. The frantic movements and baffled expression belonged to none other than Vanir.

Dare made as if to confront him. To talk him down or take him on, Anna didn't know, but she worried he would only incite

Vanir further. "Wait. Don't move," she called to her friend. Because she could tell Vanir's mind was working.

Greatly outnumbered and clearly desperate, he was strategizing a way out.

And judging by the white illumination filling the palm of his free hand, he was channeling a great surge of magic.

"Get back!" he shouted at them, waving the blade.

The outburst of English startled Anna, but hope rode on the wake of her realization. *Ian's still in there. I just have to get his attention.*

So that's who she would appeal to. But first, the danger Vanir posed needed to be dealt with. The knife, they could handle. The magic, however...

"Ian, you're safe. No one will hurt you." When he wrinkled his forehead and sneered at her, she decided to change tactics. "Vanir," she said gently.

When he cocked his head, curious, she took one step closer.

"Anna." Quinn's tone was subdued but strained with warning and concern.

"I have to try," she said aside to him. If Vanir engaged any of them in combat, either physical or magical, the coven and men would be forced to respond. They would have no choice but to neutralize Vanir to ensure each of the witches—herself especially—survived until Halloween.

And if it came down to an altercation, there was no guarantee Ian would remain unscathed, or even alive. But the stakes were much bigger than one man, one life.

Think. Think! Magic to magic was the only way. Ian had told her he believed Vanir to have been a man of valor, so Anna cupped her hands, palms to the ceiling, and let a gentle blue glow form.

She imbued the essence of peace and tranquility into the magic, hoping Vanir would sense her goodwill. She met his eyes, held, and then bowed her head. She might not be able to communicate with words, but she could still convey respect.

Vanir narrowed his eyes, chest heaving, but he relaxed his shoulders marginally. Despite the small concession, his eyes darted to the crowd surrounding him. He was still alert. Vigilant.

Anna had gained a degree of trust but wouldn't make much progress while he felt threatened.

She took another step.

And after one unforeseen event, chaos was unleashed.

Skid burst from the foyer, barking his arrival, with Mrs. Attinger trailing right behind him. She must have had the dog out for a walk.

But Michael reacted, jumping forward as he called the dog's name. He was too close to Vanir, and the man struck out reflexively, slicing into Michael's shoulder.

The spill of blood then sent Paige into action. In a streak of motion, she swept past Vanir and snatched the knife. Skid barked maniacally, and Vanir bellowed his fury as if he'd been duped.

His surprise at Paige's speed and his loss of the blade were the only reasons Anna gained even a second to intervene, to calm things down. And she needed to act fast, because he still had a deadly weapon.

Poised to use his magic, he raised both hands. They burned bright white, the escalation of power illuminating the grand hall with brilliant radiance.

"Vanir," Anna called urgently. She met his gaze and cupped her hands again, stretching them outward.

"Anna, don't," Quinn tried again.

She tossed aside, "Get everyone back."

"But—"

"Do it." Her voice was cool but brooked no argument. All the while, she maintained eye contact with Vanir.

She couldn't see her brother's response, but she assumed

Quinn had done as she'd asked when the mass of people slowly withdrew. She heard a grumble that had to have been Paige, but a more soothing tone persuaded the warrior's cooperation. It sounded like Hayden.

Anna eased closer to the man who was ready to strike again, though an assault with the blazing magic would surely be lethal.

When she was but a few feet away, she halted and lowered her hands. Then her head.

If he wanted to kill her now, she would be vulnerable unless the others stepped in. Given her proximity to Vanir, she doubted there would be time for them to intercede.

She allowed her gaze to creep back up to his, and in his eyes she saw bewilderment. He likely had no understanding of where he was or how he'd come to be here. Within a throng of bizarre-looking people, all of whom were dressed in modern clothing and speaking an unfamiliar language.

"Vanir," she whispered, offering the only bit of familiarity she could. His name was the only tie to what he recognized.

Between the others giving him plenty of room and Anna's lack of fear, along with her foolish yet apparent trust, Vanir let his shoulders drop, as if unburdening a great weight. Anna smiled and nodded to encourage him.

At last, he exhaled heavily, gave a sharp nod, and doused the burning power in his hands.

Anna's lips trembled from a rush of tentative relief, but she wouldn't be at ease until she had Ian back again. She took another step, within arm's reach of him now.

This time when she extended her right hand, she made sure he saw her empty palm—no magic—and leaned near enough to touch his shoulder. He shuddered at the contact.

"Vanir," she said gently, consolingly.

And when he let his eyes close, a show of trust, she moved her hand to his cheek. "Ian."

He blinked rapidly, moving his head back and forth, but she maintained contact.

"Ian," she said again, "come back." Placing her other hand on his opposite cheek, she closed the last of the distance, so they stood a breath apart.

Looking deeply into his eyes, she saw the shadows blow away and sensed Ian's return as he drew a long, deep breath. Unwilling to lose the link she'd forged, Anna pressed her lips to his, still holding his face tenderly.

She was rewarded when his arm slipped around her to pull her close. He pressed his cheek to hers. "Anna."

She wrapped her arms around him, telling herself she might never let go again. "Are you okay?" she asked so only he could hear.

She felt his slight nod. Then he pulled away from her and stared over her shoulder. "Michael." He eased around her. "I'm so sorry. I didn't mean— I wasn't—"

Anna turned to see Michael, his white shirt still torn and bloody. But Willyn had her hands around the wound, already healing him.

"No. It's fine," Michael said. "I know that wasn't you. And I can see you're back to yourself."

Willyn winked at Ian, and even Shauni smiled, though her protective hands were still on Michael's back. Anna swallowed, another level of relief washing through her as she realized the others had forgiven Ian for what he hadn't been able to control.

A light went on as she grasped Michael's meaning. "You can see his aura. You can tell a difference when Vanir is close, can't you?"

Michael pulled his mouth to the side, glanced at Quinn, and then said to Anna, "Yes. It's why I've been here so much lately. Why I took time off from the clinic."

"What's he saying?" Ian asked. He was still gripping Anna's hand tightly, as loath to end their connection as she was.

"Michael told us his concerns about Vanir a while ago." Dare stood with his arms hanging loosely at his sides, resignation on his face as he admitted what the men had been up to.

"And you didn't tell us," Willyn said to her husband.

"We didn't want Anna to know." Quinn frowned. "It was my call." Then his blue eyes met hers. "You had so much to handle already. I thought if there was a problem, we'd be ready. And if there never was…"

"I never had to know," Anna finished for him. Raising her brows, she could only laugh. "Normally, I would be offended, but right now…" She glanced to Ian, leaned against his shoulder. "I'm just glad things didn't get any worse."

Taking in Ian's downcast eyes, his miserable expression, Anna announced, "We're going to take a walk."

"Okay. I'll come with you," Paige said, her stare mutinous.

"Ian and I need to talk." Anna could see her friend was worried, that they all were.

"I'm sorry, but you don't need to be alone with him. Not now, maybe not ever," Quinn said, his jaw in a stubborn set.

"That's my decision." Anna threaded her tone with firm resolve. "And this is my trial." They might forgive, but they were still on guard.

Then she softened, allowing Quinn a margin of error for being a concerned brother. "I think time together is what we both need." She looked to Ian, who still hadn't let go of her. "Just the two of us."

~

"Let's go to the woods," Anna said as she and Ian passed over the back patio and through the cultivated gardens. She wanted no prying eyes for the conversation they were about to have, and while her friends and brother all meant well, she felt certain Ian was back in control.

Across the yellowing grass they strolled, in no real hurry, just at ease to be outdoors in the cool breeze. October was a month of change, even this far south.

And fall was the season of loss, when life slowly, painfully, gave way to death. The leaves were giving up their long, hard fight, relinquishing their green to the changing light as shorter days rang the final knell.

They'd barely made the shade of the tree line when Ian hooked her elbow and pulled her to a stop. "I want you to work your magic on me, Anna. Do whatever spell you have to. Just keep Vanir under."

He raked a hand through his hair. "I couldn't stand it if I hurt anyone." He scoffed, self-derision obvious. "Worse than I already have."

He let his arm move to her waist, "And if Vanir got loose again, if he ever hurt you..."

"Shh." She put a finger to his lips, tugged him back into an easy walk. The day had been a roller coaster of emotions. First her upset and then Ian's, culminating in a scene that could have been much more violent. Actions that might have been unrecoverable.

So she wanted the forest now, with its many layers of shade and shadow, and the soft bustle of life all around. Her spirit needed rejuvenation and would be well-served by communing with nature.

She slid a look to Ian, who was still visibly shaken. He could use a visit to the quiet world as well.

There was enough green left in the rich, thick foliage to create a haven among the pines, hardwoods, and palmettos. Veering off the worn path, Anna led him to one of her favorite places, beneath an ancient oak and near one of the island's few tidal creeks.

Once they were under the giant tree, standing on a lush bed of grass, Anna took his hands in hers. "It's over now, Ian, and

I'll help you make sure he doesn't break free again." She ran her hand up his arm to his shoulder, and despite the awful incident she couldn't contain her joy.

She was just so happy to have Ian back. Losing him, if only for a few minutes, had carved a hole in her chest. So she wouldn't waste the time she had with him, not another minute.

Gloom still pervaded him, though, and there could be no healing until he purged the awful experience. "Tell me what you saw," she urged, "when you blacked out. I think you'll feel better."

"I'd feel better if I could get a grip on this." He leaned back against the rough bark. "I have to tell you, I didn't see this coming."

"You were emotionally spent by the time we returned to the island. And our face-to-face with Ronja..." Anna shrugged. "She seems to be a trigger. Then, on top of seeing her, you found out about Vanir's presence during your childhood."

Ian let his head rest against the tree. "It's been a day. I'll give you that." Heaving a sigh, he looked up to the thick bough of branches overhead, then back to Anna. "I'm glad you weren't with me this time. You didn't need to see it."

Her chest swelled, almost burst, as agony flashed over his face. She ran her knuckles over his jawline. "What happened?"

"I died," he said simply. "Rather, Vanir did, but I was up close and personal for every bit of it. I got to smell, hear, and feel it all. Being burned alive was traumatic enough for me, but I can just imagine how it was for Vanir. We go through these things, these visions, together."

Ian's features hardened. "I'm sure reliving his worst moment was enough to jar him loose and set him free."

Anna shivered. "I can understand why."

"I'm sure the manner of his death is also why I reacted to Bastraal's fireball that day on the ocean. Vanir was inside me even then, and the huge inferno was a harsh reminder. It was just too much."

"I can't see the part he'll play, but what you said before is true. Vanir has something to do with all of this—me, you, the prophecy. I have to believe he'll serve a purpose in the end."

Ian's laughter was doubtful. "Yeah, but for us or for them?"

Anna dropped her gaze. She had no definite answer.

"I used to be afraid of fire," she murmured, wanting to reassure Ian, but deeper than that, wanting to share more of herself. "After my parents died in the explosion and the resulting flames, I was terrified to use my magic to call fire, or any of the other elements."

"But you overcame," he said, stroking her cheek.

"I had to. Over time, I realized the mantle still fell to me, with or without their presence. Becoming one of The Nine, facing the Amara, destroying Bastraal—this has always been my duty, my obligation. If I'd let fear rule me, I never would have grown strong in my magic."

She leaned forward, hands on his chest. "I owed them my bravery. I had to honor their deaths by pushing ahead and completing my training on my own."

"And you did. Even I can see how powerful you are, Anna, and not only in magic. You are the heart of the coven, the one the witches turn to when they're in need." He tapped her chest, just over her own heart. "And it's your core strength that empowers them as well."

"They do that on their own," she protested.

"You all do it, together. Don't sell yourself short. They need you."

Lifting her hand, he kissed her fingers. "And I need you too."

Who would have thought a small gesture could be so moving? Here she'd been trying to help him feel better, to heal him, and he'd turned things around on her.

"You saved me today," he said. "I heard you, even while I was lost inside Vanir. I heard your voice. You pulled me out."

He rotated her hand, pressed his lips to the center of her palm. "You did that. Not your magic, and not the coven. Only you. You aren't just a witch anymore, not to me. You're the woman I find myself looking for when I enter a room. The one I can't wait to get close to, so I can see what you smell like that day."

Her laugh was low and relaxed. "My smell?"

"How do you do that, by the way?" His mouth grazed the underside of her wrist, applying sweet, tempting pressure on her pulse point.

She was losing her train of thought, focusing on his persistent lips. Then his hands as they strayed lightly over her skin.

"In the beginning, I was so suspicious of you, feared the supernatural world you were part of." His other arm encircled her. "But now I'm a part of it, have been all along. And you're the one who centers me."

His mouth was on hers again, this time with a touch more heat, the cutting edge of insistence. One of his hands slid up her back to fist in her hair while the other coasted down to her leg. His fingers clutched there, kneading.

When she turned her head to gasp, his lips veered over her jaw, skimming lightly, promising more. "You're the one who saves me, Anna. Time and again."

When she put a hand on his sternum and eased him away, she saw that his pain, his fear, had been vanquished. The look in his eyes now was primal.

Gripping her leg, he traced his hand up to her backside. "I love the way you look in these jeans, the soft, faded denim clinging to the curve of your hips, your thighs." His long, sensuous strokes set off jagged spikes of heat.

"Ian," she began, taking a moment to draw breath, "your emotions are in an uproar."

"Yes, they are. And I know just what to do to get them under control."

She'd come out here with a purpose, but it was quickly getting lost in a haze of lust. "Before we go any further, I have to tell you something. You deserve to know the truth."

His mouth moved to the hollow beneath her jaw, and her knees nearly buckled. "Ian, listen to me." She managed to wedge her elbows between them. "There's another aspect of the trials I haven't told you about."

He sighed but didn't release her. "Okay. So tell me."

"Um...you may have noticed that none of the witches are single."

He quirked a golden brow. "I did notice an abundance of male counterparts."

She bobbed her head, trying to keep her mind clear and ignore his searching touch. "Each of the women met or became involved with the men during their trials." Anna found herself clutching him to her, hoping he didn't pull away. Because it felt so right to be in his arms, regardless of whatever force had put her there.

He gave her an impatient nod. "And?"

Was he not getting it? He still seemed so unconcerned. "It's part of a pattern," she said. "The witch at trial is destined to fall in love. It's only fair you understand what's really happening. Fate has made the rules, and each of us has fallen in line."

"Have you? Have you fallen in line?" He jerked her to him, insinuated his thigh between hers.

"Wha—Why aren't you upset?"

Now his sigh was impatient. "Do you want me to be?"

"No...but...aren't you worried about being controlled by greater forces?"

"There is no greater force than what you do to me."

Ian's admission grabbed onto her heart and squeezed.

"I know my own mind." He tilted his head. "Even when I lose control of my body, I'm still in here, and I respond to you. More than anything else. I know what I want, Anna. And I know how

I feel."

In a move that both thrilled and stunned her, he slid his hands beneath her shirt and began to trace her sides. "And what I need most is you." His palms slid down her back until his fingers slid beneath her jeans, branding her with his heat.

"If destiny saw fit to put me in your path, then I guess I owe it my gratitude."

"But—"

He covered her lips with his, swallowing any objection she might have made. To drive his point home, he stroked his tongue greedily against hers. Then he was pulling off her shirt. "So let me feel you, Anna. Give me what I need."

Her skin was bared in an instant, allowing his hands to roam freely, caressing her, sending her system into a rage. She could barely breathe, barely think.

Before she knew it, he was lowering her to the grass. He knelt between her thighs and ripped off his own T-shirt, revealing a long, toned torso with perfectly-carved muscles.

Her breath hitched as he looked down at her, his stare darkened by passion. In response, her desire rose to meet his.

And she knew she would give him anything.

Her clothes seemed to dissolve beneath his capable hands, and soon she was lying naked, safe in the forest sanctuary, and beneath the man who had changed her life.

His hands were on her breasts, followed by his hot, wet mouth. Lying half on top of her, Ian glided his skin over hers as he made his way down. "So soft," he said, trailing a hand over her hip.

Then he nudged his shoulders under her knees, lifting her, baring her to him. He lowered his mouth and kissed her there.

Anna almost came off the ground.

Pulling back, Ian blew a cool breath across her sex. His voice was low and husky when he said, "And so sweet."

All she could do was dig her fingers into the grass when he

spread her thighs farther apart and settled in.

Groaning as soon as he tasted her again, Ian clamped his hands beneath her, holding her tight against his ravenous tongue.

Abandoning all protest, Anna rolled her head to the side and lifted her hips, arched her back. His name was a whimper on her lips as she gave herself over, all but enslaved by the stunning sensation.

Ian ravished her, using his mouth, and then his hands, until Anna felt herself breaking apart. Then coming back together, coiling into a tight, heavy ache that begged for release. Her thighs trembled as he worked her to the edge.

She almost sobbed as he pushed her over. This time his name rode on a cry of ecstasy, as the forest, the whole world, shattered into bright light.

The waves crashed over her until she was spent, and glorious relaxation rolled over her. She felt weightless, languid, as if floating in the air.

Then her nerve endings began to explode again as Ian made a slow climb back up, over her skin, tasting as he went. "Open those blue eyes of yours." He pushed up to his knees and stared down at her. "I'm not done with you yet."

He flicked the button of his jeans, and Anna's body revved all over again.

She sat up to help him remove his pants and couldn't help planting her open mouth on those tight, ridged abs, before easing down the golden trail that hinted of more to come.

Then she took the length of him in her mouth, eliciting a moan from Ian. The sound of his pleasure shot straight to her core.

She had to have him inside of her, and based on the way he took her shoulders, guided her to the ground, he was intent on the same.

The light was softening as the day gave way to twilight, and

Anna couldn't imagine a more perfect time or place for what they were about to share. His heart thrummed against her chest as he settled atop her.

Slowing, gentling for a moment, he brushed a soft kiss over her lips before locking his gaze on hers. "I know who I am. And you, Anna, you are what I want."

His slide into her was slow and tantalizing. The first several thrusts were just as deliberate, unhurried, and thorough. Again he took her mouth, nipping, suckling.

And rapture began to build again.

Rising above her, Ian cupped her face, so tenderly. Then using his lean hips, he pounded into her, faster, harder, giving her unimaginable pleasure.

His scent consumed her. He murmured her name.

And bowing her back, Anna let him take control.

Ian was aggressive, yet masterful, delivering the perfect combination of tenderness and eroticism. Still moving inside her, he opened his eyes to meet hers. "Come with me," he urged, his hands supporting her back as he drove into her.

"Yes," she whispered, feeling the delicious spiral beginning to twist and curl. Ian filled her completely, stretching and teasing, until she tightened around him once more.

The deep golden light of sunset illuminated the island forest, the trees, the water, and Ian's handsome face. His neck strained as he lifted his head, and when he roared, Anna closed her eyes.

And lost herself in the brightness again.

23

Smoke drifted up from the crackling fire, through the darkened woods, and onward to the nighttime sky. Anna inhaled as she came upon the clearing, comforted by the scent of burning wood, the snap and crackle of flames, and the shift of logs as they charred into ash.

Hayden patted a folded-up utility blanket that would serve as a seat. "Here, Anna. Sit by me."

On the opposite side of the pit dug into the forest floor and surrounded by rocks, Lucia and Claudia swapped looks of resignation. "Well, this wasn't exactly what I pictured when Shauni and Paige suggested a girls' night out." Claudia tossed up a hand and lowered her tall frame to her own folded blanket. "But," she added with a devious smile, "now that we're here, it does seem rather exciting."

"*Si.*" Embracing the outdoor activity, Lucia also dropped to a makeshift seat. "Who would have thought, after all we've been through, that a campfire and ghost stories would actually sound like fun?"

"A campfire," Paige said, carrying over a cooler she then deposited on the edge of the clearing, "with child-appropriate treats." She pulled out chocolate bars and tossed them to Willyn before swinging a plastic bag of marshmallows and graham crackers through the air to land in Shauni's lap.

Returning to the ice-filled box, Paige then retrieved two bottles. One vodka, one beer. "But adult libations."

A general cheer went up that surprised them all and sent them into fits of laughter. Stress revealed itself in many ways, thus the enthusiastic response to alcohol from a coven of witches only days away from saving the world.

"Do you have the makings of an apple-tini in there?" Kylie asked, straining her neck to see inside the cooler.

"This is as close as we could get to a portable version." Paige tossed the youngest witch a clear bottle with tiny green apples on the side.

"This'll do," Kylie chimed out.

"Anna, we even brought white wine for you and Viv, but you'll have to drink it out of plastic cups."

"Not a problem." Anna was growing fonder of the campfire idea with every passing minute. She and her friends were huddled around the flames, whispering and giggling like a bunch of girls away at summer camp. So she accepted the red Solo cup from Paige with a bright grin and happily sipped the chilled Pinot Grigio.

Once everyone was settled with their drink of choice in hand, they continued to confide and tease, joke and laugh. But then one of the women must have said something to change the mood, and a hush fell over the group.

Finally, Willyn sighed and glanced around at the others. "I guess I'll be the one to say it."

"No, don't." Kylie pouted, which prompted Shauni to lean over and rest her head on the younger woman's shoulder.

"Only a few more days until Halloween." Willyn's lower lip trembled as she reached to her right and grabbed Viv's hand. "This will probably be the last time we have one of these talks. Just us girls, wondering aloud about the current trial and what might happen."

"Our last heart-to-heart," Viv agreed. "At least while the prophecy is still ongoing. The next time we get together like this, it will all be over."

Hayden gave a firm nod, but her golden eyes shimmered suspiciously. "And I fully expect to be crowing about how we handed the Amara a well-deserved beat-down."

"Cheers to that." Claudia lifted her plastic cup. Then a little whimper escaped before she could stifle it.

"Oh, guys." Anna waved her hands at her eyes when they began to sting. "I can't stand to think about all of you leaving. I walk through the house, and every room has so many memories. I find myself stopping in my tracks, remembering all the good and bad times, and I just freeze up. I just…" The burning became brimming puddles that threatened to run down her face.

Shauni jumped up and ran around the circle to hug Anna from behind. Then Viv came over to join in, followed by Willyn and Kylie. Lucia and Claudia sat on the other side hugging each other, while Hayden sat by herself and wiped the evidence from her own cheeks.

Paige, however, just groaned. "Stop, stop. All of you." With elbows propped on her knees, she dropped her head forward before lifting it again to brush her bangs from her eyes. "This is supposed to be a last hurrah, not a damn tear-jerker fest."

She took a gulp of beer. "Haul your asses back to your spots and dry it up," she blinked rapidly, "before I start." She snorted. "And ruin perfectly good beer."

Once final squeezes were bestowed upon Anna, the women filed back to their blankets. Anna sighed, laughing through the last few tears, and realized she'd needed the quick but nostalgic cry. Judging by the more relaxed posture of her friends, so had they.

"Try to look at the bright side," Paige said. "When all this is over, you won't have to suffer through daily sparring sessions with me anymore."

"Amen!" Willyn winked at Paige and laughed when the soldier mimed punching her in the arm.

Shauni crossed her legs and gazed into the fire. "I can't help feeling like we should be spending every minute honing our fighting skills or learning new spells." She shrugged. "Even now I think I should be swinging a sword or practicing my magic."

Lucia draped an arm around Claudia on one side and Viv on the other. "But we are." The Spanish witch's brown eyes warmed with love for her sisters. "We're working our strongest magic right now."

Anna nodded. "Our bond is our greatest strength. Our unity is the root of our power."

"Oh, no," Kylie whispered, rubbing at her eyes. "Don't get me started again."

As she fingered her amulet with reverence, Anna's eyes swept the circle, meeting the gaze of each witch to convey her silent thanks and gratitude. "I couldn't have made it this far without all of you."

Paige shook her beer like a teacher's pointing stick. "Oh, no you don't. No more of this sappy stuff."

"Agreed," Anna said, clearing her throat. "Moving on." She sipped her wine again, proving her intent to drink up and have a good time. On this last night of sisterhood before the great battle.

As chatter and laughter broke out once more among the women, and s'mores were assembled methodically by Viv and Willyn, Anna found her focus drifting over their heads and out into the woods. Almost two weeks had passed since the last time she'd visited the forest, when her relationship with Ian had edged into more intimate territory.

Their lovemaking that day had been about trust and letting go of constraints, no longer allowing their individual fears to keep them apart. And it wasn't until afterward Anna realized Ian hadn't been the only one in need of release.

She lifted her red cup to hide the wicked grin playing about her lips as she envisioned Ian at his best. And how the two of them had continued the practice.

Actually, she thought to herself, they'd become quite addicted. They seemed to end up releasing *every single day*.

Of course there was more to their relationship than sex, though that particular aspect was rather...mind-shattering. Ian, it turned out, had a romantic side and had made it his mission to woo the coven's head witch.

Every moment, every minute with him, seemed to hold a new surprise. Secret smiles exchanged across a room, a soft hand on her back as they filled their dinner plates, or shadowed kisses in dark passageways.

Never had Anna been so grateful for the size of the mansion, as well as its many hidden corridors.

"You might as well put your cup down, Anna."

Startled from her musings, Anna shifted her attention to Kylie, who had her brows raised and an I-know-what-you're-thinking expression on her face.

Actually, several of the witches did.

"Yeah, we all know that look by now," Paige said, pretending to be disgruntled, but she'd given up and fallen in love, just like the rest of the women. And she was equally as happy about it.

"What?" Anna batted her eyes, going for confused innocence.

"What?" Claudia mimicked in a saccharine voice, and then she snorted. "Who do you think you're talking to?" She used her pointing finger to indicate the circle of women.

The irrepressible joy that made an appearance at least five times a day now bubbled up in Anna's chest and popped out in the shape of a wide grin. "I was just thinking about how much I love the woods," she twirled her hand to indicate the surroundings, "and all the trees."

"Mm-hm." Hayden clucked her tongue. "Especially when you come home with half their leaves stuck in your messed-up sex hair."

"Ooh!" Paige thrust her hand in the air and sent the ghost-whisperer a long-distance high-five, while the other women burst into hoots and hollers.

Deciding silence was the safest route, Anna shook her head and hid her face behind her wine again.

"So," Kylie said, her wheedling tone making Anna cringe, "have you told Ian you love him yet?"

"Kylie!" Willyn swatted at the younger woman.

"I'm betting no." Paige stood in a single, swift motion and went to the cooler. "Anybody need another?"

Seven out of nine hands shot up.

Anna still had half a cup, so in lieu of another drink, she curled her fingers, indicating to Willyn she wanted a s'more. "No, I haven't." She said the words casually, halfway hoping Kylie would miss the answer entirely. But no such luck.

"Oh!" Kylie clasped her hands to her chest. "But you do, don't you? Don't you?"

"Kylie!" several voices said in unison, just before Paige handed the persistent inquisitor another bottle. To Anna's relief, the drink served as a diversion.

She knew there was no hiding her feelings for Ian, not from her closest friends, who all just happened to be intuitive witches as well. But for some reason, she just couldn't say the words out loud.

Yes, the past two weeks had been wonderful, more amazing than even she could have predicted, but despite her blossoming affections for Ian and the confidence he had in her abilities, Anna still couldn't shake the dark sense of dread that dogged her morning to night.

This time, these days she had with Ian, were precious to her, and not only because they were priceless moments of new love that no couple would ever have again. No matter how happy he made her, or how certain he was that Anna would succeed in her trial, the clock was ticking louder and louder, and tomorrows were never guaranteed.

The countdown was almost complete, and as Halloween loomed larger on the horizon, so too did a stormy black cloud in Anna's mind. An impending sense of doom, a reality she couldn't escape.

Her psychic ability may have been put on the backburner for the month of her challenge, but her instincts were more sensitive than ever. They warned her that All Hallow's Eve held unpredictable things in store for her and her friends.

Fate was keeping secrets it seemed, and the blind spot was what worried her most.

"At least the guys have accepted Ian." Hayden's statement brought Anna back around.

"Hmm? Oh, yes. Seeing him fight his way back from Vanir's control went a long way with them. It's as if having their fear come true has allowed them to move past the unknown to deal with it if it happens again." Anna lifted a shoulder. "Men."

Willyn stabbed a marshmallow onto a stick and held it over the fire. "I'm sure your spell doesn't hurt either. Ian hasn't had any more visions, right?"

"Nope. No dreams either." Thankfully, Anna thought. Especially since she and Ian shared a bed now, and their connection was more intense than ever. Neither of them missed the nightly trips to Vanir's ancient world.

Shauni lifted hesitant eyes to Anna. "Michael's even been teaching Ian how to throw. He's been practicing a lot, in fact. Sparring with Paige, throwing with Michael." She glanced at Willyn who pursed her lips and turned to Anna.

"I can sense the question you all want to ask." Anna chose to finish her wine after all. In one huge gulp. She held her empty cup out to Paige, the evening's self-appointed server. "And the answer is no. Ian is not going with us to the final battle."

Anna had explained her theory to them, her belief that Ronja had somehow activated Vanir's resurgence. "My spell may be working now, but I can't risk having him that close to her, and especially not on that night."

Anna swallowed and downed a huge gulp of the wine Paige had handed her, hoping she too would get buzzed and no longer feel the hole in her chest. The one left by all of her unanswered questions.

She'd signed up for the prophecy years ago, and therefore, the upcoming standoff against Bastraal and Ronja. But Ian hadn't.

Anna and the coven had accepted the risk, and she knew she might have to give her life in the end. But Ian had become her heart, and she wouldn't risk that. She wouldn't risk him.

"I think he should go." Viv spoke in a hushed tone, knowing Anna wouldn't want to hear those words. "He completes the third circle."

"What third circle?" Anna set down her cup. "We are the only circle, the only ones who have been called to stand and fight. In fact, maybe *none* of the men should go."

Again the shared glances, the tightened lips. Her coven had been talking about this and were only now bringing Anna into the discussion.

"It's no coincidence we all have cats." Claudia used her teacher's lecture-voice. "Nine witches. Nine cats."

"They see demons. They protect us." Anna wasn't buying it. She refused to acknowledge the logic, even as it was being laid at her feet.

"And nine men." Willyn summed up the argument, her features gentle, concerned, because she and the other women understood the hardship that accompanied each witch's trial. The confusion and uncertainty.

"You still can't know for sure what will happen." Claudia leaned forward, her face lit orange from beneath by the glowing fire. "Remember my trial. My deception. I had it wrong the whole time, but in the end, I did what I was meant to do."

"And maybe yours will take a turn," Hayden said. "But I think we all agree that you can't afford to break the circle. The final circle," she added. "Three circles of nine. You can't deny the magical numbers."

The weight of Anna's responsibility reappeared, pressing down on her shoulders, her chest. No, she couldn't deny the symmetry, and though she'd tried to ignore exactly what her friends were now forcing her to see, the notion of bringing Ian face to face with both Ronja and Bastraal literally sent chills down her spine.

"I'll consider it," she told her coven. Then she tried to steer the conversation back to a lighter place. "But I thought Paige had called a moratorium on all things serious or sad."

"Right you are." Willyn pointed at Anna and stood. "And just to make sure I do my part, I'm going to try some of that vodka." She whirled around as if searching for something. "As soon as I decide what to mix it with."

"I'll help," Lucia said, joining Willyn at the cooler to dig through the ice.

And since her chest still throbbed with worry, Anna tossed her wine out into the grass, determined to try something stronger. "Make me one of whatever you're having," she called to Willyn and Lucia.

Out of the blue, Kylie shook her head, snapped her jaws. "Our hum is making my teeth vibrate."

When The Nine were in close proximity, they created a subtle but permeating energy, known fondly as the hum.

"You're just buzzing, " Lucia said. "And not from us."

Kylie tilted her head, thought about it, and nodded. "That might be true."

"I changed my mind," Anna called. "Give me what Kylie's having."

"Apple? We also have raspberry and..." Willyn rummaged in the cooler, "peach!"

"I'll take peach."

"Incoming!" Testing her throwing arm, Willyn pivoted and pitched the bottle, but her aim went wide, out of Anna's reach.

Paige was there in plenty of time to make the catch. "Here you go." She handed the drink to Anna and then added earnestly, "You know we've always got your back."

Just then a noise stuck somewhere between a groan and hiccup drew their attention to Viv, who wiped a smear of chocolate from her chin and proceeded to let out a low, rolling belch. The act was so incongruent with the staid scientist that Anna cut loose a belly laugh.

"Oh," Viv said, holding her stomach, "alcohol and s'mores. We're all going to be sick as dogs tomorrow."

"Yep." Claudia clinked her plastic to Kylie's glass.

As if he knew they'd made mention of his kind, Skid released a mournful howl from the general direction of the house.

"Speaking of dogs..." Anna kicked up one side of her mouth. "Why aren't any of the animals here? I think they'd love a campfire in the woods."

"I was under the impression it was witches only, so I told them all to hang back." Shauni held out her hands. "And I didn't know how our little talk would go."

"Oh. Bring 'em on." Hayden was slurring, and between that, Viv's burp, and Kylie's vibrating teeth, Anna could see how the night was shaping up. And she was more than ready to follow them all to a nice, happy drunk.

"All right." Shauni stared through the woods, sending a telepathic invitation to the pets back at the mansion.

And it wasn't long before the sound of paws pummeling the ground at a gallop echoed through the trees. Skid made his debut with his tongue lolling out one side of a mouth turned up in what could only be called a dog-smile.

Soon the cats streamed in on smaller and much quieter feet. They made their way to the witches, each going to his or her favorite human.

As Ivy came over and settled next to Anna for a purr and snuggle, she sensed an easing of the tension she'd been carrying. She looked around at all the faces, the women she'd come to love, her sisters in magic.

Paige was right. They did have her back.

And she had Ian's. She sipped the peach and let out a sigh.

So everything would work out just fine.

~

Paige stared at the blender, one finger hanging hesitantly over the puree button. Telling herself she could handle it, she gave a push. And instantly felt like her head was inside a super-fast washing machine filled with hammers and revving chainsaws.

It took her three tries to hit a button, any other button, to turn off the machine from hell.

"Here, babe." Chris's hands were on her shoulders, steering her gently away from the blender and toward the kitchen door. "You wait out there on the couch. I'll make your smoothie and bring it to you." He inhaled, waited. Then, "But are you sure your stomach can handle it?"

"It will make me feel better." Was she whispering? She was whispering. But instead of raising her voice, she held up a hand to wave backward at him and shuffled her way out to the green velvet couch. Her current idea of nirvana.

But her little piece of heaven was already occupied. Kylie and Willyn had beaten her to it, both of them looking as hung over as she felt. The coven's campfire had turned into an absolute blast last night, so much so that the cats had all run for the cover of the mansion, and Skid ended up hiding behind a tree.

Still moving cautiously, Paige made it to a cushiony chair and sat. Neither she nor the other two spoke. And none of them moved.

Soon the sound of low male voices in collaboration flowed from inside the kitchen. Glasses clinked, the refrigerator door closed three times, and the sink faucet ran for a minute straight. *What are they doing in there?*

Keeping her eyes closed, she began to drift off but woke again when Chris started poking her shoulder. "Drink this." He handed her a tall glass of reddish-orange liquid and set two pills and some water on the table next to her chair.

"That's not my smoothie," she croaked.

"No, but this is what we all decided on. Similar concoctions are being delivered to those still in bed, in addition to you three." He gently chucked her under the chin. "So do as the doctors order."

With a limp salute, she began drinking her medicine. Tasted sort of like tomato, so not too bad.

Over the next half-hour, the men came and went quietly, taking dirty dishes, bringing pillows and blankets, and shushing Skid at one point, but not before his bark sent an ice pick straight through Paige's brain.

Eventually all nine women were gathered in the grand hall, reclining on the sofa, loveseats, and various chairs. Two movies later—romantic comedy followed by horror—the witches were beginning to stir, though their movements were still creaky and trembling. Definitely zombie-esque.

And just in the nick of time, since Claire, Joe, and Joseph entered from the foyer, along with Mrs. and Mr. Attinger. The united front brought all of the women to attention.

Because clearly, something was up.

Chris hurried across the room to greet the group and had a subdued conversation with Joseph. Then he cast a glance back at Paige, one he apparently thought was covert.

But actually set every one of her nerves on edge.

Whatever hush-hush mission was going down, Chris had a

hand in it.

"Chris?" She sat up, pushing the pillow from her lap. Anna was standing as well, the other women all perking up with interest.

Claire and Mrs. Attinger took the lead, and Paige knew whatever they had up their sleeves was as good as done. Rarely was either of the older women defeated when they made up their mind on a particular subject. So both of them at once? Forget about it.

"Girls," Mrs. Attinger said, eyeing them all in their state of dishevelment, the one word laced with both censure and humor.

Claire touched the silver-haired woman on the shoulder as if reminding her of their purpose. Mrs. Attinger looked aside and nodded. "So here it is," she said, her bearing rigid as the three men moved up to flank her and Claire.

"We've all been here since you were a baby, Anna. We've lived and loved with you and your family," she gestured, "then the girls." As she spanned the room, her blue eyes softened. "And the boys."

Paige had a moment to wonder how the men felt about being reduced to boys, but considering the endearment came from Mrs. A., she figured they probably loved it.

Then Claire took over. "And all this time, we've lived with knowledge of the prophecy. We've always done our best to support you in any way we could."

Anna's face morphed into dismay. She went to Claire, took her hand and then one of Mrs. Attinger's. "Of course you have. I've always appreciated you. If I've somehow made you feel—"

"No, sweetie." Claire brushed a hand down Anna's loose brown hair. "That's not what we're saying."

"We're just laying the groundwork." When Mr. Attinger spoke, all eyes landed on the usually quiet and private man. "So you won't refuse our request."

"Request?" Quinn stepped forward from where he'd been standing at the foot of the staircase.

"We all know what's coming up in a couple of nights." Joe stood next to Claire with Joseph on his opposite side. "And we've been part of this too long to just sit by and let you all go take care of it by yourselves."

"We want to help," Joseph summed up for his father.

"Surely you're not suggesting you go out there with us." Anna crossed her arms, ready to argue for the sake of those she loved.

"No, but we want to do something." Mrs. Attinger slid a look to Claire. "And we have an idea."

Claire let a sly smile sneak out, her brown eyes twinkling. "We haven't spent all this time around magic without picking up a trick or two."

Anna had leaned in to listen, but Chris chose that moment to speak up. "On that note, I also thought we could use some additional help, maybe a new perspective."

At first he'd addressed Anna, but now his eyes were fixed on Paige. "I invited someone who might be able to offer one." He stepped forward. "But even if he can't, he still needed to come."

The first bit of apprehension began to crawl up the back of Paige's neck. Then her heart plummeted to her stomach when a tall man with dark blonde hair walked slowly into the room.

"There's no more time, Paige." Chris was resolved. She could see it in his stance, the set of his firm jaw. "And you both deserve to see each other." His tone gentled. "Before Halloween."

Paige wasn't often speechless but found she couldn't move or utter a sound. She didn't need an introduction, because she recognized her own body type in the long legs and lean torso, her own easy stride as the stranger moved closer. The nose, the facial shape.

Paige's eyes and white-blonde hair she'd inherited from her mother. But so many other features had come from the man standing before her.

"Paige," he said, voice rough with emotion.

"Dad." She swallowed. Waited. She tried to breathe.

"Don't be upset with Chris. I would have found my way out here eventually."

"And we made sure he knew he was welcome," Mrs. Attinger interjected. "So if you're going to be angry—"

"I'm not." Paige surprised herself, but her quick reply was the truth. She'd had mixed feelings where her absentee father was concerned, even after discovering he'd left her in an attempt to protect her. But over time, she'd come to accept that he did in fact love her.

And contrary to what she'd believed growing up, he had never forgotten her.

As she stared into his sad yet hopeful eyes, any lingering doubts or resentment vanished. Still, she didn't move an inch, rooted to the floor by indecision, uncertainty over what to do next.

She hadn't seen him in person for so, so long. And she wasn't a little girl anymore, one who would run freely toward him, greeting him with a smile and a hug.

"I know we've talked about Scarlett," her father said, inching closer, "and I'm glad you're safe now, that you've accomplished the goal as predicted. But I also know taking a life isn't easy."

Paige nodded sluggishly. Murder was never easy, even when the act could honestly be deemed justice.

"But you and Chris have both told me about the Daevo. And he's still out there, still a threat." Her father's tone cemented into one she knew well, one that rang with retribution. "He might not have been the one to take your mother's life, but he killed plenty of other people while helping the witch in her hunt for you."

He raised the black case he carried, held it his hands. "I've traveled a lot of places, and I've learned plenty of useful methods when it comes to dealing with the dark side."

Paige felt the eyes on her—Chris's, Anna's, those of her friends—all watching to see how she would respond.

"It's your call, but I'm here, offering what I can," her father said. "You just tell me what to do, and if it's to go to hell, well...I've already been there." His strong face flashed with pain. "Every day that I was apart from you."

Paige would swear her chest caved inward, then expanded again as pure light spread throughout.

"But I hope you'll let me stay. I want to be there for you, Paige, for all the times I couldn't before." He scowled in a way that was so like her. "And I'd really like to help your coven kick the Daevo's ass."

Now, at last, she knew what to do.

Only Paige would get sentimental over a reference to ass-kicking, but the vengeful comment sent her flying into her father's arms. She heard and felt his sharp intake of breath, then he locked her in an embrace and lifted her off the floor.

He set her back down but kept her close, his voice shaking when he said, "I love you so much, princess. And I've missed the hell out of you."

Paige didn't let go. She couldn't, not yet. Sniffing against her burgeoning tears, she pressed the side of her head to his chest.

Chris stood in her line of sight, smiling. So she smiled back at him and mouthed, "Thank you."

Then she closed her eyes and inhaled the scent of her father, one she suddenly remembered from long ago. From the times when her mother had been alive. When they'd been a family. "I missed the hell out of you too." And as she hugged him tighter, she whispered, "Daddy."

24

The following day, Ian was headed down one of the many corridors in the mansion, intent on a walk in the gardens. Anna was busy in her room meditating, as she did at least twice a day. She'd increased the practice during her time of trial but hadn't elaborated on what she was hoping to see or clarify.

But he gave her the private time, and gladly. He was in favor of anything that might lessen her stress or reduce the constant strain she was trying to hide from him.

So he'd get outside, cleanse his own mind for a while. He was almost to the doors that opened onto the back patio when Quinn stepped out from a side room.

"Ian," he said, his features stern, "if you've got a minute, I need to talk to you."

"Sure. I've got nothing pressing." Ian started toward the room from which Anna's brother had emerged, but Quinn only held up a hand.

"Not here." He said nothing more, easing past Ian to head back down the hall.

Sensing he was supposed to follow, Ian trailed along until they were back in the grand hall before curving around toward another passageway.

The one that led to the tower.

Ian didn't claim to be psychic, but he was good at reading people and sizing up situations. Still, he wondered why Quinn—so somber and serious—was taking him to the place where his and Anna's parents had died.

Quinn tugged on the heavy wooden door with Ian right behind him. The stone steps they traversed were balanced and smooth, though it was clear they'd been hand-hewn. The stairwell twisted up and around, tempting Ian to lean over the open edge and look down into the shadows.

At the top, there was a small landing and another door. Quinn went inside, crossed to the far window overlooking the gardens, and stood silently.

Since he seemed disinclined to divulge his reasons for the meeting, Ian used the time to look around. Neat and efficient though unadorned, the room was everything a workspace should be. And given the heavy cauldron, scattered crystals, and smell of sage, it was everything a magician's lair should be.

Ian picked up on other organic smells he didn't recognize, though a pile of red powder he sniffed did remind him of patchouli. And there, he saw, moving on, were fresh-cut herbs from Anna's greenroom.

Lying next to them was a white-handled boline, a knife designed for more practical uses than the ritualistic and often dull-edged athame. He'd picked up pieces of mystical trivia here and there. But how could he not, after becoming involved with a witch?

He paused, smiled, and shook his head. The reality of that no longer fazed him, and day-by-day he was growing to enjoy Anna's more mysterious side. Truth be told, he'd become quite a fan of her occasional nighttime jaunts to the balcony. Where, according to her, she called down the moon. While sky clad.

Which in Ian's world still meant naked.

So, no, he couldn't find fault with her witchy pastimes. They only added intrigue to a woman who already held him rapt and mesmerized, simply by being herself.

Still circling the room, he came across a pad of deep blue

velvet, covered by several richly-colored stones. Some were worn smooth, others jagged, but Ian could identify neither names nor purpose.

"It's clean now but it was a mess for years." Quinn spoke suddenly, so Ian stopped his perusal and put his hands in his pockets.

"For most of my life this place was locked up tight, because none of us wanted to deal with it." He finally turned to meet Ian's gaze. "And I'm not talking about the cleaning up."

Ian nodded to show he understood.

"Anna was older than I was, but our parents' death affected her...differently. For her, the loss was two-fold." Quinn leaned against the window now, folding his arms. "Not just a young girl who'd been orphaned, but also a prophesied witch. One who had to carry a terrible burden all by herself."

Ian studied the younger man. He'd never seen him so severe, such gravity in his voice. Apprehension began a slow stir in Ian's gut.

"Both of us lost a mother and a father that day, but Anna lost something else, something more. Their guidance." Quinn's jaw-clench was evident, even from across the room. "And with their deaths, she gained another obligation." He blew out a breath. "As if saving the world wasn't enough."

Pushing away from the window, Quinn eased to a table and ran his fingers over a large pink crystal. "That's what makes this all so wrong, so unfair. Anna is not only duty-bound to the prophecy, but also to our parents."

Ian puzzled over his strange behavior and was growing impatient with the obscure lead-in. "What's this about, Quinn? Why are you telling me all of this?"

"Because you need to understand that Anna has no choice."

Ian went rigid. "No choice about what?"

"If you're going with us tomorrow night, which I know you are determined to do—"

"I'm going." Ian heard the obstinacy in his own voice. "I won't let her go alone."

"Then you need to know what to expect." Quinn's features morphed from stern to hesitant, as if he too faced a difficult decision. "Anna will be angry with me for telling you, but she's carrying so much dread and worry into this battle. And she needs to have her mind clear, not clouded by any extra worries."

He faced Ian fully. "The battle is simply too important, so I intend to unload some of her anxiety. And you're going to help me."

Ian's confusion rolled over to frustration. "If you want my help, you're going to have to start making sense."

"What do you know about what will happen tomorrow, on Halloween?"

Ian raised a hand, dropped it. "The coven will face off against the Amara, Anna against Ronja, and then Anna must destroy Bastraal." How casually he spoke of such things, Ian noticed. But his concern was no longer for himself or what the mystical world had in store for him.

He cared more—especially after this cryptic conversation— about what the supernatural forces wanted from Anna.

"Anna has to kill Bastraal," Quinn said bluntly.

"Good. Fine." Ian scoffed. "He *is* a demon."

Quinn's featured settled into a blank, emotionless mask. His tone was just as flat. "But she can't kill him until he enters a human body."

Shock assaulted Ian, flooding through him with sharp, electric jabs. His mind raced, trying to comprehend Quinn's words, and hoping he'd misunderstood. Because as far as he could tell, they meant only one thing.

Ian sucked in a shallow breath, then another. He hadn't realized he'd been holding it until his lungs had begun to sting. "No," he expelled. "No. She would never do that."

"She doesn't have a choice."

"There must be another way."

"She's been looking, we all have, but there is no alternative!" Quinn's angry voice filled the room. "See that, the look on your face?" He thrust a finger at Ian. "That's exactly why I brought you up here. You can't judge her, Ian. None of us can."

"I don't...judge her, but she must be overlooking something."

"She isn't. The directive was clear."

"But maybe if—"

"There's no other option." Quinn gritted his teeth. "We only have one more day, Ian. Nothing is going to change between now and then, no matter how badly we all want it to. I know this is a shock, but you have to get it right in your mind and accept what's going to happen. Just like the rest of us. Anna has to do this horrific thing to save thousands of other innocent lives."

Quinn's shoulders sagged, defeat scrawled across his face. "The least we can do is support her. You especially."

Ian would support her, all right. He would do so by protecting her. He wasn't a witch and had little knowledge compared to Quinn, Anna—hell, next to any of the others—but he wouldn't let her suffer this fate. He knew her, heart and mind, and the atrocity of such an act would alter her forever.

She was too beautiful, too pure, for him to allow that.

"You have to be there for her, Ian. If you love her..."

Ian startled, glanced to Quinn.

"If you love her," he said deliberately, "then you have to tell her you understand. Make her believe that nothing she does tomorrow night will change how you feel about her. She needs you. In some ways, she needs you more than anyone else."

"I do understand," Ian whispered. But he didn't. Not at all. Still dumbfounded, he staggered to a table and leaned against the edge. "Why didn't she tell me?"

Quinn glowered and stalked to a set of wooden shelves. "Remember how you were, Ian? Think back to the things you've said to her, the accusations you threw." He picked up an oval object with a golden rim and tossed it to Ian.

"Now look, and tell me what you see."

The antique mirror was worn, black spotting at the edges that begged to be re-silvered. But as he stared at himself, he knew that's not what Quinn meant. His reflection could only be described as harsh, eyes set and hard, mouth in a tight line. Yeah, he saw it. Judgment, recrimination, reproach.

"I'm angry for her, Quinn." He looked up. "Not at her."

"Doesn't matter. She'll see it in you, and it will bleed her dry. You've got to take a step back, put her needs before your own." Quinn strode over, stood next to Ian. "And you've got to *sell it*."

Already struggling to hammer down his need to fix the situation, to angle for a reprieve, Ian rolled his shoulders as tension crawled up his back and into his neck. "I hear you, Quinn." He stood, walked toward the door. "I hear you."

~

Ian took that walk in the garden. He mulled, he brooded, losing himself within the endless green hedges. Headed for the back boundary, he found a place and stood, staring into the forest until the dim light of the gloaming encroached.

Anna would be worried, he was sure, but he'd taken Quinn's suggestion to heart and was doing his best to get his mind right. By the time darkness fell, he'd determined to skip dinner, find Anna wherever she was, tell her that he knew, and that he supported her.

But the resolve he'd managed to find was fragile and already beginning to crumble. He felt the acceptance slipping away with every step, so when he got to her door, he didn't bother to knock, just swung inside and scanned the sitting area. She wasn't there.

But his abrupt entry had garnered her attention, bringing

her hurriedly from the adjoining bedroom. "Ian?" she asked, her brow marred by worry.

"You can't do it." The mandate escaped before he could gather a better, more appropriate introduction.

"What are you talking about?"

In three steps he was with her and took her by the shoulders. "Tell me you aren't going to kill a man tomorrow night."

Her mouth fell slack, eyes shadowed over with fear. She shook so violently, his hands did as well. "How did you find out?"

"It doesn't matter. I'm just glad *someone* told me." Hearing the censure in his tone, Ian readjusted. "But I don't care about that, Anna. Frankly, I don't blame you for not doing it yourself."

Her voice was strained. "It's not what you think."

"It's exactly what I think, and it's not right. You shouldn't be put in this position. No one," he slid his hands down to cup her elbows, still holding firm, "*no one* can force you to go through with it. Not Fate, not magic."

"You don't get it, Ian. I'm not being controlled. I have the option to refuse." Misery coated her voice, filled her stare. "But what will happen if I do? Can you really expect me to save one life, yet sentence hundreds of thousands more to death? And not just death, Ian, but savage torture, depravity at the hands of demons. Every hideous creature you can imagine, and countless others you can't. Your mind can't comprehend the evil that will occur if Bastraal rises to victory. He'll make the bloodiest rulers in all of history seem tame by comparison."

"But that's not your doing."

"Isn't it? If I don't finish him while I have the chance, it will be!"

"You can't do it, Anna. It's still murder."

She tried to pull away. "And that disgusts you."

"No." Ian released her arms, but only to grasp her face between his hands. "It *terrifies* me." He pressed his lips to hers, felt the tremor when they met. "Because I know it will destroy you."

She shook her head, tried to block the sob that burst from her chest. "There's no alternative. Nothing to be done. Halloween is the only night Bastraal can enter his chosen vessel. The only chance I'll have to stop him. He'll take over the man he wants to claim, giving me my one and only opportunity to end him.

"The dagger must pierce his human heart," she hissed out a breath, "once the possession is complete. Some poor guy who's probably already been brutalized by monsters and suffered unimaginable atrocities. And after all that, *I* will hurt him. I will kill an innocent man."

Ian put his forehead to hers. "Please stop." He wrapped her in his arms, tried to quell the riotous tremors still racking her frame.

"I hate it!" She made a low sound in her throat, agony in need of release. "And no amount of good that results from his death will ever remove the stain of what I did." Falling forward, Anna crumpled against him.

Ian felt out of control, panicked. "No. You can't do it. I won't let you."

Her voice was a warm breath on his neck. "You would let all those people suffer and die? Your parents? Little children?"

Ian clenched his eyes shut, at last coming to grips with what Anna had been dealing with. Her moments of wandering thoughts, when she'd seemed to be somewhere else, they all made sense now. He finally knew why she'd sometimes seemed so distant, so sad.

An image popped into his mind's eye, from the day they'd decorated the house. Her sudden crying jag hadn't been only for herself. She'd been tormented by the barbaric task set before her. "Oh, Anna. How long have you known?"

Her words were muffled. "Since the beginning of my trial. Almost a month."

Ian had been so concerned about the danger she would face when confronting the Amara. Now he was equally fearful that if she survived, if she did what she was supposed to do and triumphed...

"I've never cursed or regretted my destiny," she spoke softly, her head still resting on his shoulder, "but this last month, I've had moments, horrible, dark moments when I've resented my gift. When I've damned myself for having magic."

He held her away from him, so she would have to look at him. "No. Don't do that. You may be obligated to perform an act you despise, but don't confuse the vagaries of Fate with who you really are."

Lifting his hand, he stroked her cheek with the back of his finger. "You would never create pain or give in to the darkness. Not by choice. Your magic is a reflection of you, Anna." He cradled her cheek. "That's why it's so beautiful, so pure. And nothing you do will ever change that."

"How can I do it? How can I look into his eyes, a man who's done nothing wrong, and stab him to death?"

Anna rarely revealed weakness, but Ian could see the anguish within her. The pain and guilt. She'd been enduring her own kind of torture, all this time. And his ignorance gutted him. "I don't know, but whatever happens, I'll be there with you. I'll be there *for* you."

Damn it. Quinn was right. I've been such an ass. But he would make up for it. He would erase everything he'd said before.

Tears ran freely down her face, so Ian wiped them dry. "You told me once that magic required balance, and from where I'm standing, you've done nothing but good. You've been true to your craft."

He led her back toward the other room. "You deserve to have a good life in return. Years, you've spent *years* serving the prophecy, so I know it will all make sense when it's done. You deserve nothing less. Magic fucking *owes* you, Anna. That's all there is to it."

Fingers locked in his, Anna gripped tightly, refusing to sever their connection. "I just don't know anymore."

"Well then, maybe that's why I'm here." He stopped beside her grand bed, brushed her hair away from her lovely face. "I can see your conviction is being tested. So I'll be the one to have faith for a while. But not in magic."

He put a hand around her neck, held her gently. "Because I believe in you." He lowered slowly, slanting his mouth across hers.

She kissed him back tentatively, but then lowered her face. "What will happen to me afterward? To us?"

"Don't think about it. Time is short, but we have tonight." When her eyes lifted, he saw relief, and even more satisfying, he saw trust. "Let me love you, Anna. And know that whatever happens, I will keep loving you.

"Because no force from earth, heaven, or hell can stop me."

"Ian." It was her turn to capture his face. "I love you, so much."

In answer, he took her mouth and kissed her deeply. He drew back, drank her in. Anna, with the pretty blue eyes.

Through the wide windows, Ian could see a fat white moon peeking over the tree line. He touched Anna's chin. "Wait." Then he went to the writing desk where she'd introduced him to her hidden life only weeks ago. He lit the three tapered red candles nestled in crystal holders. Then he turned off the lamp.

"What are you—"

He held up a finger, paused. "Wait." Continuing on, he entered the sitting area and turned off the overhead lights. Mission accomplished, he returned to her, the woman he loved.

The witch he would never leave.

"Moonlight and candlelight," he whispered as he eased up to her, hands going straight to the tie of her robe. He considered himself lucky to have caught her in the cobalt blue silk, the royal color that so befitted her station.

For she was regal, carrying both prestige and duty with grace.

She drew in a shaky breath. "You won't despise me?"

"Never." He stroked her chest, encircling her amulet. "You are the strongest person I've ever known. The most loyal." He parted the robe with his hands. "And by far, the most enchanting. So I want all of you, Anna."

He whispered a kiss across her cheek. "Will you share your magic with me?"

Because he had no choice but to touch her, Ian trailed his hands down her sides, cherishing the soft skin and subtle curves. He could see the steady rise of passion within her, was gratified when it overwhelmed all hints of fear and sorrow.

Her hands were at the hem of his shirt then, pulling it gently up over his chest and head. Tonight was a different tempo for them. Where the love they'd made in the forest had been heated, fraught with the jagged edges of need, tonight the energy between them shimmered softly.

The link their bodies forged was almost palpable, the air between them silken and warm.

Naked now, she slid onto the bed, turned the covers back— all the way down and off to the floor. Satin sheets gleamed, a streak of moonlight slicing across the deep blue, and then over her lithe, supple figure.

Ian divested himself of his pants and joined her. He could see the rapid pulse in her neck, feel the shiver run up her body. "Are you cold?" he asked, blanketing her with his own heat, providing shelter.

Whatever she needed.

"No. Not cold." She nipped him under the chin. "I carry your taste with me." She suckled his neck, pulling a groan from him. "And your scent, clean male skin."

Ian's stomach tightened, he hardened in a rush. "I smell

clean?"

"Mm-*hmm*," she murmured with enthusiasm.

"And that's sexy to you?"

She reared back, seared him with her eyes. "You have no idea."

Ian made a vow then and there to shower at least twice a day for the rest of his life.

Grasping behind his neck, she brought him down to her and nibbled his ear, then proceeded to do tormenting things with her tongue. When her hips arced up to meet his, he barely held himself back.

He desired her above all else. He wanted to take, needed to plunge.

"I'm going to need years to do all the things I plan on doing to you." Knowing she liked it, he ran the stubble of his jaw across her breasts, causing her nipples to pucker into even tighter peaks. "And then, when you're all relaxed and liquid," he cupped her ass, held her against him, "I'll do them all over again."

The lines of her body were taut beneath him, her flat belly tempting him, driving him to distraction. Inserting himself between her legs, Ian readied himself, but Anna gently propped him away with her hands in the center of his chest.

"Wait," she said, the devil in her eyes as she echoed his earlier command. "I want to see your face, look into your eyes when you feel it."

"Feel—" Ian began, but he was struck mute when a glorious sensation flowed into him, a deliciously tingling wave that surged from her palms and straight to his heart. Remembering her request, he kept his eyes open and on hers.

Until he couldn't wait another moment. "Anna," he breathed, speaking her name with reverence, both a plea and a prayer. She was sharing her magic with him, and it was magnificent. Letting her power run through him, Ian absorbed the amazing gift until everything inside of him was touched by her warmth, by her love.

Already joined by magic, Ian drove his hips forward to fill her, and reveled in her cry of pleasure.

~

Anna fought for breath, felt her pulse jump when Ian entered her. Each time was as magical as the last, but tonight they shared another level of intimacy. And the love they'd spoken of heightened her awareness, sensitized her skin.

Moving in sync, hard against soft, they touched, they sought, they treasured each other. Anna was overwhelmed by Ian, his scent, his taste, his texture. And he seemed to know every sweet spot she possessed.

He put his mouth just under her jawline and slid his hand between their grinding hips. "I can't give you magic," he said, his voice hoarse in her ear. "But I can give you this."

Anna threw her head back when the orgasm broke over her. Yes, he knew her body, her secret desires, and every single one of her weaknesses.

Yet still, he loved her.

His thrusts grew longer, touched her more deeply, until her blood burned from the inside out. "Ian," she said on a ragged breath, feeling the delicious tightness building again. "Stay with me."

And when he grasped her hips, buried his face in her hair, she burst with ecstasy. Just as she heard him swear to her, "Always."

25

Standing on her balcony, Anna watched as light appeared on the brightening horizon. She wondered how the breaking dawn could be so beautiful, so peaceful, on what would surely be the darkest day of her life.

The pristine light spread slowly, waking the ocean waters as it made its journey to her island. So she took advantage of the moment, drinking in the cool morning air and absorbing what energy she could from the great rising orb.

She continued to sun gaze until the warming rays filled her with serenity and a cleansing sense of renewal. Then she turned to go back inside, to Ian, and yet another source that had transformed her and made her feel reborn. His unconditional love.

Pausing inside the bedroom doors, she took a moment to appreciate his sleeping form. He lay sprawled on his back, arms slack by his sides, and his legs... *Hmm, that doesn't look comfortable.*

Nearing the bed, she found the reason for his awkward position and laughed softly. Once Anna had cast her spell and bound Vanir from resurfacing, Ivy had flipped a switch. Her cat had become Ian's staunchest supporter, and even now was curled up to enjoy the warmth of his body.

Flooded with tenderness for both man and feline, Anna rounded the bed and perched next to her lover. She stroked the blonde hair away from his face, watching as he slowly began to wake. Then his eyes sharpened and fixed on her, a smile spreading over his face.

"Good morning," she said.

Ian rubbed his face. "What time is it?"

"Just after dawn." She traced a finger up the line of his arm and then down over his chest. "We have a lot to do today, preparations to make, but I wanted to have some time alone with you first."

The granite-blue of his eyes grew stormy as he recalled the date. "Today is Halloween."

Anna nodded. "It is," she sighed. "And because of you, I'll go to my fate better prepared and far more accepting."

He tried to sit up but quickly adjusted when he noticed Ivy stretching her feet across his shin. "I wish I could keep you from it all," he said, lying back down. "But since I can't, I will give you my support. And no matter what," he gazed at her adoringly, "you will keep all of my heart."

"I know." She feathered a finger over his mouth. "That's why I'm ready for whatever comes."

"But I will be going with you."

A thin needle of fear pierced Anna's chest. "Is there no way I can change your mind? I don't want to be responsible for putting you in danger."

"You aren't. You don't control all the strings, and I understand your fears." He reached up, pulled her down for a kiss. "But I have the same concerns about you. How can I let you walk into the most important, most dangerous night of your life, without me?"

"This is my job, my duty. I've always known I would face this battle." Her lips tingled, urging her to feel his mouth on hers again. Once again, before the night came crashing in. "Ian, I love you so much. Please stay here where you'll be safe."

"Only if you do."

"You ask the impossible."

"Then you understand how I feel. We have to stay together, Anna. Don't you believe I'm meant to be by your side?" He gripped her hand. "By the way, I've been let in on the three-circle theory, so that clinches it. There is *no way* I'm staying behind tonight."

Anna's throat seemed to make a noise of it's own accord, one of reluctance and defeat. "You'll carry a weapon?" she asked in a small voice.

"I'll carry a damned arsenal. Anything to protect you." He sat up fully, carefully extricating his legs from beneath Ivy. He cupped Anna's face. "I don't fear anything anymore, except the idea of losing you."

Touched more than she could adequately convey with words, Anna ran her fingers through his hair, just as the sun climbed higher, burnishing him with golden rays. "You won't lose me."

She stood, took a step away from the bed, and dropped her robe.

"Anna," Ian's stare grew heated, "why don't you put the cat out?"

~

Breakfast was a subdued event, with hushed conversations and little laughter to fill the kitchen. Anna could sense the mixed emotions of her friends—eagerness to be done, concern for the safety of all, and an unquenchable thirst for final vengeance on the Amara.

But underneath, another sentiment flowed—the ever-present dread of the looming sacrifice and how it would ultimately affect her.

After catching several worried glances, Anna set down her coffee and announced, "If you're all going to stare at me all day, it will only make me nervous. So please, just be yourselves. I need the normalcy, now more than ever."

A few nods and increased conversation told her the little guilt trip had worked to get them all back on track. Just as she'd known it would.

Despite the jangling nerves and anxious sighs, everyone ate heartily, digging into Mrs. Attinger's delicious country breakfast. They did the same again at lunch. The witches and the men who loved them would be trekking through the woods and into ferocious combat by night's end and would need every last ounce of reserve energy. So no one skimped on the meals.

By late afternoon, everyone was dressed comfortably, weapons were stacked in the foyer, and Anna was returning from the tower with a brown canvas bag.

Paige flicked shrewd eyes at her. "Are those the—" She choked off the words and glanced to Ian.

"Yes. And he knows what they are," Anna replied, flinching when she heard the clank of chain on metal. Inside the bag were charmed bindings, specifically created and spelled to hold down a demon. Rather, just a man, but one imbued with the soul and strength of a very powerful demon master.

She had worked tirelessly with Quinn and Ethan to ensure the bindings would hold. They'd also molded and poured their own stakes, made of steel and infused with white magic to be both sharp enough and resistant enough to pierce the flat black stone on which the victim would be restrained.

Paige's father had also come up with a few ideas, proving Paige came by her war planning abilities naturally. But tonight he would be taking on another, more docile role. That of Tadd's babysitter. Matthew would stay behind at the mansion to watch over Willyn's son.

And Skid would remain to watch over both man and child.

The Attingers were there now as well, assisting in whatever way they could, along with Claire, Joe, Joseph, and even Sylvie. The former Amara member insisted they let her help, claiming she still had debts to pay, and smudges to cleanse from her spirit.

When the sun began to sink in the west, Claire, Mrs. Attinger, and the others prepared to leave for the mainland. The two women had a plan to enact, and would be sending out their own small army to get it done.

But as they readied to leave, Anna went to the women and embraced them as one. As she hugged them, she reached behind to take the hands of Joe and Mr. Attinger. "I owe you all so much," she whispered. "I owe you everything."

She saw Joseph and Quinn share a look before they came over and wrapped their arms around them all, even tugging in the older men for one group hug. A family hug.

"Now," Claire said, patting Anna's shoulder, "we will see you as soon as it's done." Her cheery voice and confidence were much-needed balms for Anna's disquiet.

"Yes," Anna said, swallowing the hint of grief. She would see them tomorrow. She *would.*

Mrs. Attinger tugged on Anna's long ponytail. "And you, my sweetheart, will have the first truly relaxed day of your life. You will start anew, and you will have earned every second of happiness you can reap from then on." She stomped her foot.

"I will," Anna said with a laugh. "I promise." But inside she could only pray she spoke the truth. So she placed one last kiss on each cheek of the women who'd raised her. Then she let them go, waved goodbye, and facing her coven once again, she prepared to do murder.

"I'll be back," Dare said, having volunteered to ride along and then return with the boat. There were two vessels used as transportation between the island and the mainland, but both would be needed to carry the large group all at the same time.

Chris was coming down the stairs with four backpacks in his arms, prompting Paige to call out, "All packed?"

"Yeah. I think this will do." He carried the full packs with ease. "What about the crates?"

"All filled up and waiting outside."

"We need to get the carriers too," Willyn said. "Just to be safe."

"Wait a second." Nick paused with a bottle of water midway to his mouth. "You mean cat carriers? They're going with us?"

"Of course they are," Viv told her boyfriend. "This is the battle of all battles, the end of the whole war. And the cats are not only our familiars, but also our defenders."

"I thought that's what we were for." Nick stepped to Viv, put his hand on her back, a light kiss on her lips.

"You are as well," Hayden said with a laugh. Then she rolled her eyes. "Goddess save us from fragile male egos."

"Is that what we have?" Trevor asked, creeping up behind his girlfriend to sink his fingers into her sides, tickling her until she begged for mercy.

Once he'd let Hayden catch her breath again, he held up both hands in surrender. "Whatever the sanctified witches request." He frowned. "But I call shotgun."

"What?" Nick asked, after finally taking the sip of water. "Shotgun where?"

The blonde cop cocked a brow. "In whichever vehicle that's not hauling nine carriers of wailing cats."

Hayden punched him lightly in the shoulder, holding back though he was twice her size. She lifted her nose and said haughtily, "Our cats do not *wail*."

"That's right." Paige strolled in with an array of knives in her hands, as if she were having trouble making up her mind. "But you're going to love the sound they make when they're sinking fangs into a demon's ass."

Trevor nodded, crossed his bulky arms. "Now that I'd like to hear."

Grateful for the humor and the mild relief it gave, Anna turned around and sought out Ian. He was standing in a corner with Michael, loading up his belt with throwing knives on one side and a mean-looking, curved dagger on the other. And was that a gun holster at the small of his back?

Anna shook her head. Well, he'd said he would carry an arsenal, so she couldn't fault the man for not keeping his word.

At last he was ready, and with serious eyes he crossed the grand hall to Anna. "How do you feel?" he asked, rubbing her arm.

"Like a woman in love," she answered truthfully. After all, that was what mattered most, and the wondrous sensation was what she'd carry with her, what she would hold close when she faced the worst, most horrifying moment.

Ian's love was her new talisman and one that would ride just beneath her amulet, inside her heart.

Ian pulled her into his arms, and there she happily stayed for a long, sweet moment. Until she heard Dare returning through the front doors.

From then on, they all moved quietly and efficiently, loading weapons, cats, and any other necessities onto the island truck. While Quinn drove the vehicle around, the others cut through the forest on foot. Once at the docks, they performed the loading procedure again, only this time everyone climbed on board afterward.

The drive through Savannah went smoothly and without distraction, but Anna found herself both thrilled and disheartened by the homes and businesses decked out in Halloween decor. Jack-o'-lanterns glowed a warm yet menacing orange, some smiling, some leering with wicked intent.

As they headed west out of the city proper, fewer and fewer residences dotted the roadside, until soon there were no more houses. Only the road before them surrounded by the deep, impenetrable darkness of the forest.

The vehicles slowed, veering onto a desolate dirt road before they came to a halt. Anna climbed out and, without a word between them, she and the other witches lined up to stare into the eerie autumn woods.

"This is it," Kylie said. She reached out and took the hands of Viv and Claudia who stood beside her. They continued the linkage to Hayden and Willyn, then those two with Lucia and Shauni. Lastly, they went on to connect with Anna and Paige.

The headlights behind the women cast their shadows across the tall trees. And even against the towering pines and hardwoods, the Savannah Coven, united in magic and sisterhood, appeared as giants.

Anna was the first to sever the link by dropping Shauni's hand. Then she turned to the raven-haired woman and stared into her emerald eyes. "First and last," she said with meaning. "Are we ready for this?"

Shauni's smile could have cut glass. "Abso-fuckin-lutely."

The profanity from the coven's pacifist gave Anna her final boost, and after checking again to make sure the ancient dagger was securely attached to her belt, she returned to the cars to begin unloading carriers.

When Paige released the lock on Tiger Lily's cage, she announced in a deep and accented voice, "Release the Kraken!" pulling mischievous grins from Lucia and Kylie. Soon all nine cats were milling around the forest floor, stopping to dig the occasional hole in the feline version of you-better-go-while-you-can.

Then they were ready, and the mood grew somber. For safety's sake, they used flashlights to see their way. Anna looked up, tracking the white orb that hovered far above, satisfied that once they reached the clear-cut area of the stone yard, the bright, watchful moon would provide all the light required.

Silently the group progressed, listening for any sign of approaching threat. The cats moved with even more stealth, weaving around tree trunks, darting back and forth, but never straying too far from the perimeter around the humans.

The felines were the exterior wall of defense and formed an outer circle, with the men serving as the next layer, shielding the women in the middle. Protecting the coven was paramount, and for the first time ever the witches would be the ones to strike last, reserving their stores of power for the battle royale.

Footsteps crunched on fallen leaves as they traversed the stretch that would lead them to the old house with the cherry-red door. The one built long ago by the Hidden Creek Congregation, a secret society headed up by a black-hearted preacher. He'd also been the man who'd tracked down Willyn's ancestor and sentenced her to death for the crime of witchcraft.

For centuries Bastraal had manipulated people, other supernatural creatures, anyone or anything that would help him achieve his goal: everlasting life within a corporal body. One stolen from an innocent male victim, but what did such trivialities mean to a beast like Bastraal?

"What are those?" Nick halted, shone his light up into the trees. The pale white illumination revealed strange figures, made of sticks and hanging by twine. He shifted the flashlight to reveal tree after tree with the unsettling creations hanging haphazardly.

Even for a lifelong witch like Anna, the scene was disturbing—a midnight-blue sky seen only through the semi-bare branches above, and the occasional patch of electric light, making the woods beyond the beams that much darker.

"Scare tactics," Quinn finally said. "I recognize most of the symbols, and some of them don't even belong together."

Kylie gave her boyfriend a grin filled with pride. "That Ronja." She winked at Quinn. "She forgets with whom she messes. And that we have an expert on occult linguistics in our ranks."

Ethan edged up to study the unnerving shapes. "Yeah, well, I've seen similar things in other parts of the world, but none ever creeped me out like these do."

A twig snapped somewhere deeper in the darkness, and every witch, every man, froze where they stood, except for the flashlights that swerved to aim in the direction of the sound.

"Think it was just an animal?" Claudia whispered.

"No." Shauni shook her head, her face eerily shadowed by Michael's beam. "I'm tuned in to all the forest creatures."

Anna remained immobile, holding her breath, listening, searching as far as she could see.

Up ahead, a cat hissed and growled. So she inched her hand over to the dagger at her hip. Not the silver with onyx stones, the one created for the specific use of destroying demons, but the other one, plain and unadorned. But still imbued with coven magic.

She would use the weapons she carried before tapping into her innate power, because she would need to save that for Ronja and Bastraal. The two greatest opponents she would ever face.

Snowball had been the one to sound the first alert, but in seconds her snarling voice was joined by two, then three, until all nine cats were giving the alarm. Anna's hackles rose as the air reverberated with the sound, the angry cries that warned of danger.

Her skin chilled, ran with bumps, and her heart began pumping pure adrenaline.

Suddenly there was a rush of movement as many bodies sprang into action. What sounded like an army of giant feet trampling across the ground. And they seemed to be moving fast.

The cats formed a barrier. The men pulled their weapons. And within their circles, the witches prepared.

When vicious war cries and animalistic roars blasted from the dark, Viv drew both swords from the scabbards on her back.

"Jesus," Cole said, clutching a long knife in one hand and a pistol in the other.

Then from her position on point, Paige turned around and

looked to her friends. She firmed her mouth, raised a dagger, and growled, "Here they come."

26

Nothing could have prepared Ian for what he saw bearing down on them now. A legion of creatures utterly foreign in shape and size, with varying body structures and manners of movement. Freakishly huge beasts with brown skin were wearing tattered clothing and carrying equally-large weapons—maces, clubs, swords.

The sight of the massive instruments drove a solid rod of terror down the length of Ian's spine.

But those creatures were slow, unlike those that darted through the air, with their serpentine bodies and gaping mouths of teeth, teeth, and more teeth. Others slunk on the ground, hyena-shaped and with no apparent outer flesh, only ropy brown sinews.

"Be ready!" Quinn yelled next to him, breaking Ian from his horrified trance. He couldn't count or categorize the many demons he saw approaching. And though he'd been warned—even been *shown* Anna's drawings—he couldn't wrap his brain around the existence of the horde now closing in on them.

One of the cats, the white one in front, launched at the first monster to reach their group. With snowy paws straight out and claws extended, she flew at the demon's face. But instead of swinging in defense, the creature simply covered its head and screamed, sidestepping and avoiding all contact.

And now Ian began to understand the cats' usefulness. Demons were scared shitless of the pretty kitties.

The men, however, didn't seem to have the same intimidation factor.

Ignoring Chris and Ian, the giant hefted its sword high, aiming to split Paige's head in two. The beast's long arms afforded it an extended reach, but Chris's speed swiftly brought a dagger to the fiend's gut. The demon exploded into ash just in time for Tiger Lily to fly through the cloud, a moment too late.

Grunts and groans rang out on all sides as the melee ensued, so Ian grabbed a throwing knife from his belt. With the men on the outside and no women in harm's way, it was the perfect time to test his aim.

A bellow that was decidedly human brought him around with a jerk to see a man running straight at him. A young, college-aged man. Ian stalled the arm that had been poised to throw, and for a moment he stared, reluctant to hurt a human. Even one possessed by a demon.

"Ian, your bag!" Ethan yelled as he brought a sword up to fend off a flying creature, channeling blue down the blade to send the beast to an ashy grave.

Remembering the special bag of enchanted herbs, Ian pulled the burlap on the end of a small retracting cord attached to his belt and slammed it into his attacker's face. The young man collapsed to the ground, just as a snakelike demon slithered from the unconscious body.

So Ian nailed it with the knife he still held, and experienced the rush of his first demon kill.

"Ian!" Anna yelled from somewhere in the center of the chaos. He whirled, looking for the threat, and came face to face with one of the hulking warrior-caste.

The brute was swinging a mace so quickly overhead that the spiked ball whistled through the air, but when Ian faced it the creature only stared him down and let loose a mighty roar— until a sword pierced the hulking beast from the back, to run him through and emerge from his chest.

The mace soared through the air to embed its wicked spikes into the bark of a nearby pine. And through the gray plume that now surrounded him, Ian nodded his thanks to Dare.

Then he returned the favor by pulling another knife and hurling it into the face of a leech intent on biting Dare from behind. Some of Anna's drawings and lessons were coming back to him, and he recalled the coven's name for the ropy creatures with three sharp teeth. Leeches. Ugh. Aptly named.

Gaining confidence, Ian turned in search of the next available target but was surprised to see a number of the demons scurrying away, retreating into the trees. Instead of taking time to question their intent, he immediately scoured the area for Anna.

Ash filled the air, catching the cross-beams of flashlights that had been tossed on the ground, and the previously-structured assemblage seemed to have shifted somewhat during the brief confrontation. Ian couldn't pinpoint her.

"Let me light it up." Quinn's voice.

"No!" And there was Anna. "They're leaving. Don't waste an ounce of your magic on creating light."

A chill wind chose that moment to rustle through the forest, helping to dissipate the dust. As soon as Ian laid eyes on Anna, he ran to her. "You're okay. You're okay." He realized the mantra was more for himself than her, but he'd just survived his first supernatural skirmish and figured he was due one delayed—and very minor—reaction.

"What was that supposed to be?" Nick asked. "They didn't give us much of a fight."

"No, they didn't," Michael chimed in. "It was half-hearted, as if for show."

Anna nodded, touched Ian's face. "Everything Ronja and Bastraal do is to mislead, especially now."

Ian remembered the guy who'd run at him. "What about these people?" He noticed two more passed out on the ground, a man and a woman.

"We leave them for now." Trevor was standing next to Hayden, his right forearm bleeding. But Willyn wasn't healing him, nor was she tending to the fallen.

"None of their injuries are life-threatening. Save your strength," Dare was saying to her as she glanced at the inert bodies. "They'll be fine until this is over."

Willyn didn't look happy with her pursed lips, but she nodded, clearly disheartened at leaving the people and not using her gift for its intended purpose.

"Maybe they were playing with us," Quinn reasoned, staring into the shadows where the demons had disappeared, "or maybe just tenderizing us for the next fight. But either way, we keep pushing on. We can't let anything throw us. Not creepy stick-figures, and not demons and their psychological warfare."

"Right." Ethan had his hand on Lucia's shoulder. "The beasts have brought a version of hell here tonight, and you can expect to see, hear, and feel strange things. But Quinn is right, we can't let ourselves over-analyze or become distracted by every move they make."

Anna looked to Ian and gave him a quick, soft smile. Then she hardened her features again and nodded. "You're both right." She started forward. "We can't let anything stop us."

~

Joseph gazed down into the tall mug of untouched beer. He too had a role to play, but as of yet, he couldn't get enthusiastic about it.

The soft touch on the back of his neck was Sylvie's personal calling card, so he leaned into her gentle fingers. "Hey, baby." She kissed him in front of his ear and leaned in. "You doin' okay?"

Tossing her a sidelong glance, he refocused on the beer,

running an agitated finger around the rim. "No. No, I'm not. This just doesn't feel right. I'm not doing enough."

"We're doing exactly as we were asked." She slid onto the stool beside him.

"I know, and this is important too, but my gut is churning. My chest feels empty." He angled to face her. "Being here, tonight..." He slammed his fist on the gleaming oak bar. "It's all wrong!"

Sylvie's soft brown eyes filled with sympathy. "You're scared. I know."

"We should be with them," he insisted.

"But Anna agreed with your mother and Mrs. Attinger. They want us here."

"They want me safe."

Sylvie touched his cheek. "So do I."

Taking her hand, he pressed it against his face before wrapping his fingers around hers. His voice was broken when he explained. "I was raised with Anna and Quinn. They had their magic and it never daunted me. They were just Quinn and Anna." He grinned. "Q and A, as I used to call them."

When Sylvie listened patiently, Joseph continued. "Over the years, we grew closer, and I made the choice to stick around, to have their backs during this time of prophecy, in any way I could. I was there for them, and they were there for me."

Joseph studied the scene around him, happy-go-lucky partiers out for a Halloween celebration. "So how am I supposed to stop now? How can I sit here," he snarled at the mug, "having a damned beer?

"I never thought that in the end, when it mattered most, I would just run and hide."

"You aren't hiding."

"But that's what it feels like. They're fighting for their lives tonight, Sylvie. They're fighting for *all* of our lives."

Her eyes were steady on his. "Yes. They are."

"And I should be with them. They're my family. It's not just a coven fulfilling its duty," he lightly thumped his chest, over his heart, "it's my brother and sister out there." The last was said softly, but he could hear his own driving pain.

Sylvie only stared at him, her brown-sugar eyes flickering, as if she were deep in thought. Finally, she kissed him, and sniffed at what he suspected might have been tears. She leaned back. "I love you, Joseph. Don't you ever forget it."

"I won't, but why—" He broke off when she waved over the bartender. Steve was the new manager, hired in the last several months once Nick had finally found the strength to replace Jen, the woman brutalized and murdered by the Amara during Viv's trial.

"What's up?" He leaned against the bar, towel in hand.

"You know what we had planned, right?" Sylvie darted her eyes between Steve and Joseph.

"Yeah." He gave a slow nod.

"Well..." She trailed off, waiting for Joseph to fill in the pause. The open-ended statement her way of asking if this is what he really wanted.

And hell yeah it was.

Joseph's misery dissolved as hope flared. "I'm going to need you to do it without us," he told Steve, a grin stealing across his lips. "You good with that?"

Steve reached across the bar and clasped Joseph's shoulder. "For you and your friends. For Nick?" He grew serious. "You got it."

"Thanks, man." Joseph slid off the stool. "I'll be in touch."

With that, he and Sylvie bolted for the front door, but as soon as they were out on the sidewalk, he grabbed her hand and tugged her to him. "In case I don't have time later, I want to tell you now." He kissed her greedily, and then, "I love you too." Still holding her hand, he started running. "And don't you ever forget it."

~

Ian climbed over the fence of rough posts and followed Quinn, who was now in the lead. Many of the hardwoods were losing their fall leaves, but there was a distinct difference, an ominous feeling, when they came to a pathway running between rows of dead, gray-tinted trees that emanated the smell of rot.

"We're almost there," Kylie said, her monotone causing Ian to grip his knife more firmly.

Finally they came upon a small house with a bright red door. The building's simple architecture spoke of age, but the wood and other materials were unblemished. Protected for centuries by black magic.

This was part of the property he had helped Ronja acquire, albeit under false pretenses.

So that meant they were close to the stone yard.

Ian had a sudden urge to grab Anna and run, but he stifled the compulsion, reminding himself there was no true escape. If Anna and the coven failed, the world they lived in would turn to ruin. And she would forever blame herself.

Assuming she was still alive at that point.

So no. This is where they would make their stand, and though Ian had been the last to join this clan, he was just as determined to do his part, to help in whatever small way he could.

The large group rounded the house, heading out back where a great stone monolith loomed in the distance. Where Ronja and Bastraal presumably waited.

Ian could see the top of the towering edifice and, though forewarned, he was stunned by the mountain-like structure, here in the flat, flat lowlands of Georgia. Silently, they streamed toward a thick wall of evergreens, a barrier of tightly-packed hollies, cedar, and other prickly-leaved trees and hedges.

Several yards away, Quinn paused, and breaking rank,

Kylie moved up to stand beside him. They turned back, eyes expectant. Ian wondered what they were waiting for.

Then Anna made her way to the front as other couples paired off. Pausing, she looked over her shoulder and met Ian's gaze.

So he went to her, taking his place by her side. And sharing nothing more than a meaningful glance, they both breathed deeply and began to press their way through the trees.

Once beyond the greenery, they found a wide, open space that was serene and peaceful, wholly unlike the hell-on-earth Ethan had predicted. No living thing stirred within the huge oval of trees. The ground was barren, nothing but dirt and rocks, surrounded by lit torches positioned every twenty feet or so along the outer edge.

The landscape was mottled by an irregular patchwork of immense stones, their overwhelming number responsible for giving the place its name. In assorted formations and of various base compositions, the large rocks differed, with some as big as boulders erupting from the ground, contrasting against others in the shape of dolmens or crypts. Several were tall and narrow as if balanced by mystical forces, while a few lay flat and closer to the ground.

Still, Ian realized with a shudder, one stood out among them all.

In the center of the stone yard, Ian could make out a shimmering pool of black. Orange danced across the surface, images of the torches reflected in its uneven edges. And then he saw the illusion.

Upon closer inspection, he could tell the smooth object was solid, but the texture was so glossy, the composite so shimmery, that beneath the dancing fire it seemed to flow and undulate, like the darkest oil.

Ian inherently knew this was the site prepared for Bastraal's transformation, his intended place of rebirth.

Far past the would-be altar, the rocky megalith dominated,

topped by jagged ridges. The shape was almost aggressive, its height and mere presence casting a portentous shadow over the area.

"Help me!" Ian whipped his head around when a man screamed from across the clearing. From behind one of the larger stone structures, three Amara members sauntered out.

Jack, Carson, and Ross strolled behind the tethered man, herding him, while a gorgeous woman who was likely the succubus, Valentina, sauntered behind the group as if without a care in the world

When the man met Ian's eyes, he yelled again. "Help!"

Ross shoved his shoulder, pushing him onward, but the ropes that trussed the poor man's wrists and ankles hindered his progress.

Ian jolted, as did some of the others, when instincts to defend kicked in.

But he quickly got himself under control and studied the captive. Other than his bound state—and the fact he was imprisoned by supernatural beings—the man appeared to be unharmed; no blood, bruises, or even rips in his clothing. In fact, he was rather well-preserved, as if he'd been cared for.

As if his body had been protected.

"The vessel," Anna whispered beside Ian, her hand grasping his as she first set eyes on the man she would be forced to kill. She trembled, swayed on her feet. So Ian stepped closer, sliding his arm around her back, encouraging her to stand strong.

The trio of Amara thugs all but carried the man to a stake firmly driven into the ground. They secured him before encircling him again, both to ensure he didn't escape as well as deter any who might attempt to free him.

The man stared across the vast space to the group of newcomers. "Please!" he yelled, but Ross turned and spoke harshly to him, promising something so dire the terrified man promptly shut his mouth.

But his eyes fell upon Ian, and still they pleaded for help.

Ronja chose that moment to stroll from behind the same huge stone. A woman in jeans and a black hoodie followed, along with a younger girl with long brown hair. Judging by descriptions he'd been given, Ian deemed them to be the notorious Searenn and Beth.

The woman hiding her face under the hood was a Droehk, an ancient class of people gifted with the ability to summon and command demons. *More demons.* Ian heaved a breath.

The task before them suddenly seemed insurmountable, and he was again filled with the desire to shove Anna behind him, to protect her from all harm. Though he knew she and her sister-witches were the only ones on earth who could see this night to victory.

"Vanir," Ronja called out cheerfully, as though this were nothing more than a happy reunion. She strode with self-assurance in every step, crossing the desolate ground in a long-sleeved gown the color of quicksilver.

She slowed when Anna stepped forward in a threatening pose, ready to defend, to strike her foe down. Tilting her head, blonde hair flowing, Ronja glared at Anna momentarily before shifting her gaze to Ian.

The Nordic witch extended her hand. "Come now, Vanir. It's almost over."

Ian gestured toward the prisoner. "Don't let this happen, Ronja. It's not too late, and I know you can somehow make it right."

Furrowing her brow in confusion, she laughed lightly. "But it *is* right. Everything is finally perfect." She lifted a shoulder. "I've learned to be more patient. I've been compelled to do so," she added with a forced smile.

"So if you don't see the error of your ways tonight, you will in the future." She lowered her head, stared at him from shadowed eyes. "Because it's going to get very dangerous soon, very bloody, and I'm sure you'll see the wisdom of garnering my protection."

Ian puzzled over her continued misconception. How could she not see he wasn't her brother? Couldn't she differentiate? Or was the likeness between him and Vanir just too much to see past?

Then an idea blossomed, and he thought... Why the hell not? He'd encourage her delusions. Maybe it would help in the end.

He put a hand on Anna's elbow, whispering he would be fine as he stepped around her and closer to Ronja. "I realize this has been difficult for you, because I don't know you in this life. But if you were ever truly my sister, then please stop this now. You can still choose to do what's right."

He fixated on her eyes, held them with his own, mirror images in shape and color. "You were once good, Ronja. I know you were." He gulped. "I *remember* you were. You helped people, served them. Until that terrible day when I was too late to save you."

Ronja's arrogance faltered. Her face dropped into sorrowful lines. Then she grew emotional, clasping her hands together. "You *are* Vanir!"

As if she'd had any doubt?

"Not exactly. I *was*, but that life is over. I can never go back."

"But we're meant to be together. It's why you were allowed to come back again." She swept a hand up and down, intimating his form. "Your shape and visage are the same."

"But we can't be together." Ian shook his head and lifted his hand to the bound man, the sacrificial lamb. "Not if it's going to be like this."

Ronja's features morphed into fury. Her eyes glowed from within as she curled her hands into fists. "There is no other way!" Her words were an uncanny echo of what Quinn had said that day in the tower.

"You would see that," she continued to rage, "if you hadn't

chosen *her*!" The finger she pointed at Anna crackled with black energy, a small bolt of lightning that leapt through the air but didn't strike. "We shared a womb, Vanir. We shared blood, and even more than that, we shared power!"

Ronja curled her hands against her chest. "How can you betray such bonds?"

"No, Ronja! How can *you*? I'm not the one who betrayed what we were meant to be. Power comes with responsibility, and you've shown none. You've abused your gift." Ian raised his voice, but the small hope he'd had of getting through to her was dying. Ronja had been hardened too long ago to soften up now.

"Do you remember Vanir? How good and valiant he was?"

She nodded, smiled. "Of course."

"Then do you really want him to serve Bastraal? To change into an evil version of himself?" Ian struck for the heart. "Do you want him to become like you?"

Ronja actually gasped and stepped backward. "You wound me, Vanir."

No, that will be Anna's job. And Ian was done trying to reason with the witch. "For the last time, my name is Ian. And I'm only trying to reach out to you, because that's what Vanir would have wanted."

"Stop speaking in riddles." Ronja shook her head violently. "You *are* Vanir."

Ian glanced back to Anna, but she too seemed baffled. Was Ronja losing sight of reality? Had the desire—and failure—to regain her brother's love snapped what sanity she'd maintained over the centuries?

"You have made your choice, Vanir." Her cold, tempered voice was back, as if the brief interlude with madness was but a moment of panic. "As have I!"

With a whirl of her long silver dress, Ronja stalked in the opposite direction toward the far edge of the stone yard. She yelled to the hooded Droehk. "Searenn, don't let your pets touch my brother!"

With nothing visible on her face but a wicked smile, the other woman spoke in a ruined, raspy voice. "Oh, don't worry about that. I wouldn't dare." Then she raised her hand and began to chant in a low, guttural tone.

"Get ready," Hayden called to the others, prompting them all to reach for their weapons, still loaded with a good reserve of coven magic.

Which would be needed to destroy whatever demons Searenn called forth.

But a strong male voice bellowed, "Hold!" The fierce directive brought Ian around to see who'd issued the command. And when he did...

Oh, shit. Is it time for this already? Ian instinctively edged back to Anna as Tyr strode boldly to the middle of the battlefield.

Per his usual, he was attired in nothing but short brown pants. His thick bronze torso was bare, but he'd painted symbols on his chest and lines on his face, war paint drawn in thick streaks of red, yellow, and black.

He seemed bigger than the last time Ian had seen him. Or maybe his recall had just been tainted by fear.

Ronja stood calmly in the background, apparently unafraid for Tyr. Certain the powerful Daevo would take out most of the coven.

Though not Anna, Ian thought with an inner growl. He knew the Amara witch wanted the opportunity to face her St. Germaine nemesis. After all this time, and all her failed attempts, Ronja couldn't wait to kill Anna...all by herself.

Ian studied the woman he'd judged at first, come to trust, and had finally fallen in love with. He was ready to shake with trepidation, fear just for her, but Anna held her head high, her royal blue eyes blazing with power and fury.

So Ian didn't insult her by asking if she was prepared for this—the clash of coven witches against the mighty Daevo. He only gave her a nod and stepped out of her way.

Looking again to the brawny man, he saw Tyr had already summoned a swirling mist. One that would transform into some sort of monster.

So he joined the cluster of men who were now gathering behind the witches, as one by one, they took up positions alongside Anna. As they flanked their leader.

The night was far from over, and more battles were still to come, but the women had stored their magic carefully thus far. And were more than ready to deal some out.

As Ian stood in the rear, he heard Anna say to the others, "Time for Plan B."

It was then Paige yelled, "Hello, Daevo!" She drew out the words to rhyme the *oh* sounds in a mocking manner. "You think you're a real badass, don't you?"

Tyr grinned at her and gave a laugh that was clearly meant to be patronizing. He raised his hand toward the coven's warrior, leisurely but with menace.

"Oh, what, big boy? You want to shoot your magic at me? You want to knock me down?"

Paige taunted the Daevo mercilessly, and Ian started to worry when the fog in the evil man's palm began darkening to a deep red.

Ian shifted his feet, keeping one eye on Tyr's building power, the other on Paige. *Move, girl. Move!*

But Paige held her ground. "Is that all you've got? A little strawberry cloud?" She shook her head. "You became the big, bad Daevo, and the best you can do is imitate Scarlett?"

Now Tyr roared, his countenance changing swiftly from humor to rage.

Ian sensed movement and realized Chris was edging toward the action, skirting around the left side of the coven. He came out in front of Shauni and started a rant of his own. "Hey, asshole." He flicked a crude hand signal at Tyr, effectively diverting his attention from Paige.

But even with his eyes on Chris, Tyr released a crimson burst that fell to the dirt between him and Paige. The red dust dropped gradually, floated down, and hit the earth gently.

As Ian stared, several mounds began to rise, morphing into ruby-hued creatures. Once fully formed, their insect-like bodies resembled both scorpions and centipedes. They had many, many legs, and long, vicious tails with huge barbs on the end. The sharp points glistened with what had to be poison.

"Lovely," Cole murmured near Ian. Then he shook his head and shuddered unapologetically.

Ian could sympathize, because those bastards were massive, yet still imparted that creepy-crawly sensation like all their bug brethren.

Paige didn't look too thrilled either. Yes, this was part of the plan, but instead of having only one fiend to dodge, she now had four. And they were still growing, their legs clicking and snapping as they scuttled toward her.

So she zipped to the side and tossed a small bolt of coven magic at the nearest insectoid. It sizzled and popped, evaporating into blue sparks. Paige threw a relieved glance to Anna before dashing around behind Tyr to begin jeering at him again.

Still intent on Chris, Tyr threw an undulating wave of magic at the Ranger, as though not wanting to waste one of his pet beasts on anyone other than a coven witch.

Chris easily dodged the blast but kept his eyes on Tyr. As the man spun to locate Paige, Chris tensed, readying himself for what was coming next.

The Daevo now had his back to the coven, and Ian also felt his muscles grow rigid with expectation. This had to be the moment they'd been waiting for.

And it was. Chris confirmed when he shot a look to Viv. Gave her a quick nod.

The Asian witch with her stubby black ponytail stepped

forward out of the coven line and reached into her pocket. The shining gem she retrieved was a brilliant yellow, flawless, and the size of a baby's fist.

Paige's father had discovered the rare artifact, one of many in his special black case of tricks. When he'd referred to helping defeat the Daevo, he'd had the unique jewel in mind.

Viv held the bright stone up, a signal to the other women. And to Chris, who fell back on an old-school trick and simply picked up a rock. He threw it at Tyr's head, smacking him hard in the skull.

When the Daevo whipped around to growl at Chris, Paige lifted her hand.

As did the eight other witches.

The stone had once belonged to a Druid, one with an affinity for all things mineral. According to legend, the gem amplified magic.

Of course, Anna had given the stone a trial run, and the scorch mark on the mansion's exterior wall attested to the claim.

With Tyr's glare still on Chris, Viv tossed the jewel into the air and held it steady with her telekinesis. Then she shot the dazzling indigo stream that denoted the coven's magic and lit up the stone with a wash of crystalline blue light.

All of the witches did the same, until the vivid yellow was overrun by their pure, special blue. A single blast of magic shot from the opposite side, and with Viv still controlling the flow, she directed it through the air and straight into Tyr.

The Daevo was lifted off the ground, his body arching backward as the surge of energy coursed through him. Shaking violently, he emitted a loud groan, and as he was doubled over backward by the current the sound of pain escalated into a scream.

Ronja stared in disbelief, her shocked expression proving she'd believed the Daevo to be invincible. "What is this? It's not possible!"

With Paige busy channeling her magic, she didn't notice the red insect scurrying toward her, so Ian whipped out a knife, flooded it with emotion as he'd been trained to do, and sent the blade flying. The knife nailed the hellish bug, and the coven's signature blue skittered throughout its shell before sparking it into non-existence.

Michael and Dare made short work of the two remaining creatures, guarding the borders while the witches continued to channel their power into the floating stone.

"Anna," Quinn called out, his tone concerned.

"Not yet," she replied, her voice cool though lifted to carry back to her brother. "Just a few... more..."

When Tyr's head lolled to the side, Anna gave the word and the coven drew back their magic. Released from the power that had been holding him up, Tyr collapsed to the dirt where he lay in a heap.

Seconds passed as the witches and men stared at the crumpled form, wondering if he would open his eyes and leap up to resume his assault. But he didn't twitch, didn't moan, and Ian wondered if the man even still breathed.

"Get him. Get him." Ronja ordered Ross to go to Tyr, though the shifter appeared nervous about getting anywhere near the coven.

"Ross..." Ronja pointed her fingers at him, her hand flat and knifelike. So the buzz-cut blonde hurried to Tyr and grabbed him beneath the arms, dragging him across the ground.

Though not necessarily to safety. The coven had come to the stone yard, and the events so far said Amara beware.

A completely foreign and unanticipated sense of triumph exploded in Ian's chest. While the witches were still stoic and composed, there was a definite current of excitement running through the men.

Ian turned to Dare and they shared a high-five. "That worked better than I thought it would."

Dare crossed his arms. "Without a doubt." He gave Ian a crooked smile and said, "One down."

Trying to contain his relief, Ian reminded himself there were more obstacles to overcome, including the sacrifice that still seemed unavoidable. Just as the depressing thought filled his mind, he heard Ethan say, "Now, if only they could all be that easy."

But Ian's gaze was drawn to the tower of stone. He caught a glimpse of movement in the dark hole at the bottom, the cavern entrance he'd heard Quinn describe. He felt a chill of premonition—or of memory—when a figure suddenly appeared, and stepped out into the moonlight.

Swallowing the burn of apprehension in his throat, Ian watched as the silhouette began moving toward them. Easy? he thought, echoing Ethan's statement.

Then Ian locked gazes with Dare and said, "I don't think so."

27

Anna sensed the demon's arrival the instant he emerged from the base of the towering stone mountain. He didn't walk so much as he lumbered over the ground, and as he drew closer, three hundred years of enmity swelled within her.

Bastraal must have felt her perusal, or the whip and crack of her building magic as he neared, because he angled his head and zeroed in on the modern-day St. Germaine witch.

And Anna finally met the eyes of her ancestors' enemy. Now hers.

He stood at least seven feet tall, and his body was human-like in form, replete with torso, arms, and legs. His flesh, however, if it could be called that, was distinctly demonic—black and slick, yet ever-changing. Luminescence rolled over him in a constant flux, even along the tentacles protruding from his wide back.

The squirming appendages were long and thick but tapered at the ends. They writhed and curled of their own accord, like a larger, more sinister version of Medusa's mane of snakes.

Ian grunted, bringing Anna's eyes to him in a snap. "What is it?" she asked as he rubbed his sternum.

"Bastraal—his nearness. I don't know how to describe it." Ian's chest rose and fell as if he warred against something within himself. "I remember the pain of his attacks and the fire he created. So does Vanir. He's…reacting."

Anna clenched her hands. She'd been worried about Ronja's

proximity affecting Vanir, and now Bastraal's presence warranted concern as well. "You can hold him down," she encouraged Ian. "Don't let him rise."

Ronja, overhearing their exchange, came running back toward them. "Yes! Let him. I'm here, Vanir! Push your way through!"

Grinding her teeth, Anna shot a scathing glance to the witch, then to the demon, before turning troubled eyes back to Ian. Destiny had decided to hand her an ever-more-complicated trial. But she conceded that a witch in her position, armed with both her unique ancestry as well as a lifetime of training in the craft, would be the one best equipped to handle such obstacles.

For the moment, however, Bastraal seemed completely disinterested in Anna or her coven as he shot a gleefully sinister look to his favored servant. "Ah, Ronja, you disappoint me so. Even now, your weakness undermines you."

Ronja didn't realize her master had addressed her at first, so intent on urging Vanir's resurrection that she failed to notice. When finally she glanced to the hulking demon, her mouth fell slack. "What? Are we not here on the fated night? All of this," she flung out an arm, "is by design! Why do you say I am weak? I did as you asked."

"Yet here you stand, on this most auspicious night, and your only concern is your feeble, white mage of a brother!" Bastraal's voice was thunder, bouncing off the craggy setting.

Ronja cowered from the sound. She held out her hands in appeal and shook her head wildly. "I don't understand."

As he stomped over the bleak and infertile earth, Bastraal's skin began to pulse more rapidly, the oscillation of colors almost blinding to the eye. His laughter scraped the inside of Anna's skull, yet she couldn't look away. She had to watch.

Advancing on Ronja, the monster sent out a flurry of tentacles to stroke her hair, her face, before wandering over her body to every sensitive area. The fondling, however, was not an act of love. But a molestation.

"No. Stop! Why?" Rarely had Anna seen the harsh woman reduced to incoherent speech as she was now.

"Why?" Bastraal's booming question was threaded with incredulity. Then he shouted, "You dare ask me why? Because I *can*, you worthless slattern!"

Casting her eyes about, Ronja looked for an ally, but Tyr was still out cold, and the other Amara members wisely remained on the sidelines. And far out of Bastraal's sight.

"Never fear," Bastraal crooned suddenly, curling a tentacle around the witch's neck. He squeezed until her eyes bulged before releasing her just as abruptly. He withdrew every tentacle from her body and retreated. "I promised I would give you your brother. Did I not?"

Ronja managed a limp nod.

"And so I shall." Now Bastraal turned to Ian, his cold perusal sending sharp jabs of fear through every part of Anna. When he cocked his huge head and lasered his slanted black eyes at the man she loved, the entire scene became surreal, fuzzy at the edges, as if she were stuck in another of Ian's dreams.

"Ian," Bastraal rumbled. "Or Vanir." He laughed derisively and shifted his focus back to Ronja. "Soon, my submissive witch... Soon it will make no difference."

Her mind reeling in confusion, Anna inched closer to Ian, but Ronja's demon master had averted his attention once again. He strode to the other Amara cohorts and bellowed, "Searenn!" He indicated the human captive. "I need another soldier!"

A slimy smile formed on the Droehk's face. "Yes, my lord," she said with sickening obedience. Then she thrust a hand into the air and began to murmur in her demon-speak.

Anna and her friends readied themselves for combat, waiting for the arrival of a beastly swarm. But the only demon to appear was of the eel-shaped variety, the kind that could slip inside humans and take control.

With a flick of her wrist, Searenn sent the beast hurtling toward the innocent man still tied to the stake. He gave a brief yell but was quickly silenced as his head dropped forward onto his chest.

When he lifted it again, his face flickered and changed. A sure sign of demon possession.

"What are you doing?" Ronja stared, bewildered. "You need your vessel."

"I have one," Bastraal replied, his tone rolling with subversive pleasure.

And the first true spears of terror lanced Anna's heart, her gut. Surely he couldn't mean...

"You will have your brother." Bastraal's enjoyment grew, his laughter intensifying with the raucous sound of a hundred vicious voices. "You will have him in the manner I deem to give him to you."

The massive beast lifted his arm, a long finger pointed at Ian.

With a shout of pain, Ian clutched at the base of his neck. "No!" Arching his back, he staggered but managed to stay upright. Through clenched eyes, he kept his gaze on Anna.

She was at his side in a heartbeat as her sisters flew into action. The coven surrounded them, with the rest of the team following their lead. One of them was being attacked, so each man, witch, and cat was up in arms.

Anna tried to get a hold on Ian to see what was wrong, but he thrashed and twisted. All the while, his awful cry of pain streaked across the dark sky, up to the huge Halloween moon above.

"The burning!" He groaned and doubled over, gasping for air. "My neck," he rasped as he started to calm down, his hand still clamped to his skin.

"Let me see." Anna pried his fingers loose, brushed aside his golden hair.

"The pain is like the night he attacked me in my home. It's the same."

"What are you doing to him?" Ronja screeched, charging forward, but she was effectively blocked by the frontline of coven men and women.

"Quinn." Anna scrutinized the strange mark on Ian's neck, red and welted as if burned, and oddly enough, resembling a sun. "What is this mark?"

"What is it?" Ronja was beside herself, clasping her hands together. But amazingly, she didn't try to force her way through the protective barrier of coven allies.

Quinn was at her side, and with one look at the symbol he swore beneath his breath. "The *Fylfot*." His blue eyes were heavy with dread when he whispered to her, "An ancient symbol of evil. And ownership."

Anna's mind went numb. Her system staggered as denial flooded her brain. "What? Why would be it there?"

"Annaaaa!" Ronja was almost crying now "Please, let me see him. Let me look. I swear I would never hurt him."

Quinn seemed undecided, but he raised his voice to the Nordic witch, their sworn enemy who was now horrified and worried about their friend, their loved one. He shouted one word. "Fylfot!"

Ronja reared back in shock, her eyes widening before she keened, "Noooo!" Falling to her knees, she rocked back and forth, while over and over she said, "You can't have him. You can't have him."

Then in a flash, she was on her feet again, leaping toward the still-smug Bastraal. "You lying bastard!"

"No." He spread his hands. "You shall spend the rest of your days gazing upon your brother's face. I kept my word."

Ian had gone stock still, but he slowly looked to Anna. "What does it mean?"

But as she locked eyes with the man she loved more than

herself, Anna knew he already understood.

Ronja's wails echoed still. "I want Vanir, not you!"

"Anna?" Ian was still staring back at her. He cupped her face. "Anna. Tell me. Just tell me."

Quinn had stepped away, leaving the two of them alone.

"Bastraal—" She couldn't speak, her vocal cords unwilling to utter the awful truth. "Bastraal has marked you." Lips quivering and hands shaking, she grasped Ian's shoulder. "Oh, Ian."

"Just say it." His voice had lost all life.

Anna nodded, strengthened by his fortitude in the face of such atrocity. She almost whimpered but caught it and quashed it before she whispered, "Bastraal has chosen you... to be his vessel."

Ian's pupils dilated, and the thrum in his neck picked up as his heart rate accelerated. He shook his head, disbelieving. But just as quickly, he clenched his eyes shut and nodded.

Still stunned, still rejecting the truth, Anna collapsed into his arms, refusing to let him go.

"But why? Why?" Ronja was still screaming, releasing all the pent up frustration and sorrow that also pounded inside of Anna.

"All those times I left you with no explanation, I went to your brother. Your precious Vanir that I've heard you cry for and mourn all these years." Bastraal slammed his foot on the ground, shaking the very earth beneath them all. "And when I did, I hurt him. I despise the idea of your brother ever taking a piece of what I've fought for. Victory is rightfully mine, and mine alone!"

"You hurt him? My twin?" Ronja put her knuckles to her temples. "When you knew how much I loved him?"

"No. Because I knew how much you worshipped him. As you should have only worshipped me!" Bastraal's spherical black eyes seemed to narrow. "My visits to him served another purpose as well."

Ronja remained mute.

"I tortured him, terrorized him." Bastraal's smile was a flash in the dark. "And to whom did he run?"

Ronja jerked her head to Anna, eyes closing to hate-filled gashes on her pallid face.

Listening to the demon's explanation now, Anna loosened her hold on Ian. She stared at the monster who was joyfully ruining her life, piece by piece.

"He went straight to the witch. I simply gave their destinies a push in the right direction." Bastraal tossed a hand toward Anna. "And where is Vanir tonight, of all nights?" He spread his long, powerful arms. "He is here! Standing in the heart of darkness, the one place in which I will have the power to return."

Anna clutched her stomach. *Goddess, what have I done?* She'd convinced Ian he would be safe with her, that she would protect him. That he didn't need to be afraid.

As long as he was with her.

But all along, she'd been Bastraal's toy. And she had played right into the demon's hands.

No. No! her mind shouted. She couldn't let this happen! All at once, everything inside her revolted. She tugged on Ian's hand, trying to pull him with her, but he was listless, staring at the ground in a daze.

What was happening in his head? How did one prepare to die? Prepare to be consumed by evil?

Only to then be murdered by the woman who claimed to love him?

While Ronja continued to rail at Bastraal, Anna fled to Quinn and the other men. Panic was a visceral force in her body, shutting down her blood flow, clogging her throat, freezing her brain. Mindless, frantic, she reached out to the men, touching a hand here, a shoulder there.

"Take Ian away from here," she begged. "Dare, Michael. You have to help him."

They didn't speak, only gazed at her with despondency.

"Nick? Cole?"

All they could do was watch and agonize, as competent and capable Anna fell apart right in front of their eyes.

Deep inside, a voice told her they were too distraught to say or do anything, but that didn't keep her from grabbing each one of them, continuing to plead. "I've always been loyal to magic. I've always had faith."

She went to Ethan. "This can't be right!"

Finally, she turned to her brother. Rushing to him, she clutched the front of his shirt with both hands. "Quinn, help me. Please."

He wrapped her in his arms and held her close. But her heart broke anew when she felt him shaking, realized he was crying. For her. For Ian.

Devastated by grief, Anna implored again, her voice breaking on a sob. "Help me, Quinn." She cringed and shook her head. "I don't know what to do."

"Yes, you do."

Still holding onto her sibling, Anna turned her head to Ian. He was standing there, so still and calm. His face was ghost-white, and though his eyes were flat with acceptance, they also held a glint of determination.

He released a shaky breath and held out his hand to her. "You knew what you would have to do when you came here tonight."

Releasing Quinn, she crossed to Ian and threw herself into his arms. "No," she spoke against his neck. "Please, not this."

Because there were no other words, because there was no other way, Anna and Ian clung to each other. And as she cried, as she twisted inside with misery, Ian did just as he'd promised. He was there for her, supporting her.

With all that he now faced, he still kept his word. He didn't run or try to dissuade her. He did what an honorable and valiant man would always do. He thought of her and all the lives they would save. Together.

Anna with her dagger. And Ian falling under her blade.

Soon she felt a presence and raised her eyes to see Quinn standing near. Without a sound, he enclosed both her and Ian in his arms. Then Kylie was there, and Dare with Willyn. Shauni and Michael, with the others closing in all around, building a wall to surround the grieving couple.

For that moment, for the few precious minutes that remained, they sheltered Anna and Ian.

They protected them from harm.

But Anna's head jerked when Ronja's scream crescendoed into a terrible sound of anguish and fury. With arms flung wide apart, the *seiðr* turned her face to the sky and shrieked, her hair a gold waterfall over her silver dress.

Unnatural strikes of lightning rent the dark expanse, crackling bolts of black—white—gold, Ronja's wrath unleashed as she realized the depth of her master's cruel deceit.

Ian held Anna's chin in his hand. He cleared his throat. "You still have work to do. Remember what you told me. Your needs can't come first." He cradled the back of her neck with his strong fingers, his voice shaking. "*Our* needs can't come first. Too many other lives are at stake. One for thousands, Anna."

His eyes stormed with compassion tempered by loss. "One for thousands."

He kissed her, with all the love and passion that could be instilled into one kiss. Then he let her go.

Nodding, she wiped the final tears from her eyes. She could practically feel the jagged edges of her broken heart piercing her, killing her slowly, but she forced her emotions down, did her best to wrap them up into a tight ball and hide them deep inside.

"Damn it!" The oath from Trevor was filled with a noxious blend of alarm and anger. He too displayed the deadened eyes of all who'd felt this devastation. All who cared for Ian and Anna. But his concern now was for something else.

The big cop chin-notched to indicate the other side of the stone yard. "Look who's awake."

With a fresh curl of dread in her belly, Anna followed his line of sight. Tyr was on his feet again. And based on his intense snarl, he was also ready for retribution.

But his heated glower was not for Anna or any of her friends. He was fuming as he stared at Bastraal.

With a ball of energy now swirling around her instead of striking above, Ronja leaned her body forward, hands open and fingers curled into claws. "I only ever asked you for one thing!"

She shouted at Bastraal. "All these years I served you, and you would do this to me? To *me*?" With one great scream, she flung a torrent of her deadly magic toward her master.

Bastraal carelessly waved his hand to deflect her sorcery. But her actions had insulted his pride, his unassailable arrogance as her master. So he sent back a wave of energy that flung her across the stone yard where she smashed into one of the upright monuments.

Ronja's body transferred the magical current when she hit, and a burst of sound filled the air as the stone split down its length and cracked into two.

Tyr was fully charged, his muscles taut as he curled his beefy arms and blasted a roar of vehemence toward the demon.

Bastraal curled his fingers in a come-ahead gesture.

And Tyr swiftly complied. The atmosphere around the Daevo swirled with colored mists as he summoned his wealth of stored-up monsters.

As he and Bastraal began to circle each other, Searenn dashed out to the center of the battlefield. She tossed back her hoodie to reveal her tattooed face.

And Anna began to draw her magic, because she knew that gesture well. The Droehk was about to call forth a shitload of demons.

"It's time!" Anna shouted, and fear for her friends as well as for Ian allowed her to shift into another state of mind. This was what she'd been born to do, and no matter how her heart ripped, she had obligations that were larger than herself.

The Nine still stood. They had yet to fall.

And they still had a prophecy to fulfill.

Shauni nodded to Anna, confirming she had reinforcements on hand.

The other witches and their men circled up, while the cats spread out to defend the coven boundary.

And when thunder rolled across the sky, Ethan was proven right. Because all hell broke loose on this Hallowed Eve.

Just as Joseph and Sylvie dashed into the stone yard.

28

Anna sucked in a quick, sharp breath when she saw Joseph and Sylvie bound into the rock-strewn battlefield. Her stomach clenched when he slowed to meet her eyes, then give her a shrug and a boyish grin.

But as frightened as she was for his and Quinn's safety—for all of her friends—she understood why Joseph had come. Just as she knew that Sylvie would never have let him face this danger alone.

And despite her worry, their gesture touched her heart. It bolstered her spirit. So shaking her head, she raised a hand of welcome and gratitude. She winked at him and called out, "You'd better grab a sword."

Then she turned to face the monsters.

The coven allies formed a curved line of defense as demons came from every corner. They stalked across the unfertile ground, crawled over the rock formations, and slithered through the dark air of night.

Anna and the others had the dense tree-line barrier at their backs, but a veritable army of beasts was closing in from both sides. And while the numbers were terrifying, it was the faction of enemies moving in from the front that troubled Anna most.

From behind one of the large stone dolmens, a tide of human warriors flooded onto the field. With bloodthirsty leers or hostile scowls, the crush marched forward, bearing down on the coven with lethal intent.

Were these simply the hellspawn that were able to mimic human form? Or did their ranks consist of victims? Humans who'd been possessed?

The mob was moving at such a fast clip, using the coven's charmed weapons to differentiate would be nearly impossible. The horde would be upon them before the first sword could change colors—blue for true human, red for demon imposter.

"Send the cats back!" Anna shouted to Shauni. The scene was quickly turning chaotic with too many creatures to keep the felines safe while underfoot.

Shauni issued a telepathic command to the animals, and like the good soldiers they were, the cats retreated to sit by the trees until they were called upon.

"There are so many," Paige said from next to Anna, a wrinkle of concern on her forehead.

Paige was the coven's warrior, the fiercest combatant, so her concern was chilling. Still, Anna faced forward, with no option but to hold her ground.

If more than one human life was sacrificed before the night was over, that was just a loss she would have to learn to accept.

This was the night of prophecy, the one she'd prepared for— both magically and mentally—her entire life. Her parents had died while working toward this very goal, and Anna could do nothing less than see her trial to the end.

She may despise herself when it was all over, but no matter her personal devastation, she couldn't deviate from the plan. Ending Bastraal was paramount, because if he lived past this night and came to rule in this realm, millions would fall to his bloody and violent reign.

And the sacred book had asked for only one human life in exchange for a coven victory. One sacrifice to prevent mass murder.

Anna shivered, kept her sob from surfacing. Because now Bastraal had decided that life would be Ian's, stolen here, on this forsaken piece of land. A heinous death beneath the ever-watchful moon.

The throng of humans was getting closer, and the demon troops on each side were pressing in, ready to maim and kill.

"Anna?" Willyn called from several yards away. "What do we do?" The healer was clearly distraught by the idea of cutting down the human regiment coming straight at them. The coven existed to help people, and the idea of taking lives, even if necessary, was appalling to them all.

Anna grabbed the bag of herbs attached to her belt, wishing for a way to spread the exorcising mixture. If only the concoction was in an airborne form.

A breeze tickled her cheek, and then... *That's it!* Still holding the bag, she turned to the men who were again positioned in front of the coven. She met Ethan's eyes to find he had registered the same idea.

"Herb bags!" he cried to the men. Then he lifted his own and sliced open the top, severing the sack and its content from the retractable cord. "Cut them free!"

Each of the men did as instructed, no questions asked. Sylvie and Joseph hadn't known they'd be here tonight, but Joseph carried the charmed bags in his SUV and they had each brought one with them. They too cut open their sacks.

Now the scores of bodies moving en masse caused the ground to quake and thunder. The scent of sulfur was rolling in from both sides.

Anna flashed her eyes to the approaching human mob before her gaze landed on Ian. He seemed to be functioning, mind on-task, despite having learned he wouldn't survive to see another dawn.

As soon as the realization punched Anna in the stomach, she forced the thought back down. She didn't have the luxury of grief at the moment. Neither did Ian, which was probably enough to explain his intense focus.

None of the witches were immortal, so with the demon army greatly outnumbering the coven and the men, death was a valid threat to each and every one of them.

Once each man had his herb bag cut open and in his hand, Ethan led them all forward to form a line in front of the women. "We need wind!"

And that was the cue for the coven's best elemental witches to step up to the plate. Claudia and Lucia took up positions on either side of the men and awaited his command. Ethan pulled his arm back, preparing to throw. The other men did the same.

"Magic on the flanks!" Paige yelled. The demons from the two sides were almost on top of them.

And though Anna was the coven leader, she deferred to Paige's military experience and expertise in battle strategy. After all, each of the women served a special purpose, and their union had created a force to be reckoned with.

Their unique gifts were why prophecy had chosen them.

But their love for each other, their bond of sisterhood...that is what made them The Nine.

"Now!" Ethan yelled as the human front roared closer. The men and Sylvie launched their bags of herbs into the air, and as the contents rained from the open burlap, Lucia and Claudia kicked up a gust to drive the mystical blend straight toward the humans.

The witches used their current to scatter the mixture all across the horde. One by one, people dropped to the ground as the demons inside them were expelled.

That left only pure-bred demons, and they were swiftly advancing on the coven allies.

The men drew their weapons to fight off the remaining threat. And almost like clockwork, the mob clashed with the frontline of men, just as two walls of demons struck from the sides.

Moonlight had previously covered the stone yard, but now

a new source of illumination filled the battlefield. A brilliant blast of coven blue lit up the night as the witches called forth their sacred magic. This was the weapon only they had been blessed with, and the crystalline energy served one unique purpose.

The destruction of demons.

Ash burst into the air as Anna channeled her power and sprayed the advancing throng. But even as she took out dozens of the beasts, hundreds more moved up to take their place.

Knives zipped through the air and swords swung, but soon the men were depleting their stores. "I'm out," Michael yelled, referring to his throwing knives. "I'm getting the packs!"

Anna threw out another blanketing coat of blue and demolished another wave of marauding fiends, while beside her, Kylie, Lucia, and Hayden stood with her to defend their side of the stronghold.

The cats were all staying back, though Kiko and Tiger Lily both gave angry yowls, as if barely restraining themselves from leaping to defend their humans.

"Anna, fall back," Kylie yelled, her voice almost lost beneath the sound of blasting magic, trampling feet, and explosions of ash. "You need to save your strength!"

"I'm fine," Anna gritted through her teeth, but her voice didn't carry over the cacophony created by hundreds of charging monsters and surge after surge of coven blue. Not to mention the roars and bellows from the monsters, or their keening cries as one of the men drove a blade home, putting an end to yet another beast.

Gray and black dust filled the air, the haze growing thicker minute by minute and death by death.

"They're opening the packs," Kylie insisted. "You and Viv should help them."

Anna sent out another wave of energy as she considered the young woman's words. Relenting at last, she nodded and yelled to the others holding their section of the line, "I'm falling back!"

But before she went to the back, Anna ran to the other side to shout to the animal-whisperer. "Shauni, how long?"

Shooting forth a line of blue like fire from a flame-thrower, Shauni looked upward, concentrating. "Less than a minute!"

Satisfied with her answer, Anna dashed back to the trees where the packs they'd carried in had been set aside. Cats mingled restlessly on the edges as Michael unzipped the bags, exposing the spiked metal balls within. The barbs covering the projectiles were curved, allowing easy handling.

But once made airborne, the balls would spin, turning the barbs into hooks for demon flesh. When they made contact, the magic imbued into the metal would be released.

The coven had been creating stores of weapons for the past few months, and given the size of the Amara's demon militia, the coven allies would likely exhaust their supplies.

As Anna neared the backpacks where Trevor and Cole were now loading their arms alongside Michael, she gave a shout. "Viv! We need you!"

Claudia and Lucia had become as strong as their leader in controlling the elements of earth, air, fire, and water, but Anna and Viv were still the most adept at telekinesis.

Anna stood poised, ready to fire. "Cole, will you load for me?"

"You got it," the dark-haired detective replied. This was a drill they'd practiced outdoors at the mansion, though with dummy wooden balls in lieu of the real thing. Cole knew exactly what she was asking and knelt beside the bag, spiked demon-destroyers at the ready. "Just say the word!"

Anna nodded and yelled "Ready!" her eyes on the creatures still raging against her line of witches. And as Cole tossed the lethal spheres into her line of sight, she sent them rocketing toward the swarm of beasts.

One after the other, she shot the metal missiles past her fighting coven and into the throng. She never missed a target, adding plume after plume of ash to the already dust-laden air.

Soon Viv was next to her, facing away at a forty-five degree angle. Between the two of them, they covered the spectrum and provided backup to their friends on the frontline.

Meanwhile Quinn, Ethan, Joseph, and Nick had come to join in, pelting the demon forces with more of the lethal balls. Hand to hand combat was becoming more difficult as the throng of monsters continued to push forward.

Despite their small victories, the coven allies were losing ground.

Only Chris and Ian were still able to fight with handheld weapons. Chris because of his exceptional speed and strength, Ian because the demons had been forbidden to do him any harm.

Ironically, Bastraal had given the coven another weapon. Choosing Ian for his vessel had made him untouchable.

And Ian was making the most of his advantage, slashing and stabbing with a dagger in each hand.

Anna almost lost her focus when she glanced over to see him fight. No, he wasn't Vanir, but his tall, strong body revealed an ancient lineage of Viking warriors.

In a word, he was magnificent.

And on the heels of her admiration came a swift blade of heartbreak. As it pierced her chest, she wondered how she could bear to lose him. How could she go on without him?

She hurled two more balls into the faces of rushing demons, as fury with Fate, Bastraal, and the universe in general fired within her. Because, how—*how*—could she ever kill the man she loved?

An October breeze streamed across the stone yard, the cool draft helping to clear the ash. As the haze lifted, Anna caught a glimpse of Bastraal and Tyr. The two brutes were barraging each other with blows of magic, while Tyr released his inner devils to assault the mighty demon from all sides.

She was stunned to see the Daevo still on his feet, holding his own against the exceedingly powerful demon, and for a split-second something inside her flared with hope. Maybe Tyr would defeat Bastraal, thereby eliminating his ability to take possession of a vessel.

Ian would be freed from danger, and Anna from duty.

But just as quickly, her optimism crashed. She was the one destined to end Bastraal, and Fate wasn't kind enough to allow for loopholes.

"Incoming!" Shauni shouted from the left side of the coven formation. "Kylie!" she yelled to the younger witch. "We need to push them back!"

With her tumble of golden curls tied back in a tail, Kylie gave a hard nod and tossed her a smile. "I'm on it!" She pulled back from her defensive position, allowing Viv to step in and hold the line. Then she moved to the middle where Ian and Chris still fought and pushed a slow-moving spread of coven magic through their still-battling forms.

Kylie's blue energy saturated the foremost soldiers of the demon horde. Viv, Lucia, and Hayden did the same on their side, while Claudia, Paige, Willyn, and Shauni mirrored the attack from theirs. Once the leading edge of the demons turned to ash, Kylie jumped in front of the men.

Taking advantage of the gap she and her sisters had created, she spread her arms and screamed, "Eat this, you slimy bastards!" Then the youngest witch released her own version of the perfect storm.

Lightning cracked and sizzled, bolts zigzagging on a path parallel to the ground to create a blockade of searing electricity.

Demons might not be obliterated by lightning, but while in this world they were still subject to the laws of physics. And Kylie's light show not only stopped their forward motion but threw their bulk at least ten feet backward.

And that was all the separation they needed for Shauni to

take over.

Lifting her gaze to a sky now peppered with dark objects, the animal-whisperer sent out a silent command to rally.

Various species swooped and dived, but all of them had one thing in common. The specially-crafted spheres clutched in their talons.

Crates had been brought from the island and left beside the vehicles in the woods. With the lids removed, all the birds had needed to do was land and take one of the orbs, bombs filled with coven magic.

And now the sky above darkened as the aerial combatants arrived. In droves. Hundreds of birds flew in from all directions, their sheer quantity blotting out the moon.

Shauni could have given the order with her mind, but a sly smile lifted her lips as she yelled to her winged friends, the coven's reinforcements. "Release at will!"

The assault of beasts had been nothing short of bedlam, but as the bombs began to land, the stone yard radiated a bright, glorious blue. Explosions of sapphire light burst at random, while numerous billows of demon ash erupted.

Hundreds of creatures had been advancing on the coven, but in less than a minute the field of battle had become a wasteland of evil residue. As the last explosives lit up the scene, a heavy coat of silt glowed an eerie twilight gray.

From across the stone yard, Anna heard Ronja's violent scream. Again the Nordic witch's efforts had been defeated. With fists pressed against her stomach, she shot daggers at Anna with her eyes. Then black sparks began to shoot from her skin, her hair, as she started to cross the graveyard of vanquished monsters.

The atmosphere was thick, dense with demon detritus. So this time Claudia and Lucia were joined by Willyn and Hayden as the four women stirred the air and whirled the ash upward to the midnight blue sky.

Clearing the way for Anna to meet Ronja's hate-filled stare.

The dark-hearted seiðr pointed her arm at Anna and opened her mouth to speak.

But a bellow of pain diverted her attention, just before her face contorted into a mask of distress. One word burst free from her as she turned to run. "Tyr!"

29

Ian jolted when he heard the anguished cry. He'd just offed one of the demon stragglers that had managed to survive the bird-delivered bombshells.

The ongoing battle between the Daevo and Bastraal had just landed Tyr a terrible blow. The Native American man was lying on the ground at the base of a huge boulder, his neck twisted at an impossible angle and blood spilling from his open mouth.

The Nordic witch had screamed and run to her fallen lover, so Ian took advantage of the Amara's inner-circle drama to seek out Anna. When his gaze locked with hers, she nodded that she was fine.

With a fresh wave of loss washing through him, Ian shifted away from her and continued to make his rounds. Despite a successful tactic on Shauni's part, a number of hell-born creatures still roamed the stone yard.

And keeping busy was best for him right now. If he spent too long thinking about what was coming, the terror started to seep in.

Yes, he recognized the importance of the impending sacrifice, but that didn't mean he wasn't still sick inside. Devastated that his life ended here. Now. Unexpectedly.

But he'd already accepted that someone would die tonight on the sinister black stone, and he'd allowed for the necessity, understood the awful need. He couldn't just change his mind because he had ended up being that person. The chosen vessel.

Revulsion rolled over him at the idea of being possessed by that tentacle-ridden spawn from Hell. He couldn't stand the thought of it, and in a twisted way, Anna would be doing him a favor.

But then an image of his parents flashed in his mind, and he wished for a moment to call and speak to them, to tell them both goodbye. Though what could he say? I love you and I'm going to die, but hey, that's actually the better option?

No. That would be cruel, and frankly, hearing his mother's unavoidable tears might push him past the point of courage.

He might just cut and run.

So he forced himself to think of them in another way. His mother's kindness to those in need or his father's lifelong career defending those who had no other advocates. Special interest groups, lost causes, civil rights—his father had championed them all.

So Ian wouldn't try to escape. Instead he would pull strength from his parents' example and prove himself to be the son they'd raised. Even if he had to give all in his effort to save the citizens of Savannah.

Even if he had to make the ultimate sacrifice.

He stopped and stared up at the moon as emotion swamped him. In a way, it was poetic.

Anna would be honoring her parents tonight. And Ian would be honoring his.

He shook off the misery that pressed in on him and searched for another demon. At last he saw one, the gigantic type with a sword the length of Ian's leg. The wretched creature tried to run away, to avoid the one man he was prohibited from killing.

So Ian chased down the hulking fiend, driving a dagger into his chest and venting his fury into one of the monsters that had come to destroy his world.

The beast puffed into ash as so many of his brethren already had, but as Ian looked down at his blade, he saw a flicker of pale blue and sensed the magic inside was dwindling.

He turned to check the status on the field, relieved to find Chris and Paige cleaning up the last few remaining demons. The rest of the witches and their men had formed a loose semi-circle behind Anna as they all cautiously observed the unfolding Amara tragedy.

Without realizing it, Ian had worked his way to the western end of the field, far from any of his friends. He stood largely isolated and near the towering mountain of stone. So he stealthily began easing toward the group, keeping his eyes on the massive demon that still had his back to him.

Bastraal was standing immobile, his focus on Ronja as she stroked Tyr's hair and appeared to be murmuring to him.

Choosing to opt for safety, Ian veered in a wide arc to keep his distance from the strange scene playing out beneath the bright white moon. The entire night was so surreal, and he felt as if his entire body had gone numb. As if none of this were really happening.

He welcomed the cold detachment; he prayed that it would stay with him. Right up until the end.

Movement on the Amara side of the yard caught his eye, and he instinctively halted, like a cat who'd sensed a predator.

The woman with the tattoos, Searenn, had turned her head in his direction.

As Ian watched, as he held his breath, she spoke to the underworld master. She nodded her head in his direction.

And Bastraal eased around to level his black stare on Ian.

Still frozen, he watched as the demon lifted both hands, palms facing outward. A distortion appeared around his torso, and Ian felt a jerk on his hip.

He looked down to the dagger strapped to his belt. The blade was tugging itself free, inching upward to slip out of its leather sheath. Before he could think to grab hold of the hilt, the weapon flew up and out, straight through the air to Bastraal.

Then the knife still in Ian's hand started to shimmy.

Too late he realized Bastraal was trying to disarm the coven. He'd created a gravitational pull to attract the metal, sucking them in and effectively taking them out of commission.

Ian couldn't hold on to the dagger. He gripped tightly with both hands, but only succeeded in being dragged across the dirt in his efforts to hold firm. At last he released it, and his only remaining blade shot into Bastraal's hand.

The demon tossed the two daggers aside to the black-haired woman named Jack. Then he faced the coven allies and raised his hands again.

Ian was still thirty yards or so away, but he yelled across the now-quiet stone yard, "Hold on to your weapons!" Then a new thought struck. It terrified. "Anna!" he shouted, now running toward her. "Your dagger! Protect the dagger!"

He spared only a second to consider that he was telling her to keep the weapon in her possession, only so she could soon drive it into his heart.

His shouts, his movement, prompted a response from Bastraal. The demon jerked his head toward Searenn. "Take him now!"

Employing her own magic, Anna was buffering herself against Bastraal's magnetic force. But the men all lost their weapons in short order, with Joseph being dragged across the field until Chris caught up to him and broke him free of the sword and scabbard strapped to his back.

Searenn started chanting in the demonic language that only she seemed to speak, channeling more creatures to do Bastraal's bidding.

Ian stalled as he realized exactly what that meant. She was calling forth monsters. So she could send them for him.

This was what had to happen, and his logical mind had processed that fact. Bastraal would need to invade Ian's body if Anna were to banish him forever.

But instincts kicked in, and Ian just couldn't stand still. He simply couldn't wait there and allow those underworld sons of bitches to put their filthy hands on him.

So he spun on his heels and started to run. He had to get to Anna.

There was more he wanted to say. *I love you. I forgive you.*

He ran faster.

Please don't forget me.

But the thing about conjured demons is they could appear anywhere, and three materialized directly in his path. There was no slowing down or changing his course. He plowed into their open arms, three of the warrior-caste. They towered over him, trapping and subduing him with their unearthly strength.

Anna cried his name, but she was still struggling to keep her dagger from Bastraal.

Too much was happening at once for Ian to keep track, especially when his world abruptly turned upside down. The beasts had hauled him up between their bodies and slung him over one of their arms so that he dangled, head below waist.

He heard Paige shout for the coven to turn their magic on Bastraal. And while his gut roiled with fear, he understood they had to protect the sacred dagger above all else. Anna had to retain the dagger, to have it in her grasp. At all costs.

Ian was tossed none too gently onto the glistening onyx plate in the center of the stone yard. Having landed on his knees, his face close to the dark misshapen plate, he could make out millions of tiny particles, glistening preternaturally.

He'd swear they glowed from within, and as he watched, the illumination increased. Whatever insidious power was confined within the flat black stone, it seemed to be stimulated by Ian's presence. Or provoked.

He leapt to his feet and found himself surrounded by even more of the massive demons. He reached for his daggers, then remembered they'd been ripped away from him. But standing, he could at least see some of what was happening beyond the wall of monsters.

"Don't let anyone past the boundary!" Bastraal ordered Searenn. The Droehk was still chanting, but she gave a slight inclination of her head in response.

So the beasts around Ian were in essence his guardians. Bastraal was now protecting Ian; rather, he was protecting his body.

The brutal irony of it all?

He was protecting Ian from Anna.

A full-body tremor passed over him, and he found himself unable to blink. Reality was sinking in, sinking down. And it was taking him with it.

As more and more demons appeared to thicken the barrier around him, Ian curled his hands into tight fists. As his breathing became shallow and his heart kicked in his chest, he did his best to channel resolve. He tried to stay calm.

Closing his eyes, he pictured Anna.

~

At last Bastraal was pushed back several feet as the eight other witches pummeled him with magic. The magnetism he'd been sending out diminished, and Anna felt the dagger on her hip drop safely back into place.

Her breaths were ragged from the exertion, her fight against Bastraal's unimaginable power. Thankfully, her sisters had acted and had saved the sacred blade.

But while the coven allies had been struggling to keep their weapons, Ian had been overtaken by Searenn's fiends. Now he was barricaded within a demon fortification.

Worse still, he was trapped on top of the evil stone.

Ronja's angry voice dragged Anna's focus away from Ian. The Nordic witch stormed toward Searenn, clearly incensed by

Ian's treatment.

"Droehk!" Ronja screamed at Searenn. "You betray me as well?"

Finally lowering her hands, Searenn took two threatening steps toward the blonde woman who had once been her leader. "Bastraal is right," she said, her hoarse voice dripping with disgust. "You've become weak, Ronja. You are no longer suitable to lead the Amara."

Pulling up her black hood, she all but growled when she added, "And you definitely aren't worthy to order a Droehk."

"You are nothing but a mongrel stealing scraps from my table!" Ronja flicked a single finger and thrust a visible wave of magic toward Searenn.

But Bastraal moved like lightning, using his body to intercept the deadly flow.

Ronja clamped a hand to her stomach as she stumbled backward.

"No, Ronja," Bastraal thundered. "She serves me now."

"Liars and deceivers!" Ronja lifted a hand as if to send forward another wave of energy, but instead she crossed her arms over her chest and made a low, keening sound. "Don't do this, Bastraal. I don't understand."

The huge demon turned away, the pleas of the witch who'd aided him for a thousand years seeming to mean nothing to him now.

A streak of green soared through the air and plowed into Bastraal's back. A thin creature with an elongated head latched onto the demon's shoulder and began ripping at his tentacles. The alien-esque form pulled at him with multi-jointed arms and chewed with elongated fangs.

Bastraal roared and spun in a circle as he tried to grab the thing eating into his back.

Anna and her friends were all standing at the ready, not sure when or from where a threat might emerge. And since the men and Sylvie were now without weapons, the coven had taken a stand in front of them.

Anna swung her head to find the source of the entity. Though she knew who'd sent the beast that was now devouring Bastraal's tentacles. Tyr was standing again. But his head was still angled sharply to one side as if his neck had been broken.

Alive but twisted and mangled, he was forced to walk by unnatural means, his weight supported by the devils residing within.

Ronja had backed away from Bastraal, but the expression on her face was one of shock. Her arms were slack at her sides, eyes wide and impassive as the creature she'd answered to for a millennium now fought to defend himself.

Moving as if his limbs were disjointed, Tyr ambled forward, throwing out another strange being to attack Bastraal. Then another, until the mighty demon was roaring with fury, spinning and biting, a ferocious dog in a fight.

Then the demon tucked his arms against his strangely glowing body, tensed all over, and released a blast of power so cold it instantly froze every beast within a five-foot radius.

Anna was still a distance away, but she felt the frigid wind from his potent release.

As soon as the creatures clinging to him broke into icy shards and fell to the ground, Bastraal turned his wrath upon the still-approaching Tyr. The demon held out his hands and curled his fingers as if gripping the air.

Then he twisted his hands, and Tyr screamed in agony.

Anna watched as the Daevo was lifted into the air, as his body crumpled beneath an invisible crush of power. And she flinched when Bastraal thrust his hands apart, and ripped Tyr's body in half.

Blood spurted a dark purple, turning Tyr's mangled form into a grotesque imitation of a fountain. The two pieces of him sailed through the air in opposite directions, both landing with sodden thumps.

The gory sight was too much for Ronja. Again and again she'd been deceived or thwarted, and the loss of Tyr seemed to break her last link with sanity.

The Nordic witch dropped where she stood, channeling her rage into a nearby column of stone. On her knees, she beat and scraped her hands, her nails, until her fingers and knuckles were raw and bleeding. "No! No! I won't accept it!"

Wailing and crying, she spent her rage on the inanimate rock before abruptly lurching to a standing position. Her silver dress was dirty and blood-spattered as a result of her outburst.

"I will not stand for this!" She fixed a demented stare on Bastraal, and then Searenn. "Do you hear me?"

The Droehk looked mildly apprehensive, for gaining Ronja's hate was no small thing.

But Bastraal seethed just as Ronja did, baring his long, pointed teeth, spittle flying when he roared furiously, "Witch! You will obey me!"

"Never! Never again!" Ronja threw another burst of magic at Bastraal, but he moved out of the way long before the stream could strike.

With a final look of loathing for Ronja, Bastraal shook his head. He turned to Searenn. "You know what to do."

Searenn bowed her head. "Yes, Bastraal."

Then the demon master focused on Anna. He fixed her with a heated glare.

Unafraid of the great beast, Anna stood her ground.

But then his glower morphed into an evil smile.

And that worried her more than his hate.

As if sensing the meaning behind his smirk, Anna leapt forward. "Bastraal! Face me now!"

But he flashed up into the air, his shape turning to a blur as he soared up into the dark sky, hovered tauntingly, and then zoomed in a downward spiral.

Straight into the black stone where Ian was being held.

"No! Ian!" Anna looked to her sisters. "The demons!" And that was all she had to say.

Her friends flew into action, and while they might have lost their metal blades, they still retained their weapon of choice. The coven magic.

Taking out the demons should have been a simple task, but every time one was destroyed, Searenn would cry out in her demonspeak. And two more would appear in its place.

Shauni waved her arm like a commander calling forward her troops, and the nine cats bounded across the stone yard. The small but fierce warriors leapt over boulders, kicking up dust as they streamed into the fray.

As the sounds of battle renewed, Searenn tossed a worried glance to Ronja. Then she ran to the remaining Amara members who—much like the coven allies—had been watching, stunned, as the bizarre events had unfolded.

They appeared to be on tenterhooks, strained and ready to leap into defensive mode. "You must make a choice," Searenn demanded of them in her scratchy voice. "I am with Bastraal, and I suggest you make the same decision."

"I think you're all crazy!" Beth started backing away, her eyes darting around as if she'd just found herself in a place she didn't want to be. "I never should have joined you. I never should have come out here to this dirty place!"

As a wicked grin curved her mouth, Searenn fixed her mismatched eyes on the younger girl. With her one-blue-and-one-black orbs fixated on Beth, she rolled her hand in a circle and flung her fingers toward the mare, whose talent for bringing bad dreams wouldn't help her now. "I never did like you, devious little mouse."

Out of thin air, an acid demon appeared and locked his long gray arms around Beth. The younger woman shrieked and writhed as the creature's caustic fluids soaked her skin.

And she was still screaming when it dragged her behind one of the crypt-like stones.

"Carson!" Ronja yelled, her voice strong as her usual arrogance returned. The witch appeared to have regained control of her wild emotions, but the hand she ran through her hair was caked with gore. Ronja didn't seem to notice.

"Do not listen to her." Ronja sent a black bolt of lightning toward the ground at Searenn's feet, causing the Droehk to dance away.

Knowing she faced a much stronger foe this time, Searenn wisely bolted, running toward her mass of summoned demons. It seemed her intent was to get past them, to seek safety on the other side, despite the fact the beasts were engaged in combat with the coven.

Before the Droehk made the safety of her demon servants, another woman sprinted after her. Like a runner off her mark, Sylvie chased Searenn down, and launching herself into the air, she tackled the Droehk and they both went tumbling.

Joseph ran to help hold the Droehk down, flanked by Nick and Michael. If they could restrain Searenn, then she couldn't call forth any more demons.

The witches continued to destroy the ring of fiends around Ian, while the cats leaped and scratched, driving the huge beasts into a frenzy of panic.

Finally, the remaining Amara crew seemed to make a decision. Their fear of Ronja had been long-ingrained, so now they burst into a run, heading straight for the coven men.

Anna had guarded the sacred dagger from Bastraal, and in doing so had managed to save the other knife on her belt. "Trevor!" she called, tossing the weapon to Hayden's boyfriend, giving him an added measure of defense.

They would need everything at their disposal to take on Carson, Jack, and Ross.

Trevor snatched it from the air, his eyes hard, no sign of fear.

As if sensing the renewed turmoil, birds began flocking back to circle over the stone yard, their caws and cries filling the air.

But all Anna could think about was Ian. With all the commotion, she'd lost sight of him.

Bastraal had gone into the stone, but had he already come back out? Was he inside Ian now?

Panic choked her, wrapping around her neck like bands of steel.

She had to get to Ian.

Anna faltered as she realized the futility of worrying over his safety.

Touching her amulet, she closed her eyes. Because what she would be forced to do on that wicked plate of stone all but tore her heart into jagged pieces.

No! I won't think about it. Please, Goddess, find me another way.

Forgetting everything else, concentrating only on the man she loved, Anna begged the deities for help and guidance. Once she stopped shaking, she moved to go aid her sisters in the fight.

But a strike of inky electricity landed at her feet.

She whirled to find Ronja stalking toward her. "You," the Nordic witch hissed, eyes wild and blonde hair streaked with her own blood. "You did this. You did *all* of this."

With one last fearful glance toward her friends and Ian, Anna drew a deep breath.

Then she opened her arms, let her magic flow, and turned to face her lifelong nemesis.

Alone.

Ronja and Anna. The time had finally come.

30

"From the very beginning, you have stolen what belonged to me." Energy crackled around Ronja as she and Anna circled each other. "First you take Sylvie, you and that ghost-talker of yours. You convinced one of *my* people that she needed to be a better woman, a kinder person."

Ronja tossed back her head and barked a short, derisive laugh. "Well. Her loss. I could have given her eternity."

Shadowing Ronja's every step and matching with one of her own, Anna wondered if the witch had forgotten Bastraal's betrayal. Even if the coven were to be defeated, Anna suspected any promises made by the demon were now obsolete.

But she wasn't surprised. She knew too well that deceit and treachery were inherent to a demon's very nature.

"You encouraged Sylvie's defection," Ronja said as winds began to whip and churn, "and that would have been insult enough. But then she killed RJ, in defense of your despicable coven. And the worst, the very worst! You allowed your soldier to kill my Scarlett. My dear, sweet Scarlett!"

Anna kept her expression neutral, hiding her reaction to hearing one of the most vile, cruel witches to have ever lived being described as "sweet." Then there was the fact she needed to push her opponent, but push her carefully. Ronja was already walking a thin line between anger and *madness*.

No matter how strong or how prepared Anna was, a witch was always more dangerous when they cut ties to reality. More lethal once they'd gone insane.

Even now, the sky was beginning to boil with sickly green clouds. This was a favorite trick of Ronja's, but Anna wasn't intimidated. *Let her waste her energy on theatrics.*

She'd studied Ronja for years on end, scrutinizing her decisions, learning her habits. And though the witch had remained elusive in many ways, one thing could always be counted on to make an appearance when things got too intense.

Ronja's vanity. Her arrogance.

Anna had always planned to counteract with patience, to let the seiðr drain herself in a fit of fury. But that had been before she'd known what would happen on this fated Halloween night. Before she'd known time would become such a precious commodity.

Ian was trapped on a source of evil, a malevolent stone that, as far as she knew, travelled down through the earth and straight to the netherworld. So she was having a hard time maintaining her patience. She'd waited years to face off with Ronja, and now she just wanted it to be over with.

So she could go to Ian.

"And now!" Another of the bolts Ronja favored snapped to the ground between Anna's feet, a lesson on why she had to keep her mind on the fight she was facing, instead of on others elsewhere in the stone yard.

"Now," Ronja screeched, "you've gotten Tyr killed as well!"

Anna worried again about Ronja's grasp on what was real. How could she blame her for Tyr's death when Ronja had been the source of that conflict?

The Nordic witch pounded her fists to her chest. "But why must I also lose Vanir? Why? *Why?*" she wailed as her features grew taut, as they turned stark white from grief.

But in a flash, Ronja was furious again, lashing out at Anna with another bolt.

Anna easily sidestepped, but she felt the heat as it passed

too close for her comfort. *I have to keep moving, run her down, wear her out.*

But Ronja was fueled by a deadly mix of agony and fury. Mists began to curl across the ground, the color of a day-old bruise, deep purple with a putrid yellow tint to the edges. The fog spat and hissed, enshrouding the two witches as they circled and sparred.

Anna felt cut off from her coven, but this was a task meant for her alone. Just as she'd always known it would be.

"Your magic has soured, Ronja." At last, Anna allowed her power to magnify in her outstretched palms, her hands glowing with a brilliant, dazzling white. "You turned your back on the tenets of our craft long ago."

Anna flashed her energy so quickly toward the Nordic witch that Ronja was forced to lunge to one side, almost losing her balance in the process. And for the first time, the ancient seiðr showed a hint of fear.

"Harm none!" Anna surged again, this time before Ronja had a chance to dodge.

Just as Ronja had regained her feet, the blast catapulted her backward. But where another would have flown far, the seiðr summoned her gift to catch and cushion her, before setting her gently on the ground.

"I hope you have more than that." Ronja's voice was low and rough with animosity, heavy with the hate she'd carried for Anna since the trials had begun, and the prophecy had been set into motion.

"I have plenty." Anna struck again, shooting forth a pure stream of white power with silver strands running throughout. Ronja barely made it out of the way in time.

Anna felt a renewal of hope, a sense of justice. "Tonight you don't answer to me alone. Tonight, Ronja, you will be revisited by your ill-spent past. Every evil you've done for centuries will come back to you. Every sin, every pain you've inflicted, all will converge here."

Anna lowered her head and let her own fury seethe. She allowed her vehemence to build, to rush through her veins and multiply her power. "Three times three, Ronja." She sent forth a swell of magic. "You know the rules."

Waving her hand in a smooth motion, Ronja deflected Anna's attack. "You think I should fear you?" She laughed caustically. "No. I have no fear. Nor do I feel any remorse for the life I've led, or for the lives I've *taken*. I am the one who has wrought payback, vengeance for what was done to me! I delivered what was deserved to all those worthless humans you feel inclined to protect! And why? When they hate our kind? When they murder us and burn us?"

Blonde hair flowed about her head as her summoned breezes turned to a blustering gale. Ronja spread her arms wide. "I made them pay tenfold for the pain they caused!"

"The entire world isn't to blame for what happened to you and your brother, Ronja. That was a millennium ago." Anna released a shimmering shield of crystalline magic when the seiðr tried to catch her off guard with a slap of power.

"You have become the very thing you claim to despise. A murderer!" Anna stepped forward, refusing to be intimidated by the other woman's show of strength. Ronja might be a thousand years older, but Anna was a thousand times more righteous.

And the essence of magic was on Anna's side. The doctrines demanded that those who were bestowed with magic use their gifts for worthy purposes. As witches, she and Ronja were bound by honor.

Ronja had broken that faith centuries ago.

Her punishment was long overdue.

With justice winging through her blood, Anna channeled another torrent of energy. "You twist and warp your magic. You defile the gift you were blessed with." She thrust a quick blow toward Ronja, then another, the second rush of magic making contact with Ronja's left arm, singeing her skin and ripping the silver of her dress.

Spinning to escape another hit, Ronja turned full circle and faced Anna again, her nails elongated into thick, curving black claws. Her chest heaved as her long strands of golden hair whipped madly in the raging storm of her own creation.

With eyes lit an otherworldly blue, Ronja let her anger build her magic.

Just as Anna did.

But where Anna had shown restraint, had maintained control, Ronja had foolishly let her power explode from within.

And Anna wasn't done goading her yet. "You say you have no guilt?"

Ronja lashed out at her with dual lances of the dark-as-pitch lightning. "Never!"

Anna pushed her backward with a massive pulse, a current that swelled outward from her body, like a heart pumping its lifeblood. "No remorse? Not even for the cruel fate that you... *you!*...have now brought down upon Vanir?"

Anna's accusation had the desired effect, and Ronja opened her mouth to release a vicious scream. Her body shook as she dealt blow after blow to Anna, strikes that were easily avoided or repelled.

Ronja didn't seem to notice that her target remained uninjured. Her eyes had sheened over with hatred and bloodlust.

Aside from her vanity, another characteristic of Ronja's could always be counted upon.

Her temper.

And now it raged out of control. "You simpering little bitch. The St. Germaine blood runs thin in your veins! You aren't worthy to stand against me!" Again, two streaks of inky electricity arced from Ronja's hands and through the air.

This time, however, Anna was hit. Heat tore through her side as an excruciating burn traveled along each individual rib where she'd absorbed the lightning.

But she couldn't let the pain distract her. Ronja was still a powerful witch, and despite the magic she'd squandered thus far, she possessed deep wells of resources.

Anna was well-trained and prepared for this battle. But Ronja had lived a thousand years and likely knew things Anna had never conceived of.

So she couldn't spare a single second to address her wound or steady her now-ragged breaths.

Ronja was rearing back a hand, and by the look in her eyes, she was routing a massive amount of magic into that one arm. She was building a death-blow.

And this was where their combat would take a turn. One of them would gain the advantage.

Anna was determined to be that witch.

"It's your fault Vanir will be taken over by Bastraal!" she yelled at Ronja. "You brought that devil back into our world, and now your twin will suffer for all eternity!"

Anna had no intention of letting that happen, but she needed to prod the seiðr, to push her into a mindless frenzy.

Ronja was so incensed she could only bellow a guttural sound of rage. Then she pulled her arm back another fraction of an inch.

But Anna saw the motion. She anticipated her foe's next move as Ronja's arm pitched forward.

No lightning sprung forth this time, but an undulating wave of deep green and black magic. The surge was so powerful, it spread wide to easily encompass Anna and burn her entire body, just as the lightning strike had seared her ribs.

She would be dead before the power dissipated.

But she'd seen it coming, and she was ready. Anna cast her own wide net of magic, only this time the energy came from another source. The sheltering force of magic was sapphire blue, like the center stone in Anna's amulet. It carried with it the power of the coven.

Even when her sisters were far away, the bond they shared stretched through time and space, giving her the strength she needed to intercept Ronja's dark power.

And giving her time to dive to the side, out of the strike's deadly path.

She landed hard on her shoulder, but rolled quickly and leapt to her feet. Palms aimed, heart pounding, and magic coursing, Anna stood and waited.

When the malicious surge of Ronja's magic faded, the witch stood there, smiling, a gleaming look of triumph in her eyes. Along with the madness still burning bright.

She didn't see Anna until it was too late.

"By the power of love, the power of Fate, my light of truth will banish all hate." Another line of magic burst from Anna's right hand and struck Ronja in her stomach. The blonde witch doubled over with a cry of pain.

Using her magic, Anna sliced open one of her own palms. And with her bleeding hand, she sent a final, blazing stream of power to her enemy's chest. "By my blood and by my heart, I now will finish what three sisters did start."

Ronja lit up, her skin radiating a pale blue from the coven magic streaming through her. The Nine had been handed down a prophecy, an obligation, and the magic to see it done.

Now all of it rushed through Ronja's body as she was lifted off the ground where she jolted and trembled, as if a hundred hands were shaking her at once.

Rubbing her palms together, Anna created one final ball of light. As Ronja began to moan helplessly, still shuddering violently in the air, the coven's leader, the St. Germaine witch, flung the dazzling sphere toward her family's ancient foe.

The momentum of the blast caught Ronja in the center of her

gut and carried her across the stone yard. She hurtled through her own purple mists until she struck a dolmen and slid down its stone wall to crumple in the dirt.

Anna didn't need to examine the witch to know she was finished. The sickly-colored fog disappeared almost instantly, and a sheen of light beneath Ronja's flesh went dim.

Anna had never truly noticed the subtle glow until it was doused. And this was the confirmation she needed to be certain that Ronja's great power, the magic she'd cultivated for a millennium, was gone.

Satisfied her enemy wouldn't be getting back up, Anna turned in search of Ian.

The rings of demons that had surrounded him had been decimated. And with Searenn restrained, there would be no more summoned from the underworld.

He was still standing on the black plate of stone. He was staring at her.

And Anna was reminded that the worst was yet to come.

Tearing her eyes away, she searched the grounds. There were still a few Amara to deal with, and even as Anna had the thought, Carson ran across the battlefield and fell to her knees beside Ronja, just as Valentina slipped behind a massive stone formation and disappeared.

After a brief moment with her fallen leader, Carson stood. Fists at her sides, she cast a fuming look to Anna.

But when Anna took a step toward her, the Amazonian's countenance shifted from ire to apprehension. She spun and sprinted in the opposite direction, fleeing the stone yard and the coven's retribution.

That left only Searenn, Jack, and Ross. But the shifter had also seen the scales tip and all the power roll to the coven's side. Per his norm, he fell back on cowardice. He transformed himself into a bird before flying up into the sky.

Unfortunately for him, he speared straight into the thick

flocks of Shauni's winged soldiers, and a hawk swooped in to snatch the smaller bird out of the air.

And that was the last of Ross.

Jack, though, was moving with the blur indicative of her exemplary speed, the kind she had in common with Paige and Chris. Anna would have shouted a warning, but Paige had already seen the other woman's flight and had burst into a run.

The coven's warrior was on the opposite side of the stone yard. The witches had spread out in a wide circle around the black stone, in case any more of Searenn's demons popped into existence. Before Paige could catch up to Jack, the quickest of the Amara veered toward Sylvie and the men who were helping to hold Searenn down.

With a swift drive of her palms to each of their chests, Jack sent all four of them—Sylvie, Joseph, Nick, and Michael—flying backward. Then she reached down to help Searenn stand.

Anna was closer and had her hand raised to intervene. But Jack stunned her when she spat in Searenn's face and yelled, "Traitor!" just before using her strength to snap the Droehk's neck.

Jack leapt over Searenn's falling body and zipped toward the tree line to make her escape.

Paige skidded to a halt, apparently torn as she glanced back to Ian and then to the trees again. But she too knew the order of priorities and wouldn't leave her sisters alone. She wouldn't abandon Anna or Ian. Not now.

They would both need the support of the witches and all of their friends, because as Anna realized with a catch in her breath, the Amara had all finally been vanquished.

All but one.

Slowly, Anna pivoted to meet Ian's gaze. Then she broke into a run.

Her time with Ian was growing short, and she had to hold him.

One last time.

31

Anna rushed to Ian and fell into his open arms. Despite the imminent heartbreak and terror they would both soon endure, he was filled with pride after watching her battle against Ronja.

But he was sick with loss as he felt her tremble, so scared and uncertain. No longer the bold, confident witch he had observed mere moments before.

She was broken now. She knew what was coming. Just as he did.

Because the freezing pains had already begun.

Ian felt as if icy needles were pricking his skin, then driving deeper to pierce his muscles, his organs. He recognized that hellish cold, and was sure Bastraal had begun whatever process was required for him to transition to his chosen vessel.

Ian's body was undergoing an invasion, and he was afraid he didn't have much longer.

The bouts of agony came and went, and now he was just grateful that the pangs had subsided. He held Anna, stroking her back and murmuring soft words. He kissed the top of her head as she quaked within his embrace, as she shuddered and hugged him to her.

"Anna—"

"No." Her voice was muffled against his neck. "Not yet. Please, I just need to hold you."

"I would hold you forever," he squeezed her tighter, "if I could."

Anna let a sob slip out in response, but she choked down the sound and kissed his cheek, holding her lips to his skin as if memorizing the way he felt.

A knife of cold suddenly sliced into his stomach, and he couldn't hold back his groan.

She lifted her distraught face to his. "What is it? Are you hurting?"

He nodded, breathing deeply to try to quell the terrible ache. "It's starting," he whispered.

When Anna's face fell, Ian's heart plummeted too. He hated that their last moments together would be so anguished. That their goodbyes would always be tainted by the presence of that demon bastard.

"We have to get you out of here!" she cried, yanking on his shirt, urging him to move.

"No, Anna."

Her eyes were wild with horror, but he held onto her wrists until the fervor broke and she let her head fall forward. "I can't do it." She shook violently. "I can't!"

"You *must*." Ian firmed his tone, because only he would be able to get through to her. To convince her that his death was inevitable.

"I love you too much to lose you." Raising her beautiful blue eyes to him, Anna touched his mouth, his face, as if she couldn't get enough of him. Then she laid her hand over his heart and shivered. "It's not fair, and I don't care what happens. I won't do this!"

Wiping her tears with his thumbs, Ian centered his gaze on her. He spoke evenly. "You know that's not true. You came here with your decision made. You'd accepted your fate, as terrible as it is. This changes nothing."

"It changes everything!" Now she cupped his face, looked adoringly at him as her breath stuttered, her eyes flooded anew. "It's also my destiny to find love, and I have. Don't leave me, Ian. You can't."

Lowering his head, Ian ignored the next stab of cold and pressed his lips to Anna's. He let the warmth and love of their kiss flow through him and bolster his courage. Just having her near dampened the pain growing inside him.

Then cramps assaulted his stomach. A headache came upon him as if a vise had been strapped to his skull and was being tightened. But he forced aside the discomfort.

"I'll always be with you." He put his forehead to hers and whispered, "I know you can do this."

"Please, Ian."

Over her shoulder, Ian looked to the other men. All of their friends were gathered around, solemn expressions on their faces, and many of the women in tears. He spoke with authority to Trevor and Cole. "Get the bindings."

Anna's arms were around him again, her mouth near his ear, whispering of her love.

But Ian took comfort in the fact that she was no longer begging him to run. No longer telling him she couldn't do what must be done.

Because as much as it tore at him, and as unfair as all of this was, Anna was the only one fated to do it. The only one tasked with ending his life, thereby destroying Bastraal forever.

Each of the men stepped forward, and Ian saw in their serious faces and efficient motions that they all intended to take part in the binding. Each man would participate, so all of them would forever share the weight of that awful burden.

Anna startled when Quinn drove the first of the charmed stakes into the black stone.

She flinched with every successive blow.

With the pain in his head building, Ian held Anna's chin in his hand, forcing her to look at him. To hear him and keep his words with her, long past this horrific night.

"I know now that it had to be this way." He stroked her cheek with his thumb, offered a loving smile despite the cleaving sensation in his gut. "It had to be me."

"Why do you say that?" Anna had one hand on his face, the other in his hair.

"Because I'm the only one who can give you permission."

"What?" She shook her head, heart still denying what her mind had accepted.

"I can tell you it's all right." He kissed her softly. "So let me do this one last thing for you. Anna, I love you." He caught her sob with his next kiss. Then he rubbed his cheek to hers. "I absolve you, Anna. I set you free."

For a moment, they simply clung to each other. No words spoken, but an embrace meant to last her for the rest of her life.

Another twist in his gut, and Ian wheezed out a breath. "Promise me you'll find a way to forgive yourself. Be happy, Anna."

"Not without you."

"I love you, and I know you love me. So I'm telling you to finish your trial. Fulfill your destiny."

Finally Ian broke down and let his own tears fall. "You are the strongest person I've ever known. Fate chose well, my amazing witch." He kissed her, with all the passion and tenderness he could.

Then he stepped away from her and felt as if his soul had been torn from his body. "Don't let us down, Anna." He gave her a meaningful look. "Don't let any of us down."

This time when the pain came, Ian buckled and fell to his knees.

But when he looked up and met Anna's stare, he saw a resurgence of the serene strength that was so much a part of her. And knowing he'd done his part, that he'd done all he could, he lay down on the cold, unforgiving stone…and let the demon take him.

~

Anna was still gripping Ian's hand when he was overcome by agony. The evil rock glistened in the moonlight, and as she watched him suffer, the weight of the prophecy pressed down on her shoulders.

It crushed her heart.

Her duty settled upon her like a cloak of inescapable misery and grief. And though she had accepted her destiny, watching Ian endure such pain almost destroyed her.

She was the witch of prophecy, but her heart still broke, and her tears still flowed. The drops fell and sizzled where they landed, her white magic offending the sinister stone.

Ian's body torqued, and seeing his agony wrought a cry from Anna. Even if he'd displayed no outer signs of torment, she still would have sensed the black soul of Bastraal.

The beast was drawing near, and the higher he rose from the hidden abyss below, the more Ian thrashed.

"Ian!" She couldn't help herself, rubbing his hand, his arm, hoping to help in some small way.

Damn you, Fate! How could she let him go?

His gorgeous eyes—the strength of granite, the beauty of a blue sky—fixed on her one last time. His teeth were clenched, his jaw tense. But he held her gaze. "I love you enough for ten lifetimes, and I will see you again, Anna." His hand reached for her as he began to seize and shake. "I *will* see you again."

"I love you, Ian! I love you!"

His head kicked back against the hard plate of rock, and this time his words were for the men. "He's coming! Hurry!"

Chris and Ethan dropped beside Ian and began to affix the charmed metal, the chains and cuffs that would hold a mighty demon like Bastraal. At least for a short while.

"Anna, I have faith in you!"

Ian's eyes rolled back in his skull, and she was shaken to the core, terrified he was gone for good. "No! Ian!"

His tremors grew and his words became garbled. The seizures were so intense, the men, Chris included, were having trouble holding Ian still.

Anna couldn't bear to watch, but she couldn't look away.

This was her lot. Her cruel destiny.

So as the man she loved suffered and convulsed, she forced herself to watch everything, to remember every jerk, every cry. She wouldn't forsake him by averting her eyes.

Finally, after the worst had passed, Ian's clenched muscles relaxed.

Chris, Ethan, and now Trevor—who'd jumped in to help— were all breathing heavily.

And yet, one arm remained free, one wrist untethered.

Ian expelled a long, thin breath. His body stilled.

And when he opened his eyes again...they were no longer blue.

The orbs were stained a color so dark that iris couldn't be distinguished from pupil. And deep within the soulless black, Anna saw flames. Fire.

Ian was gone.

Bastraal had arrived.

"Witch," he drawled, his deep voice thick with deviant pleasure. "How long I've waited to taste St. Germaine blood, to gnaw on your frail bones."

Chris's movements were a blur as he swiftly fastened the final cuff.

As if made aware he'd missed his chance for freedom, the beast inside Ian's body yanked his right arm, trying to break the newly-latched chain. Then he pulled again, harder, as a growl built in his chest.

The metal had been created to hold an unwilling man, but even bespelled as they were, the chains would hold the demon inside him for only so long.

Just long enough for Anna to do her duty.

"Anna, don't let him get free!" Paige was on the perimeter of the sacrificial stone, her face wet from crying. And though Anna's sister ached for what was about to happen, Paige was a soldier and knew the repercussions of setting monsters loose on the world.

Another strong yank and a link on one chain began to weaken, to stretch and lose its shape.

All Bastraal needed was one free arm, and Anna was as good as dead. The veil between the spirit worlds was at its thinnest, and the Halloween moon was full in the sky.

The beast would never be stronger than he was at this very moment. Or as vulnerable.

Sick in her heart, Anna reached for her dagger.

She could wait no longer.

~

Joseph drew a ragged breath as he pulled his phone from his back pocket. This part had been intended for Cole, but now that he was here, he wanted to be the one to send out the call.

The contacts were already typed into the bar at the top of the screen. And the message box contained one word—Now.

Joseph hit Send. Then he looked back to Anna as she positioned herself over Bastraal.

He hoped everyone got the word in time, because Anna, the coven—all of them in this dark, abandoned place—were in desperate need of their help.

~

Downtown at Nick's pub, Steve felt the vibration in his pocket. He read the short message and quickly climbed on top of the bar. "Hey! Hey! It's time!" And in that long-honored tradition, he and every patron inside the pub lifted a glass.

They remembered a friend on the night it counted most, and sent their thoughts to others who'd lost her but couldn't be there tonight. Including his boss, Nick.

The music was quickly shut off, allowing a hush to fall over the room. Holding his own mug, Steve raised it high. As one, the crowd said, "For Jen."

~

Deeper in the heart of the city, Joe and Mr. Attinger were with a much larger group, and they all gathered around the fountain of Forsythe Park. Almost every Ranger from the 1/75 was in attendance, as well as many Savannah Metro P.D. officers who were off-duty.

Friends and family of missing loved ones stood in silence, several holding pictures in frames. Among them, a mother held a child in her arms. The same woman who'd almost fallen to her death from the Talmadge Bridge.

Joe and Mr. Attinger received the text, then lit the white candles they held in their hands.

One by one, flames blazed into existence, lighting the faces of soldiers, friends, children, and parents. Some of whom had come to mourn, others who'd come to pray.

And as the candlelight vigil flared brighter than the sun, many simply bowed their heads, and offered their thanks to those fighting in the dark.

~

On the lawn outside a college dorm, SCAD students amassed. The crowd here was exceptionally large—for no one believed as easily as the young. Coming together for a moment of silence, they remembered their friends, the missing and the lost.

And in that crowd were some who'd undergone one terrible night. They'd run through the halls and hidden from the monsters that had invaded their world.

And somewhere deep inside, part of them remembered.

~

In various places across the country, people were coming together in support of the Savannah Coven.

A group in Hayden's hometown of San Francisco sent positive energy all the way across the continent, while in the Midwest, Viv's parents held another park vigil in the heart of Chicago.

Claudia's parents had traveled far, and now stood holding hands with Mrs. and General Worthington.

All the animals in the Cheyenne Mountain Zoo were quiet and still as Shauni's parents gazed up at their daughter's beloved peaks.

And even down in Alabama, a prayer group sat in a little brick church, sending love and hope to Willyn and her circle of friends. The ones she called "sisters."

~

Two women stood within Savannah's grandest cathedral, leading hundreds of their fellow worshippers. The call had gone out a week before, and though many here tonight had not set foot inside a church for years, all the strange events in Savannah could no longer be ignored.

So many had come tonight, on Halloween. Scores and scores had answered when help had been requested.

Sylvie's grandmother, a hoodoo priestess, sat in the front pew. She lifted her eyes when Claire's cell phone emitted the sound of a bell. And along with the endless rows of believers behind her, she stood, channeling strength and energy to those in need.

Mrs. Attinger reached out for Claire. They had organized it all and now faced a crowd so large that many spilled out the open doors.

The two women clasped hands in solidarity. They started the prayer.

As hundreds of voices merged to become one, Mrs. Attinger squeezed the hand of her long-time friend. And in a voice choked with emotion, she whispered, "For our girls."

~

Help me. Help me. Clutching the dagger in her hands, Anna prayed to any power that might deign to listen.

On the wicked stone, Bastraal still struggled, and with a terrible jerk on the chains, he managed to loosen the manacle on one ankle.

"I'll drink your blood! Suck on the marrow of your loved ones!" The demon's rage was violent, and it was all Anna could do to keep away from his thrashing body.

She raised her arms, fingers clenched around the blade. Tears threatened when she gazed upon Ian's face. Though distorted and twisted with fury, she still imagined his blue eyes, still heard his deep, soothing voice.

So she looked up to the sky instead and was stunned to see falling stars streaking yellow lines across the midnight blue. The universe seemed to be giving her a sign, and the final push she so badly needed.

Steeling herself, she stared down into the blazing eyes of evil incarnate. She suddenly felt a rush of power, swells of love and support from sources she could not name.

The onyx stone on the dagger's hilt began to warm. Then the metal surrounding it heated in her hand.

Just before the blade burst into flames.

As she glared at the demon, she remembered the night before. All the sweet yet feverish moments she'd shared with Ian.

Never suspecting those would be the last.

Choking back her sorrow, Anna gripped the dagger until her knuckles screamed from the strain. Gritting her teeth, she lifted the flaming weapon, heartbroken that after Vanir's traumatic death, fire would once again claim an honorable man's life.

Tensing every muscle in her arms, shoulders, and torso, Anna stared directly into Bastraal's hateful eyes. She sucked in a breath.

And the demon froze. He stopped his frantic actions as if sensing his end.

Over his roar of fury and denial, Anna raised her voice as she raised the dagger. "This is for Ian!"

As another cry of pain burst free, she closed her eyes and plunged the blade.

At first, the beast only arched his back, an expression of shock on his face, and disbelief in his soulless eyes.

Then the dagger's magic began to spread, snaking through his flesh in meandering lines of silver and black. Finally, Bastraal screamed and began writhing with what Anna hoped was excrutiating pain.

At least as much as he had caused Ian.

The demon's multi-layered voice rose in a bellow of denial. His wide, round eyes disavowed the fact that he'd wasted three hundred years. Though he lay dying, Bastraal still seemed to reject the truth.

That another St. Germaine witch had been victorious. And he would never achieve the eternal life he sought.

The fire of the dagger spread outward, burning in the wake of the silvered trails. The flames traveled through Ian's poor body, but the damage done was to Bastraal alone.

Fire and magic converged to eliminate his essence, and as the beast realized his failure, his inescapable demise, he kicked his legs and flailed his arms. But the chains held him, and the magic continued to course through him.

His body went suddenly rigid as a warm breeze blew through the stone yard, then whirled around Bastraal as he lay bound and dying.

Anna lifted her head, sensed a benevolent force, and watched as the last of the demon's dark power was stripped from Ian's body and dispersed by the cleansing winds.

As she stared into Bastraal's shadowy eyes, she saw the flames begin to flicker and fade into black.

But as the fires were extinguished, as the beast drained away, he carried with him the love of Anna's life.

When Bastraal's stolen body slumped against the stone, his features relaxed and again became Ian's. Blood from the wound in his chest trickled down his shirt in a thin, peaceful stream.

And as the beast died, as Ian died, the sound of a high, sweet note emanated from the necklace hanging around Anna's neck.

The gravity of what had occurred, of what she had done, simply swamped her. The sense of loss burned her mind and squeezed her lungs, while the song of victory—so long awaited—now mocked her pain. It harmonized with the cry rising in her throat.

In one brutal motion, Anna ripped the amulet from her neck and hurled it across the stone yard. The delicate silver piece smacked against something in the distance, but she didn't see. She didn't care.

Finally able to acknowledge her grief, she dropped to Ian's chest and wrapped her arms around his lifeless body. She caressed his pale face.

And as she caught the scent of his blood, Anna finally broke, dissolving into deep, wrenching sobs.

32

It was all over, Quinn thought to himself. Feeling hollow and completely gutted, he stood by silently as the women huddled into tight groups, hugging each other, crying on shoulders, or staring listlessly into space.

Anna was still bent over Ian, her ragged sobs now reduced to softer cries.

The expected question had already been asked and answered. Kylie had tearfully begged Willyn to check on Ian. To just see if there was anything she could do to heal his body, to bring him back.

But the coven healer had only shaken her head before pulling the younger witch into her arms. Then Dare had enfolded them both and held them as they cried together.

Quinn had been foolish enough to shoot a hopeful look to Michael. But Shauni's boyfriend gave the same negative reply. There was nothing to be done. Ian no longer had any aura.

His soul had flown.

Quinn ached to see his sister so distraught, but he didn't go to her. He didn't offer words that would do no good.

Willyn and Shauni had tried to soothe her, touching her shoulders and speaking her name, but Anna had turned even them away. Her grief, her guilt, consumed her completely.

Quinn swallowed a suspicious tremble in his chest, a burn behind his nose. It would only hurt Anna more to see him cry.

But like everyone else, Quinn was utterly devastated. His

spirit, his peace of mind, and his joy of life had been destroyed. Because Anna's had been.

He worried as he looked across the barren stretch of land. He was afraid she would never be the same again.

But there was at least one thing he could do. Setting off across the stone yard, he determined that he would recover her amulet.

Anna might despise it now, but he would still find it. He'd hold on to it for her. The necklace represented the connection she shared with her sisters, and maybe, just maybe, there would come a day when she could bear to look at it again.

Regardless, he couldn't leave it here. The amulet meant far too much to be discarded in this bleak place of death.

Quinn sighed, his throat thickening as sorrow welled within him. Anna wasn't going to recover from this night any time soon.

And he knew without a doubt, as he glanced back at the wreckage left behind by the prophecy, that she would never be able to love another. Her heart, her shattered heart, would always belong to Ian.

Concentrating on the rocky ground, Quinn followed the arc through the air the amulet had taken. He was sure it had bounced off the large stone that looked like a crypt. The one with a hole on the front side.

So eyes on the ground, he scoured the terrain, until finally, he caught sight of a glimmer. There, half-buried in the dirt, lay Anna's amulet.

Sniffing back the emotion that still threatened, he bent down and pulled it by the long silver chain, freeing it from the dry earth. He carefully wiped away what he could and stuffed it into the front pocket of his jeans.

Turning to head back, to do whatever he could to ease his sister's pain, Quinn still kept his head down. But he paused mid-step. He strained to listen, swearing he'd heard a voice.

"Youuu."

There it was again, weak and breathy.

Then again, he heard, "You. Boy." A soft cough followed, drawing his attention to the form crumpled on the ground.

But Ronja had managed to lift her head, and her focus was all on Quinn.

"Pleassssse." Her words were little more than a hiss.

Striding closer to where she lay, he raised his hand, channeled the magic he possessed. Though not as strong as his sister or the other coven witches, he had enough to do some damage. Stopping yards away, he told the hated witch, "Female or not, I won't mind killing you."

This time when she coughed, red spittle splayed across the soil. "No need," she rasped. "I'm already dying."

Quinn looked down on her with revulsion. "Then I'll leave you to it."

"No!" At last she showed some vigor, but as soon as she lifted her arm, she collapsed again in a fit of coughing. "Please." More spasms wracked her body. "Please. You must help me."

"No." Quinn laughed, but the sound hurt his already aching chest. The pain of this night's loss would follow him for years. "I don't think so."

"Your sister."

Ronja's words gave him pause, and though he had his back to her, he listened.

"You know the love between siblings. You understand. So, please, I beg you. Take me to him."

Quinn whirled on her. Voice low, so as not to carry, he still ensured she heard his disgust. "You're the reason he's dead."

"Please, no. Oh, Vanir." She lifted teary eyes to Quinn.

And goddess help him, a shaft of sympathy opened inside. She looked so pitiful, lying there in the dirt, abandoned by all, and dying a slow, lonely death. It was no more than she deserved, but no matter how wicked Ronja had been, no matter her terrible deeds, Quinn couldn't just walk away.

She was too pathetic.

"I take you to him and then what?"

"I just want to be with my brother. As I should have been, so long ago."

Quinn swore beneath his breath and then looked over his shoulder to where Anna was still slumped over Ian's lifeless body. Having Ronja near him might cause his sister to fracture, to break what little of her still remained.

But no matter how he reasoned with himself, he knew there was no way he could kill Ronja. Nor could he leave her broken and bleeding to death.

He couldn't be so callous. Even to her.

Wondering if he'd completely lost his mind, Quinn bent down on one knee and slid his arms beneath her. As he lifted her, cradling the witch who'd harmed so many people, Ronja grimaced.

Quinn ignored her gasp, knowing the jostling pain couldn't be helped, as he strode over the craggy land with a dying and feeble Ronja in his arms.

As he drew near the sacrificial stone, Dare was the first to see him. And he was the first to react.

Tossing a quick, anxious glance to Anna, the male witch slipped his hands from Willyn's shoulders and hurried to intercept Quinn. "What the hell are you doing?"

"I honestly don't know," Quinn ground out. "But I'm doing it anyway."

It wasn't long before a few others noticed the odd sight, and murmurs started to roll through the group. Half of them looked horrified, while a few seemed confused. Then there were others who were downright furious. Paige being one of them.

She rushed over, blocking Quinn's path. Then she actually reached for Ronja, as if she would take the witch away and get rid of her for good.

"No," Quinn barked abruptly. And his harsh response caused Anna to raise her head in a sharp, startled motion. Her eyes were swollen and red, her clothes mottled by the transfer of Ian's blood.

Stunned for a moment, Anna only stared. Then her eyes sharpened as they fell upon Ronja.

Instead of rising to meet him, Anna spread her hands protectively over Ian's bloody chest. "Take her away from here."

The words were soft, but no less a command.

"Vanir," Ronja whined, lifting one weak hand to stretch toward Ian.

"Anna's right," Shauni said. "Don't let her do any more harm."

"Quinn." Kylie's mouth was slack with shock. "What are you doing?"

With no better answer than before, he simply shrugged. "She's no longer a danger. Her magic is gone. She's dying." He indicated Michael with a nod. "Ask him what he sees."

All heads turned to the vet. With a frown, Michael nodded. "Quinn's right. Her aura is mild. She wants nothing more than to be with..." He trailed off, unable to call Ian by any other name.

He would save his friend that final insult.

But Ronja had no problem with it as she began to move in Quinn's arms and moan, "Vanir. Vanir."

Taking pity on her, and following an instinct he truly didn't comprehend, Quinn walked slowly to the stone. He knelt—all the while meeting his sister's outraged stare—and set Ronja gently on the hard surface.

Everyone seemed to freeze in place, watching to see what would happen next.

And everyone gasped or cried out when Ronja ripped the dagger free of Ian's chest.

Pushing Ronja back, Anna wrested the weapon from the her

hands. "Don't you touch him!"

Straining for every breath she took, Ronja managed to rasp, "You fool." Then she held out her hand. "Give me your blade."

"No!" Claudia shouted, as Hayden turned to Trevor and started to cry.

"I won't let you harm him. Not anymore."

"I never did him harm." Ronja coughed, a deep crimson bubble forming on her lips. "Fine. Hold onto your knife." She thrust out her arm. "But cut my wrist."

When Anna shook her head, retracted in revulsion, Ronja sucked in a deep breath and demanded, "Do it!

Surprising himself one more time, Quinn knelt behind Ronja. He locked eyes with his sister and said, "Do it."

~

Anna gaped at her brother, and then shifted her bewildered gaze to Ronja. What was happening? Why couldn't they just leave her alone?

She wanted to be with Ian.

"Now, slice my vein." Ronja glared at Anna. "You were meant to take my life, and so you have. But if I want to give my brother one last gift, who are you to deny me?"

"A gift?" Viv asked, putting her hand to her mouth.

"Oh, no," Lucia said. She and Shauni were holding hands, clinging to one another. "Her blood. It's been tainted by Bastraal."

Ethan rushed forward then. "No. It's been blessed. Maybe by an evil force, but blessed just the same."

Anna felt a tiny spark inside but didn't dare give it a name. Not yet.

But Ethan was suddenly excited, his dark brown eyes alive with...*hope*. "It might work, Anna." He too came over to join them on the soot-colored stone. "I'm sorry to be crass, but..." he glanced at Ian, "it won't hurt him."

Hayden turned within Trevor's arms. "Try. Please try."

Waves of fear and optimism rammed at each other inside Anna as she studied her friends. But even Kylie and Paige were nodding.

Urgency exploded inside of her, and she didn't want to wait another second. Without warning or apology, she grabbed Ronja's wrist and slit her white skin until blood gushed out.

Holding the other witch's hand steady, she guided the stream into Ian's mouth and let demon-enchanted blood flow down his throat.

This same blood had given Ronja immortality, and when shared with Tyr and Scarlett had made them impervious to death as well.

But would it work now with Ian? Was it too late?

Ronja's eyes began to flutter, and as her head drifted down she cast a strange look to Anna. One of commiseration, and other unidentifiable emotions.

The Nordic witch then slid her eyes to Ian again. She put her hand to his face and slowly nestled into a sleeping position beside him.

Except…she wasn't asleep.

"She's gone," Anna whispered to no one but herself.

Placing her fingers on Ian's neck, she felt for a pulse. Then she put her head to his chest and listened for a beat.

There was no sound, no movement, no breath.

After achingly long minutes passed by with no change, Anna felt the grief begin to creep back in. And this time when it swallowed her, she didn't think she would ever come back.

She put her palm to Ian's cool, cool skin. Feeling no warmth, she dropped her head and let the tears come again.

"No. No. No." Kylie's sweet young voice.

Then Anna heard Quinn's deep rumble as he held his girlfriend and tried to console her.

Movement began around Anna, but she couldn't lift her head or pay attention. She just wanted to lie with Ian, until her heart stopped as well, and she had no memory of either his love or his death.

"Wait!" Michael's voice sounded, startling Anna so she jerked upright. He sounded far too animated. "I see something. Color. I think... I'm not sure, but..."

Then the usually placid man slammed his hands together with a booming clap. "It's Ian! Not Bastraal and not Vanir, but Ian!"

He rushed to Anna's side, dropped to the hated stone.

And the first man who'd come to the coven through love laid his hands on the one who'd come last.

"Willyn!" Michael cried. "Now! Now!"

The healer was at his side instantly, her hands forming a circle around the wound in Ian's chest. Then Shauni came over and put her arm around Michael, while Dare moved in to send his energy into Willyn.

Viv came next, kneeling on Anna's other side. When she placed her palms on Ian's shoulder, Nick was standing behind her, his fingers resting lightly on her arms.

The pattern repeated with Hayden and Trevor. And the line-up continued as Lucia fell in with Ethan by her side.

Almost everyone was connected when Claudia and Cole joined the expanding linkage of love and magic. And Quinn trailed a hand down his sister's brown hair as he and Kylie took up positions across from her.

Ronja's body still rested next to Ian, and after long, hate-filled years, her face looked peaceful at last.

Finally, Chris and Paige united with the rest, and once they formed the last connection, a surge of energy flooded them all. It rolled in a circuitous route before coalescing and rushing into Willyn.

The wound made by Anna's dagger sealed itself before her

eyes. And as she watched, something in her chest squeezed tight. It pulled inward.

The strange sensation released with a sigh as Ian drew a breath. His skin flushed pink again, while his eyes fluttered as if they thought of opening.

Then they did, and the grayish-blue Anna loved so much was back. With a sound that was part joy, part shout, Anna let the love continue to flow from her hands into Ian as she cupped his handsome face.

He seemed dazed and slightly perplexed. So Anna kissed him until his confusion melted away and a smile began to form. "Anna," he said with relief.

Through laughter and tears, she looked at the man she loved and whispered, "I missed you."

33

They'd given themselves one week.

As Ian stood on the walkway above the grand hall, he smiled at the gathering of women below who'd spent the last seven days kicking back, relaxing, watching movies—and now probably held a world record for pizza consumption.

Even the cats had seemed more at ease since the conclusion of Halloween night, while Mrs. Attinger and Claire were bustling around their "girls," ensuring every small need and desire was met.

Ian, for one, felt they deserved the pampered treatment from now until the end of time. They had, after all, helped bring him back from the dead.

The Savannah Coven, nine marvelous witches.

And their men. Ian grinned and scanned the huge room. He couldn't forget his new band of brothers.

And he refused to acknowledge the little tug in chest as he continued to take in the scene on the level below. The assembly of all involved, as they came together...to say goodbye.

Even after the week-long party they'd spent being drunk on relief, camaraderie, and...other female pastimes he'd rather remain ignorant of, the women couldn't seem to stop hugging each other. All eight were milling around the great room as the men made multiple trips outside with luggage.

All of the coven laughed, chatted, and shared their favorite stories a final time.

All but one.

He shifted his eyes to Anna, standing on the landing at the top of the stairs. Even from a distance, he could see her struggling to contain her sorrow.

Yes, she and Ian were about to start their life together, and yes, he loved her more than seemed humanly possible. But her life would go on without her coven family in residence, and what she was dealing with gave a whole new meaning to the words "empty nest."

He heard another woman say, "Awww," down below, and remembered Anna wasn't the only one facing that emptiness.

Silently he walked to her, moved up behind her to wrap her in his arms. "You ready?" he asked, putting his face closer to inhale the lovely scent of...gardenias.

Ah, the magic of Anna.

He felt her chest rise and fall as she drew a deep breath. "As ready as I'm going to be." Turning to face him, she looked up with liquid blue eyes. "I know this sounds silly after all we've been through," she lifted a shoulder, "but will you hold my hand?"

With a knuckle beneath her chin, Ian not only took her hand but lifted it to kiss her fingers. "Until you tell me to stop."

~

Descending the wide mahogany stairs, Anna prepared to say farewell to her friends, her sisters. But with each step, she reminded herself of all that she had gained over the last year and a half.

Touching her amulet, she gave yet another silent thanks to Quinn for retrieving the necklace and making sure she got it back. She and the other women would forever be bound by magic, and now by love, and the nine stones joined by silver knots was an apt representation.

As she gazed upon the smiling faces that greeted her, she swore never to part from her amulet again.

Nor from the man who was steadfastly—and miraculously—at her side.

With Ian's warm hand on hers, Anna managed to catch Mrs. Attinger's eye. The older woman winked and grinned, but she couldn't quite hide her own feelings of melancholy. She and Claire had come to think of the witches and the men as their extended brood of children.

That's why days like today were that bittersweet mixture of joy and sadness. It was natural to want your family to be happy, even when they had to go separate ways.

Tissue boxes sat atop every flat surface, and judging by the overflowing basket near the green velvet couch, plenty had been used so far.

"Anna," Shauni said, coming over to stand before her. And with no words needed, the animal-whisperer gave her a hug before pulling back to let the others have their turn.

Parting with Shauni and Michael and Viv and Nick wouldn't be quite so hard, since both couples would remain in Savannah where the men had their businesses. Or where one would soon exist, as in the case of Paige and Chris. Anna planned to be the nursery's very best customer.

Hayden and Claudia would also stay close, with Trevor and Cole still serving the city. The two detectives had no plans to leave any time soon.

Lucia and Ethan, however, already had a flight booked. The Spanish witch was having her plane—a replacement for the one lost in Peru—readied for the long trip to the Philippines. "I was this close to Yamamoto's gold," she'd told them one day earlier this week. And since Ethan hadn't yet visited that corner of the world, the tropical paradise would be their first shared adventure.

Well, the first that didn't include demons.

Willyn and Dare wouldn't be too far either. They'd decided to settle in Charleston. Where Dare could have his city, and Willyn could have her South.

Despite having hugged each of her friends numerous times over the last week, Anna still pulled each of them close one more time, then knelt to give Tadd a big squeeze.

At last she came to Quinn and Kylie, and though her brother was so excited to get out and see the world, her heart pinched the tiniest bit to see him go. The boy-turned-man, who had always been her sidekick, staunchest supporter, and ever-reliable pain in the ass.

She looked to the woman beside him. "Take care of him, Kylie."

The youngest witch gave a wide grin. "You know it."

"And, Quinn," Anna said, "keep her out of trouble." With a sly grin toward the savvy fashionista, she added, "And away from the shopping malls."

The trio laughed as Anna's brother tugged her to him and held her tight for a few extra seconds. Then he pulled back and cocked his head. "I've had plenty of experience keeping a willful witch in line."

Anna shook her head and rolled her eyes. "Yeah well, me too."

Once the bags had all been carried out and everyone knew it was time to go, Viv adjusted the black glasses she wore, sighed deeply, and said, "We've come so far, and done so much."

Nick put his hand on her shoulder.

"So why does walking out that door feel like the hardest thing we've ever done?" Hayden rested her head on Trevor's shoulder.

"Don't make me cry again." Lucia was waving at her eyes. "I've got to be able to see where I'm going."

"I thought your plane had instruments for that." Ethan gave a playful pull to his girlfriend's ponytail of long brown curls, trying to get a smile out of her instead of tears.

Joseph and Sylvie were there too, both planning to relocate to Atlanta. Close enough to keep Claire happy, but far enough for the young couple to truly set out on their own. Anna put an arm around each of them.

"Yeah. Me too," Joseph said in answer to her unexpected sniffle. Then he patted his front pocket. "I'll go start the car."

Michael lifted a hand. "And I'll take the truck." Multiple vehicles were needed to transport the baggage created by eight couples and one small boy. Including, of course, the eight cat carriers.

As general acceptance fell over the group, they all gradually made their way to the front doors and out into the pleasant midday sun. Joseph and Michael had already left in the vehicles, so the other men strode in that direction, not wanting to dawdle and leave them to heft all the luggage by themselves.

Left behind, the nine witches gathered into a tight circle. Without a sound, they linked hands, shared glances, and reveled in the magical hum they created together.

"Think we can actually avoid conflict for a while?" Shauni asked, looking up as a blue jay flew by.

"Well, I don't know about all of you, but I certainly plan on leading a peaceful life." Paige drew her head back when they all laughed at her. "What? You think I'm going to pick a fight with a tree?"

"If anyone could…" Claudia smiled at the fierce warrior who would soon be gently tending to plants.

Knowing she needed to be the one to do so, Anna let go of Kylie's and Lucia's hands. "I love you all," she said softly. "And I'll never forget the time we've shared."

Willyn wiped her eyes. "Neither will I."

"Me either," Hayden said, just before Viv echoed the sentiment.

Anna received a teary round of hugs and goodbyes before

they turned to leave. The remainder of the men were waiting on the edge of the woods, and as the witches went to join them, Anna walked back up the stone steps to where Ian waited.

No hand-holding would do it this time, so she wrapped her arm around his waist and leaned into him.

One by one, the women looked back to her just before entering the shelter of the trees. Anna's throat closed for a moment, but she shoved aside the urge to cry for the past and focused instead on what lay ahead.

Life with Ian. She squeezed him tighter. A happy and preferably *long* life.

Because now she knew to cherish every single second.

Ian rubbed her back as Kylie, the last of the women, disappeared into the shadows. Quinn stayed behind for a moment, staring at the mansion, the home where he'd grown up.

Anna lifted a hand. And waved a final farewell to her brother.

And once he'd done the same, he turned away and vanished inside the line of trees.

Ian's voice was a warm, rich timbre and comforted her as she watched her brother disappear. "You're a traditional woman, Anna, but one with your own twist."

Caught off-guard by the strange observation, Anna looked up at him.

"So if I'm right," he continued, lowering his gaze to her left hand, "I think a sapphire will look perfect on your hand."

Her ring finger seemed to warm as she registered his meaning, and the love blooming inside her was simply immeasurable. Now they faced each other, and she stared deeply into his eyes—sun-kissed granite backed by clear blue sky.

"A sapphire?" She put her hand to her chest, imagining the gem that would exactly match the center stone in her amulet. The man was not only handsome, reliable, and wicked smart, he was also sentimental.

Reaching up to meet him, she pressed her lips to his. And any lingering sorrow was seared away. "I love you, Ian."

He tightened his arm around her. "I love you too. And I promise you," he kissed her forehead, "I won't let you be lonely."

"And you *are* a man who keeps his word." Turning thoughtful, and not quite as sad anymore, Anna listened to the island sounds, birds calling and the distant rush of waves.

"You made me another promise, out there, in the stone yard. You kept that to me, so now I'll make a similar one to myself."

"What promise is that?" he asked softly.

With the gentle sun on her face, and Ian's love surrounding her, Anna stared at the forest trail that her friends and her family had followed. Then she vowed, "I will see them again."

But until that day, she thought as she took Ian's hand to lead him toward the doors, she definitely wouldn't be lonely. She had the love of an honest man, and the sisterhood of the bravest, most amazing women in the world.

And if she ever found herself in need, she could call on any one of them. Or all of them. The bond of The Nine could never be broken.

Anna had dedicated her life to magic. She'd sworn her oath to prophecy.

And for her loyalty, they both were paying her back. Tenfold.

As she turned to Ian, she left the past behind and gladly opened her heart to the future. Magic would always be a part of her life, but now it was tempered, it was balanced...by love.

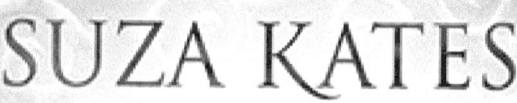

CALL TO THE EAST

WATCHTOWER MAIDENS

For a special sneak peek
Sign up for the Suza Kates Newsletter

Suza Kates writes both paranormal romance and romantic suspense. She lives in Savannah, Georgia with her family and four ridiculously spoiled cats.

For more on Suza and her books visit

www.suzakates.com